"I never want to know who you are," he murmured softly,

kissing the corner of her mouth, her chin, the hollow of her neck. "St. Laurent was so dazzled he could not remember what you were called. And you will never know who I am."

"We shall never hear of each other again," said Lila. Tears appeared and he gently kissed them away.

"Tell me your first name though, for I shall never forget you. When I am old, I shall remember this night and draw comfort from it. I must know your first name."

"Lila," she replied.

"Lila," he said.

"And your first name?" she asked.

"Napoleon . . ."

LILA

Maureen Lee

CHARTER BOOKS, NEW YORK

LILA

A Charter Book/published by arrangement with
the author

PRINTING HISTORY
Ace edition/May 1983

ISBN: 0-441-48325-9

Charter Books are published by Charter Communications, Inc.
200 Madison Avenue, New York, N.Y. 10016.
PRINTED IN THE UNITED STATES OF AMERICA

*Dedicated to my sons, David
Paul and Patrick, without
whose constant love and attention
this novel would have been written
many years ago.*

Chapter One

Miss Lilian Ward ran as fast as her feet in their blue satin shoes would carry her. Skirts held high, revealing a froth of creamy lace, she fled until she could go no farther, and at the far end of the orchard she sank down thankfully onto the warm grass. The sun was dipping behind the apple trees on the very fringe of the orchard so that the dazzling pink blossoms and soft green leaves became stark black lace against the shimmering orange ball.

"I can go no farther," Lila declared aloud, and she was glad it was the truth, for Ralph was chasing her, was bound to find her any minute, and if there was one thing she could not stand, it was girls who just pretended to give in. Girls like her cousin, Rosalind, who, after teasing her fiancé Simon (just as Lila had done Ralph, having poured a few drops of apple juice down his neck as he lay on the lawn feigning sleep), would run just a few yards and then collapse giggling, shamming exhaustion.

If Lord Ralph Curringham intended to chase Lila Ward, for whatever trifling reason, then Lila would give him something to reckon with. Her heart beat fast and furiously, and she conceded, with some slight satisfaction, that this was not merely due to her recent flight but was also in anticipation of Ralph's impending arrival.

"Lila!"

From the other end of the orchard his voice sounded light and clear on the still, evening air. She lifted her head a little and watched him approaching through a veil of tall grass.

He was slight of build, but strong; she knew that only too well from the power with which he so frequently tried to pull her to him. What a struggle it was to escape from his grip! His hair was chestnut and a lock was forever falling onto his fore-head, which he would impatiently brush away. Lila admired his hazel eyes, his pale, aristocratic face with its fine nose and thin mouth.

She was lucky to have been betrothed to someone she found so attractive. Rosalind's Simon was nearly twenty years older than his bride-to-be, small and weedy and always acting in the most juvenile manner, playing up to Rosalind's silly behavior in a way Lila found obnoxious. But then Rosalind didn't seem to mind him, which was all that mattered, Lila supposed, though for herself she couldn't stand the thought of being wedded to someone whom she did not find physically attractive. At the age of not quite eighteen, the idea of intellectual compatibility did not yet seem important.

The match with Ralph, she knew, was of some advantage to Papa. Ralph's father, the marquess of Rawlesbury, was a leading Whig, and a union between his son and Miss Lilian Ward would be bound to further Papa's political career. Sir William Ward was at present a very insignificant back-bencher—in fact, this rather inconsequential position had been his lot since his entry into Parliament many years ago.

This train of thought vanished from Lila's mind instantly, for Ralph had caught sight of the blue of her dress in the long grass and came bounding up, falling down beside her, only a little breathless.

"Lila! You minx!" he cried. "I'd like to bet you'd not come far behind if we ran a race together."

"I'll lay you ten to one I'd win," Lila said smartly. "I'll race you tomorrow if you like."

"Nonsense, minx." Ralph took her hand. "I'll have your mother accusing me of being a bad influence if I take you at your word. Perhaps when we are married and you have only me to please..."

His words were spoken in jest, but their unintended, deeper meaning was apparent to both of them and for a few moments they were silent. Lila was flushed from the strange, tumultuous feelings evoked by the touch of his hand on hers and by his words. Ralph, looking down and imagining her pleasing him, felt an urgent thrust of desire and longed to take her, there and then.

How deceptive her appearance was. She looked like an angel, with that thick, golden hair falling into a mass of ringlets on her slender, white neck. And those eyes! Blue, with a hint of violet, just like that china doll of his sister's, and fringed with long lashes which were a reddish, deeper gold than her hair; lashes which now rested demurely on her pink cheeks as she looked shyly down at the grass.

Indeed, she was almost like a doll herself, her nose and mouth as perfect as his sister's plaything. But there was nothing doll-like about her character. There was fire within. He could sense it when a light kiss turned to something more passionate and he tried to force his tongue between her lips. Or when the caress of a shoulder became the caress of a breast. She wanted to respond, he knew, but convention and upbringing stopped her. Her mother, Lady Catherine Ward, had brought up her three daughters with much stricter injunctions on how to behave than most parents.

Catherine Ward was half French, and in her youth, when her incredible beauty was at its height, she had been mistress of Louis XV of France. On a visit to England, she had met William Ward, a man in most things hard of head and heart, who had fallen so deeply in love with her that his previous intention of acquiring a bride who would further his political aspirations was swept aside and he had married Catherine Lescaut, who some said had a strain of Medici blood in her veins. But that was all she could offer him, having no money or political influence with anyone in England.

Lila's mother always knew she was regarded by other women either with an unhealthy interest or with scorn and had taken the utmost pains to appear worthy of the man who loved her so. And she took the same pains with her daughters, so far particularly with Lila, the eldest, who must never give anyone the opportunity of saying "like mother, like daughter," or "bad blood coming out." Lila, who had been told of her mother's past, as her younger sisters would be one day, must appear to be the epitome of virtue.

But Lord Ralph Curringham was not interested in the problems of mothers—though he professed that even though she neared forty, he could well acquire an interest in Lady Catherine Ward if the opportunity arose. At present, however, he wanted only Lila.

Her bosom rose and fell swiftly, the blue silk of her dress tightening with each intake of breath. His hand stroked her arm, her shoulder, then her breast, and with a gasp of desire he pushed her back onto the grass where she lay staring at him wildly for a second. Then he flung himself on top of her, his lips seeking hers, one arm thrust behind her, his free hand running over her body.

For the briefest of seconds she lay there, passive, though he felt sure she wanted to respond. Then, "No!" With enormous strength she sat up and pushed him away. "No," she said again. "You must not."

Resignedly, Ralph pulled away and sat and watched her. Never mind, the day would come when she would not resist. In the meantime, he would have to make do with black-eyed Mathilda, the blacksmith's daughter, who welcomed him with open arms in the barn loft behind her father's cottage. Mathilda was a willing partner to any of his fancies—a willing partner to anyone who wanted her, he knew, but satisfying and very cheap.

When the matchmaking was going on, his father had said to him, "For God's sake, be careful with this girl. Her father thinks the marriage is his idea and all to his advantage. He doesn't realize I had people working on him, urging him to approach me. We need his money."

"I know that, Father," Ralph grinned.

"And don't smirk at me like that, my boy. One of the principal reasons for needing his money is the debts you continually run up with your betting, your drinking, and your women. You *need* a rich woman for a wife."

"I know that too, Father." Ralph had grinned again. "I also need a pretty one, and by gad, Lilian Ward is that."

"You're damned lucky. It's not often riches go with such

a pretty face. So, as I said, be careful. No rough stuff. I don't want her father coming here raging because you couldn't control yourself."

"Don't worry. I'll stick to Mathilda for the time being," Ralph had answered.

"Be careful, even with her," his father had said warningly. "The blacksmith knows his place, but he just might forget it if you go too far with his daughter. He might end up doing *you* more damage than you've done to her."

"It would be impossible to go too far with Mathilda," Ralph chuckled. "You must try her sometime, Father."

There had followed a discussion about women which would have shocked anyone within earshot. Lord Guy Rawlesbury and his son got on very well indeed, and Ralph's rather unusual and excessive sexual needs were in no small respect due to his premature introduction to the female sex by his father—an introduction enjoyed every bit as much by the senior member of the family as the junior, for the former obtained a great deal of gratification as a voyeur.

In the orchard, remembering his father's words, Ralph got to his feet with a smile that was not quite genuine.

"Come along, minx," he said, taking Lila's hand and pulling her to her feet.

Lila could sense the insincerity in the smile and knew she had displeased him, but she didn't care a jot. She knew that however much one desired the pleasures indulged in between men and women, no decent girl would let a man enjoy such pleasures until they were married.

Hand in hand they walked slowly back to the house.

Grassbrook Hall, home of the Wards of Grassbrook, of which village Sir William was the squire, was an impressive residence. The three-story mansion, built of warm, red, Yorkshire stone, was set atop a gentle hill, from which the county of Lancashire was visible on a clear day fifteen miles to the west. Rich lawns surrounded the house. On one side was the beautiful kitchen garden; on another, a rose garden which was now a rainbow of budding flowers. A commanding row of luxurious lime trees at the rear guarded the house from northerly winds.

The orchard from which Lila and Ralph emerged was at the front, and before them on the gently sloping lawn sat Cousin Rosalind and her fiancé, Simon, for once quietly engaged in conversation together. They were to be married in two weeks' time. Lila's two young sisters, Hettie, fourteen, and Mary, two years younger, sat tossing a ball to each other in a desultory fashion, tired after such an unnaturally hot June day.

And Mama! Lila's heart gave a wrench to see her, for her mother was not well. She said nothing, but Lila knew she was in pain from the way her beautiful face would flinch when she thought no one was looking.

There was no sign of her father, and she noticed another carriage in the drive, behind those belonging to Ralph and Simon.

"Papa has a visitor," she said.

Ralph glanced over.

"That is my father's."

His heart sank a little and he hoped it wasn't a sign of trouble that his father's carriage was there, but common sense prevailed and he realized the only sort of trouble he was likely to get into would involve Sir William going to visit *his* father, not the other way round.

Lila's Irish maid, Norah, approached them from the French windows of the drawing room. She gave a little curtsy as they met and said, "Sir William wishes to see you, Miss Lilian. He said you were to go to his study the minute you came back."

"And Lord Ralph?" queried Lila.

"He didn't mention him, miss." Norah shook her head.

Ralph looked puzzled.

"Is my father here?" he asked Norah.

"Yes, milord. Lord Rawlesbury is in the study too."

Lila and Ralph looked at each other and then Lila shrugged.

"I shall see you at teatime, Ralph. I cannot think what Papa and your father want of me."

Turning to Norah, she said, "I am going to my room first. Lay out my green and white muslin dress, please."

Norah looked anxious. "Sir William said you must go to him immediately, miss. He was most insistent."

Lila pouted. "I would have liked to change my dress first. I feel so hot and sticky in this."

She brushed away a few pieces of grass which had clung to her skirts, and as she walked quickly towards the house Norah ran behind.

"There's more bits on the back, miss," she called, picking

them off and wondering what her young mistress had been up to in the orchard with her handsome fiancé.

In his study, lined with the leatherbound books which he had never read, Sir William Ward could not hide his elation. A man of medium height with thinning, sandy hair, his face reflected his insipid character. The only thing of significance he had ever done in his life was to make Catherine Lescaut his wife.

Now he pressed yet another glass of his best port into the hand of the marquess of Rawlesbury, his daughter's future father-in-law. He'd known this would be a good match, but had hesitated to make any advances until several acquaintances had urged him on. The acceptance of his suit on behalf of his daughter had exceeded his wildest dreams. With Rawlesbury as his ally, joined by blood in fact, surely there would be an improvement in his political career which had remained stagnant for so long.

Why, oh why, had he become a Whig? This question had tortured the mind of William Ward for years. When he had decided to enter Parliament thirteen years earlier in 1782, the Government was led by Lord Rockingham, and fellow Whig Charles James Fox was hypnotizing members with his oratory. The Tories were in the doldrums, Lord North having been forced to resign due to his mismanagement of the American war.

With political convictions as irresolute as his character Sir William had allied himself to the winning side, which seemed the sensible thing to do. But the Whig ascendancy was short-lived, for in 1783, young Mr. Pitt had ousted Fox from office and from then on the Tories remained in control. True, Fox and his friend and fellow member Richard Brinsley Sheridan caused many a stir in the chamber with their wit and their oratory. Due to the close friendship they both enjoyed with the Prince of Wales they wielded no small influence in the country, but William Ward had sat, unnoticed, causing not a ripple in the affairs of state during his thirteen years as representative for northwest Yorkshire.

That this dull progress was because he was a remarkably dull fellow did not enter Sir William's head. In his view he had entered politics a year too soon—or a year too late. With the Tories, who knew where he would have been by now?

But never mind, here was Lord Guy Rawlesbury, undisputed leader of the Whigs, diplomat and orator, financial genius— some said William Pitt secretly sought his advice on behalf of the treasury—asking a favor of him. Well, of Lilian, really, but, her participation in the plan was up to him, her father. Inwardly he squirmed a little. Yes, indeed it was a "plan," and a very good one, at that, though a little voice told him it should really be called a "plot."

Where was the girl, anyway? He'd sent for her nearly half an hour ago. He aired his impatience aloud.

"I am in no great hurry," Rawlesbury replied easily, reckoning it was probably his own son who was preventing the girl, albeit unwittingly, from attending the interview with her father.

At that moment, Lila entered and Rawlesbury rose swiftly to his feet, marveling at her beauty. Gad! Ralph was a lucky man. Who would have thought they'd win such a prize as this?

His aristocratic face showed no sign of any thoughts other than those befitting an elderly gentleman of state as he took Lila's hand and she curtsied prettily.

"I'm sorry I am late, Papa. But I was at the far end of the orchard and Norah had no idea where to look for me."

As she showed no signs of distress or damage, the marquess assumed his son had behaved himself and wondered if the marriage could be brought forward a year, or even more. The strain of worrying about Ralph was too great to endure for another two years.

Sir William cleared his throat and spoke.

"Daughter, Lord Rawlesbury has come here to ask you to perform a duty which will be of great value to this country."

Lila looked at them both with astonishment.

She was seventeen years of age, had only set foot out of Yorkshire twice in her life, had never been to London, and knew nothing whatever about politics. What favor could a country bumpkin like herself possibly do for her country?

Curtsying again, more out of confusion than politeness, she murmured, "What duty is this, sir?"

"First, how would you like a holiday in London, girl?"

Lila's eyes lit up with excitement. She had always longed to visit the capital, which seemed the only place in the world where truly exciting things happened. She loved Yorkshire, and Grassbrook Hall was the only place she had ever wanted to live; her friends all lived nearby and there were numerous parties and other social functions. But London was the place where *real* life was lived. Where the Prince of Wales held his fantastic parties—in fact, some people hinted they were really orgies—and where Mrs. Fitzherbert, his secret wife, lived. Where the poor king suffered his strange illness, and where all manner of scandalous and wonderful things took place. Yes, she would dearly love to visit London.

"That would be very pleasant, sir," she answered demurely, thinking it would be unladylike to show her delight.

Sir William felt a twinge of conscience. His daughter looked so young and vulnerable, so childishly pleased at the idea of a holiday in London, while although Rawlesbury had not used the words, she was being unwittingly led into playing a major part in a rather underhanded and sordid plot. Yes, damn it, to put it bluntly, it *was* a plot. They wanted to use his daughter as a spy.

For the briefest moment, Sir William felt the urge to withdraw the offer, or at least suggest the idea be given his wife's approval—approval he knew would not be forthcoming if Catherine knew the facts. But what kind of fool would he appear to Rawlesbury if he withdrew Lila now? And to suggest his wife should give permission gave the impression he was a milksop, unable to make decisions without her consent. He would have to lie to Catherine—as Rawlesbury intended to lie to Lila.

"The Prince of Wales, as you know, recently married," he was saying.

Lila nodded. She had heard rumors about the strange, late-night marriage with the prince so full of alcohol he was scarcely able to stand, for it was said this was the only state in which he could bring himself to face the ceremony, so abhorrent did he find his bride.

"The marriage is a mere six weeks old, but already the prince is talking about maintaining a separate establishment for his wife—he wishes her to move away from Carlton House."

Lila gasped. So the rumors were true. How appalling to think that newlyweds should despise each other so much they could not bear to live in the same building!

"Mind you, girl," Lord Rawlesbury was saying sternly, "this is in the strictest confidence. Don't go tittle-tattling to your friends with this story."

Eyes flashing with the anger she could not very well express,

Lila answered as boldly as she dared, "I would not dream of *tittle-tattling* as you call it, about anything, milord, never mind a matter of such import as this."

"Sorry, girl," laughed Rawlesbury. "I was forgetting all young women are not like me own daughter, Margaret. She prattles and gossips all the day long."

Lila knew that well. The only possible drawback she could see in having Ralph for a husband was gaining the vain and silly Margaret for a sister-in-law. And there was no love lost either, for Margaret made it plain that she had little time for Lila whom she considered far too pretty. Margaret would have much preferred a dull and drab sister-in-law who would boost her already inflated ego.

Pride filled Sir William as he regarded his daughter's pink cheeks. The nagging question of why Rawlesbury was not using his own daughter was answered. Margaret was not sufficiently trustworthy to carry out such delicate work. But his Lilian was a sensible girl, obviously intelligent, and he was sure they could rely on her to act with all the wisdom she had acquired in her short life.

"As you know," the marquess continued, "the prince has always had the good sense to place his sympathies with our party. This has not endeared him to his father, an ardent Tory-lover. George III is a hard, narrow-minded man who cannot bear to think any person has an opinion different from his own, particularly when that person is his eldest son."

Inwardly Lila felt a thrill. To be confided in in this manner was indeed a privilege. That a gentleman of such high esteem as Lord Guy Rawlesbury should speak to her as though she was an equal was a rare and most unexpected honor. She nodded in what she hoped was a grown-up and understanding way as her future father-in-law went on.

"It might not be known to you, but since the prince and his 'secret wife,' Mrs. Fitzherbert, parted, he has formed—what shall I call it?—an alliance with Frances, countess of Jersey, a notorious and bigoted Tory."

"That rumor is rife, sir," murmured Lila.

"Huh! Who would have thought the intimate goings-on at court would reach the wilds of Yorkshire," said Lord Rawlesbury with a sardonic smile.

Anxious lest he thought his host to have been indiscreet, Sir William interrupted, "May I assure you, the news has not reached the household from my lips."

"Oh, no, Papa," Lila assured him and turning to Rawlesbury she said, "Indeed, I was told this by your daughter, Margaret, who keeps us informed of all the London—news."

She nearly said "gossip" which would have made her former indignation at the idea of tittle-tattling look rather hollow, but it was not exactly gossiping merely to listen to Margaret airing her knowledge of the capital and the goings-on at court, gleaned no doubt from her brother, who in turn heard the tales from his own father. It made Margaret feel superior to this country mouse who was to become her sister in two years' time.

Lord Rawlesbury laughed heartily at her revelation.

"So, me own daughter spreads the scandal around in these parts, eh! Well, most of it is true, anyway. Lady Jersey is ensconced at court, in Princess Caroline's entourage, much to the chagrin of the latter. It is bad enough for your husband of six weeks to have a mistress, but to have that person attending upon you is surely more than flesh and blood can stand."

"Disgraceful!" spluttered Sir William.

"The activities of the Prince of Wales have always been disgraceful," said Rawlesbury smoothly. "But he is our principal supporter and we in turn must support him, no matter what antics he engages himself in."

Sir William didn't answer, feeling himself rebuked. If only, thirteen years ago...He dismissed this chain of thought. He needed all his wits about him at the moment. This was no time for regretting past mistakes.

"Who can tell where the loyalties of Lady Jersey lie? Is her allegiance now to the prince—or still with the Tories and Mr. Pitt?" The politician's eyes narrowed and he looked cruel. "It is an impossible situation having that Tory harlot in court. The prince is so easily led. God knows what she might talk him into. And what influence does she have on Princess Caroline? Might she turn her Tory? We *must* know what goes on in that court. We must have someone from our side there." He turned to Lila and beamed upon her, saying, "And that, young lady, is where you come in."

"Me!" gasped Lila. "In court?"

"Precisely," smiled her prospective father-in-law.

"But"—Lila struggled for words, not wishing to offend—"wouldn't I be a spy, an agent for the Whigs?"

His Lordship laughed heartily.

"Bless you, no, my child," he said easily. "Princess Caroline has repeatedly asked for Lady Jersey to be removed, but the prince refuses. It is convenient to have his mistress legitimately under the same roof. Caroline called for Pitt to remove her, but naturally he also refused. He gave some milk-and-water excuse, but one takes for granted that he likes to have his representative so firmly entrenched in court."

Lord Rawlesbury stretched out his hand which held an empty glass and asked, "Could I have a drop more of your excellent port, Sir William?"

As William Ward scurried about refilling the glass Lila could not help but notice his obsequious behavior. This seemed un-usual in her rather staid and distant father. Presumably the task she was being set would further his career, make him happy, and therefore make her mother happy. In that case, she would do it, whatever doubts she might have about its rather dubious nature. And doubts she certainly had. Still, Lord Rawlesbury had not finished and things might sound quite different when he had.

"Yesterday," he went on, "Caroline sent for Charles Fox and myself. She asked if we could arrange for another lady-in-waiting so that she could relieve Lady Jersey of some of her duties. There are other ladies, of course, but she trusts no one. The princess was not willing to make this request to Pitt who would almost certainly provide yet another Tory spy, nor to her husband who could well take the opportunity of installing another mistress."

"Does she not assume Charles Fox and yourself will present her with a Whig spy?" Lila asked innocently.

"I do not doubt it," replied Rawlesbury. "But in order to forestall such a plan, she has stipulated that the lady provided must be less than eighteen years of age. No doubt she considers a gal of sixteen or seventeen is likely to have her head full of other things than politics."

"I see," Lila nodded sagely.

"A very wise move on the part of the princess," said Sir William, anxious to make up for his tactless interruption a few minutes ago.

"Exactly," Lord Rawlesbury agreed. "Last night, Fox and I met with Richard Brinsley Sheridan and we racked our brains trying to think of a young lady suitable as lady-in-waiting to the Princess Caroline. Who knows? If the king is ill yet again, she might become our queen at any moment. Me own daughter, Margaret, is too featherheaded to be considered. Then I thought of you, and Fox and Sheridan both agreed you sounded like the ideal person."

Lila felt flattered beyond belief. To think that three such distinguished statesmen and friends of the prince had actually been discussing her and approved of her being chosen for this important role!

"So you see," Rawlesbury was saying, "there is no question of you being a spy. The princess has asked for someone and we have chosen you. And it may not be for long. Some say the prince already tires of Lady Jersey and has thoughts of Mrs. Fitzherbert once more. The situation at court could change drastically at any moment."

"I see," Lila nodded again. "Then it is all quite acceptable."

"Of course," the marquess assured her in smooth, unctuous tones.

Sir William Ward felt pricks of shame for committing his daughter to all this politicking. She was honest, straight as a dye, he knew, and it would be quite against her nature, once she was taken into the confidence of the princess, to tell tales behind her back, to reveal the names of her visitors, her behavior, opinions, conversations. And what would Rawlesbury say if Lila's integrity stood in the way of his plan? Sir William wondered uneasily.

"How soon can you leave?" the marquess was asking Lila.

"I shall have to talk with Mama," she replied. "There is nothing to delay me at this time."

Sir William hastily interjected: "Your mother is not well, Lila. Do not burden her with all the details of this arrangement. Just the fact that you are for a short time to be lady-in-waiting to the Princess of Wales should suffice. That should please her."

Lila would have liked to discuss the matter in detail with her mother, but no mind. She could tell her some other time. The vague doubts disappeared when she began to think of how exciting it would be. Visiting London, seeing in the flesh all the people she had hitherto only heard mention of—it would be wonderful beyond her wildest dreams.

"What about Ralph?" she asked suddenly. "May I tell him?"

"Yes. Yes, of course," answered Rawlesbury. Ralph certainly wouldn't mind the girl being in London, but it meant she was more at risk from him than at home. He would have to have a very stern word with his son. Which reminded him, now was an appropriate time to bring up the idea of the marriage being brought forward a year or more.

He turned to Sir William, raising his eyebrows in such a way that his host realized the interview with Lila was at an end.

"That will be all, Lilian," Sir William said. "I think I heard the bell for tea."

Lila curtsied and left the room with a soft "Good-bye, sir."

Rawlesbury turned to William Ward, holding out his glass for another fill of port and began, "Now, about this wedding . . ."

Chapter Two

"I do declare, this is the most boring and tedious place in the whole world!"

Lady Sylvia Beauchamp pouted at the jade inkstand which sat on the bureau before her, then with a sigh drew the thick, crested paper towards her.

"I must do at least another ten of these silly letters before midday. Fancy sending a chamber pot for a wedding present. How do you thank the sender? Do you say 'I'm sure it will come in useful' or 'Every time I use it, I shall think of you'?" With an exaggerated gesture of despair she flung down the pen which emitted a series of blots onto the cream stationery.

Lila laughed. "Sylvia! They did send a matching water jug and bowl and they are quite beautifully hand-painted and made of Sevres china too."

They were sitting in the morning room of Princess Caroline's apartment in Carlton House. In Lila's view, the room was decorated in the most appalling taste. In her Yorkshire home Mama had thin silk curtains in the morning room with lemon-colored walls and the chairs and cushions covered in the palest gold satin. A bright, cheerful room it was, that made you feel the sun was shining even on the dullest morning.

But here! The drapes and most of the coverings were of plum-colored velvet, the carpet a rare Persian design. Ornaments were crammed onto every inch of surface of every shelf and table: marble busts, candelabra, girandoles, clocks of a variety of shapes and designs, priceless porcelain. Paintings which Lila recognized as being by artists currently in vogue, such as Vermet and Claude, covered the walls, not to mention many gloomy family portraits in frames of the most ornate and heavy design. On one wall hung a collection of miniatures of the Prince of Wales' sisters, all six of whom looked unbelievably pretty and angelic.

According to Lila's newfound friend Sylvia, the Princess Caroline also hated the room, as indeed she hated her entire apartment and, apparently, the whole of Carlton House. It was so different from her German home, she constantly announced, where the accent was on comfort rather than show. And on dirt, Sylvia had told Lila. Rumor had it that her German castle was indescribably squalid for a royal household.

As yet Lila had not encountered the princess. Lila had arrived in London the previous day, having driven down from Yorkshire in the marquess of Rawlesbury's carriage, accompanied by the marquess and her father. They had gone straight to Carlton House, Lila's eyes bright with interest as they passed by the Tower of London, then the Houses of Parliament, practically shimmering in the brilliant June sunshine. Londoners looked different from Yorkshire people, she thought. More flamboyant, they strutted about in a jaunty fashion, with cocksure expressions on their faces.

And the noise! Apart from the clip-clop of horses' hooves and the wooden cartwheels rattling over the cobbled streets, it seemed as though everyone was selling something and was determined to shout the loudest. Even a tiny girl with a box hung around her neck in which was heaped a pile of lace, hawked her delicate wares in a shrill and penetrating voice.

Soon, she would be able to walk these streets, thought Lila, sample the sweets a ragged boy was making in a pot suspended

over a fire in the gutter, buy some of that lace or any of the
hundreds of other articles for sale. She hugged herself with
glee. She had forgotten the sad parting from her mother and
two little sisters, and was thinking about the wonderful time
ahead.

The outside of Carlton House fairly took her breath away
with the simplicity and dignity of its Corinthian portico, but
the interior was quite a different matter. She entered to find
an extravanganza of light and color. The prince had already
lived there twelve years, yet workmen were everywhere, busily
toiling away to satisfy His Royal Highness's yearning to have
a home comparable to Versailles. Privately, Lila thought it
vulgar and ostentatious in the extreme. She preferred the quiet
and simple decoration of her own home.

In the carriage she had said a tearful good-bye to her father,
and then Lord Rawlesbury had taken her into Carlton House
where he placed her in the care of Robert Swann, secretary to
Princess Caroline. Lila's arrival seemed to put him in a flutter.

"Her Highness is at Windsor today, milord," Swann lisped
distractedly, his wishy-washy face frantic, as if he were somehow to blame for his mistress visiting her in-laws, who happened to be the king and queen of England.

"No matter, no matter," Rawlesbury snapped. "This is Miss
Lilian Ward and she is expected."

Swann scurried off and fetched Miss Sylvia Beauchamp, an
engaging young lady with a mischievous face and a tumble of
black, frizzy ringlets. She seemed delighted to take this Yorkshire ignoramus under her wing to regale with her formidable
knowledge of Carlton House and its residents. Sylvia was at
present involved in the endless task of writing to thank all those
on the princess's side who had sent wedding gifts. Although
in reality Robert Swann was secretary, he dealt only with matters of state and business. Lady Sylvia had a smattering of
German which suited her to the monotonous task.

"I do hope they don't compare letters," she complained
bitterly. "I cannot think of five hundred different ways of saying
'thank you' in less than four lines."

Lila was helping. She knew no German but copied from
Sylvia's letters. She suspected Sylvia was not as bored as she
made out. It was merely a pose that perhaps everyone adopted
in court, and soon perhaps she herself would be tut-tutting over

the tedium of life in what was probably the most exciting city in the world, in a house with an unchallenged reputation for wit and good company.

On her first night Lila had found it hard not to cry herself to sleep, for she felt very lonely even though she was sharing a bed with Sylvia. This morning she felt much happier, despite the overpoweringly ornate room. She longed to go out exploring—to see all the sights which, apart from the brief glimpse she'd had from the carriage, she had only read and heard about. It was with trepidation, however, that she looked forward to meeting her royal mistress. She said as much to Sylvia as she addressed an envelope.

"Oh, she's a decent old soul," said Sylvia with complete lack of awe and respect which Lila, in her innocence, thought was quite genuine.

She was therefore surprised when the door opened and two ladies entered and Sylvia nearly fell off her chair to curtsy and utter unintelligible replies to the guttural *"Gut morgen"* which the foremost of the new arrivals said in greeting.

Untrained in such matters, Lila hastily bobbed a curtsy on the assumption that this was the Princess Caroline of Brunswick, now Princess of Wales, and perhaps soon the queen of England.

The first thing she noticed about the princess was her ruddy complexion. She had the reddest cheeks Lila had ever seen, the redness accentuated by a mass of unbrushed auburn hair. She wore an ill-fitting gown of dark blue, most unbecoming on her rather dumpy, shapeless figure. Nevertheless, she seemed friendly and open, and Lila took to her at once.

"You help with the letters, *ja?*" she queried and Lila nodded.

"Yes, ma'am." She hoped her voice sounded firm and unafraid, for Sylvia's nervousness seemed childish and unbecoming, and she had no wish to appear so awestruck.

The woman accompanying the princess did not give out the same warmth. She was matronly, a cold-looking person with graying hair, and the glance she gave Lila was icy.

"So this is the person sent by Rawlesbury?" she inquired in clipped, precise English.

"Ja! Lilian Ward, is it not?"

Lila nodded again. The pronunciation of her name—*Leelian Wood*—made it sound so odd and exotic that she smiled and the princess smiled back.

"You are nice, friendly girl, Lilian. Tomorrow, you will

come in my carriage when I ride through the park." She patted Lila on the shoulder in a rather clumsy manner.

"There is no need, ma'am," said a chill voice from behind. "I am always at Your Highness's disposal to accompany you in your carriage."

Without turning, the princess replied, "I am sure, Lady Jersey, you must be as sick of my company as I am of yours," and then gave Lila a grin, aware of the cold looks being bestowed upon her back but quite indifferent to them.

Excitement coursed through Lila's veins. So this was the infamous Lady Jersey, the Prince of Wales' current favorite. How could this plump grandmother have supplanted the lovely Maria Fitzherbert in his affections? Her reflections were cut short by a crushing glance from Lady Jersey as she left the room with the princess.

Lila thought she could detect the smell of cabbages cooking—a sour, rather distasteful aroma—and she sniffed, wrinkling her nose questioningly. Lady Sylvia saw her and giggled.

"So you noticed. Dreadful, isn't it?"

"What is it?" Lila asked.

"Our dear princess, of course. They say she has not bathed since the wedding. It is unhealthy, she tells them. And I don't know what objection she has to changing her clothes, for she is reluctant to do that also."

"She is very nice in spite of it," declared Lila stoutly.

"She liked you, I could see that," Sylvia said cattily. Privately, she was irked by Lila's composure during the princess's visit. "So therefore you have made an enemy of Lady Jersey. That will do you no good."

Lila was upset at Sylvia's reaction.

"I have done nothing wrong," she said indignantly.

"What difference does that make?" Sylvia answered smugly. "You caused the Princess of Wales to like you, and that is wrong in the eyes of Lady Jersey."

"Shall we get on with these letters?" Lila suggested stiffly, disappointed with Sylvia whom she had regarded as a friend. They sat down again at the beautiful little mahogany bureau set with mother-of-pearl—a gift, Sylvia had informed her, from Louis XV of France on the birth of the Prince of Wales. Lila did not mention her mother's relationship with that notorious French monarch.

* * *

No one had as yet told Lila what her duties were to be, and that afternoon she felt a little lost when Sylvia disappeared. She sought out Robert Swann who could usually be found in his little room near the entrance to Princess Caroline's apartments. She knocked, waited, and then opened the door. Like all the rooms in the house it was opulently decorated, with dark blue hangings and heavy, cumbersome furniture. But the carved desk where Robert Swann should have sat was empty, so Lila wandered off down a corridor. Her heart lifted slightly when she saw a door at the end which led out to a garden. She realized she had not set foot outside since her arrival.

Like the inside of Carlton House, its garden was, in Lila's opinion, far too elaborate. The scent of flowers jostling for space within the neat borders was almost overpowering. Roses the size of cabbages, suspended from wrought-iron lattices, dangled before her eyes. It was claustrophobic. Tears came to Lila's eyes as she longed for the wild abandon of the garden at home, where flowers were allowed to spread and thrive at will, and where her mother let nature's colors match of their own accord. *Oh, to see a familiar face,* she thought sadly, and as if in answer to her prayer, her father appeared at the end of the path on which she walked.

"Papa!"

Sir William Ward felt almost unbearable pangs of remorse as his daughter's slight arms were flung around his neck and she hugged him with all her might. He was not a demonstrative man and his daughters had learned not to expect much in the way of affection from him. This involuntary show of love from his eldest daughter made Sir William aware of how lonely she must be. He did not fail to notice the trace of tears on her thick golden lashes.

"There, now," he said gruffly, disentangling himself from the white arms. "I've come to see how you are getting along."

"Very well, Papa," Lila assured him, but her father knew full well this was not true. If only he could raise the courage to pack her into the carriage which waited for him outside and take her back to Yorkshire, to her mother and her sisters. But what would Rawlesbury think of him then? And Fox and Sheridan? The home secretaryship which they had promised him when the Whigs came to power would be lost. Indeed, his political career as it stood now would be jeopardized if he withdrew Lila. He should have stood firm in the first place, he realized, but it was too late. She was here, his precious Lila, planted unknowingly in this hotbed of intrigue as a spy for the Whigs.

"I'm to ride in the park with the princess tomorrow," Lila told him proudly.

Sir William's heart sank a little lower. His one hope, after weakly committing Lila to the scheme, had been that the princess would dislike her and she would have no opportunity to discover anything. But if Princess Caroline took a fancy to her—well, the Whigs would be delighted, expecting no end of information. Sir William changed the subject.

"Do you know why I have come here?" he asked. "I suddenly realized my little girl was probably not fitted out to be a lady-in-waiting to royalty. So, I have arranged for a seamstress to call tomorrow. What time would be suitable? She will make you a wardrobe fit for a princess. Just tell her what you want—expense is no object."

These words were strange coming from the normally careful Sir William. Although by no means tight-fisted, he could scarcely be said to throw his money about, and until now Lilian and her sisters had been dressed carefully but not extravagantly. Unaware that this generosity was to salve his conscience, Lila once again threw her arms about her father's neck.

"Oh, Papa! You dear, dear Papa," she cried, and to Sir William's awful surprise, he felt tears come to his own eyes.

"There, there," he said patting his daughter's shoulder awkwardly and wondering why a presentiment of doom descended over him.

"My carriage awaits," he said, unable to stand being there a second longer. "What time do you wish the seamstress to call? Her name is Prymm, by the way. Miss Annabelle Prymm. She has made clothes for the royal family for many years."

"Early afternoon, Papa. There doesn't seem to be much to do in the afternoons."

"I will see to it." With a perfunctory kiss on Lila's forehead, Sir William hurried away.

Lila felt indescribably sad to see his figure disappear round the corner at the end of the rose-covered trellis. She had never felt particularly close to her father, but now he was her only link with her dearly loved home and family.

She wondered if Ralph would soon come to see her for he was frequently in London. She turned off at an angle down a path lined with yet more roses, all planted with monotonous regularity—one red, one white, one yellow. What would happen, she thought with amusement, if the gardener made a mistake and a yellow rose grew where a white or red one should be? Would he be beheaded, sent to the tower?

Smiling at these absurd thoughts she skipped along the path to suddenly land sprawling at the feet of an elegant gentleman seated on a beautifully carved wooden seat in a little alcove that Lila had not noticed. His immaculately shod feet, stretched out in front of him, partially covered by Lila's skirts, were the cause of her fall and she stared at them indignantly as she half sat, half lay on the ground before him.

"What!" the gentleman declared in a lazy voice. "Is the prince allowing his cherished gardens to be used as a playground for children now?"

Lila shifted her gaze from the feet, which had not moved, to the man's face. It was difficult to tell whether the deep brown of his skin was natural or caused by overexposure to the sun, but whatever it was, it made him look quite unusually attractive, particularly as his eyes were a deep, startling blue and looked as though they always held the same amused sparkle that they did now. Yet at the same time his face had a sternness about it that told Lila that in a different situation he would stand no nonsense. Contrary to the modern fashion for gentlemen to be clothed in decorative brocades and laces, this man was plainly though elegantly dressed in black.

She began to struggle to her feet.

"Wait!" ordered the man, and removing the pile of papers from his knee and placing them on the seat beside him, he withdrew his feet from under Lila's skirts and stood up. Then, with a barely perceptive effort, he bent down, and putting both hands around her waist, he lifted Lila and placed her unceremoniously down in front of him.

"What do you mean, children?" she demanded angrily, conscious of the fact that his hands were still on her, almost meeting round her narrow middle. The man's eyes raked her lazily from head to toe and Lila found herself flushing and feeling a surge of anger at the same time. How dare this arrogant stranger treat her in such a familiar manner? She struggled to free herself from his grip. He gave a deep sigh.

"I leave go with reluctance," he told her solemnly. "Though why such a child should object to the caresses of a man old enough to be her father, I do not know. Methinks I saw you not a minute ago showering hugs and kisses upon a man who cannot claim many more years than I."

"Don't be ridiculous, sir," Lila cried scornfully. "That man *was* my father. Whilst you . . ."

She paused and looked into the man's face. He could scarcely be more than thirty and must think her young indeed if he considered himself old enough to be her parent.

"I am Miss Lilian Ward, sir," she said, drawing herself to her full height. "Lady-in-Waiting to her Royal Highness, the Princess Caroline. I am nearly eighteen years of age and engaged to be married."

Lila felt this speech to be full of dignity and was sure it would impress this impossible stranger. She was mortified when he laughed aloud.

"Bless me! It seems I have not only quite literally upset your pretty little body, but your dignity too. My apologies, Miss Lilian Ward. Do you accept them?"

He held out his hand and Lila grudgingly put her small one into it. With what she considered a mocking gesture, he kissed her hand, and she could not help but retort.

"I do accept your apologies, but only because it would be churlish not to. But I dislike your manner, sir. I see nothing amusing about being seventeen, and there is not an older man or woman in the world who has not been so during their lives." She regarded him coolly. "Did you encounter such hilarity when you were unfortunate enough to be my age?"

For several seconds the man looked quite astounded, even faintly angry, yet his blue eyes sparkled still and Lila was acutely aware of the fact that his large brown hand still held hers warmly. She wanted to pull her hand away but at the same time enjoyed the protective feel of his hard, leathery skin. His hands were well cared for, the nails polished, but they looked as though they had accomplished hard, physical work recently. The skin on the palms was tough, even calloused.

"No, sir," she said in a steady voice, "if you will allow me my hand I will make my way back to my cradle."

The man released her hand with another laugh which irritated Lila still more. He let go of her hand and bowed.

"Farewell, little maid. Perhaps we shall meet again under more dignified circumstances." His voice was deep and Lila thought there was a trace of an accent.

Her eyes flashed. "I assure you, sir, *I* have felt no loss of dignity."

She turned and walked away, head held high, then spoiled the effect by tripping over a stone which she kicked angrily aside, hurting her toe in the process. For several minutes she marched, even when out of the irritating man's sight. If only he hadn't been so attractive her anger would not have been so confused. If it had been, for instance, Robert Swann, she would have known exactly how she felt, but the memory of those penetrating blue eyes, the feel of his hands on her own, the firm pressure on her waist—all this stayed with her and she wished they had met under more auspicious circumstances.

Were these wrongful thoughts, she mused, for a girl engaged to be married?

Her temper was not improved when she discovered that after walking blindly for so long, she was now lost, once again in an enclosed corridor of trellises, this time covered with a sweet-smelling vine she did not recognize. For several minutes she wandered along until she came to a summerhouse constructed in the manner of a small Greek temple. Lila was about to thankfully enter and rest when she heard voices from within, so she turned away to resume her search for a way out of the garden.

At that very moment a man emerged from the opening in the little temple and stood looking right and left. Some sixth sense made Lila step back and enter a passage she had just passed on her right, and in her green dress she was well nigh invisible behind the trail of vine leaves.

There was something about the stranger which took her breath away, though in quite a different manner from the gentle-man she had recently met. It was frightening the way he filled the doorway where he stood, his head only inches from the roof of the opening, his massive shoulders nearly broad enough to touch the marble sides. He wore a cream shirt opened at the neck and pulled out at the waist of his tight, green britches, and as he stood looking about him, he yawned and began to tuck the shirt in. The sleeves were rolled back to reveal thick, powerful arms. Lila was glad she had hidden, glad she had not been caught up in the penetrating gaze with which the man swept the garden in front of him. She could not see the color of his eyes, which were little more than slits in his craggy face, but his hair was blond, almost white, and cropped unusually short.

He turned and spoke to someone behind him in the summerhouse, and Lila, who could scarcely hear the words, had a feeling they were not English. She desperately wanted to move away but was terrified of making a noise and revealing herself to the man in the doorway—though why she should not be free to walk where she liked in the grounds of what was now her home, she knew not. This was silly, she told herself, yet she remained planted in the same spot.

Then the man's companion joined him. At first all she could see was a head of hair, but that vivid auburn was enough to raise suspicion, and the suspicion was confirmed when he turned aside and the person was indeed revealed to be Caroline, Princess of Wales.

But what horrified Lila was that the princess was fastening the front of her dress which was opened to the waist, and that the man threw his arm familiarly about her shoulders.

Throwing caution to the wind, Lila turned and ran.

Chapter Three

Lila spent a miserable night. She did not know why they had given her a room to share with Lady Sylvia Beauchamp, but tomorrow she decided to insist on a room of her own. She longed to be alone with her thoughts, and Sylvia's chatter irritated and bored her. It was mainly gossip about people Lila had never heard of, and though she was dying to inquire about Princess Caroline and the blond man in green, she was reluctant to raise Sylvia's suspicions.

Later, as she lay abed beside her sleeping companion, Lila's mind buzzed with the image of what she had seen in the summerhouse. Margaret, Ralph's sister, had told her that the princess's moral character was not all it should be, and that she frequently boasted of the many affairs she had enjoyed back in Germany. One in particular had come to nothing because the man concerned was not of royal birth. It was said that the princess had been outrageously familiar with the sailors on the ship bringing her to England and that at Carlton House she indulged in the most coarse conversation at mealtimes. It was supposedly this latter habit more than any other which had turned the prince against his bride.

Lila had listened to these stories, as she had listened to those wilder and even more fantastic tales about the prince himself— the orgies, the incredible extravagances and affairs—without really believing them. It did not seem possible that a woman destined to become the queen of England could behave in such a vulgar manner. Would the authorities, those distant, lordly creatures who organized the affairs of the country, allow such a thing to happen?

As she lay tossing and turning she made up her mind to have no part in spreading the tale. In her mother she would confide, and perhaps Ralph, but not in Sylvia, snoring beside her, or any of the other ladies of the court.

When she finally managed to make the image of the princess's lover disappear from her mind, it was replaced by the equally disturbing recollection of the irritating gentleman in black, and she blushed, imagining again his hands on her waist as he stared down at her with tolerant amusement.

She longed to seek the advice of her mother. How was she to cope with the drive in the princess's carriage the following morning knowing what she had done? She would have to act as if nothing had happened. Did she have sufficient guile?

At last, in the early hours of the morning, Lila fell asleep.

The princess was as friendly as ever. Despite everything, Lila could not help liking her open, hearty manner. She wore a rather dusty-looking dress of purple, and her hat sat rather awkwardly on her abundant auburn hair. Lila wondered why Lady Jersey, who stood glowering in the background, had not advised the princess to use more hatpins.

"*Gut morgen,* Miss Lilian," the princess greeted her, pleasantly, ignoring Sylvia, who stood behind Lila. "And what a pretty dress you are wearing."

At home, her blue dress had been considered the height of fashion, but Lila now saw that her father was right to be sending her a seamstress, for here the dress was quite out of date. She had already noticed several frocks of quite a different style. That morning, for instance, Sylvia had on a thin muslin dress of cream, embroidered with blue forget-me-nots, gathered under the bust with a cream satin ribbon. Underneath, she must have had on only the thinnest of petticoats. By contrast, Lila's dress with its bustle, panniers, and layers of petticoats was far too elaborate. Lila knew she must write her mother and inform her of the new fashion.

As they walked towards the door of the apartment, the princess astonished Lila by putting her arm around Lila's shoulders in a hearty fashion.

"Come, Miss Lilian Ward. Let us see what fine men are on show for us this lovely morning."

Lila would have frozen in her tracks had she not been swept along by the princess's muscular arm but froze instead minutes later when they emerged from the front of Carlton House, and there, standing on the steps leading to the gothic columns before a black and gold carriage, was the massive blond man she had seen in the summerhouse the previous afternoon. Today he wore a tricorn hat and a tight-fitting jacket over the green britches.

He leaped towards the carriage door when he saw them, and perhaps if Lila had not observed them together the previous day, she would not have noticed the way the coachman, when taking the princess's arm, pressed his knuckles into her breast. Lila hung back, reluctant to let the man touch her.

Sylvia, who had come out with them, glanced at her and asked, "What is the matter, Lila?"

"Who is that man?" Lila asked.

"Ludwig Something-or-other. The princess brought him with her. Some people do say . . ."

But what it was people said, Lila did not have the opportunity to hear, for the princess shouted to her to come along, and Lila crossed swiftly to the carriage and leaped in before the man could help.

For most of the ride, Princess Caroline conducted a conversation in German with her coachman which seemed to afford both of them great amusement. When she laughed, Caroline threw back her head and opened her mouth wide, showing two rows of beautiful, white teeth. Her laugh was deep, like a man's.

The Mall and Hyde Park were crowded with open carriages, for it was a beautiful June day. Lila looked about her with interest. This was what she had come to London for. This was a scene quite unique in her experience: the many ornate carriages bearing ladies and gentlemen with powdered hair, which was an uncommon sight in Yorkshire. She noticed the smartest ladies did not wear a hat, but merely two ostrich feathers pinned in the back of their hair, which rippled and swayed.

She sat facing the back of the carriage so it was not until people had passed by that she could see them properly. Therefore, a maroon carriage containing two couples had gone some way along before she noticed that one of the men was Ralph. She could see that one of the women, wearing a vivid, strawberry-pink gown, was quite beautiful, her hair a deep, luxurious red, and lips rosier than any Lila had ever seen.

The princess turned to see what was claiming Lila's attention.

"Two—what you call them—young blades?" she remarked. "With their *filles de joie.*"

"Ma'am?" Lila asked, puzzled. The expression was strange to her, although her French was good.

"They're strumpets, little Miss Innocence," laughed the princess. "Did you not notice their painted faces?"

Lila's heart began to thump. Ralph, her fiancé, with a woman like that! Of course, she had heard of such women. There was Mathilda, the blacksmith's daughter at home. Everyone knew she sold herself for a few coins, and Lila knew there were women at the other end of the scale who sold their favors for immense riches. Indeed, her own mother, through no fault of her own, had been given to a king. But what was Ralph, who loved her, doing with such a woman? And to think he was in London too. Her departure from Yorkshire had been so swift they had only been able to exchange a few words after his father's visit. He had not mentioned any intention then of coming to London so soon.

The rest of the ride was a nightmare. Fortunately, the princess was not interested in conversation with Lila. She bowed with mock graciousness from time to time or waved in a wild manner when they passed someone she seemed to like. All these gestures were accompanied by a string of German to her coachman.

The rich extravagance of color all about, the muted clip-clop of the dozens of horses, the buzz of chatter from every quarter, the bejeweled ladies and gentlemen, the glittering carriages—all was lost on Lila. Indeed, Carlton House seemed almost like home when they returned. Lila left the princess as quickly as possible to go to her room, praying Sylvia would not be there so she could be alone with her thoughts.

She sped up the stairs, two at a time, and had almost reached the top when she collided with someone in the most unladylike fashion, her head meeting the stomach of the person descending, and she would have fallen backwards had not two hands quickly grasped her and held her steady.

Looking up startled, she met the amused eyes of the man whose feet she had fallen over the day before in the garden.

"Glory be! Miss Lilian Ward. Do they not teach children how to climb stairs nowadays? 'Tis sensible to look where one is going, not where one has been. You are more likely to reach the top that way."

Inwardly, Lila groaned. It was true that she had been bounding up the stairs looking down at her feet instead of in front of her. And of course this awful, arrogant man was coming down just then.

"I beg your pardon, sir," she said stiffly.

"Our entire acquaintance seems to rest upon my lifting you from the ground or saving you from falling there."

This day, the man was dressed in military uniform. He wore a white shirt and britches and a red frock coat with gold frogging. A sword rattled at his side. Lila wriggled free from his grip and saw that in one hand he carried a gray plumed hat. She had no idea what regiment he belonged to. Once again, the infuriating man smiled down at her.

"Here, let me escort you to the top of these stairs so that I may leave with a mind relieved by the knowledge of your safety."

Taking her arm he helped her with exaggerated care up the final few steps until she eventually stood on the landing above him. In a teasing voice he added, "Now, I trust it is not necessary for me to carry you and place you in your cot."

Suddenly, Lila felt it was all too much. What with the loneliness of her position, the burden of her secret knowledge about her royal mistress and the German coachman, the cold dislike of Lady Jersey, not to mention the humiliation of seeing Ralph with those—those women, and now, to cap it all, to have this dreadful man making such fun of her. To her horror, she felt tears prick her eyelids and she blinked furiously to drive them away.

"I say, you're not hurt are you?" The man's voice changed

completely and was full of concern. Lila was disgusted with herself for giving the impression she would actually resort to tears because she had hurt herself.

"Of course not," she answered coldly, holding the tears in check with grim determination, though the effort it cost her was obvious to the onlooker.

"Shall I call someone?"

At least he didn't look amused anymore, though Lila would have preferred humor to pity, which she could not stand.

"I am perfectly all right, sir. Pray concern yourself no more with me. I shall retire to my room—to my nursery—and hope never to bother you further."

At that moment Sylvia appeared at the bottom of the staircase and climbed it in a far more ladylike manner than had Lila, glancing at the pair curiously as she reached the top and passed them.

"May I assure you, Miss Ward, that both our encounters have caused me much pleasure. Unlike you, I look forward to our meeting again. *Adieu*—until our next collision."

He waved a gloved hand and, tucking his hat under one arm, went smartly down the stairs. Lila couldn't help wishing he would trip and fall to the bottom.

"Who is that infuriating man?" demanded Lila, entering the bedroom where Sylvia sat patting her hair in front of a mirror.

"My dear! Infuriating? Never. That is Captain Phillip Grenville. An utterly delicious and adorable man whom the entire court—the ladies that is—have set their caps at whether they be married or not."

"Oh!"

Lila sat down on the corner of the large bed a bit troubled, for Captain Phillip Grenville was practically a national figure and had been for several years now. Being part French and having relatives there at the beginning of the revolution, he had traveled across and snatched them from under the noses of their captors with the greatest daring. As time went on he had returned again and again to bring back to England refugees who would otherwise have been bloodily executed. Not only the titled and illustrious nobility, but their servants too, all destined to suffer the same fate, were rescued by the redoubtable Captain Grenville. On two occasions, Lila had been told, he had himself rowed a small boat containing several small children across the Channel. Wild tales circulated, as they

always do about such figures: He had delivered a baby in a
carriage fleeing from Paris; had been involved in an abortive
attempt to rescue the executed King Louis XVI and had almost
lost his own life in the process.

Even Lila, who had never seen a likeness of the captain,
had felt her heart swell when reading or hearing of his exploits.
His uniform, then, would be of the Prince of Wales' Own
Regiment, the Light Dragoons, for it was well known that the
Prince had taken the captain under his wing and obtained his
transfer to his own troop, which was officered almost entirely
by his personal friends. Of course, being part French, Grenville
would not have been expected to participate in the present war
against France. In any case, the prince's men were not ever
likely to take up arms in battle.

This was the man Lila had tripped over and collided with.
This hero of the people! Waves of burning shame swept over
her. "The Black Arrow" they called him. Yesterday he had
been dressed entirely in black and she had thought him, with
his papers, to be some sort of clerk.

Really, it was impossible for things to go more wrong. She
wished she could confide in Sylvia but remembered her pleasure
yesterday when Lady Jersey had disapproved of her. How Sylvia would love to hear of her embarrassing encounters with the
famous Captain Grenville and of her glimpse of Ralph with
his *fille de joie*.

Oh, Mama! If only she was there to talk to.

Just then there was a knock on the door and a tiny maid
entered to tell them that there was tea in the drawing room.

Lila had forgotten all about Miss Prymm. She was about to
set out again in search of Robert Swann in another attempt to
discover the exact nature of her duties at Carlton House when
she was informed that the seamstress had arrived and was
waiting for her in the bedroom.

Miss Annabelle Prymm was a stocky little woman, surprisingly light on her feet. She darted to and fro like a plump
sparrow, her bright eyes looking Lila up and down expertly.

"An eighteen-inch waist, I do not doubt."

Confirmation of this with a tape measure drew a sharp gasp
of envy from Sylvia who had followed them upstairs with
interest.

"Well," snorted Miss Prymm, "much good will it do you,

for you are about to lose it completely. You will have noticed
ladies no longer have waists—those who must be stylish, that
is. For myself"—she patted her ample, tightly corseted middle—"I shall keep my waist until the day I die, but if you wish
to be in the latest fashion—"

"Which I do," Lila interrupted eagerly.

"Then your waist must go and *this* becomes your middle."

She tied a ribbon tightly around Lila, directly underneath
her bosom.

"See? Did you know this is called the Empire line? Now,
your father told me you need an entire wardrobe. Two ball
gowns, two dresses for walking and at least six day dresses,
and three of them out of silk or satin so they will be suitable
for receptions and the like. That should do for now. And, of
course, some shawls. I will leave you some samples. They are
made in Paisley and you can choose once you know what colors
your dresses will be." Miss Prymm paused and deliberated.
"You will need a cloak for evening. They are not so full now,
as they used to be. Would you like velvet? I have some beautiful
crushed strawberry velvet out of which I was to make Princess
Augusta a cloak, but she did something quite naughty and the
king canceled the order."

"You make clothes for the princesses?" Lila asked in awe.

"All of them. And I sewed for the Princess Dowager of
Wales who used to live in this very house, though I must say
it was very different when I used to come here years ago."
Miss Prymm sniffed disdainfully. "See, here are some samples.
Most of the material I already have. The rest is stocked by
Messrs. Hodges and Woolf, from whom I buy all my goods.
Do you like any of these?"

She emptied the contents of a cotton bag onto the bed and
a rainbow of small squares of stuff spilled out. It reminded
Lila of the magician who sometimes entertained at their parties
at home who produced endless silky scarves from his sleeves
and pockets.

"Oh! This is pretty. And this. And this too."

She picked up one piece after another, each of them seeming
more desirable than the one before. Sylvia joined in and the
two girls became totally absorbed in trying to pick out the
pieces which appealed to them most.

Miss Prymm watched them with narrowed eyes. Carlton
House she knew was a hive of plots and crossplots. Everyone

there, she reckoned, was there for some ulterior motive, to keep watch on somebody else. Lady Sylvia Beauchamp was the daughter of Lord Barnaby Fernicrust, the member of Parliament who until recently had been foreign minister. There was no doubt in Miss Prymm's mind what his daughter was doing there—a scheming minx if ever she saw one. She had to be a Tory spy—after all, the chief representative of the Tories at Carlton House was Lady Jersey, but she was frequently off with the prince at Brighton. Lady Sylvia was no doubt there to report on happenings when the prince's mistress was absent and in all likelihood told tales on that lady herself, for who knew which way she might jump in view of her close relationship with the Whig prince?

The sharp eyes of Miss Prymm had noticed the real jealousy with which Sylvia was observing Miss Lilian Ward. But what was *she* doing here, Miss Prymm wondered. Appearances were deceptive, she knew. She had not reached nearly seventy years of age (though there was no one but herself familiar with *that* piece of information) without learning that the most innocuous-looking individual could be the most dangerous. But there was something about this girl, with her angelic face, that made Miss Prymm feel sure her presence in the court of the Princess of Wales was quite innocent. The child's blue eyes were so open, and she looked at people so directly and spoke so firmly that the seamstress could not imagine her being party to any court machinations. She could, of course, be an unknowing tool in some intrigue, and the thought of this being the case made Miss Prymm feel angry. Nowadays when she got angry, though, Miss Prymm's heart beat faster than it ought to, so she shrugged and told herself it was no business of hers. She was only there to make the girl clothes.

Lila had at last, after anguished deliberation, chosen several pieces of cloth.

"Could one dress be ready by the end of next week?" she inquired. "My cousin Rosalind marries then and I am to go home to Yorkshire for the wedding."

"Of course, young lady. Which one would you like me to begin with?"

Lila picked up a piece of delicate yellow silk, almost transparent.

"This, I think. With ribbons the same color. And you will make me a new chemise?"

The thick cambric ones trimmed with heavy lace which she now wore would be useless under such flimsy material in its simple, flowing style.

"Of course, miss. You'll need several."

She arranged to come the following afternoon at the same time.

"We are going to be busy, Miss Lilian, over the next few weeks. Each dress will require three or four fittings."

Lila was sorry to see the comfortable, homely seamstress pack up her bits and pieces and leave. It had been nice to see such a friendly, trustworthy face, and Miss Prymm reminded her of her old nurse, Lucy, back in Yorkshire, and indeed had the same manner. Not at all servile or familiar, yet somehow giving the impression of caring.

"What are we to do tonight?" Lila asked Sylvia after dinner that same day.

"We may accompany the princess almost anywhere she goes—except for private visits or calls on the king and queen. Then she chooses whoever she wishes to take with her. Tonight there is a reception in the home of Colonel St. Leger. The prince himself returned from playing at army maneuvers especially for it."

"Indeed."

Lila was anxious to view the Prince of Wales, but he had not been residing in Carlton House since she arrived. She longed to see for herself what the most talked about man in England looked like.

"Are you coming to the reception?" Sylvia inquired. "The princess is most easygoing and never insists on anyone going with her."

Lila shook her head. Much as she would have wished to have gone out that night, she decided not to show herself in public until she had her new wardrobe. And she wanted to do something with her hair too. The frizzy, short curls or alternatively the smooth upswept styles adopted by the ladies of London were quite different from her own girlish curls and waves. Perhaps Miss Prymm could advise her. Whilst Lila did not expect to take London by storm, at the same time she did not wish to make her first appearance in out-of-date clothes and be immediately put down as a country bumpkin.

So, what would she do tonight? She had an irresistible urge

to go out. The coach ride that morning had not really provided much enjoyment, trapped as she had been between the princess and her coachman, then the shock of seeing Ralph riding past. For three days now she had been closed in the claustrophobic atmosphere of the court; it felt more like three weeks, and Lila longed to get away, if only for a few hours.

Sylvia spent the next hour changing into a beautiful gown of rust-colored lace, primping and patting her hair into shape and pinching her cheeks to make them rosier still. Then, draped in a fluffy white shawl and exuding a strong smell of rosewater, she departed with a cheery wave.

Immediately, Lila sprang to the closet and took from it her old blue serge cloak and minutes later was creeping out of a side door and was soon in the Mall. Why she crept, she knew not, but felt she should be asking permission to leave.

There were a few people still parading, one or two grand carriages about, but the Mall was quiet. Lila hurried in the direction of Charing Cross where London entirely changed character, and here indeed, when she reached it, was the city of her dreams. Here were the lace-sellers, the boys with boxes hung about their necks selling no end of things, little shops with their dim interiors already lit by candles despite the bright sunshine that remained. A pharmacy with colorful bottles on every shelf, a pie shop—Lila held her nose passing this, then held it tighter when she passed another selling eels. She wandered along, jostled by the crowds who took no notice of her in her old cloak.

Leading off the Strand were little streets which looked interesting, some with stalls selling vegetables, fish or meat, but Lila decided it would be safest to stay on the main thoroughfare and continued on, regardless of time, drinking everything in, until a vague darkening of the sky reminded her that it was time she turned and went back to Carlton House, for she must have walked nearly two miles. It was then she noticed the street sign BLACKFRIARS and with a quick thrust of fear realized that this was the very worst part of London. Here it was that all types of blackguards hung out and that the most sordid crimes took place.

Lila became aware that the people around her had changed character. The men were sullen and dirty, staring at her suspiciously. Women, some to Lila's horror dressed only in soiled and tattered chemises, lolled in doorways and one or two muttered obscenities at her when she passed.

She turned swiftly to return to the safer, more respectable streets and had scarcely gone a step when each of her arms was seized and she was prevented from moving. Looking up in terror she found herself held fast by a man and a woman. The man was evil-looking enough, unshaven and pockmarked, with a deep scar running down one cheek, but it was the woman who struck the most fear in Lila's heart. Almost six feet tall, she was even uglier than her companion, with sallow, almost gray skin covered with sores, and a nose hooked like an eagle's beak. When she opened her mouth to speak, numerous gaps showed between her yellow teeth. It was difficult to see her eyes, hidden as they were by the lids which drooped down in a loose, gray fold over each of them. Coupled with the nose, this made her look like some nightmarish bird of prey.

"Not scared are you, dearie?" she croaked in a deep, rasping voice.

"Of course not," Lila replied boldly, though the quaver in her voice betrayed her.

The woman laughed, a hoarse, cackling sound.

"Where are you off to, dearie?" she inquired.

"To Carlton House," answered Lila, "where I am lady-in-waiting to Princess Caroline of Brunswick."

She was sure this statement would soon put the two vagabonds in their place. Surely not even the scum of Blackfriars would dare to meddle with a resident of Carlton House, but to her amazement this announcement merely produced a paroxysm of mirth in the evil pair.

"Well, that's the best yet," the man said conversationally to his mate. (Even in her panic, Lila could not help wondering if they were man and wife.) "Ladies' maids, yes. Ladies-in-waiting, well, you're our first, luv. And to Princess Fleshpots herself! Sure it isn't our dear queen, now?"

The woman laughed her coarse laugh.

"I likes her spirit, though, Alf. If you're going to lie, well go all the way and be really outrageous."

"I'm not lying."

Lila struggled in their grip, but they turned her round and headed back into the Blackfriars district. People by the dozen passed by, but no one took any notice of her plight. Terror gripped her and she opened her mouth to scream, but the woman's hand was immediately clapped across her face with such force that tears of pain sprang to Lila's eyes. Lila could scarcely breathe, and the smell of the woman's hand made her retch.

"Careful there, Lil," said the man, "else she'll only be fit for the doctor to buy as dead. We'll get a good price for this one. Look at that hair. Like pure gold it is. And young too. No more'n sixteen, I reckon."

"This is a good dress too," the big woman said, glancing down at the maroon silk peeping through the blue serge of Lila's cloak. "Though not in fashion now. Got it off her mistress, I'll bet. Not much of an accent, but what's there is of the North. Run away from service, I'll wager a pudding to a pea."

They dragged Lila round a corner into a narrow, dark street, unlit and uninhabited.

"Let's rest awhile, Queenie," said the man, puffing. "I'm fair whacked."

"You shouldn'a drunk so much with your dinner," the woman told him harshly, but nevertheless they pushed Lila into a doorway and released her. They stood in front of her, and Lila knew she would never get past them. It was not much use to scream, so far away from the crowded street—though she doubted anyone would have come to her assistance anyway. They had all looked as though they would wish Lil and Alf good luck in whatever ill deed they were carrying out.

"What's your name, duckie?" The woman sniffed and wiped her nose on the back of her hand.

"Miss Lilian Ward," Lila announced firmly. "And you will get into a great deal of trouble if you do anything to me. My father is Sir William Ward, Squire of Grassbrook Hall in Yorkshire."

"Lilian, is it?" the woman remarked conversationally. "Now, there's a coincidence. I'm a Lilian from Yorkshire, myself, better known as Lil nowadays. Though when I was your age I was Lady Lilian, not miss. I bet you don't believe that though, do you, duckie?"

Lila's first reaction was to assure the woman that it was quite unbelievable, but she paused, for on reflection there was something about the voice that all the harsh overtones could not disguise. Something almost indiscernibly cultured underneath the London slang, as though somewhere in the past she'd been taught to speak properly.

"Yes, I would believe it," Lila told her. "You talk as if you might have been born a lady."

The man chuckled.

"There, Queenie, I told you. It still shows. They don't call you Queen Lil for nothing. It's 'cuz you deserve it, my gal."

The woman preened herself.

"Lady Lilian Rawlesbury I was born and bred. Perhaps you've heard of my brother? A bigwig in Parliament, he is."

Lila was recovering from the shock of this shattering announcement when there was a commotion at the end of the street and three men ran towards them, yelling and brandishing clubs.

"Be off with you."

"Scat!"

Without a moment's delay, Queen Lil and her swain took to their heels and fled. Lila stood undecided for a second wondering whether to join them in their flight. Was the approaching danger greater than that she had just been in? But it was too late to change her mind now, for the three men had reached her and one of them took her arm comfortingly.

"Are you all right, miss? I saw Queen Lil go off with you and it took some minutes to get these stout chaps to come and back me up. It was no use me tackling those two wicked 'uns on me own."

He handed the two men accompanying him a coin each and they touched their foreheads, muttered, "Thanks, guv" and slouched off into the night. They walked back towards the main street, and Lila was relieved to reach the bright lights and crowds again.

"How can I thank you?" she cried.

The man did not reply. At any other time, Lila would not have liked the look of him; he was middle-aged, dressed in a well-worn leather jerkin and dirty britches, with an unnaturally thin face, his graying hair in a pigtail. In her present state, however, he was as welcome as an angel from heaven.

"Sir," she said, "if you would call me a carriage, I would be grateful."

"'Tis not safe to call a carriage hereabouts, miss. Let's walk awhile, then I'll get one for you."

Lila allowed herself to be led along the road, back in the direction of the Strand. All she wanted was to be back in Carlton House in her bedroom. To be safe again! Even the inane chatter of her roommate would have been welcome at that moment.

Well, she would soon be there and was actually on her way. Her rescuer would soon be calling a carriage. Already the surroundings were looking more respectable, the people better dressed and the shops cleaner.

"Sir, would you call me a carriage now?" she asked, and to her surprise, his grip on her arm tightened as she spoke. A fresh fear took hold of Lila. Surely *this* man was to be trusted? After all, he had rescued her from that dreadful woman and her partner.

"I've got friends just around the corner. They will lend us their carriage," the man answered curtly, his hand gripping Lila's upper arm through her cloak like a vise.

She wanted to struggle, but the man was now leading her at such a speed that it took all her energy to keep up with him. Indeed, she was almost running, but at least in this part of the city people stared at them, clearly wondering what was going on. He couldn't just abduct her in full view of all these people. Suddenly he turned a corner and swiftly crossed the road to a tall, imposing house where he hammered on the door. Thankfully Lila realized he must have been speaking the truth and no doubt would ask here for a carriage to take her back to Carlton House. She sighed with relief.

A maid answered the door. She was dressed in black with a frilly cap and apron.

"Madam Isabella," the man demanded, and the maid stood back to let them enter.

Rubbing the arm which the man at last freed and which she felt was surely bruised, Lila stared at her surroundings. Grand, yes. Too grand in fact. Not in the way Carlton House was, but opulent in the most atrocious sort of way. A rich, blood red carpet matched the silk wall coverings. The chairs were covered in white satin. Everywhere were mirrors in gilt frames and paintings in which—Lila blinked—everyone appeared to be naked.

There was definitely something wrong with the place. Yet strangely she felt no fear. At least these surroundings were civilized, unlike the dark doorway where she had recently been held captive in Blackfriars.

The attitude of her rescuer had completely changed. The courteous helpfulness he had shown at first had gone and now he spoke only in a rude and surly fashion.

The maid returned.

"Madam will be here shortly," she announced. "There is a party upstairs."

They waited in silence for several more minutes. Lila knew it would be useless to demand she be allowed to leave. She had not been asked to sit down and was conscious of how tired she was. She must have walked many miles that night and her feet and legs throbbed.

Upstairs a door opened and the sound of music and laughter was briefly heard. Then a woman appeared at the top of the stairs. Lila gasped. She was one of the most striking women she had ever set eyes upon. Dressed entirely in black, her jet hair was smoothed back and piled into a huge chignon at the nape of her neck, and a jet necklace and earrings gleamed against her alabaster skin. As she came closer, Lila gasped again, for the bodice of the lace dress was completely sheer and the woman's ample, well-formed breasts were provocatively visible through the flimsy material.

Face to face, the woman appeared older than at a distance. Fine lines crisscrossed beneath her large, gray eyes. She regarded Lila for several minutes without speaking, then turned to the man, who stared lasciviously at her bosom.

"Where did you find her?"

"Blackfriars. Tuttle Street. Queen Lil and Alf'd got hold of her."

"She's a lucky girl then, to be rescued from those two."

Lila felt stirrings of anger. She resented being talked about as though she were an object.

"What's your name, girl?"

The woman was well-spoken in a deliberate sort of way as though she had to concentrate to keep from lapsing into the cockney of which there were faint undertones.

Lila threw back her head and answered haughtily: "I am Miss Lilian Ward of Grassbrook in Yorkshire. At the present time I am residing in Carlton House where I am lady-in-waiting to Her Royal Highness, Princess Caroline of Wales."

This explanation caused as much merriment as it had done earlier. Madam Isabella said with scorn, "And what would a lady-in-waiting to royalty, a member of the court, be doing wandering alone on the streets of Blackfriars in the late evening?"

Lila could not think of an answer. She walked at home, long solitary walks at all hours of the day. It had not seemed at all unreasonable that she would walk around London.

"I'd been tailing her for some time," the man said, and Lila stared at him in astonishment. She had not known she was being followed. "Thought she looked new like, and lost, and might be just right for you."

The woman studied Lila, appraising the blue, golden fringed eyes, the cheeks, pinker than usual from the still suppressed anger which also made her full young bosom rise and fall swiftly. She took in the blond hair which fell in natural ringlets onto the girl's shoulders. Damp tendrils clung to her forehead like threads of gold.

"Yes. I think she'll do," the woman said eventually. "More than do, in fact. You've done well, Roger."

"The usual payment?" asked the now perspiring Roger, still unable to tear his eyes away from Isabella's provocative breasts.

"Yes, twenty-five pounds if she stays a month."

"And in the meantime?" The man was almost panting by now.

Madam Isabella laughed. "Oh! You men! It's all you think about. All right, you can stay awhile—but belowstairs, mind. Upstairs is only for gentlemen."

Eagerly, Roger went to the end of the hallway, opened a small door and Lila could hear his footsteps hurrying down the wooden stairs.

"The entrance to downstairs is really outside," said Madam Isabella conversationally. "Down the basement steps."

For several seconds, Lila stared at her. She realized what sort of house this was and why this Roger had brought her there. They no doubt considered her, just as Queen Lil and her swain had done, to be some young girl who'd run away from home and come to London in search of adventure. It was a well-known fact such girls often ended up on the streets—or were even abducted to foreign parts for the use of men whose desires were quite unspeakable—or so Margaret, Ralph's sister, had told her. No doubt, thought Lila, if she had been the sort of girl they thought she was, she would have considered herself lucky to have landed in this house which was almost a palace.

They wanted her to be a courtesan! What was the expression Princess Caroline had used that very morning?—a *fille de joie*. Despite herself, despite her protective upbringing, a faint thrill stirred through Lila which she quickly suppressed, and this was immediately replaced by the anger which had been flickering in her breast for so long and which now burst into flame. She *wasn't* that sort of girl. She hadn't run away from home. Nor was she in search of adventure, at least not *this* sort.

In her frostiest voice she told the woman before her, "I shall soon be missed at Carlton House—that is if I am not already. People will be looking for me. The Marquess of Rawlesbury, the gentleman who brought me to London, will cause a great deal of trouble for you if I come to any harm."

If Lila thought the name of the noble lord would cause the woman any alarm, she was mistaken, for instead she laughed aloud.

"Rawlesbury!" she said scornfully. "Well, Miss High-and-Mighty, that gentleman happens to be upstairs at this very moment. If you knew what he was up to, you wouldn't talk such nonsense. When it comes to causing trouble, *I* would be the cause of it for him—if I wanted to, that is, which I don't. You don't cause trouble for your best customer."

Lila stared at the woman, perplexed. "Lord Rawlesbury? Here?"

"Taken you back a bit, hasn't it, Miss Lilian Ward?" the woman spat contemptuously. "Who are you? A maid from his Yorkshire estate he's brought down to have a bit of fun with? Where does he keep you? Got a little hideout on the side, no doubt. So, he's keeping secrets from his little Isabella, is he?"

"How dare you, madam!" With equal contempt Lila drawled the last word and then went on, "Fetch Lord Rawlesbury here immediately and he will vouch for who I am."

For a moment Madam Isabella looked nonplussed. Then she said admiringly, "You've got guts, my girl. And cheek. I'll give you that."

She took a step towards Lila and made to link an arm through hers. Lila was conscious of the all-but-naked breasts pressing against her.

"Come on, Lilian whatever-your-name-is. Come down off your high horse. You'll have a good time here. You'll—"

Lila pulled her arm free and lunged towards the door. Madam Isabella almost fell to the ground as Lila pulled at the great brass knob and was about to open the door when it was pushed from outside and she was knocked backwards to land squarely on her rear on the floor.

"What's this? Keeping open house tonight, Isabella?" said

a lazy male voice. The tone changed to one of utter incredulity when Lila was observed in her undignified position. "Miss Lilian Ward! By all that's holy. Will the day ever come when I find you in an upright position?"

Lila stared up into the amused eyes of Captain Phillip Grenville.

"Oh, no! Not you," she groaned. While she desperately wanted to be rescued, Captain Grenville was the last man on earth she would have wished for a savior. Two large hands, the touch of which were becoming embarrassingly familiar, grasped Lila round the waist and hoisted her to her feet.

"If this task were not so pleasant, it would become monotonous," drawled the captain, his face inches from Lila's own. She felt herself blushing.

"She really is a proper lidy, then?"

In her surprise, Isabella's cockney accent had come to the fore.

"She most certainly is, and whilst I am getting used to picking her up from the grounds in or around Carlton House, I confess myself somewhat mystified to find her here. Would it be carrying humor too far to ask if she had just dropped in?"

"Much too far," Lila interrupted stiffly. "I find myself in no mood for jokes. Will you kindly call a carriage on my behalf and instruct the driver to take me to Carlton House?"

"I will do better than that, my child. I will personally take you there and place you in your—nursery?" Gently he removed his hands from her waist. "Perhaps on the way you might like to tell me exactly what you are doing here."

"Jenny will be disappointed, captain. She's been waiting all evening." Madam Isabella seemed in no way apologetic for Lila's presence. Indeed she was quite amused at the situation. "As for this young lady, why, it's a crying shame she can't stay. Business would have doubled with such an attractive tidbit on offer."

"Enough, Isabella," Captain Grenville snapped. "I am afraid Jenny must remain disappointed for I will not have time to return tonight. I am expected at a reception at Colonel St. Leger's."

"A pity, captain," said Isabella huskily. "Tomorrow night, I hope."

"We shall see. Come, child."

Captain Grenville put his arm around Lila's shoulders and

was about to open the door when suddenly the air was rent with abrasive laughter and shouting and a crowd of people began to descend the stairs, all apparently taking part in some sort of strange, devilish dance.

Lila gasped, for the woman leading the procession was none other than the girl she had seen in the carriage with Ralph that morning.

Tonight she wore green. A bright apple green dress of diaphanous material which clung to her body like a second skin, showing every luscious curve, while the artificially red lips and cheeks and the golden brown of her skin completed the picture of garishness.

But what made Lila's heart seem to turn over completely was the fact that Ralph was behind the girl, his hands clasping her hips, and farther back in the chain of dancers was his father, the marquess of Rawlesbury.

What a different picture the illustrious Whig politician presented now! The dignified elder statesman, the immaculately turned out gentleman who could quell opponents with a glance, now practically staggered down the stairs, jacketless, his shirt undone, minus his wig. Straggly wisps of hair stretched across his bald head and his arms were about the neck of a pretty, brown-haired girl who was naked from the waist up.

"Hmm! You mentioned that noble gentleman, didn't you?" sniggered Madam Isabella. "Your protector, I think you said he was."

"Lila! What the hell—?"

Ralph had seen her! Pushing aside the green-clad girl, he stared in Lila's direction.

Turning to Captain Grenville, Lila implored, "Please let us leave immediately. I do not wish to talk to anyone."

The captain's reputation for escaping from tight corners was evidently well-earned, for he whisked the door open and had Lila outside within seconds.

"Hurry!" he urged as they almost ran towards the Strand where the captain hailed a passing cab.

Dimly Lila thought she heard Ralph's voice calling her as the door of the carriage slammed and the horse trotted off. She sank back into the seat and closed her eyes with a relief so great that she didn't even think about Ralph and his father and their grotesque dance.

Captain Grenville leaned forward. "Kindly do not go to sleep on me," he ordered sternly. "Not only do I not wish the embarrassment of carrying your recumbent form into Carlton House, but I am eagerly waiting to hear the reason for your presence in Isabella's House of Sin."

What an appropriate name, thought Lila, wanting to laugh as she opened her eyes and stared into those of the man she found so irritating, despite the fact that he had just rescued her from an extremely difficult situation. Why, oh, why did it have to be him? Once she told him her story, he would think her even more childish and immature than he had before. She sighed deeply. Well, it had to be done. He was entitled to an explanation—after all, she had spoiled his night out with Jenny. Strange that she should feel a pang, almost of jealousy, at the thought. *Where to begin?* she wondered ruefully. At the beginning would be appropriate.

"I am waiting," the captain said expectantly.

"Well, you see," Lila began haltingly, "I decided to go out for a short walk. . . ."

Chapter Four

The midafternoon sun shone down, accentuating the red and the pink roses that bordered the lawn where the wedding guests were standing.

Rosalind was being married at the home of her uncle, Sir William Ward. Her pleasant rosy face had acquired bridal loveliness and her plump figure seemed stately, almost regal, in her smooth-fitting gown of white Nottingham lace. Her new husband, Simon Creffield, a junior clerk in the treasury, appeared totally engulfed by his wine velvet coat and the enormous burst of starched ruffles at his throat.

Lila could not help but wonder yet again what Rosalind could possibly see in him. True, he seemed pleasant enough, but when compared with Phillip Grenville...On her swing seat in the corner of the lawn, Lila paused in her reverie. She had no right to compare him with Captain Grenville, for the captain was nothing to her, and really it was quite wrong to give the man room in her thoughts.

"Are you all right, Lilian?"

She looked up to find her father gazing at her anxiously.

"Yes, of course, Papa," she assured him. She knew he was worried about her and could not help but smile to think what he would say if he knew about her escapade in Madam Isabella's House of Sin! Her father took the smile at its face value. If things were fine on the surface, he certainly was not going to probe deeper and perhaps discover problems.

Despite inward disapproval minutes before, Lila let herself live again through the coach journey back to Carlton House on that fateful night two weeks before. Didn't she know, the captain had told her sternly yet with a twinkle in those penetrating blue eyes, that ladies, young or old, simply did not promenade the streets of London without an escort? And that any escort worth his salt would not permit his companion anywhere near the district of Blackfriars. It was a plague-spot, where only the vilest specimens of mankind were to be found. He himself would think twice before penetrating the streets of Blackfriars, even in broad daylight.

Lila felt embarrassed at her naivety at the time, but the following morning she wanted to rush back to Yorkshire in shame when Captain Grenville appeared unannounced in Princess Caroline's apartment. First he routed out Robert Swann whom he dressed down in no uncertain manner for not paying more attention to the new arrival. Then he had a frigid confrontation with Lady Jersey, which Sylvia had heard from the next room.

"Their voices got colder and colder," she giggled to Lila. "I could feel the iciness wafting through the open doorway and had to put my shawl on."

"Really, Sylvia!" Lila demurred uncomfortably. Lady Jersey and Robert Swann had not welcomed her presence before. Now they would dislike her even more.

"He said that as the eldest of the princess's ladies she had a duty to advise young girls, particularly young innocent country girls such as you, Lila, in the ways of the big city. I think it was the way he referred to her as the eldest that offended the old Jersey cow the most."

"Really, Sylvia!" Lila said again, shocked at such language from a titled and educated young woman.

"Anyway"—Sylvia paused as though reluctant to part with the next bit of information—"I must say, he likes you a lot, Lila." She sighed wistfully.

Lila nearly said, "Really, Sylvia," again, but mumbled something incoherent instead and turned away to hide her blush.

"He really was angry," Sylvia went on. "But far more angry than he would have been if it had been *me* he'd found wandering about Blackfriars. He was mad because it was you, Lila."

"Lila! Your mother wishes to speak to you."

She returned to the present to find Ralph standing before her, looking apprehensive. He was still not sure how she regarded him. How utterly delicious she looked today in that filmy lemon dress which draped softly over the curve of her hips and revealed the shapely line of her thighs when she walked. What a pity she had that frill of lace at her bosom, giving only the barest, most tantalizing hint of creamy breasts beneath. Little did he know that the frill had been added at the last minute because Lila had felt naked in the new low neckline. Miss Annabelle Prymm had given her firm approval.

Ralph took her arm as they strolled across the lawn to the drawing room, and she could not help but be aware of admiring glances from the wedding guests. For the first time in her life, Lila was in the forefront of fashion. Her thick golden hair was too heavy and silky to frizz, but she had cut a fringe, and frothy curls framed her face, while the remainder of her hair was tied in a knot, high on the back of her head. Here she had affixed two yellow peacock feathers, which, although they created a stunning effect, made her feel like a ship under full sail. Rosalind's elderly aunt who sat in an armchair enjoying the day to the full was heard to remark as Lila passed, "How regally Lilian walks since she entered court," little knowing that Lila walked so straight for fear her feathers might collapse!

The French windows of the drawing room were thrown open to the warm midday sun and there Catherine Ward sat in an armchair which had been placed in the cool shade, her beautiful face tightly drawn with pain. However, she gave a glorious smile when she saw Lila.

"Mama!"

"I will see you later, Lila." Ralph gave a slight bow and left them.

Lila entered the room and picked up a footstool on which she tenderly placed her mother's feet. Then she kneeled beside the chair, her elbows on the arms, and gazed into the beautiful face. She would never be as lovely as Mama. The high, aristocratic cheekbones, perfect nose, and porcelain skin were the envy of all the ladies who knew her, but even those features were overshadowed by her exquisite eyes which were a unique shade of violet, deep, warm and unforgettable.

Catherine Ward's father had been an English nobleman of high standing, who, when visiting the court of Versailles had fallen wildly in love with the daughter of one of King Louis's gamekeepers, making her pregnant. The girl's mother had been rumored to descend illegitimately from a Medici. Even if the aristocrat had not already been in possession of a wife, marriage to someone so socially beneath him would have been out of the question. The mother gave birth to her bastard, then disappeared, leaving the girl with her grandparents in their little cottage in the woods of Versailles until, inevitably, her ravishing beauty came to the attention of that expert judge of womanhood, King Louis XV himself. Within a short time, the grandparents were able to retire to a finely furnished house in a village nearby. The king kept a kindly eye on the young Catherine, who was being brought up as royally as possible, until at the age of sixteen, when she was taken and presented to the king by her grandparents.

"Never," the king would often declare, "has any one of my subjects presented me with a gift so fair. A jewel to outshine all others."

All this Catherine knew was no fault of her own. But what no one knew, and what had shamed her inwardly all her life, was the fact that she had loved the king and all he had done to her. This inborn, unwelcome sensuality worried her, for her daughter's sake.

It was William Ward who had completely stolen her heart, though in an entirely different way from the king of France. He seemed not to care about the damage she might do to his political aspirations. Marrying her was, she knew, the only really unselfish act of his life, and she was glad to be the recipient. The king had relinquished any claim on her, and the last twenty years of her life had been extremely happy.

But the pains, which at the beginning of the year had been only niggling and unpleasant, now frequently engulfed her entire body so violently that Lady Ward felt she had not long to live. This awful knowledge worried her all the more because she was concerned about her eldest daughter. What had William, with his political maneuvering, involved Lila in?

"Does everything go well in London, my dear?" she asked with a slight frown. "Have you settled there?"

"Yes, Mama," Lila assured her. "I have settled very well indeed. The Princess Caroline is very friendly and warmhearted."

She would have loved to confide in Mama. The night after seeing the princess with her coachman in the summerhouse, she had longed for her mother's advice, but one look at that beautiful face making such an effort to hide the suffering within dissuaded Lila from any confidences. She knew Mama would be terribly worried if she learned what was going on in the court of the Prince of Wales and his bride—and that her daughter, albeit unwittingly, was involved.

"Have you made any friends, my dear?" asked Mama. "I hope you are not lonely amongst all those strangers."

"Not at all," Lila assured her mother stoutly. "I share a room with Lady Sylvia Beauchamp, a very pretty person a year or two older than myself, and we have become good friends."

This was not altogether a lie. She and Sylvia were on good terms most of the time. Her friend's cattiness and spite, when directed at Lila herself, was often distressing, but Lila supposed, with a wisdom beyond her years, that it was not always possible to have perfect friends.

"And Mama," she cried excitedly, "I told you briefly in one of my letters about Miss Prymm. She made this dress and is in the process of completing an entire new wardrobe. It is all quite beautiful, Mama. And Miss Prymm is so kind. So like Lucy. I have truly taken to her and she to me. And she has made me promise that, should I ever be in trouble whilst in London, I must go to her immediately, no matter what time of day or night."

Miss Prymm had made Lila promise this when she had brought the nearly finished lemon dress to Carlton House for a fitting. She had made inquiries and discovered Sir William Ward to be a Whig backbencher of great insignificance and had no doubt he had something to do with planting the poor child there. Miss Prymm, for all her outward cheerfulness, was inclined to look on the morbid side of life and she was worried about Lila. She had a strange, awful presentiment that something untoward was going to happen to the girl and it was then that she elicited the promise that Lila must turn to her if in trouble.

Lila might well not have wanted to worry her mother, but retelling these words of Miss Prymm's caused great inward alarm. Why, wondered Catherine Ward, should this woman who sounded a stalwart of common sense advise her daughter so? There was something going on, she was convinced of it. What on earth had William done? That very evening she would ask her husband for the truth.

She listened to Lila's chatter about the latest fashions, the incredible interior of Carlton House, the bustle of the capital's streets.

"But Captain Grenville says one must not walk them alone— which is a shame, for they look so interesting."

"Captain Grenville?" queried Mama gently.

Lila got to her feet and began to walk to and fro across the room.

"He really is the most infuriating man, Mama. Yet..." She paused. "He is also rather disturbing in a strange sort of way which I cannot define." Lila grinned. She was so consumed with worry about everything she had seen and heard at Carlton House that she was terrified of telling anybody anything! But her brief relationship with Phillip Grenville was in no way connected to the scandalous goings-on she had witnessed. She could tell her mother, amuse her with the adventure she'd had, without causing any worry.

Although alarmed by what fate might have befallen her daughter, Catherine Ward could not help but laugh when Lila finished.

"What an escapade!" she exclaimed. "But promise me you will be more careful, my dear. And tell me, this Captain Grenville, is he the one they call 'The Black Arrow'?"

"Yes, Mama. I suppose you could say he was attractive, but in quite a different way from Ralph."

Catherine Ward had never been at all keen on Lord Ralph Curringham as a match for her lovely daughter. She knew all about men and had observed the way in which that young man watched her own forty-year-old body; it was not how one should regard a future mother-in-law. And his father, the bird-of-prey father—the expression in his eyes insulted her. How much nicer this Captain Grenville sounded. Lila was obviously attracted to him, though she didn't seem to realize it. Was it too late? she wondered; But her thoughts were interrupted when her two younger daughters ran into the room demanding that Lila join them.

"Cousin James has already quickly sketched the wedding party for a pastel later on. Now he wants to do a likeness of you, Lila, for he said you look so pretty in your dress," cried Mary, her cheeks as rosy as the pink flowers in her hair and adorning her bridesmaid's dress. Hettie regarded her elder sister with discernment.

"Mama, could Lila's marvelous new dressmaker come to us? I know it is a long journey, but our dresses are so . . . so overdone compared to hers. I feel like a Christmas parcel."

"There is no need to have Miss Prymm here. Tomorrow morning, before Lila leaves, we will send for Mrs. Baker and let her examine this lovely yellow frock and the simple dress Lila traveled in. I am sure she will be able to order these fine materials from London."

"I will order them for you all, Mama," Lila exclaimed eagerly. "And have them sent at the earliest moment."

"Only if you shop accompanied by a chaperone," said Lady Catherine with a secret smile at her daughter. She fingered the filmy yellow fabric of Lila's frock. "This must be so cool and comfortable to wear. I admit I am looking forward to throwing away all my stiff taffetas and oiled silks."

The three girls ran out onto the lawn and Lady Ward sank back into her chair, realizing she had not felt the stifling, searing pain in her chest for at least ten minutes.

It was odd, thought Lila, but she didn't feel any less afraid of Lord Guy Rawlesbury, despite the fact she had seen him in the most unbecoming and undignified position a mere two weeks before. In fact, it was well nigh impossible to believe this stern, impassive individual sitting opposite her in the coach returning to London the day after Rosalind's wedding was the same person she had seen dancing down the stairs in Isabella's House of Sin.

He stared out the window, quite clearly not taking in the haunting desolation of the Lincolnshire countryside where the broad river shimmered like a satin ribbon in the sultry midday sunshine. Beside her, Ralph pressed his body close to her, his face almost touching her own from time to time when the carriage lurched. She could tell this was deliberate, and a few weeks ago she would have been thrilled by it. But now . . .

He had come to see her the day after their encounter. Even in her thoughts Lila hesitated to use the words "bawdy house" for Madam Isabella's grand establishment, but she could think of no better term. He confessed he had been weak-willed and talked into going there by friends. Of course, he insisted, it was his first visit and he promised faithfully he would never go again.

Ralph attributed her aloof reaction to shock and disapproval at the idea of her betrothed setting foot in such a sinful place, but he was wrong. After much thought, Lila had decided Madam Isabella was providing a much-needed service, without which young girls of virtuous disposition, such as herself, might well be in great danger. There was no doubt that men needed ladies to sleep with from a very early age. Madam supplied these ladies and therefore everyone was happy. The men satisfied their needs, the *filles de joie* earned their fees, and girls like Lila were left in peace. She was not sure, however, whether this bit of charitable philosophizing was influenced by the fact that she had seen Captain Grenville in Isabella's House of Sin. She thought no less of *him*.

No, it was the fact that Ralph was quite clearly lying that caused her to feel a coldness towards him. Had she not seen him the very morning of her fateful stroll to Blackfriars riding in a carriage with the young lady he had been with that night? Lila had not told him this, feeling unwilling to tolerate further embarrassment and lies. Nor did she mention that she had seen his father in the notorious establishment. But since then her feelings about Ralph had been fraught with doubts and worries about what their life together would be like. She could not stand the idea of being unable to trust her husband.

So, on the few occasions Ralph had called at Carlton House asking to see her, she had sent word that she was busy and although she could have left what she was doing, this was indeed the truth. For Lila had been given a daunting task.

Queen Charlotte, wife of George III, was a person of rigid morals with deeply held Protestant views, bringing up her fifteen sons and daughters in such a joyless and unnecessarily callous manner that the boys had rebelled against the unnecessary discipline as they grew older, and all were leading lives of wicked abandon. Their parents had become resigned to their sons' various dissolute life-styles, but now the Queen was absolutely horrified by her new daughter-in-law.

Reports from Lord Malmesbury, who had been dispatched to report on the princess, had been good, and he had raved about her good looks and pleasant manners. Lord Malmesbury must have been drunk or temporarily insane, Queen Charlotte decided, for Caroline was a German wanton, and though her eldest son, George, did not deserve any better wife, the country had a right to a queen beyond reproach in every respect.

There was not a great deal Queen Charlotte could do about the way in which the princess behaved, but she could do something about her wardrobe, which was quite disgraceful. Immediately following the princess's last visit, the queen sent a stern message to Robert Swann to say something must be done to remedy the problem. Swann received this communiqué while still quaking in his shoes from Captain Grenville's tongue-lashing. Therefore, what better task to keep that adventurous young lady off the streets of London than to supervise the complete overhaul of her mistress's wardrobe?

Thus for the week prior to the wedding Lila had been engaged in this job, which would continue for several more weeks. So when Ralph called again and again, she was quite honest when she sent word that she was up to her ears in work.

The existence of such a handsome fiancé in Lila's life quite sent Lady Sylvia Beauchamp into a tizzy of jealousy. She could not understand Lila's unwillingness to see him and found her reasons childishly moral.

"Poo!" she remarked inelegantly. "How childish you are, Lila."

Lila shrugged and said, "Next time he comes, *you* entertain him."

Sylvia decided to take her friend at her word, but Ralph hadn't appeared again.

Yesterday at cousin Rosalind's wedding, he had been a model escort, holding Lila's arm in the most gentlemanly manner, fetching food, drinks, shawls for her with alacrity, even though Lila had not expressed any wish for any of these things. Now, thinking he had charmed his way back into her good graces, he was pressing himself against her, holding her arm and caressing her skin with his thumb. Lila held herself stiffly, unwilling to give in to him. The coach was now entering Kings Lynn, rattling over the cobbled streets, and drawing to a halt in the courtyard of an inn.

"We change horses here." The marquess of Rawlesbury had come out of his reverie and adjusted his wig. "I think we shall partake of some refreshment."

The food was good, simple though rather heavy for such a hot day. The roast beef was deliciously tender, but Lila had to leave a great deal of her food.

After the meal, Rawlesbury said imperiously to his son, "There is a jeweler in this town who mends timepieces with great skill. Take this enameled watch of your sister's to him and request an estimate for its repair. The stupid girl dropped it and although the casing is not damaged, the timekeeping has gone haywire. You will find the watch repairer in Bury Street."

As Ralph left obediently, Lila's heart sank, for this was quite clearly a plot to get Lila alone. She had a strong inkling of what the marquess would want to say to her.

"Does life at court agree with you, Miss Lilian?" he asked almost impatiently, as though begrudging the need to approach tactfully or cautiously.

"I am finding it strange, sir, but then I have been there only a few weeks. I am sure I shall become more used to it in good time."

She waited, dreading his next question.

"Has anything—of interest happened, miss? I am not in court much, but I find tales of the ups and downs there quite beguiling."

Lila sat mute, feeling his mud-colored eyes boring into her. What could she say? If she had stumbled on a murder plot or a plan for revolution, she would have been anxious to convey her knowledge to anyone in authority who could foil the plotters, but she was quite definitely not going to reveal her knowledge that the Princess Caroline was having a relationship with her coachman. What good this information would be to Whig or Tory, she knew not, except as an instrument of blackmail. These thoughts brought back the image of the huge, half-bare man in the doorway of the summerhouse and the princess in disarray behind him, and a blush came to her cheeks. It was then obvious to her questioner that she knew something.

"Come, girl!" he snapped. "You have not been blind these past weeks. You must have observed something. Does the princess have callers? What does she talk about and who with? Does the prince visit her? Surely you can tell us something?"

"Sir!" Lila drew herself up stiffly. "You did most positively assure me I was not a spy. I find it most distasteful being cross-questioned in this manner. I will tell you, however, that except when addressing the English members of her entourage, the princess converses in German, which I do not understand. As to callers—yes. The queen herself came last week, though I was not privileged to meet her."

"You are hiding something, miss!"

Rawlesbury's voice was an icy snarl and he was about to be even more offensive when he remembered he wanted more from this girl than information from the court. She was to be his son's wife and her father's money was needed, both for the maintenance of his son's extravagant tastes and for his own political aims.

"If I hide something, then it is my own affair," Lila was saying haughtily and Rawlesbury decided he had better make amends quickly.

He put his hand on Lila's, not noticing the way in which she shrank from his touch.

"I'm sorry, m'dear. Affairs of state weigh heavily on me at the moment. I forgot myself. Of course you are not a spy. There was never any suggestion of such a thing."

His stern face twitched into an unnatural smile. He would have to get Ralph to work on her, for she knew something. Of that he was certain.

In one way or another, the girl had to be made to talk.

Chapter Five

The Prince of Wales was most happy to be flirting outrageously with the delightful eighteen-year-old wife of the middle-aged Bohemian ambassador in whose honor he was holding a reception. He had heard tales about this little black-haired Bohemian wife who was willing to go to any lengths to further her husband's career—with his full approval—and he was only too anxious to favor the couple. Trade, a treaty, a pact—anything to make the ambassador happy, if the wife would make the prince happy.

It was therefore a rather suspenseful situation when a footman announced that Caroline, the Princess of Wales, was about to enter with her ladies, and then there she was in a horrible green dress, her cheeks like two over-ripe apples and her hair looking as though it had not seen a brush for a week. Behind her was Lady Jersey. He could not deny he was fond of her, but he would have preferred her to be absent this evening, as his sights were set on the fruits of foreign soil. His thoughts became even more disloyal when he observed the two younger members of his wife's entourage: a pretty dark-haired girl, in rust lace, whom he had seen before, and a beautiful, golden-haired young woman in a thin red silk dress. Her enticing form walked sedately behind the squat, ugly figure of his bride.

Caroline approached him, baring her teeth into what he supposed she considered a smile.

"Hello, George," she called.

Oh, that voice! Was it the voice, or the manners, or the smell, the dress, the face? What was it that revolted him most? No one would ever know what he had gone through those first few days of his marriage to this—to this fat Brunswickian gorgon. How on earth had he managed to... well, love the woman on the first night, which had proved to be their last night. He had been quite intoxicated, virtually unconscious. They'd carried him in to do his duty and carried him out again, duty done.

Well, never again, though it was a pity, for his father desperately wanted him to sire an heir to the throne. London, indeed the entire country, was littered with the illegitimate offspring of his brothers and perhaps of himself. But what was this his bride was saying—so loudly the entire room could hear.

"A little baby is on the way, George. Tell your mama and papa. I've been a good girl, eh?"

His jaw dropped so far he worried it would not return to its proper place.

Caroline laughed and said, "You don't understand, do you, George? You've put a bun in the German oven!"

Sir William Ward had once remarked that just one of the Prince of Wales' frequent parties would keep the entire village of Grassbrook in food for a year. Lila felt that such extravagance was shameful, and she felt guilty at her pleasure when she received an invitation for the evening's entertainment in the Chinese Room. She assuaged her conscience with the thought that it was inevitable, given the irresponsible nature of the prince, that such elaborate entertainments were going to be held, and since she couldn't prevent them, she might as well enjoy them.

Miss Prymm brought her new dress that very afternoon. It

was fine red silk with a deep band of gold silk embroidery at the hem and gold ribbons gathering the tiny, puffed sleeves. She blushed when she looked in the mirror and saw the low neckline revealing the creamy swell of her breasts.

Marveling at the fact there was a female in Carlton House still capable of blushing, Miss Prymm told her sternly, "There is no time to sew a band of lace on that. Anyway, it is time a little of your bosom was exposed to the world. You cannot hide it forever. Besides, I can assure you yours will be one of the most modest outfits at the reception tonight."

Lila reluctantly agreed this would probably be the case.

"Have you ever met the Princess of Wales?" she asked the dressmaker as she was packing away her sewing things.

"No. And I have no wish to, either," Miss Prymm replied firmly. "She sounds quite unsuitable to become queen of this great country, and I only hope I'm dead and buried before she does—though perhaps I shouldn't express such a forcible opinion in front of one of her ladies-in-waiting."

"I would never betray a confidence," Lila assured her earnestly. "It's just that I find it difficult to judge what she is really like."

Initially, she had taken to the princess, but as time passed she was more and more shocked by her behavior. Lila had begun to wonder if she should confide her secret knowledge in someone of authority, someone who could advise the princess now and perhaps avoid some great scandal later on. The only person she could think of was Phillip Grenville. Although he belonged to the prince's regiment, she got the impression that he had no political ties and could be trusted to be impartial. She felt sure he would know exactly what to do.

Observing the girl's worried face, Annabelle Prymm placed a hand on her arm. "Is everything all right, my dear?"

Lila stoutly assured her that everything was as well as it could possibly be, and Miss Prymm, not wanting to worry her further, merely said, "Don't forget now. My little cottage is twenty-four Cotterell Street. That is in Chelsea, not too far distant from here. If I am not there, my maid Ada will let you in."

Privately wondering why Miss Prymm had twice told her this, Lila thanked her and felt it comforting to find someone who cared about her for herself, not for what she could do for them.

After dressing for the reception, she went into the fragrant garden of Carlton House and plucked a deep red rose from a bush, hoping she was not committing some unforgivable crime, and back in her bedroom she pinned this to the knot of hair high on the back of her head. When she stepped back to regard her reflection in the mirror, she could scarcely believe her eyes. Was this really the Lila Ward who had left Yorkshire, an unsophisticated country lass, no less than three weeks before? The hairstyle made a vast difference, making her look older and adding a look of maturity to her features she had not yet earned. The soft lines of the dress gave inches to her height, making her feel like a stranger to herself. Could it be possible that she was beautiful? Lila wondered. She had never thought of herself as such before, merely feeling glad her hair was gold and her nose straight. Now this strange new figure excited her, and as she contemplated this, the thought that Captain Grenville might be attending the forthcoming reception made her heart leap. The thought that her fiancé might be there did not enter her head.

To Lila's chagrin, when she arrived at Princess Caroline's apartment, she found her dressed in a soiled green frock which was split under one arm. Perhaps Lady Jersey was responsible for this, Lila thought exasperatedly, for she seemed to be bent on ensuring that her mistress was turned out as shabbily as possible. Lila had seen to it there were many cleaned, pressed, and mended frocks Caroline could have worn, not to mention dozens of pairs of new stockings and freshly sewn handkerchieves. Reticules had been repaired or replaced and lace darned. Twenty white petticoats were yet to be made; four others already delivered lay neatly folded on a shelf in the princess's wardrobe. After all Lila's hard work, the princess's appearance was discouraging.

Lila never dreamt that their arrival in the Chinese Room would cause such consternation. When the footmen announced them, every eye in the room turned in the direction of the doorway. There was silence, followed by gasps, and a buzz of excited conversation, until the princess caught sight of her new husband. As she strode towards him her ladies had difficulty deciding whether to keep their dignity and walk sedately behind or hurry to keep up with their mistress.

They heard the princess say something about buns and ovens

which Lila found quite inexplicable. Lady Jersey gave a horrified little shriek and everybody else looked either shocked or amused.

"So! The child has become a woman in record-breaking time," murmured a lazy voice behind her, and Lila turned to find Captain Grenville regarding her with a look that thrilled. Naked admiration shone in his eyes, though his mouth curved in its usual sardonic fashion. He wore black from head to toe, except for the white collar of a shirt beneath his velvet frock coat which gave him a vaguely priestlike air. Lila gave a shy smile and did not speak, for a strange, indefinable emotion affected her so deeply she knew she would not be able to reply to his remark in a sane and sensible fashion.

"What do you think of our prince?" the captain asked, as though aware of the embarrassment he had caused and wanting to make amends with a change of subject. Maybe he was not used to conversing with inexperienced country girls, as yet unable to flirt or engage in small talk.

Lila regarded Prince George with interest. Whatever his wife had said had shocked him greatly, and he was taking rapid sips of brandy. He was as tall and as handsome as Lila had been told, yet there were signs, even at the age of thirty-two, of the dissipated life he led. A slight sagging of the facial muscles, the spreading waistline, the air of weariness that emanated from this man who had everything, all seemed to indicate that he had tired of all his indulgences and there were now no more experiences for him to have.

"I think I feel sorry for him," Lila told the captain, contrasting his firm, weathered skin with the waxiness of the prince's, his sober clothes to George's richly embroidered white satin coat.

"That is not the proper reaction for an impressionable young woman to have," Captain Grenville told her with a smile. "You should fall in love with him instantly. Most ladies do."

Lila felt a surge of irritation.

"I am not most ladies," she told him. "You must not put everyone into the same box in your mind and expect them to jump out in the same way. The prince looks pathetic to me, and—"

She stopped, about to say something tactless about his regrettable marriage.

Captain Grenville raised an eyebrow and smiled his sardonic

smile. "I consider myself rebuked. At seventeen, nearly eighteen, you must of course know far more about life than an old
stick-in-the-mud such as I."

"Sir, you tease me," Lila replied stiffly. "Of course you
have more experience of life than I, but it does not mean your
common sense surpasses mine on every issue. You assume
most ladies fall in love with the prince. *I* have not and I know
many more who would not be stricken either. Therefore, in
this one thing at least, I am wiser than you."

Her eyes sparkled with anger for she hated to be made fun
of and she was unaware of the electrifying effect she was having
on several gentlemen standing nearby, including the prince,
who was only too pleased to be distracted from his bride. The
pink of her lips and cheeks was accentuated by the deeper red
of her dress and the rose in her hair, and by the creaminess of
her arms and neck.

"By Gad! Who is she?" asked someone several feet away,
and Lord Ralph Curringham replied, "She is my fiancée."

"Then hurry, sir, and claim her. I've never seen our proud
Black Arrow so captivated before. The good captain professes
himself to be bored by society females. I would say boredom
is the furthest from what he is feeling at this moment."

Ralph hesitated. He had never dreamt Lila could look so
lovely, and his heart had jumped when he saw her enter and
observed the many glances in her direction. He had wanted to
go proudly to her side then and there so all present would know
she belonged to him. But this was her first meeting with the
Prince of Wales. The prince's weakness for a pretty face was
well known; it would be politic to leave his fiancée for a while,
for if His Majesty did fall in love with her—and fall in love
was something he did with monotonous regularity—and wanted
a relationship with Lila, then their marriage could be arranged
immediately. The prince would not want an affair with a single
woman if it could possibly be avoided, for there were dangers
from paternity suits, broken marriage promises, all sorts of
likely complications. A willing wife with a cooperative husband
was the ideal arrangement, with the prince paying handsomely.
Ralph would be only too willing. Also, his father would be
pleased at the idea of a Whig supporter in the prince's bed.
Ralph waited and watched Lila curtsy low as Captain Grenville
presented her.

The prince held her hand far longer than he should have.

Lila was conscious of Captain Grenville's smile and wanted to tell him that she still was not captivated, and that his hand was hot, sweaty, and far too soft and white. Nevertheless, she would enjoy telling Mama, Hettie, and Mary about meeting the Prince of Wales and about his most gracious compliment.

"Every time I see a red rose in the future, Miss Ward, I shall think of you—and wonder why it is not as beautiful."

Lady Jersey, her face mottled with fury, almost dragged the prince away, and this reminded Lila of her resolve that afternoon.

"I wish to confide in you," she told Captain Grenville, who was still at her side. He regarded her with mock surprise.

"You regard me as worthy of your confidences?"

Frowning slightly, Lila said, "I am serious, sir. A matter of great import has—has come to my knowledge and I am in a quandary as to how I should deal with it. You are the only person I can trust to advise me with impartiality."

"I take it you do not wish to discuss this important matter here," he said. "Shall I call on you tomorrow afternoon?"

"By all means," Lila told him.

"Lila."

Ralph bowed before her, and she felt conscience-stricken, for she had forgotten his very existence.

"My fiancé, sir." Lila glanced at Captain Grenville. "I do not know if you have met."

"Lord Curringham, is it not?" The Black Arrow gave a nod in Ralph's direction.

"Captain Grenville." Ralph bowed stiffly. What a good thing this chap was a gentleman and could be trusted to be discreet. He'd seen him dozens of times in Isabella's House of Sin where Jenny, the brown-haired girl, was his particular favorite. The captain never joined in the more advanced entertainments offered there, but he was bound to know, Ralph reckoned, of the Curringhams' participation in Isabella's more unusual offerings.

Lila immediately sensed the antipathy between the two men and vaguely wished Ralph would go away, when Sylvia came up to her.

"Lila," she whispered agitatedly, "do look at the princess's dress. People are beginning to notice. Should we do something? For Lady Jersey will not."

The green dress, only slightly split at the beginning of the evening, now exposed several inches of her petticoat under her arm. Lila remembered a lovely silky rainbow shawl, whose tassels she herself had patiently unraveled only the day before, and which she had put away, cleaned and pressed, in the wardrobe.

. "I'll fetch something to cover the tear," she said quietly to Sylvia.

Reluctantly excusing herself from Captain Grenville and Ralph, she left the room, not noticing the princess's giant footman who stood impassively, arms folded, beside the door. Lady Jersey did, however, observe the man's presence, and also noticed that the princess had suddenly decided to leave, just after he arrived.

"*Gutt* night, George," Caroline said, waving in the direction of her husband, who merely looked pained.

Lila was by now out of earshot. If she had known that the princess was about to leave, and no longer needed a shawl, the entire course of her life would have been changed.

The princess's wardrobe was not, as Lila had first expected, a piece of furniture, but an entire room about twelve feet square leading off from the main bedroom. Clothes were hung in rows along two of the walls, while the other two were covered with drawers and shelves. Helga, the princess's maid, was as untidy as her mistress, and had thrown several items of clothing onto the floor. These Lila swiftly sorted out, hanging up some, folding others and putting them away. Then she took from a drawer the glossy, multicolored shawl she had come for.

As she turned to leave, she heard a man and woman enter the bedroom, both of them laughing and speaking German. Lila paused, unsure, then resolutely went to the door of the wardrobe where she stopped, staring in disbelief at the sight before her.

Princess Caroline was removing her final item of clothing, which within seconds rendered her plump form naked, while on the bed lay Ludwig, nude, his arms outstretched. Into these arms the princess launched herself, and the two began to make love. Neither had observed Lila, who stepped back into the wardrobe, immersing herself in a row of dresses, hands on her ears.

Please, please, make them go away. Make them be quick, she prayed. *Please!*

This couldn't be happening. She clamped her hands over her ears so tightly that her head started buzzing, and she couldn't think straight. When she removed her hands she felt light-headed, and then desperate when she heard the same noises coming from the bedroom.

But now they were mixed with other sounds. The wardrobe adjoined the corridor, and there Lila could hear footsteps and voices, among them Lady Jersey's saying imperiously, "I saw them leave together. They are both in this apartment. I insist that you enter and confront the abominable pair."

The Prince of Wales could be heard protesting, fruitlessly it would seem, for the party continued past the wardrobe and along the corridor towards the door of the apartment. In the future, Lila could never decide why she wished to save the princess from discovery and subsequent embarrassment. She put it down to the automatic reaction anyone would have to grab at a person about to fall under the wheels of a carriage or into a fire.

Realizing it was a matter of less than a minute before Lady Jersey and her entourage entered the door of the apartment, walked through the drawing room, and reached the bedroom—and also realizing the princess would not have thought to lock doors—Lila snatched at a robe hanging nearby and rushed into the bedroom.

"Quick, madam! Put on this robe and tell the man to hide. The prince is about to enter."

The group could be heard not too far away. The two regarded her with dazed eyes until comprehension dawned. The princess said something in German to her lover, leaped from the bed, and seized the robe from Lila.

Then their actions took her entirely by surprise. The princess disappeared into the wardrobe, while Ludwig towered above Lila, his naked body glistening with sweat, and put both his huge hands to her breasts. She gasped with horror as he took hold of her red dress and ripped it down the front like paper. Her torn underwear fell away. The dress was flung into a heap on the floor, and Lila stood there petrified in only her stockings and garters.

He threw her onto the bed and lay on top of her, one hand over her mouth. His skin slid along hers, his hardness thrusting against her, making her give a silent scream of pain. When the door eventually was flung open, it was Lila who lay virtually naked on the princess's bed with the coachman lying over her, and it was Lila who stared, speechless with shock, embarrassed beyond belief, into the eyes of Lady Jersey and Prince George, who stood, stunned, at the foot of the bed.

Someone from the accompanying crowd giggled. Lila, her eyes huge and brilliant with fear, looked for a friendly face— Sylvia, for instance, who could say she had left only minutes before to fetch a shawl. Sylvia was not present, but Lila did meet the eyes of Captain Phillip Grenville, and he stared into hers with a coldness that made her shudder. His face was hard and unforgiving, and he was the first to turn away and walk swiftly from the room.

Then, one by one, they all left until she was left with only the coachman to share her nightmare.

Chapter Six

It was only when the footsteps faded, the apartment door closed, and Ludwig laughingly pulled Lila back down onto the bed beneath him and started to kiss her and fondle her body that her speech and her senses returned.

"Let *go* of me!" she screamed. "You beast! You animal! Do you realize what you have done?"

The man laughed, not understanding a word she said, but nevertheless released her. She sprang from the bed, picking up her torn dress and underthings and covering herself as best she could. Before leaving she made a move towards the door of the wardrobe which had remained firmly closed throughout the proceedings, but the huge coachman lunged from the bed to stop her and she ran from the apartment before he could touch her again.

Fortunately she met no one as she ran back to her own room. There she emptied the water from her jug into the basin and washed herself thoroughly from head to toe, sobbing as she did. The cold cloth helped to calm her, and then self-reproach began. Why hadn't she shouted to someone, when Ludwig had removed his hand from her mouth, that the princess was in the wardrobe? Why had she helped the princess in the first place? The woman was committing adultery. Why not let the prince find her? What an idiot she was. How naive and stupid.

These questions and recriminations chased themselves around in her mind until she felt her head would burst. She pressed the cold cloth to her forehead hoping to quell the tumult there. Then she went to her closet and took from it one of her old cotton dresses. The tears returned as she put it on, remembering how Hettie had made her a little drawstring bag from the remains of the material. If only she were home now . . .

Abruptly she cut herself off from such thoughts. She must now concentrate on extricating herself from the awkward situation she was in. It was no use, she felt sure, approaching Princess Caroline. There was her intended father-in-law, the marquess of Rawlesbury. He would know she was innocent, and would help her. . . .

This chain of thought was interrupted by a tap on her door, and she opened it to that very gentleman.

"I know it is unusual to see a lady in her bedroom at such a late hour, but the circumstances are, shall we say, unusual."

Lila stood aside silently for him to enter, not sure of what to say. Would he blame her or sympathize with her?

"A messenger came to my London home less than fifteen minutes ago," the marquess was saying, "sent by Charles Fox, who was with the prince when they visited the princess's apartment and found you—*déshabillé*."

Rawlesbury paused. The child was flushed and trembling, but she held her head proudly and the look she gave him was full of dignity. He felt a pang at what he was about to do to her, but a momentary pang only. All that mattered to him was power and Lila had proved a more useful tool in its attainment than he had ever envisaged.

Lila glanced at the clock, amazed to see it was only just past the hour of ten. It seemed an eternity since she had left the Chinese Room on such an innocent errand.

Rawlesbury continued, "I have spoken to the princess—incidentally, she is packing and will leave with her entourage before midnight—and she is horrified at what has happened."

"She will own up then?" Lila interrupted eagerly, sinking onto a chair with relief. "You've no idea how glad that makes me feel."

"I did not say that," Rawlesbury said smoothly. "The princess may well be horrified, but she is also scared. The prince is saying that if she had been found on the bed instead of you, he would have immediately sought divorce. He quotes Henry VIII, and you will remember that that monarch dispatched some wives in a rather more cruel fashion. Her Highness realizes she has been foolishly indiscreet, but feels that as a princess she is less able to bear the brunt of the inevitable scandal than you are."

Lila choked with rage.

"That is no doubt true," she observed angrily. "But I have done nothing whatsoever to deserve such scandal. The princess has, and I have no intention of taking blame upon myself."

"I'm afraid that remains to be seen," the marquess answered. "Her Highness has let it be known that she will come out fully in support of the Whig Party if we can arrange this unfortunate affair to her satisfaction."

Lila gasped. It was quite beyond her experience for people to behave so deceitfully. She threw back her head and announced to Rawlesbury, "Tomorrow it is my intention to seek out the Prince of Wales and inform him of what truly happened this evening. I have no doubt that he will believe me."

Rawlesbury had no doubt either. Lila was quite obviously a more honest and trustworthy person than the princess, and rumors about Caroline's relationship with her servant were already rife.

"Both the princess and Whigs will make it worth your while, my dear girl. Monetarily and in other ways." His voice was soft and cunning. "Don't forget your father, for instance. He will benefit enormously from his daughter's cooperation."

"Sir, you overestimate my father's quest for power," she said coldly. "Above all else in this world he loves my mother, and for her sake alone, neither he nor I will aid you in this affair. It would kill Mama."

Rawlesbury was biting his lip when Lila spoke again.

"Tell me, sir," she said with a sardonic smile. "If I agreed to take this disgrace upon me, would I still marry your son?"

With reluctance the marquess of Rawlesbury admitted, "It is most unlikely."

Lila smiled again. "Then surely you must understand, sir, that if I love your son I must insist on clearing my name so that we can be wed as planned."

The little minx was playing with him and for the briefest of seconds, the marquess was visited by an overwhelming sexual urge to fling her onto the bed and beat her. Indeed, he even reached out to take her arm, but he restrained himself and used the gesture to adjust his wig. He moved towards the door.

"You will regret your obstinacy, miss," he said frigidly. "You will find yourself with blame and no benefits."

Lila followed him to the door, and said in puzzlement, "Sir, I do not understand how your power can give you satisfaction when it is earned by causing suffering, and by lies and deceit. Surely power which has come honorably sits on a person more easily and with more dignity."

Lord Rawlesbury did not reply. He merely bowed stiffly and left. Almost immediately Sylvia entered the room.

"I heard someone in with you and did not wish to interrupt," she said hurriedly. "Lila, I am so sorry...."

"Sylvia. Come with me tomorrow when I see the Prince of Wales and tell him I left only to fetch a shawl. Say you yourself drew my attention to the princess's torn dress."

In her anxiety, Lila had grasped both Sylvia's arms. It seemed such a simple thing to ask, such an obvious favor for her friend to agree to, but here nothing was predictable. Everything was governed by undercurrents of politics. She was right to have been concerned about Sylvia's support, for her friend's eyes dropped and she looked ashamed.

"I have been jealous of you, Lila. I freely admit that. And glad sometimes if you have got into trouble, but I would never willingly let you be blamed for this evening. I was told about it in the Chinese Room later. Everyone was laughing and I even argued with several. Then Lady Jersey told me in no uncertain terms to be quiet."

"But why, Sylvia? Why?"

"I don't know. She says I must say nothing until she has evaluated the position and sent for my father."

Sylvia went over to the small cupboard on her side of the big bed and took out her sleeping gown and cap. Lila stared at her in astonishment.

"I'm sorry, Lila, but Lady Jersey says I must stay only a minute to get my things. She is providing a bed in her dressing room for me tonight, for I cannot stay with you."

After Sylvia had gone, Lila felt overwhelmed by loneliness. For a moment, she considered packing her bag and going home, then and there, to Yorkshire. To be safe within the bosom of her family would be bliss. But it would be an admission of guilt. She would stay and fight. Her chin went up as she determined to clear her name with all possible speed.

Strangely enough, Lila fell asleep more quickly than she would have supposed. The sheets were cool and soothed her aching body, relaxing her and affording an escape from the torment of her thoughts.

But a sharp, insistent banging on her bedroom door woke her and filled her with dread. This could not be good news. A glance at the clock, shining in the light of the moon, showed it to be ten past three. The banging became louder. Whoever it was considered their business to be urgent. Lila drew back the bolts and Lady Jersey swept into the room without a word, followed by a cowed and quivering Robert Swann.

"Pack your bags, miss, and get out," spat the lady. "If you are not gone by half past three, I shall fetch a footman to help you on your way."

"I do not understand. What does this mean?" asked Lila in bewilderment.

"I do not know, miss, whether you came here to spy on me or the princess, or to seduce the prince—"

"I came here for none of those things," Lila interrupted indignantly, but Lady Jersey ignored her.

"—but whatever the reason, you've gotten more than you bargained for, I'm sure. If, as Rawlesbury says, you won't cooperate, then we want you out before you get in our way. Now, get dressed and begone."

Despite the muddle in Lila's brain, she could not help but wonder what Lady Jersey and the Tories were gaining from the situation. Earlier that evening, Lady Jersey had been all set to confront the princess and her lover, with the prince as witness. That plan had backfired, due to Lila's misguided goodness. Yet, despite the fact that the tables had been turned on her, Lady Jersey was able to swiftly twist matters back to her own advantage.

Lila trembled with fury. She wanted to scream at the injustice of it all. Then, almost as a sort of protection, her fury was replaced by a numbness, and she moved about collecting her things, asking in an emotionless voice, "Do you intend to remain while I dress?"

The couple left the room without a word, and Lila put on her old dress, shivering, despite the fact that the July night was hot and clammy. Even her old blue cloak could do nothing to warm her.

She was about to depart when she noticed out of the corner of her eye, her red dress, lying where she had flung it, its soft folds like ripples in a pond. Only someone of great strength could have ripped the garment completely in two like that, she thought as she lifted it slowly, the silk soft and sensuous against her fingers. This would be her proof when she told what had been done to her, and she would keep it until her innocence was known to the world.

Outside her door she could hear Lady Jersey and Robert Swann conversing in low tones and she opened it to ask, "Am I expected to carry my trunk or will you make arrangements for it to be sent to me?"

"We will make any necessary arrangements," Lady Jersey told her briskly. As they marched towards the exit, Lila marveled that they could turn her out in the middle of the night like this. She was a stranger in the city. It was as though she really had committed some awful crime.

Robert Swann cringed behind Lady Jersey, yet had the grace to look uncomfortable, and even muttered, "Is it safe? Something might happen to the child at this hour."

"Apparently Miss Ward is used to walking the streets of London at a late hour—according to our beloved Black Arrow, that is. Even if she does come amiss, that would suit our plans even better. Who would care after what she was up to tonight?"

Lady Jersey flung open a side door and Lila stalked out, her head high despite the dizziness she felt. The door slammed, reverberating on the still night air. Two guards outside regarded Lila with curiosity as she wandered towards the Mall, wondering if there was a person in the whole of London she could turn to.

Miss Annabelle Prymm bathed Lila's fevered brow as she lay on the bed in the spare room, moaning and rocking her head violently from side to side. She had been in this state almost continuously since her arrival in the early hours of the morning two days before. Dr. Plumpton had pronounced it shock, and said that rest and care were the only remedy. Miss Prymm had provided these, and she felt that finally today there had been an improvement in the child's condition. Lila had slept quietly for nearly two hours at midday and it was only now that she began to show signs of her inward agitation.

"Shush," soothed Miss Prymm. "There now."

Wild rumors had spread around London about the goings-on at Carlton House two nights ago. Friends had conveyed the essence of these tales to the seamstress, of how Lady Jersey had sought to expose to the prince his bride's adultery with the coachman, but instead had surprised the latter with a young lady-in-waiting, Miss Lilian Ward.

Miss Prymm believed not a word of it, and her heart bled for the young girl lying before her. Lila's eyelids fluttered at that moment, and she opened her eyes and looked up at the woman who was so tenderly stroking her forehead. For quite some time her eyes were blank and showed no recognition and for an awful moment Miss Prymm thought she had lost her memory.

But then Lila cried, "Miss Prymm! Oh, dear, dear Miss Prymm!" She sat up and flung her arms around the plump figure, and that person who so prided herself on her toughness and composure felt tears well up in her eyes.

"There, there," she said comfortingly, as much to herself as to Lila. "There, there now. You're quite safe."

Later on, as Lila sat up in bed sipping a bowl of hot broth, a knitted patchwork shawl about her shoulders, she told the entire tale to her protector.

"As soon as I am well, I must go to see the prince. I shall take the red dress, for surely that is proof that I was taken to the bed against my will. I feel sure he will believe me."

The prince was kind, and he had quite clearly taken a liking to her. He would at least give her a hearing. She deliberately shut from her mind the disdainful face of Captain Grenville as he had turned to leave the awful scene, but then cried out as another thought occurred to her.

"Mama! I must write to her immediately. She will be out of her mind with worry."

Miss Prymm patted her hand. "I wrote to Lady Catherine

within hours of your arrival here. She knows you are safe, but I am sure she will be relieved to receive a letter in your own hand."

Lila thought of how it would break Mama's heart to hear all the supercilious ladies she had met in England saying, "Of course, she must have had it in her. Bad blood coming out."

For Mama's sake alone, it was imperative that she clear her name.

The following day she was on her feet and seemed to have recovered completely from her ordeal, though Miss Prymm noticed a look of determination in the pretty face, a firm set to the chin that was not there before and which gave her an air of maturity. The childish impetuosity, she suspected, had gone forever.

Less than half the clothes Miss Prymm had been making for Lila had been finished. The remainder were in the basement workroom in various states of completion. That morning, a day dress of mushroom-colored silk was hastily given the finishing touches, and the lining of the little matching velvet cloak tacked in. Lila was dressed to call on the Prince of Wales.

"Try not to let the stitching show," pleaded Miss Prymm as Lila tied the satin ribbons of the bonnet beneath her chin. "Or my reputation will suffer."

"Then you will be in good company."

Lila laughed a little too brightly, thought Miss Prymm, and she said warningly, "Do not expect too much, my dear. The prince may not be at home, or he may have company or even be in bed. They say he spends an enormous amount of time there, for if he is not eating, drinking, or indulging in some fort of debauchery or other, then he is prostrate in bed in a state of recovery."

"Pray, do not look so worried," Lila urged. "I have inflicted too much anxiety on you already. From now on, things *must* improve."

But Miss Prymm, with her long experience of life, knew better. She said nothing, however, as Lila climbed into the carriage, but merely wished her good luck.

That afternoon, the seamstress's lifelong friend, Miss Esther Larkin, called to bid farewell before taking a month at the waters of Bath, and Miss Prymm told her the entire story.

"And I'd like you to witness this, Esther. It is my last will and testament. George, my brother's child, is, as you know, my only heir, and I have not seen him in ten years. I feel Miss Ward will benefit far more from my little house and its possessions than a man who is almost a total stranger to me."

"But, Annabelle, you said her father was wealthy," protested Miss Larkin.

"It is not the money, Esther. It is somewhere for the child to live, for she will never return to Yorkshire until she clears her name, and somehow I have a feeling that that is going to be more difficult than she thinks." Miss Prymm folded the will and put it carefully into her bureau. "Of course, she can stay with me as long as she pleases, but it would seem I am her only friend in the capital.

"I shall take the will to my solicitor tomorrow. Ada witnessed it also this morning. Esther, dear, may I share your carriage as far as Berkeley Square?—for I am in the throes of making a magnificent ball gown for Lady de Vere Lowdry and I have an appointment for a fitting after tea."

Lila returned to the little house in Cotterell Street not very long after its owner had departed for Berkeley Square. Ada admitted her and told of her mistress's absence. She was barely civil for she disapproved of Miss Prymm's charity, but Lila did not notice her rudeness. She was feeling far too despondent after her visit to Carlton House. The place which until a few days ago had been her home, where she could come and go as she pleased, was now out of bounds. The guards on all the entrances had quite clearly been told not to allow her entry. They had been polite but firm. Under no circumstances could the prince be disturbed, and when Lila demanded to see his secretary, she was told that he was too busy.

Any further visits, Lila could see, would be dealt with in the same fashion. Of course she could write to the prince. In fact, she would compose a letter this very minute, but it was unlikely that he opened his own correspondence, and who could say whether or not his secretary could be trusted to hand the letter over.

It was surprising that her father had not contacted her, and Lila was wondering if he could present her case to the prince when Ada entered the room and grudgingly announced there was a gentleman to see her. At that moment Ralph Curringham entered the room.

Ralph's carriage had passed Lila's in the Mall and he had

instructed the coachman to turn and follow. He knew the stories circulating about his fiancée and the German servant were untrue, although his father had not bothered to share the facts with him. Nevertheless, Lila's situation added a certain spice, a piquancy, to her already delectable person. He remembered all the hot, covetous glances in her direction at the reception in the Chinese Room and a wild, throbbing desire had possessed him ever since. Now, as he stared at her across the room, he could scarcely prevent himself from crossing over and taking her on the spot.

Why, thought Lila, was she not throwing herself into his arms, sobbing for his protection and telling him how glad she was to see him? She could not say what prevented her. After all, she was to marry this man when her name was cleared. It was no use, she thought cynically, to imagine that Ralph might defy his father and go right ahead and marry her without giving a damn about public opinion.

I suppose I do not truly love him, she told herself regretfully, *and he does not love me. It was arranged because it suited our fathers, and I was so thankful that he was young and handsome I made believe I was in love.*

"Why have you come?" she found herself asking coldly. Then fearing to sound rude, she added, "Please sit down."

Ralph sat in an overstuffed velvet chair, unsure of what to say and not really knowing why he had come. Last night at Isabella's he had made love only to blond girls, for Lila was all he could think of. Had he really come for that? Damnit, yes he had. Who was she to refuse him? Her reputation was now as black as could be. She should be glad he wanted her. He crossed the room, knelt before her and placed his hands on her waist. She had a faint, careworn look that made her look vulnerable, more desirable than ever.

If only he could get his hands on her. She would succumb, for she was hot-blooded, like her mother, no matter how coolly she might act. Some said the German coachman had actually penetrated her the other night, so she was not a virgin anymore, and what right had she— His hands fumbled with the buttons on the front of her dress.

"Ralph!"

She was totally astonished. She pushed him away but he held on and undid more buttons as he pushed her back into the chair. Her dress was undone to the waist, and he pulled it off her shoulders along with the lacy camisole. Her white breasts were exposed, causing his insides to leap. He nearly choked with urgency.

"Let me go!" she screamed. "Go away! I beg of you."

Surely Ada would come to her aid, Lila thought frantically, but then she remembered that Ada was slightly deaf, and she was all the way down in the basement kitchen. Ralph was raining kisses on her shoulders, her bosom. His hands were struggling with the skirt of her dress when she tried to bring up her legs to kick him off. Her chair toppled over and they fell onto the floor, his body heavy on top of hers.

She tore at his hair, but grinning he freed her dress for a moment and imprisoned both her wrists in his left hand so she was completely helpless. She managed to bite his ear, but it seemed to incite rather than hurt him. Her skirt was at her knees and Ralph was beginning to undo his own clothes when something large and bulky struck him on the side of the head and he fell sideways onto the floor, slightly stunned.

Miss Prymm stood above him, her face beet red, with her bag containing Lady de Vere Lowdry's ballgown, several pairs of scissors and numerous spools of thread, raised ready to strike again.

Ada could be heard ascending the stairs, and Ralph scrambled to his feet and hurried out without a word, adjusting his clothing as he went. Lila struggled into her dress, watching Miss Prymm with anxiety, for her face had turned purple and her chest rose and fell at an alarming rate.

"Sit down, pray." Lila led the plump little woman to a sofa where she collapsed.

"My heart . . . is not strong," gasped Miss Prymm, her breathing now hoarse and labored.

"Water, Ada! Quickly!" shouted Lila to the maid who stood helplessly in the doorway. But as Ada left, Lila realized water would be of no use, not because the noisy, gasping breaths had quietened, but because they had ceased altogether.

Chapter Seven

Ada arranged for a messenger on horseback to take news of Miss Prymm's death to the nephew in Maldon. George Prymm, a thin, rodlike figure in musty black, arrived in the early afternoon of the following day, regarding his aunt's house with satisfaction, as he calculated the rent it would fetch. Before he viewed the body, Ada gave him the will she had witnessed which there had not been time to deposit with the solicitor.

"Who is this Esther Larkin?" he asked.

"A friend who has gone to Bath until the end of August," Ada told him with a sly look. "If she asks questions I can just say this will wasn't found. After all, the mistress could have changed her mind again and destroyed it."

George Prymm slipped several gold pieces into Ada's hand, and after she had left the room, he put the stiff white paper roll in the cheerful sitting-room fire and watched it burn brightly. He did not leave the fireside until the paper was reduced to gray dust. Then he sought out Lila and told her stiffly that she must pack and leave the house that same day.

Lila had scarcely anything to pack. She had arrived in her oldest clothes with only a small bag of personal possessions including the torn red dress. Now she was wearing the new day dress and cloak that Miss Prymm had all but finished only yesterday. She was ready to leave within half an hour, and as she sat alone in the tiny attic bedroom she wondered in desperation where she could go.

The death of her dear friend and ally was a dreadful blow, worsened by the fact that Lila felt partially responsible. If she had not come to this house, Miss Prymm would be alive now, bustling about, her determinedly cheerful face glowing with energy and good will. Strangely, though, Lila felt no urge to shed tears. The events of the last few days had shocked and drained her system, and although she was immeasurably unhappy about Miss Prymm's death, she was unable to grieve.

She wrestled with the problem of where to go, but with no intention of going back to Yorkshire. She was afraid that once ensconsed within her loving family circle she could easily be persuaded never to leave. So immersed was she in her predicament that she did not hear the light footsteps on the stairs, and the tap on the door made her jump.

"Simon!"

She wanted to throw her arms around her cousin as he stood in the doorway, enveloped by his coat.

"They told me downstairs what has happened to Miss Prymm," he said as she pulled him into the room. "And I read her letter to your mother yesterday when Rosalind and I called at Grassbrook Hall. We were on our way back to London from our honeymoon in Scotland. Rosalind has stayed to care for your family, and I came immediately to see how you were."

"How is Mama?" Lila asked anxiously.

"Bearing up remarkably well, under the circumstances," he told her. "But your father was present when the news came of your misfortune. He was quite devastated. Lila, he has suffered a stroke, and he has been bedridden since then."

Lila was trying to digest this news when Simon said, "If you are ready and packed, Lila, we can begin our journey home straightaway."

How could she explain her feelings to this kind, considerate man to whom nothing tragic or even dramatic had ever happened in his entire life? Could she make him understand her desire to stay in London? Surprisingly, it was easier than she thought.

"I wrote to Mama yesterday," she said. "I told her I intended to stay in London until my innocence in this awful affair is proved without doubt. I cannot return home with you."

"In that case, we must find somewhere in London for you to stay," Simon said calmly. There was more to him than Lila had ever imagined. "You will soon be able to stay with Rosalind and me in our new home in Hampstead. We plan to lodge with my parents until it is finished, and they could not accommodate an extra person, but I have a friend who is on holiday in Vienna for a few weeks, and he left the key to his room with me. I am sure he would not mind if you used it. It is only a back basement, I am afraid, and it is apt to get damp, but it is a place to stay nevertheless."

He picked up her small bag.

"Is this all you have?"

"I am afraid so. I do not know what has happened to all my clothes at Carlton House."

"No doubt they are being sold for large sums to souvenir hunters," Simon said drily as they descended the stairs.

"Why on earth would anyone want to buy my things?" asked Lila in surprise.

Simon didn't answer for a moment, then said slowly, "I'm afraid, Lila, that over the last few days you have become... famous." Simon had been about to say "notorious," but stopped himself. "You must be prepared for unpleasantness if you are recognized. You know that the *Times* wages constant war on the prince. Well, they have leaped onto the incident, featuring you, the prince, the princess, and the coachman in cartoons which are not exactly in the best of taste."

Surely, Lila thought miserably, *there cannot be room for my heart to sink yet further?* This awful news made her resolve even more strongly to leave no stone unturned in her quest to remove the blight from her name.

The basement room was tiny and dark, but comfortable.

"A bit different from Carlton House," Simon said apologetically.

"Simon! I hated Carlton House. It was far too grand and not at all like a true home."

She threw herself down onto the shabby sofa nd heaved a huge sigh of relief.

Simon stayed with her for several hours, listening to her whole story from the beginning to the end with remarkable sympathy and understanding. She began to feel envious of Rosalind for being married to such a dear man, and wryly remembered feeling superior because she was engaged to Ralph, who was so much younger and more attractive.

I've learned many lessons over the last few days, she thought to herself, *and here is yet another. Looks are not everything— it is only now that the true meaning of that has come home to me.*

Eventually Simon left for Yorkshire, promising to return within a few days to see how Lila was getting on. After he had gone Lila prepared to bed down on the sofa, amused by the oddness of her position. In her whole life she had never heard of a girl of seventeen living alone.

The next morning she wrote a short, explicit letter to the Prince of Wales, emphasizing the urgency with which she had to see him and took it to Carlton House, but was dismayed to see the huge wink the guard who took it bestowed upon his companion nearby. She felt a moment of deepest despair when she knew there was no chance of the prince receiving her communication. Was there anyone in Carlton House who could not be bought?

Then she recalled that she had this very same thought when faced with a problem before, and she had decided to confide in Phillip Grenville. Why not do the same thing now? No one would read his letters before they reached him. He was too intelligent, she reckoned, not to concede that there were two sides to every story. Surely if she wrote explaining her innocent role in the affair he would believe her. She started back to her room to write the letter and find out where the captain lived. This letter task proved unnecessary, however, for at that moment two young blades passed by, exuding a strong smell of lavender, their shirt fronts a mass of ruffled lace, and she heard one of them say, "Yes, the prince is not supplying alcohol tonight. He wishes to commence the troop movements tomorrow in a sober condition."

His friend laughed. "His role as colonel of the Light Dragoons is quite pathetic. He approaches these silly little maneuvers as if he were about to enter a great battle."

Suddenly the two young men became aware that Lila had stopped to listen, and they glanced at her with admiration in their eyes. Then one gave a start and whispered something to his companion, and they sniggered, looking her up and down in a suggestive manner. As Lila hurried away a foul epithet was flung at her back, and it was all she could do to keep from running back to the shelter of her little room.

For all their unpleasantness, the two young men had provided vital information. If the prince was accompanying the Light Dragoons, then wherever they were going, Captain Grenville would be with them. Therefore, it was imperative she contact him before the day was out. The Light Dragoons would certainly be based in London so all she had to do was find out where the barracks were situated and leave a note for the captain. Even if he did not sleep there, surely he would go there before the regiment embarked on maneuvers.

She scribbled away, writing far more than she had to the prince, and finished off,

I have with me the red dress, which, you may remember, I was wearing that night in the Chinese Room, and which has been ripped entirely apart. What need would there have been for such violence had I been a willing participant in the affair?

She marked the envelope URGENT, stuffed it in her bag, and stood to leave, when she found herself feeling faint and remembered she had not eaten at all that day. Hastily she made a meal from the food Simon had brought yesterday. Tomorrow it would be necessary to replenish the empty larder.

Refreshed, she left the house and asked at the first shop she came to the whereabouts of the Light Dragoons.

"Across the park in Kensington Gore," the shopkeeper informed her. "The Prince's Pets we call 'em. Never gets shot at and never gets wet."

Outside the barracks a fresh-faced young soldier told her to leave her missive with the sergeant in a nearby office.

"We expects him this evening, miss," the sergeant informed her. "I'll give him your note the very minute he arrives, don't worry, young lady."

Heartened by his friendly manner, Lila walked back to her room to wait. She did not notice a little squint-eyed man following her. In fact he'd been behind her all day, and he'd had to hurry to keep up with the spritely young lady. He felt he was certainly earning the florin a day he was being paid to keep a watch on her.

It was not until late in the evening that the golden rays of the setting sun were able to reach the lower window of the basement room where Lila sat, once again writing, this time to her mother. So absorbed was she that it was not until a beam of light crossed her face that she discovered the entire room was lit with the amber glow of the late afternoon sun. She stared about her, astonished at the transformation of the shabby room into a warm, radiant grotto.

It was at that very moment that Captain Grenville tapped at her door. She opened the door and stepped back into the room. Where she stood in the sunlight, her golden hair reflected the light and her slim, softly clad figure seemed to glow. It seemed to the captain that her eyes were a lifetime older than when he had last looked into them.

"You came," she said unnecessarily, caught unawares.

He didn't reply but went straight to her and took her in his arms, holding her close, his hand on her neck, stroking the molten hair, and Lila thought wildly that all the terrible things that had happened to her would be worth it if this were how it was to end.

For several moments they stood like that, silent and still, until he stepped back, took her hands and led her to the sofa.

"Your letter lifted from my mind the greatest weight it has ever known." He took her hands and held them to his lips briefly. "How could I have doubted you?" he murmured, half to himself.

His face twisted into its old cynical smile and he went on, "I regret, my dear child, I am too easily disillusioned by the female sex. Experiences in my youth have destroyed my faith in the purity and the loyalty of womankind. Although I saw at once that you were different, I let myself believe too easily that I had been fooled yet again. Will you forgive me?"

"It must have been difficult for you to doubt the evidence of your own eyes," she replied shakily, unable to believe that he cared for her. "I am deeply grateful that you believed my letter and came."

He leaned back, smiling into her eyes, and said, "Tomorrow

the regiment departs at noon to play maneuvers on the east coast." He gave a wry smile as he spoke. "I am to collect the prince at mid-morning and escort him to Kensington Gore Barracks. Come early to Carlton House, my dear, say at nine o'clock, and I will take you to the prince. I will show him your letter beforehand, and I know I can persuade him to listen to you."

"But they will not admit me," Lila told him. "Twice I have called, but obviously they have been instructed not to allow me in."

"I see." The captain's eyes were steely. "That woman . . ."

"Lady Jersey, yes," agreed Lila. "But Lord Rawlesbury too. Both conspired to have me evicted."

"Rawlesbury, eh? Is he not the father of your fiancé, Ralph Curringham?"

Now it was Lila's turn to harden, and her eyes flashed as she replied, "Lord Ralph Curringham is no longer my fiancé, whatever the outcome of this affair may be."

"In that case . . ." Phillip Grenville paused, then kissed her lightly and stroked her cheek, saying, "I will not inflict the question on you now, but will wait until this turmoil has subsided, which I am sure will be quite soon."

Lila wondered that a proposal of marriage from this man could be termed an "infliction." She wished he would not be so considerate. He was kissing her softly, and she guessed that he was deliberately restraining himself. Yet she had never felt so inclined to give way to wild, abandoned lovemaking. She wanted to forget utterly the ordeal she had suffered over the last few days, and lose herself in passion. But she sat there, prim and proper, while he merely folded her gently in his arms and behaved exactly as a gentleman should. Nevertheless, she felt radiantly happy, and when he left she promised she would arrive at Carlton House at nine sharp the next norming. That night Lila slept more calmly and peacefully than she had since she came to London.

The man with the squint, still waiting outside, saw Captain Grenville leave, and watched as Lila's light eventually dimmed. Then he made his way off into the night to make his report.

It was a shame, thought the squint-eyed man as he returned to wait outside the house very early the next morning. She seemed like a nice young lady and not at all the type to do anyone any harm. But when he went to see the hawklike lord in Belgrave Square, and described the soldier who'd called on her, and told of her visit to Kensington Gore Barracks, the lord's face turned nasty.

"The Black Arrow!" he snarled. "The Light Dragoons leave for the east coast at midday tomorrow with the prince in tow. I'll stake a hundred to one that the prince will see her before he leaves Carlton House."

The squint-eyed man said nothing as he didn't understand a bit of what his master was saying.

Rawlesbury continued, "She mustn't be allowed to reach there. Do you hear? Use anything short of murder. You have a free hand."

The man was relieved to hear that he wasn't to murder the girl, because he didn't have the stomach for it. Not for the mere twenty pounds he was being paid, at least.

"What happens if a carriage comes for her?" he sniveled. "And what if the soldier's in it, calling for her?"

"Then don't wait for him to arrive," snapped the aristocrat. "Get into her room and kidnap her. You can cope, I am sure."

If he couldn't cope, the little man decided, he would go into hiding and hang the twenty pounds. He didn't fancy his chances with this old upper-class scoundrel if he failed.

Lila opened her window the minute she woke and looked out on the sunlit garden with pleasure. The sweet August breeze lifted the curtains and she rejoiced that in a few hours all her troubles would be over. Then she would go immediately to Yorkshire to see Mama. And Papa too, of course. Captain Grenville, when he had finished playing maneuvers as he called it, would come to see them and...

She hugged herself in delight and wished sadly that Miss Annabelle Prymm was still there to share in the marvelous news. Now she must forget the past and live only for the future. She suddenly realized that she was starving hungry. Over the last few days she had scarcely eaten anything. Slipping on her old cotton dress, she put some money in a reticule and looked at the time. Not yet seven o'clock. Plenty of time to buy something to eat and then get ready for her visit to Carlton House.

On the corner of the street, she found a small bakery. The smell of freshly baked bread sharpened her hunger pangs, and

she entered to join the customers who were buying large supplies for their households. Going in, she had to hold open the
door for a little man with a squint who came in behind her,
followed by two old women.

On the assumption that she would be leaving the room she
now occupied that day, Lila bought only two cob rolls. She
had paid for them and was about to leave when a shout stopped
her in her tracks.

"Stop her!" yelled the squint-eyed man. "She pinched that
old lady's purse! Right before me eyes I saw her do it! Perhaps
'cuz my eyes aren't straight she thought I wasn't looking, but
took it out the old girl's pocket she did, cool as a cucumber."

He caught hold of Lila's arm and she struggled indignantly.

At the same time, one of the women cried, "You're right.
My money's gone."

"Is this it, lady?"

To Lila's total astonishment, he fished in her reticule and
took out a shabby cloth purse which he held up.

"That's it! That's my money."

The old woman came up to Lila and thrust her face close.
"I'll have you whipped for this, young woman. There's a guinea
in there, belonging to my mistress, and it would have come
out of my wages if I'd lost it."

"I'll hold her, whilst you fetches the law," the man said,
tightening his grip on Lila's arm.

"Shame on you!"

Two young kitchen maids spat as they left the shop, and
once again Lila was overcome with despair, realizing she was
powerless against the mighty forces working against her.

It was then that, for the first time in her life, she fainted
dead away.

The cool breeze had disappeared and had been replaced by
sultry, oppressive heat. It was difficult to breathe. The court's
corridor was crowded with a hundred or more vagabonds who
had not bathed for many a day, and Lila had to take deep gasps
in order to prevent herself from fainting again. It was past
noon, and by now Captain Grenville and the prince would be
on their way to the coast. What had the captain thought, she
wondered desperately, when she hadn't turn up? Had he gone
to look for her?

Even if he had, there was no one there to tell him anything.

Only the strangers in the bakery knew what had happened, and out of them, only the man with the squint and the old woman knew she was at Holgate Courts. They were to be witnesses when she was tried and they were waiting, presumably somewhere more comfortable, in the same building.

She allowed herself to be swayed and carried along by the crowd, as it surged backwards and forwards. Pickpockets, thieves, prostitutes, drunkards, petty criminals of every type surrounded her. The smell of sweat, drink, and bad breath was so overpowering she felt she would choke, when she heard her name being called, and she struggled hopefully towards the voice.

"Ward. Lilian Ward."

"Here!" she shouted back, thinking it was someone come to rescue her from this hell.

But the answering cry informed her, "Straightaway to court number three."

Captain Grenville waited for half an hour at the giant columns at the front of Carlton House. He could not understand why Lila hadn't appeared, and it worried him deeply. In the end, after giving strict instructions to the soldiers on duty that he was to be informed the minute she arrived, he had to return to the prince.

He had read to His Royal Highness the letter Lila had written to him the previous day and was faintly annoyed when his listener collapsed onto his satin-covered bed convulsed with laughter.

"That woman!" he snorted. "That odorous Brunswickian whore! Oh, if only your little friend had not been so honorable, Phillip. How I would have loved to catch that person being serviced by her animal coachman. Never mind, I shall enjoy exposing the truth, and the newspapers will find that more titillating than the fiction they have published so far."

At ten o'clock there was still no sign of Lila, and the prince, his bulging waistline emphasized by the tight-fitting uniform of colonel-in-chief, was escorted to the barracks to inspect his troops, something in which he took great delight and pride.

At noon the soldiers were mustered and ready to leave when Captain Grenville approached the Prince of Wales.

"Colonel?"

How the prince loved that title. He was softened before the request was even made.

"This is unprecedented, I know, but the girl still has not arrived at Carlton House. I left a message there that I was to be advised immediately if she came. I am convinced that something has happened to her. May I join the regiment as soon as I have investigated the matter?"

Prince George, who could understand an affair of the heart more easily than most men, readily agreed he could manage without the good captain for the time being. After all, it was only maneuvers, he thought sadly. If only his father would let him take the dragoons to France to join in the war there. But that was wishful thinking. . . .

The Black Arrow left immediately, and the prince and the Light Dragoons started on their long march to Hove.

It was no surprise to the captain to find Lila's room unlocked and empty. The sight of the silk dress, which she had told him the night before was the only good outfit she owned, filled him with fear. It meant she had not even left for Carlton House, for if she had she would have been wearing this very dress. He thought that perhaps for some reason she had returned to Miss Prymm's house, but a visit there proved to no avail. He began to feel convinced that his new love had been kidnapped for reasons which were only too obvious. Someone knew the truth was about to come out and had panicked.

He began a frantic journey amongst the underworld of London, returning to Isabella's House of Sin, where he had once found her, knowing it was in reality a foolish thing to do, yet less foolish than doing nothing at all. He could not track down Queen Lil, but he found her companion, Alf, living in a squalid room in Blackfriars, where the man informed him that Queen Lil had been arrested the day before for thieving.

"Only a bit of grub it was, general," whined the man. "We was hungry, see, and no other way of getting food than stealing."

The captain threw him a coin and returned to his carriage. It was dark by now and very late, and he could think of nowhere else to go but home. Maybe after some sleep he would emerge refreshed and be able to think of somewhere else he could search for Lila Ward.

But on awakening, very early, he had no new ideas. He went back to her room in the faint hope that she had returned, but it was empty, damp, and silent. Then a thought struck him. There were no provisions at all in the room. Surely Lila would have intended to breakfast before leaving for Carlton House the previous morning. She would not have put on her only good dress to leave early to shop.

Outside he asked a passerby for the nearest shop which sold provisions.

"There's Mother Gunter's Bakery on the corner there," he was told. "Very good she be, the bread always fresh and warm."

"Minx!" exclaimed Mother Gunter, moments later, her face red and perspiring from the heat of the ovens. "I know the young lady you be looking for, and I'm not at all surprised that there's a military man wanting her now. Stole a purse, she did, from old Nellie Dunn. Wicked! Real wicked. Though I must say she looked more like an angel from heaven than a thief." She shook her head wonderingly. "It just shows you. Looks can deceive."

"What happened to the girl?" Captain Grenville asked urgently.

"This man, a stranger in my shop he was, he got some help and she got taken to Holgate Courts. Look, here's Nellie now. She went with them."

Nellie told him she had given her evidence, which was her duty, and then come home. As long as she got her purse back, that was all she cared about.

"I expects she was found guilty," Nellie went on. "Should have been if there's to be justice in this world, stealing an old woman's purse like that." Mother Gunter nodded in agreement. "If so, you'll find her at Newgate, surely, doing penance for her crime."

Captain Grenville did not bother to stay and argue for Lila's innocence, but swiftly made his way to Newgate Prison, where a warden in a dank and dark office told him, "Yes, Captain, I can tell you straightaway the young lady you describe was here, 'cuz we weren't given no name, which is odd, and we had instructions to put her in a room by herself." He shook his head at the vagaries of the authorities while the captain waited impatiently for him to continue. "About seventeen she'd be, and like you said, her hair all bright and shiny, like proper gold it was."

"Thank God!" exclaimed the captain, feeling as though an enormous weight had been lifted from his chest. "Let me see her straightaway, please. And bail? How much is it? I'll post it immediately."

"Well now, Captain. I wish I could help, but I did say she *was* here. She ain't no more. She's gone, sir."

"Gone? Then where can I find her?"

"That's just it, sir. You can't. The lady you're looking for got sentenced to deportment. Very early this morning they took her and a crowd of other women to the *Gabriel* which sailed from Southampton little less than half an hour ago, headed for Botany Bay."

The marquess of Rawlesbury could not stop himself from rubbing his hands together with glee. Things had worked out remarkably well. The princess had promised to come out on the side of the Whigs if they successfully suppressed the truth about the scandal. Ludwig had been abruptly dispatched to Brunswick. Caroline did not care what her husband thought about her, but she desperately wanted to be queen of England some day, and as the Whigs could blackmail her at any point, it was to her advantage to cooperate with them. At the same time, the Tories were bound to cooperate, because Rawlesbury harbored a charge of serious corruption against a senior Tory minister.

It had all gone like a dream. The only time things seemed shaky was when Rawlesbury heard that the Black Arrow had contacted the girl in response to her letter, but even that matter could not have been resolved more perfectly. That little ruffian with the squint had acted with rare common sense, and the judge at Holgate—well, he had turned out to be an old friend, and having been privately assured of Miss Ward's guilt and promised a visit that very night from one of the more experienced ladies of Isabella's House of Sin, he had not hesitated to sentence the troublesome girl to deportation. Then, as though it was the icing on the cake, there happened to be a ship, the *Gabriel,* leaving for Australia the very next morning.

Perfect, that's what it had all been. Quite perfect. Now the only pressing problem was to find a rich young lady for his feckless son Ralph to marry.

The laborers at Southampton docks stared with interest at the tall, splendidly clad soldier who stood staring out to sea, a lone, strangely tragic figure.

Captain Grenville had ridden like a madman to Southampton, hoping, praying that an accident or a low tide, anything, had held up the sailing of the *Gabriel*. But he was too late. The ship could still be seen, a miniature in full sail on the horizon.

The dock workers were not close enough to see a solitary tear run down the brown cheek of the man as he stood looking out, as though his very soul had left his body and was on the ship set forth for Botany Bay.

Chapter Eight

Mama was standing in the corner of the morning room, just inside the door. Instead of looking at Lila, she was staring beyond her at some point by the fireplace, and it gave Lila the feeling of being invisible. But Mama knew she wss there because she was saying in a cold, unrecognizable voice, "I am very displeased with you, Lilian. I knew you would let me down."

Hettie and Mary had their faces buried in Mama's bosom and she had an arm around each. Lila felt she was no longer part of her family, and the way her mother was addressing her was eerie and frightening. She started to cry and Mama smiled, an evil, vicious smile. Hettie and Mary raised their heads and Lila knew they too would be smiling in the same manner.

She was wrong. Hettie and Mary had no faces at all, just smooth skin, white and blank, where their features should have been. Lila screamed and, sobbing threw herself onto a sofa to hide her eyes. She woke to find that the sobs were real, but Mama, Hettie, and Mary were just part of a hideous nightmare. Scarcely more hideous than reality, however.

She was lying on a straw pallet which smelled of vomit, covered by a coarse and grubby blanket, and although she was crying, she was making no more noise than the sleeping women all around her. About eighty women lay on the lower deck of the ship, crushed together side by side, with a narrow passage between their feet and the next row of wretched cargo. They groaned, moaned, and, like Lila, cried in their sleep. They flung up their arms, sat up straight in their bad dreams, sinking down again when they realized it was another nightmare they were part of.

Lila was on her way to Botany Bay, a convicted criminal. That awful squint-eyed man, the indignant woman whose purse had been placed in her reticule—both had sworn her guilt to the senile, mumbling judge who had sentenced her to seven years' deportation. Lila had wanted to laugh at him. What absolute nonsense! Captain Grenville, her father, Simon—the Prince of Wales himself—someone would free her before she was sent halfway across the world on some trumped-up charge.

At first she had not understood what was happening to her. She had been placed in a cell on her own, awakened when the moon was high, and put, along with a large, silent woman in black, into a carriage which raced through the night, changing horses with swift efficiency. She was not permitted to alight, nor offered refreshment. It was when the carriage jolted onto the hard cobbles of Southampton docks where the *Gabriel* bobbed lazily, and the bright morning sun was already reflecting off the water, that she realized what was happening.

She was put on board immediately! There was no way of contacting Phillip or her family. Sailors, their feet brown and bare, were already hauling in ropes, shouting to each other, getting ready to sail. For the first time in her life, Lila had hysterics. Until that moment, she'd scorned people who gave way to hysteria and inflicted their emotions on those around them. Afterwards she reflected wryly that perhaps her reason was more substantial than a spoilt dress or a lovers' tiff.

When the woman, who had scarcely spoken throughout the long journey, got out and stood waiting, hand outstretched and ready to grab her arm, Lila began to scream.

"No! Please, no!"

The sailors looked up from their tasks, startled. Some watched sympathetically, others laughed, as the girl was dragged from the carriage with the coachman's help and carried to the gang-plank.

"Please help me! You cannot do this!"

A burly marine came down the gangplank, took Lila from her captors, and threw her over his shoulder as if she were a baby. Then he walked surefooted onto the ship.

"Last bit of cargo aboard, Cap'n," shouted the marine to someone above, and as if they'd been waiting especially for Lila, there came the cranking sound of the anchor being drawn, and the gangplank was pulled away.

She was carried to the door of a cabin and placed none too gently on her feet. Inside, a man in naval uniform, with hard eyes and a sharp nose, sat at a desk with a series of lists spread out before him.

"Name?" he inquired curtly.

"Miss Lilian Ward of Grassbrook Hall in Yorkshire," Lila answered, head held high. Her hysterics were over but had left her red-faced and panting. She assumed the man wanted her to enter and stepped through the door.

"Stay outside," he snapped. "We can do the necessary business without you fouling the air of my cabin."

Before Lila could think of a reply to this insult, he went on, "Seven years for stealing one guinea off a Nellie Dunn. To be spent in Botany Bay, New South Wales."

He put a tick beside her name, which, even from her position in the passageway, Lila could see had been added to the list in a different hand from the others. She opened her mouth to protest, to plead her innocence, but closed it again. With this man they would be a waste of time.

She glanced behind her, desperately searching for some means of escape. Several sailors stood between her and the quayside. Even if she managed to dodge through them she risked death or serious injury if she jumped from the ship now, though for a brief moment the thought of death passed through her mind as being preferable to the future destined for her. Resolutely she brushed the thought away. She would win through in the end. She would return to England and prove her innocence, come what may.

"Take her to the women's quarters," the uniformed man snapped to the marine who waited behind.

Lila impatiently shook away the hand which tried to clasp her arm, preferring to follow, eyes darting everywhere trying to see a way out of her predicament, but the likelihood of this proved fainter and fainter as she was led along passages, down stairs, into the very bowels of the ship. Eventually her guide opened a trapdoor in the floor and motioned to her to descend. Lila passed halfway down the ladder, horror-struck at the sight before her.

She was at one end of a vast space which seemed to be the size of the entire ship. Dim oil lamps suspended from the deck above cast murky, flickering shadows onto the scene below her.

Women, row after row of indescribably filthy women, most of them dressed in nothing but rags, their hair matted with dirt, their faces, arms and legs covered in sores. The eyes turned to the opened trapdoor were either hopeless or smoldering with rage.

"They're not in such good shape as yourself," grinned her companion. "Most of 'em have come from the hulks, so they're not exactly spruce."

He poked his head down through the trapdoor and yelled, "Find a place for your new traveling companion!" He grinned at the barrage of obscenity which greeted him.

Women shook their fists at him, and waved arms. Others bared their bodies and leered at him. One or two, in no uncertain terms, advised him to depart.

"Gerroff, Charlie, or I'll chew yer nipples orf," screeched a hunchbacked crone.

"C'mon, now. Where's an empty spot for this young lady?"

Lila prayed she would not have to venture far into the grotesque collection of females, and was thankful when a place was pointed out near the bottom of the ladder. The man above gave her a shove and disappeared, slamming the trapdoor shut behind him.

Now that their main enemy had disappeared, the women turned their attention towards their new shipmate. All eyes were on her as she descended the last few steps, and the minute her feet touched the deck she was surrounded by a dozen or more repulsive creatures who marveled at her hair, tugging it to see if it was real. They stroked her pink cheeks with their blackened fingers, commenting in wonder at the petal-soft skin. Someone tried to drag the lace collar off her frock, and another lifted

her skirt to see the new owner's underthings. This poor soul
got a sharp slap on her ear from a now exasperated Lila. Lila
expected a retaliatory blow, but instead all the women shrank
back. There was a flicker of respect in their faces, and some
were probably too weak to do battle with this healthy young
woman.

Leaving them to stare, Lila stepped agilely over several
recumbent bodies to reach the empty spot and sat down on the
gray pallet. She was still the center of attention; lewd comments
about her personal appearance or about why she had joined
them were called from every direction, but Lila was thankful
to have reached her own bed without coming to any harm. She
was also glad to note that not all the women were as revolting
as they had first appeared.

Next to her was a girl of about her own age who, although
shabbily dressed in a dark blue frock and a worn pair of men's
heavy boots, had clear skin and clean thick brown hair coiled
into a bun on the nape of her neck.

One or two other women nearby also looked more respectable than the awful harridans who screamed and shouted still—
some at Lila, some at the captain of the ship wherever and
whoever he might be, and some at God. Lila could not help
but feel pity for these creatures.

"They're from the hulks," said the girl in dark blue as though
reading Lila's mind. "Their brains have gone rotten with their
bodies."

Everyone had heard about the dreaded hulks which lay stink-
ing in the Thames providing scanty shelter for the unwanted
remnants of English society. When the War of Independence
made deportation to America impossible, prisons began to burst
at the seams, old, rotten, and rusted hulks provided "temporary"
accommodation. For twenty years the hulks had grown more
rotten, more rusty and their scurvy-ridden, disease-ridden inhabitants more uncivilized. They were now gradually being
emptied of their wretched inmates with the deportation to Botany Bay underway.

In a while the poor women lost interest in the new arrival
and sank down exhausted after their exertions. The girl who
had spoken to Lila sat with her eyes closed and her hands
clasped around the crucifix of a rosary, the beads falling onto
her knees. At last there was time to think. She was being
launched into a new world, peopled mainly by criminals and

savages. Botany Bay in New South Wales was the place discovered a quarter of a century before by the redoubtable Captain Cook. It was only a mere eight years ago that the law had been passed permitting criminals to be sent to this godforsaken place. Lila lay back on her pallet feeling sick with despair and frustration, when suddenly several of the women gave an enormous shout.

"It's Queenie. It's Queen Lil!"

"Come and join us, Queenie, gal."

And there, coming down the ladder only a few feet away was the grotesque woman who had tried to kidnap her that night in Blackfriars. That frightful adventure suddenly seemed tame.

"Where've you been, Queenie? Entertainin' the cap'n, I'll bet."

"No, lasses," Queen Lil shouted to them in her hoarse voice with its odd, infrequent upper-class tones. "They put me in the bilges with the murderers. It took five sailors to get me aboard this ship. Chained up I was, till she sailed."

"Shame on 'em, Queenie. A nice gal like you!"

"Four foot o'water in them bilges. Those men won't see Botany Bay. Better hanging any day than months of rotting, half-drowned in a dungeon like that."

True enough, as the ugly giant of a woman reached the deck, her tattered clothes were seen to be soaked up to the waist, clinging to her legs. Lila shrank back, willing Queenie not to see her. But if Lila thought she could hide, she was sadly mistaken, for she had no hat or hood to cover her head, and even in the dim glow of the swinging lamps her head shone like gold in the midst of her yellow prisoners.

"Well! If it isn't Miss Lilian Ward!"

Queen Lil towered at the foot of Lila's mattress, her yellow, pockmarked skin glistening with fever, her hooded eyes twinkling.

"You have exalted company, dearies," she shouted. "Here is Miss Lilian Ward, daughter of Sir William of Grassbrook Hall in Yorkshire. Daddy is a member of Parliament, is he not?"

Lila ignored her, but the woman kicked at her feet, indicating she wanted an answer.

"Yes, he is," she answered stiffly.

All the women shrieked hysterically at her reply and Queen

Lil went on, "But that's not all, my gals. Here we have none other than a real lady-in-waiting." A gasp went up at this and Queenie grinned at the effect she was having. "That's right. Come down in the world, haven't we? What happened, Miss Ward? You must have got on the wrong side of our dear Princess Caroline to be in this pickle."

Another gasp from the women listening avidly as Queen Lil taunted her young victim. "That's right, dearies. Lady-in-waiting to our future queen, is this young woman. Or I should say, was. You see, we came across her in Blackfriars, did Alf and me. I didn't believe her, but Lordie me, I found out afterwards it was true. What'ya do? Steal the crown jewels?"

"Perhaps it was Prince Georgie himself she stole, Lil," a raucous voice shouted from out of the gloom.

"Not likely," sneered Queenie. "If all the women who stole him were sent to Botany Bay, there'd be no room on ship for us convicts."

"Come on, Miss Ward. We lead humdrum sort of lives. Give us a bit of court gossip and tell us how you got here."

Lila stared at her tormentor, hoping to shame her with the contempt in her eyes, but Queenie simply stared back. After some seconds, though, she began to sway, and Lila marveled at the strength of the woman who had been chained, soaking wet in the bilges for several days.

Someone else must have noticed the bout of dizziness and shouted, "Come on, Queenie, gal. You looks fair worn out. Come and lie down and take them wet clothes off."

For a moment, Queen Lil eyed the girl next to Lila who sat with her eyes closed, and for one awful moment, Lila thought that Queen Lil was about to force her away and take her place beside Lila. But the fearsome woman turned to join friends elsewhere. Lila lay back onto the stained mattress, moving her arm so that her face rested in its crook and smothered the smell of vomit. The stench in the air was hardly more bearable, and Lila wondered if they would be allowed on deck. The thought of fresh sea air, of fine salty spray on her face, seemed like heaven.

The ship was now well underway, the timbers creaking and groaning and the water lapping with soft monotony against the hull. Food was brought in by the marine. He carried down several large pots of gruel, electing three women to share it out. Lila found hers inedible. The wooden bowl was already filthy; she readily handed over her dish to the girl beside her, who was eyeing it greedily. The woman lying on her other side had already begun to be sick and was retching noisily.

Carrying away the last empty pot, the marine shouted, "Ye can all go on deck now—for exercise!"

He leered when he said this, and it was not until she reached the deck, behind almost everyone else, that she understood the reason for the leer. Women were already coupling with the sailors, beneath lifeboats, on tarpaulins, against cabin walls. One pair was comfortably ensconced within a huge coil of rope.

She averted her eyes and made for the rail taking deep breaths of the sharp, fresh air. As she stood staring into the gray, froth-tipped water, a dozen men closed in behind her, muttering the most coarse enticements, vying with each other in their indecency. Then they began to pluck at her clothes, and she turned, eyes blazing, to spit in their faces.

"Pigs!" she screamed. "Let me be!"

Frantically she wondered what protection she had. Was a convicted woman anyone's for the taking? Could these men ignore her angry rejections and just throw her to the deck? Thankfully she noticed several more respectable-looking women grouped together at the bow of the ship, so presumably it was possible to reject the sailors' advances. Nevertheless, she was such a delightful contrast to her companions, with her bright hair and eyes, her curves revealed as the breeze lifted the soft cotton of her dress, that the men would not give up. *Surely,* she thought in despair, *I will not suffer this every time we are allowed on deck?*

The men's whining voices followed her as she walked along the deck. One man crawled behind and grabbed the lace of her petticoat. And for the first time in her life Lila screamed an oath, cursing the men who scrabbled behind her.

In desperation she returned to the hold, where the fetid, suffocating atmosphere was preferable to the animals who pursued her with their foul suggestions. About twenty women still lay on their beds, too ill to move. She could see Queen Lil asleep, and she fell onto her own bed, trembling and wondering what else could possibly happen to her. The other women gradually returned.

It was the worst day of her life. Time ground slowly by

while she lay or sat, not wanting to talk to the other prisoners. No one approached her either. *It would have to be a brave woman,* thought Lila, *who would make friendly overtures towards someone publicly mocked and declared an enemy by Queen Lil.*

Barely cooked potatoes accompanied by rancid-looking meat floating in hot greasy water were offered at some time during the day and again Lila'a neighbor greedily ate both meals. Because there was no daylight in the hold there was no way of knowing the time, and with horror Lila recalled that the journey to New South Wales took between eight and ten months. If she didn't die of starvation or bullying, then she would surely die of boredom.

She lay back on her bed, drained, and before her closed, aching eyes appeared a vision of Phillip Grenville, tender and loving as he had been on that last night, and Lila realized with the utmost astonishment that from the moment he had boarded this ship, he had not crossed her mind. Nor had Mama and Papa, or her sisters. This new world she had entered was so brutal and so different from what she was used to that no room was left in her mind for anything outside it.

With an overwhelming hatred she recalled Lord Guy Rawlesbury and Lady Jersey, who, she was positive, were responsible for everything. She even began to wish she had agreed to her would-be father-in-law's proposal that night and taken the blame for Princess Caroline's immoral behavior. She would be with her parents now, safe and secure in Yorkshire. In disgrace, true. But could anything be worse than the position she was now in? Silent tears ran down her cheeks and dropped onto the rough blanket which she had pulled around her. The fact that she had not remembered her loved ones made her feel more alone than ever. *Phillip—did you look for me? Have you found out where I have gone? Mama, please don't die. Wait for me.*

Finally she felt sleep creeping up on her. Phillip Grenville would call on Mama and tell her all he knew. Of course there was Simon too. Already he would have told her family about Miss Prymm. Drowsily she prayed again, *Don't die, Mama, before your daughter is safe home again.* Of course it depended on Lila's not dying first. . . .

Queen Lil had awoken and was yelling taunts in her direction.

"Come on, Miss Lilian Ward. What was you up to in Carlton House? Got on the wrong side of someone, did you, Goldilocks?"

"Goldilocks, Goldilocks, Goldilocks..."

The shrieks still sounded in her ears from somewhere very far away, and Lila eventually escaped once again into sleep.

But there was no escape, for in her dreams there was Mama with that hard, unforgiving face, and Hettie and Mary with no faces at all, and Lila woke up—whether it was five minutes or five hours later she knew not—sobbing aloud and hugging herself.

Everywhere her fellow prisoners muttered sleepy groans and Lila sat up, heart pounding, aware that something had happened, but unable to pinpoint it. She stared around her and then turned to lie down again when she stopped, transfixed at what lay on her pillow. The same strange feeling came over her that she'd felt in her dream when Hettie and Mary had turned to her, faceless. On the bed was part of herself.

With a horrified, shaking hand she reached out and took hold of her lovely, gleaming golden hair. It lay heavy and still, curling in her palm. No longer part of her.

She clutched her head with both hands. Short, bristly ends caught on her fingertips and she removed her hands and stared at them, surprised to find they were covered with blood.

Someone had hacked off all her hair.

If they could do that when she was asleep, they could do anything to her. Cut her throat, cut off her hands, disfigure her face. Lila's first instinct was to panic, to scream at the outrage which had been done to her, but almost immediately this was replaced by an icy calm. She would not be here when all these creatures woke up to laugh at whatever apparition she now presented to the world. She would not be here tomorrow to be the butt of their jokes, to eat the odious food, to sit and lie, lie and sit, hour after hour. She would no longer be plagued by the seamen when she went on deck.

Picking up the thick golden mass of her hair, Lila stood up. It was useless trying the trapdoor she had come through for she had heard it being bolted. The women occupied just over half the hold. Crates, trunks and sacks, securely tied together with ropes, were piled at the other end, appearing to take up as much room again as the women did.

There must surely be another way out beyond all that cargo.

She picked her way through the rows of sleeping, restless women, kicking viciously at a scraggy arm which tried to grasp her ankle. She clambered easily over the heaped cargo, slipping through cracks and between boxes until she reached the far end of the hold where there was indeed another trapdoor. She prayed it would be open.

To her relief the door lifted and she climbed up into a dark passage, at the end of which were stairs going up. As she went higher within the ship, a dim light could be seen through the portholes. She guessed it was four or five o'clock in the morning, and this was confirmed when she crept out onto the deck, making sure first that no one was about.

The ship did not appear to be moving, but was just rocking gently to and fro. The deck was completely empty. Before her, a watery sun was just beginning to enter the sky, as yet only a wet, silvery line on the horizon. The sea was a dark, solid gray and Lila walked to the ship's edge and stood staring into it, so far below her. She held out the handfuls of her golden hair and gradually let them go so that the hairs separated, and by the time they reached the sea they had been blown far and wide by the slight breeze and had disappeared from her sight.

Despite all that had happened, she didn't have the courage to throw herself into that lonely gray mass. The idea of death by drowning was too abhorrent. Anyway, she'd thought of a better, easier way. She had noticed the lifeboats yesterday, hung suspended to the aft of the ship—two large ones which she reckoned would hold thirty or forty people, and beyond them, two smaller ones.

It was no easy matter hanging from the ropes and moving along, hand over hand, until she reached one of the smaller boats, where she removed the tarpaulin from the edge and hauled herself inside. She lay down between the seats, not noticing the ridges in the wood beneath her, conscious only of the sweet, salty air, of the gentle rocking of the boat and of the great weariness that had come over her.

Here she would stay until she expired. Already she felt weak from lack of food. It might take a day, a week, a month. Lila did not know, but at least here she was at peace. She closed her eyes and began to pray.

Lila woke several times. Once she heard the women on deck and wondered if her disappearance had been noticed by anyone in authority. The other prisoners would, of course, know she had gone, but would they bother to report her missing? She worried briefly that a search might be mounted for her, but drifted off into another sleep and woke again when the sun was high. It did not get too hot in the boat and the smell of scorched wood and tar was pleasant. She would have given anything for a drink and her throat felt swollen and her tongue thick and too large for her mouth, but no matter how great her thirst became, she knew nothing would make her leave the lifeboat.

When dusk fell, she glimpsed several stars in the half-dark sky and wondered if she had become delirious, for the twinkling yellow dots made her think of home and of Phillip Grenville, and despite the fact that she felt she was close to death, she also knew, just as surely, that one day she would be back in Yorkshire with Phillip by her side and—

These crazy thoughts were driven from her mind completely when the tarpaulin was roughly dragged back and someone slipped into the lifeboat and sat crouched on a seat looking down at her.

A boy, no older than she, with hair so red it stood out even in this dim light, his eyes a dancing green and his face covered with golden freckles, said in a low voice, "I say, what are you up to?"

He was well spoken and well dressed. His white shirt was rather grubby but laundered and starched recently. His britches were dark brown and well cut.

Lila stared at him, unable to speak, terrified out of her mind.

"Sorry. I've frightened you, but I couldn't knock or anything, could I? I had to get in whilst old Jacko is climbing the main mast. It's the only time till eight bells when it is safe, else he might have seen me. Just as I saw you this morning."

He wasn't going to give her away! Her fear lessened. Who was he? What did he want?

"Look, I've brought you some food and water."

Lila took the drink eagerly, gulping down the lot without a pause, then nibbled at the bread he handed her.

"Who are you?"

"So, you've got a tongue! Timothy Bateson, miss. Press-ganged into service on this darned ship, and jolly fed up about it, I can tell you."

"You don't look fed up," observed Lila, for indeed the young man seemed inordinately cheerful.

"What's the point? May as well make the best of things. Just walking along Chichester beach last Saturday night I was, on the way home from my friend Tom's, when a gang of ruffians set upon me, stuffed me on a boat and brought me here where I remained locked up till the ship sailed yesterday. My father told me I'd be press-ganged walking the Sussex beaches on me own. By danged, if he wasn't right. But, then, I suppose fathers usually are."

He smiled ruefully and Lila found herself smiling back.

It was difficult for ships, naval or private, to find crews, and when short of men a party of sailors would go ashore at night and whisk away any unfortunate, healthy-looking man they happened to come across. This poor creature was forced to do service for at least the length of the ship's voyage, often leaving behind frantic wives, children, or parents to wonder what tragedy had befallen their loved ones.

She reckoned that few accepted their fate with such equanimity and good will as Timothy Bateson.

"I say, what's wrong? What are you doing here? I've been longing to come and see you all day. It must have been about half past four this morning I was perched like a seagull near the top of the main mast—which, I might tell you, I loath, as I go dizzy up a small tree—when I saw you hide in here. Are you a prisoner? Of course, you must be. Rough down there, is it?"

"Rough is a mild word to describe it," Lila remarked, struggling to sit upright and face this young man at his own level. "It is as I have always imagined hell to be. I came into this boat to die and cannot think what help you will be to me bringing water and food, for it will only prolong my agony. You are kind, sir, indeed. From now on, let me be, I beg of you."

"Not likely!" Timothy Bateson replied indignantly. "It's bad enough keeping up me spirits on this wreck without the knowledge a pretty young gal's committing slow suicide with my connivance. Pretty, that is, despite the fact that she's got hair like a hedgehog."

Lila touched her hair.

"This is the reason I am here," she said. "I have suffered much, but this was the last straw."

"I've heard of people killing themselves, but never on account of a rotten haircut," said Timothy with a laugh.

"'Tis no laughing matter," Lila snapped indignantly, unable to believe anyone could feel amused in such adversity. True, Timothy Bateson's fate was not nearly so black as her own, but nevertheless, his future was scarcely bright. Perhaps, she thought ruefully, she did not possess sufficient sense of humor. She felt mollified when his face sobered and he apologized.

"Sorry. I make a joke of everything, or so my father says. He also says it is a grievous fault but he's glad I'm inflicted with it. He's a jolly good stick, my father."

"Won't he be worried about you?"

"Of course, but press-ganging is common on the south coast. He'll guess what has happened to me, but he'll also know I'll be back in time for university next year. That is, September 1796. He'll expect me by then. My mother is dead."

"Have you brothers and sisters?"

"Eight brothers and nine sisters. In fact, that is why my mother passed on. She swore she'd die in childbirth—she had rather a morbid disposition, you see—but she just went on and on having children hoping to prove her point and at her eighteenth she did."

"How very sad," Lila murmured.

"No, it's not sad at all. You see she died happy knowing her prediction had come true. She got one over on my father too. He swore she'd manage twenty. Children, that is." Timothy grinned engagingly. "Why are we discussing the birthrate in my family when you are in this pretty predicament, anyway?"

Lila confessed she did not know. She felt overwhelmed at this young man's cheerful eloquence. It didn't seem at all odd that he should scramble into her hiding place, her death bed, and chatter on about his mother's apparently happy departure to heaven.

"Now, what are we doing to do about you? No!" He raised his hand as she opened her mouth to speak. "Pray do not tell me to go away and let you die in peace for I shall do no such thing. Anyway, tell me what happened to your lovely hair. And what were you doing down there with those women in the first place? You clearly don't belong."

So Lila told him, right from the very beginning.

"Phew! Well, there's a tale to tell your children!" gasped Timothy Bateson admiringly when she had finished. "Wait till I regale my sisters with *that*."

Lila gazed at him with respect. Instead of being horrified

at her dire story, he was impressed! *What would his reaction be to her experiences in the hold?* she wondered, and she began to tell him of Queen Lil and the awful, filthy women down there.

"Poor souls," he murmured sympathetically. "You know the old saying 'There but for the grace of God go I'? My grandmother always used to say that. Be thankful you're not like them. As for your hair, 'twill get pretty hot on this journey. You'll be much cooler without its weight on your neck. In summer my sisters forever moaned they wanted their hair short like mine." He gazed at her contemplatively for a moment. "It could do with tidying up, though. Whoever did it must have used a hatchet or something."

Lila's stomach churned at the thought of a hatchet at her head. Her respect for this likable boy increased by the minute. He'd turned the happenings of the past few weeks into an adventure, even seeming sorry he'd not been a part of it.

"Anyway," he said reasonably, "you're lucky to have got on a ship under such a lenient captain. 'Tis much worse on some."

"Worse!" gasped Lila. How could anything be worse than the conditions in that hold? "There are men in the bilges, I am told. The food is deplorable. Men and women were—well, together, on the deck yesterday. I had to go below to be left in peace.

"But you *were* left in peace," Timothy pointed out. "Companies contract to take the prisoners for so many guineas a head and care not whether their charges arrive alive or dead. The women often have no protection whatsoever. Captain Widdicombe is an old naval captain, retired from service due to ill health. He sticks rigidly to every regulation laid down for the proper transportation of convicts. Had you not noticed only two men, ABs Packer and Hill, were allowed in your quarters? Any other man entering the lower deck will receive twenty lashes. Any man taking a women against her will during exercise or at any other time will receive fifty. You are not chained. On many merchantmen the prisoners, men, women and children alike, are chained like slaves for the duration of the journey. Captain Widdicombe is a fool, but a fair man, and he follows admiralty instructions to the letter. As for the poor chaps in the bilges—"

Lila interrupted him tartly, "I've no doubt you can think of a dozen good reasons for them to be there. Nor do I doubt the food is luxurious compared to many ships. Perhaps I am a trifle too fussy, preferring my potatoes cooked, my meat tender, and my crockery washed."

"You're cheesed off with me!" Timothy said, dramatically clasping his hands to his brow in mock despair. "My sisters always become cheesed off with me after a time. So, I shall depart. I'll try and throw in some bread and water early tomorrow morning before it gets light. I pray you are not knocked unconscious. But if you should be, 'twill help pass the time! Farewell, sweet maiden."

Chapter Nine

Lila slept soundly, remaining unscathed when a heavy leather bottle and some crusts of bread were flung through the tarpaulin opening in the first gray light of morning.

She could not but smile every time she thought of Timothy Bateson who was the cheeriest, happiest soul she had ever met. Due to him her nightmares had merely become a bad dream. As she listened to the sounds of the day, the whipping of the sails, the wind singing through the rigging, and the sailors barefoot on the deck below her, she longed for the time when her savior would return with his happy smile.

Return he did. As the stars appeared so did Timothy, with more water and some biscuits. He snuggled down beside her.

"I've thought of something. A marvelous idea has come to me. I've already told you the captain is a fool, he is also a friend of my father's. He's a doctor."

"The captain?"

"No, my father is the doctor, dimwit. The captain's doctor. Captain Widdicombe is one of those people who thinks he suffers from every ailment under the sun and for all of his distempers Papa prescribes a bottle of his seaweed physic, which invariably cures him."

His eyes shone with enthusiasm.

"He's a darned good doctor, my papa, and he's found seaweed miraculously clears up a variety of stomach and other complaints. That's why I'm going to university, to learn to be a doctor."

"What has this to do with the captain?" Lila asked with some exasperation.

"Well, he feels frightfully embarrassed about me being here. I mean to say, what is my papa going to say when he discovers his favorite son—or perhaps his least favorite son, who knows?—has been press-ganged by a patient? Well, not by the patient in person, but you know what I mean."

"I know, but—"

"Don't interrupt. Listen. He can't even let me off at Teneriffe or Table Mountain or any other port of call. The destination of this ship is Botany Bay and that's as far as I've got to go by law. If he sets me free he'll be court-martialed or keelhauled or something awful, so . . ." He paused, forgetting his chain of thought.

"So, he's embarrassed you're here," Lila reminded him.

"True. So, he'll do me a favor and that favor will get you out of this mess."

Lila said she failed to see how the captain could help her if he couldn't help the more favored Timothy. He grinned and took her hand.

"Of course, he won't do anything that isn't fair, square and aboveboard. He's a stickler for doing the right thing and he can't discover any admiralty regulation that says he's not allowed to do what I have proposed."

"And what have you proposed?" Lila asked waiting to hear he'd suggested the lifeboat be lowered and she be towed to New South Wales or something else equally outrageous.

"That we get married," he said solemnly. "I propose we become man and wife. That is, if you get your hair cut properly."

So many things had happened over the past few weeks that had an air of fantasy about them, yet nothing so far seemed as unreal as her marriage to Timothy Bateson.

Captain Widdicombe, a grim, heavily whiskered man, looking slightly pained about the heart-searching and nagging worry caused by his young, press-ganged victim, conducted the ceremony with all the gloom of a funeral.

"I now pronounce you man and wife," he muttered reluctantly, and Timothy planted a brotherly kiss on Lila's pink cheek.

She stared at him in wonderment.

His eyes danced with merriment as he stared back and proclaimed incredulously, "Odds Bodkins! I've got a wife. Just to think a few days ago I was planning my studies for the winter, my sister Emma was making me a new shirt, Becky was threatening to tidy my bedroom and Papa was lecturing me on something or other. Now, here I am, a sailor on me way to the other side of the world. Not only that, I've acquired the prettiest little wife a fellow could possibly have. How old are you, wife?"

"Eighteen in September," Lila told him.

"Darn it! I've never fancied older women and you've got two whole months on me. I won't be that age till November."

Captain Widdicombe regarded the two youngsters somewhat grimly.

"It must be said, young Timothy, that Miss Ward—I beg your pardon, Mrs. Bateson—may well have been badly treated by the law, but 'tain't my job to set things right."

He cleared his throat and looked uncomfortable. Timothy was anxious to put the captain at his ease.

"Bless you, sir. We wouldn't expect it. But as for your cooperation today, my father will be enormously indebted to you."

The captain looked sheepish. Lila reckoned he was not nearly as foolish as Timothy made out. He was good-natured and of working class origins, as his gruff Devon accent made clear. While he was a keen disciplinarian, and even with the officers of much higher birth than himself remained in strict control, he was ill at ease with young Timothy, conscious of the anguish that had been caused to his great friend and helper, Dr. Arnold Bateson.

Reams of instructions had been issued by the Admiralty and the navy board regarding the deportation of men, women, and children to New South Wales, and Geoffrey Widdicombe had conscientiously studied every word. He knew he could marry prisoners to each other, but nowhere could he recall reading what action should be adopted if a crew member wished to marry a convict. If there was no rule against it, young Master Bateson had earnestly pointed out, then surely he could go ahead and marry him to this young, much maligned young lady without delay. And indeed if no law was laid down in regard to a particular matter, the captain wished to do the fairest thing for all.

Lila was shown to the cabin which she would share with seven other women. Five were wives of marines who had decided to start a new life in the colony of New South Wales, and two young sisters were daughters of the second mate who was also settling in the new land. Most of the women regarded Lila with spite, clearly offended to find themselves traveling alongside a convict, albeit one better dressed and better spoken than themselves. But the girls, Barbara and Jessica, one a year older, the other the same age as Lila, were dazzled by their new companion.

"What is it like down there?" they inquired with morbid curiosity. "Aren't you glad to be here, with us?" they went on, without waiting for a reply.

Lila was a creature of rare interest in their uneventful lives. The daughter of a member of Parliament, an ex-lady-in-waiting, a convict from the hold, and now, a brand-new bride. Lila certainly found it difficult to believe she was now Mrs. Timothy Bateson, wife of a would-be doctor, having acquired eight new brothers, nine sisters and an eccentric father-in-law. She felt no pangs of disloyalty to Captain Grenville. He was part of a world she had left behind, and although she realized it had not been left behind forever—she and Timothy could return on the *Gabriel* once it had dispensed its cargo in Botany Bay and be back in England within two years—this seemed a lifetime away.

On her new bunk there were clean sheets and a soft, feather pillow, and during the afternoon Lila lay and worried that she had been cowardly and lacking in character by allowing Timothy to marry her in order to escape the horrors of the hold. Perhaps a stronger, better woman would have put up with the conditions there for eight or nine months rather than expect a young boy to sacrifice his future on her behalf. She confided these alarming thoughts to her new husband that night. He pooh-poohed her fears.

"Rubbish!" he snorted. "I had ulterior motives for marrying you anyway. There's no one else to talk to on this darned vessel. As to our marriage, we can get it annulled. Takes no time, Mrs. Bateson. Divorce means waiting seven years, but if we don't get up to any hanky-panky—not that it should be called hanky-panky between a respectable, married couple but I can't think of a politer word for it—then it means the marriage hasn't been consummated, and we'll get it annulled. You won't want to be married to a scatterbrained jackass like me when we get back to good old England. I'll just pop out to buy a loaf of bread one night and get press-ganged again before you can say 'Jack Robinson.'"

Lila laughed, and as the days and weeks passed by she thought of Timothy all the time. He was the dearest boy she had ever known, and if he wanted their marriage annulled, then she would be only too willing to comply with his wishes. In a way, she loved him, as she would have loved the brother she never had. If Timothy ever decided he wanted her, then he would have her, as an expression of Lila's gratitude for rescuing her from death and giving her new life and new hope. That would mean there would be no grounds for annulment, and Phillip Grenville would have no part in her life again. She would owe all her love and loyalty to young Timothy Bateson.

Six weeks ago, Lord Ralph Curringham had been her fiancé, and now Lila recalled this man with loathing. What lessons she had learned since that carefree day in the orchard of Grass-brook Hall.

Lila entered the cabin where two other wives sat sewing, and each bestowed a disdainful glance in her direction and began to make offensive remarks.

"Jake has complained several times to Lieutenant Montclair, saying he thinks it offensive his wife has to travel with a convict," said one, a plump, chalk-faced woman. "It's just not right at all. Most unfair on us respectable women."

The other woman smoothed her faded black cotton dress vigorously.

"I quite agree, Mrs. Blackstone. But the captain won't listen. My husband's quite cut up about it too."

Their nastiness had no effect on Lila. She remained quite

unmoved, indeed even felt a grain of sympathy for their attitude. These women did not know her true story, and in their eyes she was a criminal, no different from the likes of Queen Lil. She could be guilty of the most abominable felonies for all they knew.

That evening she and Timothy sat near the bow of the ship. He was pale and his freckles stood out prominently on his unusually white skin. This was because he had not long completed his watch atop the main mast, the only thing that ever dampened his bubbling good nature.

"You've no idea what it's like up there," he said once, frowning for the first time since Lila had known him. "The mast sways and creaks and you feel you're going to catapult into the sea at any minute. My stomach heaves if I look down at the deck which seems ten miles away. My heart heaves when I look about me at nothing but water, thousands of pints, quarts, gallons of gray sea in every direction. Then my brain heaves when I remember I have to do the same thing tomorrow and the next day until Captain Widdicombe considers we are quite clear of shipping."

She was glad he had her to confide his fear in and tried to cheer him up—a relatively easy thing to do—by asking him about his family.

"Oh, my sisters'll take to you like a duck to water. So will my brothers. I won't swear to my father for he's an odd sort of cove. I don't think he's ever taken to me for he dislikes freckles. But he'll be polite, never fear, whether he dislikes you or not."

Lila clapped her hands.

"I'm longing to meet your family."

"Then you'll have to wait a jolly long time, Mrs. Bateson," said Timothy, taking her hand and squeezing it.

She reckoned his family were affectionate with each other for he was forever hugging her, throwing his arm around her shoulders or kissing her without any sexual undertones. He was a pleasure to be with and she thanked God for her good fortune in meeting him on this ship.

"Lila. Come here. Look!"

Barbara and Jessica beckoned to her. They were suspended over the rail of the upper deck from where they had a good view of the main deck below.

"See, the men convicts. They are up for exercise."

With an interest she considered unhealthy, Lila joined the girls and looked down below. Like the women, the poor men were in rags. Their hair was cut so short that on many the skin of their scalps showed through, blue veined and scab-ridden. Many were too exhausted to walk but lay breathing in the luxury of the fresh, sea air, their emaciated bodies still and lifeless. A sailor went by and kicked one of them, a boy no more than twelve, with such force that the slight body lifted in the air and returned to the deck with a thud.

"I do hope Captain Widdicombe saw that," said Jessica virtuously, "for yesterday a sailor who struck a prisoner for no good reason was put on bread and water for a week."

Lila watched the boy. His pinched face was twisted with pain and he was trying desperately not to cry. She wondered how such a young child could be guilty of a crime so heinous it required he be taken across the world for punishment. Did her father know of the conditions under which prisoners were transported? Timothy had said they were supposed to have been provided with a new suit of clothes each, but none had arrived when it was time to sail.

"Yet the manufacturer will receive his payment, do not doubt it," he said. "For corruption is rampant and people are becoming rich because of the misfortune of these poor souls."

Then some of the poor souls caught sight of their fair audience and such a shouting was set up that the three girls became quite frightened and ran back to their cabin.

She told Timothy what she had seen that evening as they took their usual stroll.

"The surgeon is out of his mind, for he is a good man and wants to help but his medicines are quite insufficient. Of course, he cannot order a proper diet for the scurvy either. Already two men have died and were buried at sea."

Lila asked him when the women came up for exercise for she had been unaware of the time of day when she took part. It was at midday, Timothy told her, so the following day, she stationed herself, well hidden, in a vantage spot where she could observe her former companions.

Sailors waited eagerly on deck as the women emerged, and coins changed hands as couples found the most comfortable place for their lovemaking. Several women had more than one

customer during the exercise period. Lila tried not to watch
these goings-on. The only reason she had come was to see
Queen Lil and find out if she had recovered from her sojourn
in the bilges.

It was some time before Queenie appeared. She limped a
little, yet otherwise seemed none the worse for her experiences.
So immense and powerful did she appear that if any man had
fancied her favors, he did not come forward, and the Queen
made her slow, impressive way along the deck followed by
several obsequious friends. Queen Lil was strutting up and
down taking great breaths of fresh air, when Lila noticed the
girl who had occupied the next pallet quietly come onto the
deck, her rosary around her neck. She was immediately ac-
costed by several men. Lila waited to see the girl rebuff her
hopeful lovers, but to her intense surprise the girl took money
from two of the men and disappeared with both of them.

There but for the grace of God go I. Timothy's words came
to her. If she had not escaped by the time they reached Botany
Bay would she have come to resemble, to act and think, like
these women? It did not bear thinking about, and she decided
never again to watch the convicts, male or female. It was like
going to the theatre to see a tremendous tragedy, yet here the
principal actors could not leave.

When the *Gabriel* called first at Teneriffe, then Rio de
Janeiro and other ports, neither Lila nor Timothy was allowed
ashore. Both deeply regretted being unable to visit these strange
new places. At each stop the ship became more and more loaded
down with cargo. In the hold where three of the women had
already died, their empty places were quickly taken up by casks
of coffee, cocoa, tea and rum. Poultry littered the decks, along
with rabbits and goats. At Table Mountain where the ship
docked for more than a week, sheep and hogs, two stallions,
and a bull were taken on board, together with an enormous
assortment of plants: fruit trees, vines, sugar cane, bamboo,
and botanic specimens.

On leaving Table Mountain a curious desolation spread over
the ship. The sea was cold and gray and while a flat empty
horizon on all sides was the commonest sight of all on board
any ship, this time it caused intense depression all round. Now
they were truly on their own. The next piece of land they would
sight would be New South Wales, thousands of miles away.

Only one person aboard, the botanist, Ernest Clay, had made the journey before. To everyone else, from Captain Widdicombe down, it was a fresh experience, and although he showed it to no one, even the captain felt qualms about the responsibility of taking a shipful of human cargo into the unknown.

All the men in the bilges had died by this time, and burials frequently took place at night. Lila would occasionally hear the splash as the sack-covered body hit the water. She hoped the soul reached a more comfortable home than the body had on earth. She found it difficult to believe that a convict's soul was automatically destined for hell. Most of them had been reared brutally, knowing nothing of human kindness or compassion. Surely God would not punish his flock for not being good when they had never known the meaning of the word? It was the Lord Rawlesburys of this world who deserved hell, for despite knowing better, they manipulated people's lives, causing intense suffering or death, just to suit their own evil purposes.

The weeks wore on and at Christmas they enjoyed a fine dinner. Even the convicts were given plum pudding and a tot of rum. In the new year spirits began to revive. The journey's end was in sight with three quarters of the distance covered. They could not begin to count the days to their arrival, for the ship was making excellent time. Captain Widdicombe announced that they might even set a record. The weather had been fine so far, but a few days afterwards a storm rocked and tossed the *Gabriel* ferociously.

It was difficult to believe that such a huge, solid vessel could be thrown about the mountainous seas as if it were little more than a stick of firewood. The ship was flung this way and that and the passengers stayed in their bunks, clinging onto the sides for dear life. Lila tried to imagine what it must be like for the women in the hold who had nothing to hold onto. They would be hurled from one end to the other. She fervently hoped the freight remained securely tied, and tried to rid her mind of the vision of the carnage that could ensue if the crates and boxes broke loose and were tumbled onto the imprisoned women.

In this latitude icebergs were a real menace, and Captain Widdicombe reinstituted a watch from the top of the main mast. Timothy literally shook with fear when he was ordered to take on this duty, and Lila comforted him as well as she could.

When the storm ceased, although the weather remained dull
and cold, the sense of optimism increased. Some convicts
dreaded the life before them, but for those from the hulks, life
had already touched rock bottom and could only improve in
this new land. The sailors were glad their voyage was nearly
half over. Once they had unloaded at Botany Bay they would
return to their homeland, their wives, parents, and children.

That night as Lila and Timothy took their customary walk
on the main deck, he said, "What would you say to setting up
home in Botany Bay?"

She stared at him in surprise and he grinned mischievously.

"That took you by surprise, eh?"

"Why, yes. I have thought of nothing but returning to England to clear my name. I had assumed you were intent on
commencing your studies next September."

"I was talking to Roger Cobb this morning. He is the father
of the young girls in your cabin. He has great plans for his life
in New South Wales. He does not intend to stay near the bay,
but means to go inland or along the coast a ways, as some
other settlers have already done."

"I would need to think about such a proposal," Lila said
reluctantly.

Her first reaction was one of alarm. The idea of settling in
this strange country had not crossed her mind.

"Every cooperation is afforded by the government," Timothy explained enthusiastically. "The materials for your house
are provided and transported to the site, as well as convict labor
to erect it, along with an overseer experienced in building. You
can have as many acres to farm as you wish and are given
sufficient stock to start with, whether it be agriculture or animals or both. Just think, Lila, what an adventure it would be."

His green eyes shone as he took both her hands in his.

"It would be such a challenge. How many people are ever
given the opportunity to organize their own life to such an
extent. Their house, their land, their work."

His optimism was catching. To start life anew was strangely
appealing, though she felt she must return to England as soon
as possible.

"This stuff about clearing your name is unimportant," Timothy said derisively. "Everyone must know you are innocent.
Even I had heard of the reputation the Princess of Wales brought

with her. As for your family, you can visit them as Mrs.
Timothy Bateson in a year or two."

Lila tried to visualize life with Timothy on an idyllic farm
which she imagined would be set within a circle of palm trees
with a lagoon nearby and friendly natives to till the land. Convict labor, she vowed, was out of the question. Never again
in her life would she have anything to do with convicts.

Excitement began to mount when it was reckoned they were
barely seven days off their destination. Nine women and seventeen men had died. Even some of the animals in their pens
crowding the deck had expired, and these were cooked and
served to the officers of the ship.

Timothy's enthusiasm for founding his own particular dynasty in the new colony grew daily. Lila had written to her
mother from Teneriffe, so Mama would know her daughter
had married and was in good hands, but she did so desperately
want to see her again. This alone prevented her from joining
wholeheartedly in Timothy's optimism. She did not allow
memories of Phillip Grenville to influence her. He would forever retain a place in her heart, for he was her real, true love,
but she owed everything to Timothy now, and she felt that
loyalty even to her mother came second to her new husband.

That night for the first time she sensed a difference in his
attitude to her. He touched her hair, which by now had grown
below her ears in springy waves and curls, and there was a
hesitant roughness in his touch as if he were holding back a
bewildering emotion which he had never experienced before.

"I have been talking to Ernest Clay and he tells me in parts
of New South Wales the flax grows to eight feet in height,
whereas in Europe it is a mere three feet," he said. Then, a
few minutes later, "Lila," he went on urgently, "I have never
sought nor wanted power or glory, but can't you see that perhaps these two things will come to us unasked if we are founders
of a life in this new country? Whatever name we choose to
call our house may well be the name given to the town built
around us. A capital city, perhaps."

His face shone and he looked young and vulnerable.

"It is such a challenge, Lila. Such an adventure. I must
confess my desire to become a doctor has evaporated completely, and the idea of establishing a homestead in New South

Wales grows more appealing as I think of it."

Lila's heart went out to him. How could she dash his hopes? She surrendered.

"Of course, my dear. Then we will stay there, but you must promise me I can return home at the earliest moment."

"You dear, dear girl. Dear wife. We will indeed have children, Lila. Lots of them to play on our farm. There will be no question of having this marriage annulled."

Clumsily he drew her to him and kissed her full on the lips. At first he trembled, then with more confidence, both his arms went round her. Hesitantly she placed hers about his neck and they kissed, warmly, fondly, and with a touch of passion.

"Lila," Timothy whispered as they drew apart. "Lately I think of you quite differently. I cannot put it into words, but no longer do I consider you as I did my sisters. I think I love you, little wife."

Obstinately shutting out the unwelcome and uncalled for vision of Phillip Grenville, Lila answered sincerely, "I love you too, Timothy."

The young couple, little more than children, remained clasped in each other's arms, looking forward into the ocean to their new life.

During the night Lila heard a commotion on the ship but paid no attention, snuggling down into her bunk and lulling herself back to sleep with thoughts of the future. She had just finished dressing the next morning when a marine banged on the cabin door and shouted that Mrs. Bateson was urgently required in the captain's quarters and she hurried there without delay.

Captain Widdicombe looked sterner than ever, so much so that Lila was visited with alarm.

"What is it?" she cried. "You have bad news, I can tell. Timothy? Is he hurt? Pray, tell me."

"Sit down, Mrs. Bateson. I regret to tell you that your husband had an accident last night. He fell from the mast when coming down from the middle watch at eight bells. And he is dead. I am so sorry."

Lila stared at him, unable to believe her ears.

"But it was a calm night," she protested uselessly. "Although he had become no less terrified of climbing the ratlines to the top-most platform, he had undoubtedly become more adept."

"We do not know what happened, but the morning watch was just about to take over when he heard a splash and Timothy was no longer above him. The ship had stopped and we searched for many hours," he said uncomfortably. It was bad enough telling the poor young woman all this, but there were further ill tidings to convey.

Lila could not help but wonder if her young husband had been distracted by thinking of her and their newly discovered love. That this, in fact, had been the cause of his death.

As yet she was too shocked for tears. What was this the captain was saying?

"You must realize you are a convict, again, Mrs. Bateson. When your husband was alive, he was your protection. In all honesty I cannot land you in Botany Bay as a free, guiltless woman just because you underwent marriage and bereavement on my ship. You must take up your position again with the convicts, I regret to say."

Lila cried out in fright.

"Not in the hold, I beg of you. They will kill me. They have so much more reason to do so now."

"You may stay where you are until we land," the captain assured her. He felt anguish and guilt over this young woman. After all, she was still the daughter-in-law of his friend. He made a vow to call on the doctor himself with this tragic news rather than instruct the shipping company to send a letter.

He said gently to Lila, "Return to your cabin and take with you my condolences for your present sorrow and for all that has befallen you, Mrs. Bateson."

Chapter Ten

"Land ahoy!"

The joyous shout went up on St. Patrick's Day, March 17, 1796.

The other women in the cabin swooped as one to the door for their first sight of the new land.

The words were echoed throughout the ship and people rushed from all parts to see the longed-for coastline. Lila tried to imagine Timothy's excitement if he had been there. He would have come to find her, no matter what he'd been doing, and together they would have watched their future drawing near. It was almost impossible to believe his cheerful person was gone forever. His death created an unbearable emptiness in Lila's life. She might love another man, but no one would ever be able to lift her heart as Timothy had done.

She supposed she too should go on deck, so she dragged herself from the bunk and went to join the cheering crowds.

There was as yet little to be seen—only a thin black line on the horizon, which didn't seem to grow any bigger even though the ship was moving quickly towards it under full sail.

By evening mountains could be clearly seen in the background and before them sloping hills scattered with trees. To their left the sun had begun to sink into the gray-blue sea, unnaturally large and fiery, an impression heightened by its distorted reflection in the water. It was a frightening, alien sight and Lila wished with all her heart that her husband was there to laugh at her fears and comfort her.

Although Botany Bay was the dreadful destination to which criminals were sentenced to be deported, it was at Sydney Cove, a safer anchorage farther along the coast, that they had always been landed. Here a settlement had been established, and here the *Gabriel* docked the day after land had been sighted.

The convicts were kept confined on board while the cargo of animals, provisions, plants and seeds, building materials, and almost any item vital to man's existence was taken from the ship and moved into warehouses on the quayside.

Jessica and Barbara stood on deck with Lila, all three marveling at the warehouses, at the brick barracks visible in the distance, at the assortment of wooden and brick houses, shops and bars, already arranged in little squares and streets. It was quite beyond their expectations to find such a thriving community which already had an air of permanence about it. What with the shouts of the seamen in a variety of English accents, they felt they could almost be in a port at home.

Roger Cobb came to take his daughters away and shortly afterwards Lila was approached by the marine who had carried her on board the ship at Southampton.

"Captain Widdicombe sends a message, Mrs. Bateson. You're to go to Mrs. Oates's lodging house over yonder, the white cottage with green shutters, and you're not to move till you're sent for."

Mrs. Oates's husband, a ploughman, had died within a week of landing in New South Wales where he had hoped to start his own farm. His widow had decided to stay and make a go of it on her own and now ran a well-established lodging house which was used by many settlers while they were waiting for their own homes to be built.

She welcomed her temporary lodger but was mystified that she had no luggage, not even a reticule. She offered Lila tea and homemade jam tarts in her parlor. With the heavy, well-polished furniture and assortment of dark oil paintings, the room reminded Lila of visiting an elderly aunt or the vicar's wife in Yorkshire. From the window of her bedroom where she soon retired for the night, she could see the *Gabriel,* still being unloaded by the light of dozens of lanterns strung from her masts.

Lila had begun to doze when she was awakened by a wild shouting from the direction of the harbor. She jumped out of bed and went to the window.

On the quayside stood many hundreds of men, chanting and waving bottles of rum in the air, and after a few minutes, Lila realized why. They were waiting for the women to come ashore, and when they did it was to the accompaniment of almost inhuman whoops and screams which Lila knew would render sleep impossible. She stayed watching with morbid fascination as figures took themselves onto the sands where scenes of the utmost depravity continued until the early hours of the morning. This was almost certainly why the good captain of the *Gabriel* had let her remain in her cabin and had personally arranged for her to come to this lodging house.

Lila had grown used to Captain Widdicombe's Christian ways and had entirely forgotten the officer first encountered on the *Gabriel* who feared her presence might foul the air of his cabin. To her utter dismay, this very gentleman awaited in a shack on the quayside to which she was directed early the following morning.

"Ward?" he barked, his voice and his expression cruel.

"No. Mrs. Timothy Bateson, sir." Lila bobbed a mock curtsy, glad to see the man momentarily disconcerted at her contradiction. He remembered the reason for her change of status and inserted the correct name on his list.

"You are assigned to be a laundry maid at the farm of a Mr. Gouch over at Pitt's Plain, fifty miles from here."

"How do I travel, sir?" inquired Lila.

"On your own two feet. We do not provide carriages for convicts."

Lila stared in consternation at the kid shoes, well past repair, which she had worn for eight months. She doubted they would take her fifty miles over rough terrain, and wished she had money to buy new shoes and other personal items.

She did not know Captain Widdicombe had sent special orders that she was not to be kept in the female prison where most of the women from the *Gabriel* were now housed, but was to be dispatched immediately to a suitable post. And it had not entered the good captain's head that this order might put Lila in far greater danger.

She was given a bag of provisions and put in the care of a Jacob Evans, a tiny cripple, no taller than herself, who was already employed at the Gouch farm and had been sent to Sydney Cove to take on extra staff. The only wagon was being used to carry supplies to the farm, so she was resigned to the walk.

"Will it take long?" she asked.

"Three or four days," he answered in a Welsh singsong. "Depends on the weather. It's fine now and in this we'll make good progress, but if it gets much hotter we have to have a good rest at midday. On my way in, there was a storm and the rain came down like as if the good Lord was throwing bucketfuls at me personally. There was nothing I could do but shelter for most of one day. A'course, a lot depends on the condition of those that comes with us and whether they're fit enough to walk many miles a day."

"I am very fit, though my shoes are not," Lila said, and then asked if many others were to come with them.

"Four others, miss," said Jacob Evans with a wry smile at Lila's naive questions. "I hope they're a decent type o' man. Mr. Gouch has increased his holding by three hundred acres and is in desperate need of four more hands."

The Welshman's hopes were ill-founded, for the men turned out to be four of the most evil-looking scoundrels Lila had ever set eyes on. All were covered in scars and sores. One was missing an eye, and the empty socket was screwed closed, giving the face a fearsome lopsided look. Another was unnaturally fat, his great balloon of a face swollen and pockmarked. The third man had his arm in a filthy, blood-soaked sling, and Lila could not help but wonder what use he would be as a farm laborer. Last but not least was a youngster, little older than herself, without a hair on his head or anywhere on his face, and his skin a deep, repulsive yellow.

This boy looked at Lila, undressing her with his unhealthy

hot eyes and licking his lips as if relishing the sport to come.

She was horrified. Surely she was not expected to travel fifty miles in the company of these ruffians? Was she to be entirely at their mercy? Jacob Evans would be no protection, even if he was willing to be. Any one of them could flatten the little Welshman with a single blow.

They talked amongst themselves, their eyes on her, making no secret of their delight in finding she was to be with them. Lila knew it would be useless to convey her fear to the hard-faced officer from the *Gabriel*.

Jacob Evans noticed her obvious distress.

"Don't make a fuss, miss," he whispered urgently. "Last time I came for convict staff they sent a little girl, no more than fourteen she was, and she shouted and screamed she didn't want to go with the two big louts I'd been allocated. They just handcuffed her to one of them. So just come quietly and don't fuss. Let's hope for the best."

He didn't go into the fate of the little girl who had arrived at the farm half mad from the abuse of the two men.

Lila nodded numbly and the party set off just before midday. She walked in front, sticking close to Jacob Evans. Behind her the men shouted obscenities. Her thoughts were so upset and confused that she hardly noticed the countryside they were walking through. After a while she became vaguely aware that it was not particularly attractive. The soil was sandy and the bushes bedraggled and bare. The terrain was flat as far as the eye could see. It was warm but not unpleasantly so, and Jacob informed her that it was now autumn and that a short while ago it had been unbearably hot.

"On Christmas Day we fair baked," he told her, which seemed quite unbelievable. If it had not been for the men behind she would have enjoyed talking to this pleasant little man about the new land she was now part of.

"Don't worry, miss," said Jacob, once again sensing her apprehension. "I know a way to keep them busy for one night at least. When we stop, you go well ahead."

Lila guessed it was about seven or eight o'clock when Jacob suggested they rest for the night. She wandered further on and sat beneath a tall, bushy tree.

She wondered how Jacob Evans planned to divert the men that night and soon understood when she saw him handing round a bottle of rum apiece. Soon shouts of raucous laughter rent the still evening air as the men gradually downed their bottles of spirits. At one time the fat man made a clumsy move in her direction, but was stopped by the hairless boy who seemed to have claimed first rights. Gradually, however, the minds of the men became clouded with their drink and they forgot her.

Darkness fell and she ate some of her food. As the night wore on she found the greatest difficulty in staying awake. Her legs throbbed from the long walk and her heels were rubbed raw, and she was worried she might fall asleep despite her efforts not to. As an afterthought, she collected a pile of stones and put them within easy reach.

This was a fortunate precaution for she did fall asleep in snatches leaning against the tree. During one short nap she was awakened by the touch of a hand on her ankle. The boy was kneeling before her, drawing back her skirts, his eyes glistening with desire, his breathing wild and the smell of drink over-powering. Lila kicked at him with all her might but he caught her foot in his hand and laughed, throwing her skirts back yet further. He brought his head close, quicker than she had expected and buried his face in her neck. She reached out desperately and just managed to grab a large stone which she brought down with all her might onto his shoulder.

Blinking his strange eyes in surprise he looked up, and again she hit him, this time on the forehead, wincing herself at the awful crunching noise it made. Blood ran down his face.

Falling back he stared at her with half-conscious terror, and she sprang to her feet, glaring at him with the stone poised ready to strike if he came close, yet terrified at what she had done. He was too far gone from the spirits and the pain to realize quite what had happened, and after a while he crawled back to the other men and they lay sprawled out, dead drunk, with Jacob Evans curled up asleep nearby.

She examined the tree she had been sitting under and decided she could climb up part of the way with ease, and this would afford more safety, though no sleep. As she climbed she wondered if she would be able to find her own way back to Sydney Cove, for she would not spend another two or three nights at the mercy of these animals. She made up her mind that at the very crack of dawn, before the men woke, she would begin to walk back in the direction they had come and hope Jacob Evans would not be punished for her desertion.

Perched up the tree, well hidden within the leaves, her eyes smarted with tiredness and she imagined the weariness she would feel the next day without any proper rest. Hours passed and Lila noticed a faint lightening of the sky in the east, little more than a glimmer, and she was about to descend when she saw a movement in some bushes near the men. Instinctively she drew closer into the leaves, and seconds later a person she could only describe as a savage emerged from the bushes.

He was blacker than any human being she had ever seen before and stark naked except for a necklace made of feathers. His nose was broad, and flat and his hair was a wild and woolly black halo. Lila had never seen such a strange-looking sight, and this at last brought home to her that she was indeed in another land, another civilization, another world.

In his right hand the native carried a wicked-looking knife, and with it he gestured behind him and three more natives appeared. They were not tall, but had broad-shouldered, well-muscled torsos. They crept towards the sleeping white men and stood around them silently watching. Lila clutched her hands to her mouth, wanting to shout a warning but knowing this would be suicide.

Then the leader raised his hand and slashed at a still form beneath him. Taking this as their signal, his companions set upon the other men, hacking and butchering with a force and savagery that sent blood spurting onto their own bodies and faces.

Though utterly petrified at the sight, Lila could not take her eyes away. At last the savages ceased their slaughter, and quickly slicing off the victims' genitals, which they carried off like trophies, left as silently as they had come.

There had been no sound from the murdered men, not even a whimper.

An hour later, the savages long gone, Lila still stared as if hypnotized at the carnage before her. It was not until the sun rose, suffusing the light blue of the sky with a golden radiance and lighting up the bloody scene, that she was able to hide, burying her face in the trunk of the tree and sobbing for harmless little Jacob Evans, for the four terrible convicts who had surely not deserved such an end, and for herself, and her loneliness in this foreign land.

She must have wept for an hour. When she eventually looked up the sun was full and round in the sky and she could hear hundreds of insects buzzing round the scene of slaughter. This time she kept her eyes well averted and began to climb down the tree.

Then she screamed. Directly below her in the very spot she would have landed stood a native who grinned and jabbered at her. Her heart dropped several inches in her chest. At least this one did not carry a knife and was considerably younger than the murderous dawn visitors, but he had the same jet black skin and broad nose. He wore tattered cotton shorts.

Grinning, he held out his hand as if to help her down, but Lila screamed again and tried to scramble back up the tree. The boy shouted and Lila heard an answering voice in the distance. She shook with fright, convinced she was about to die. In her confused state, it even seemed to her the boy gabbled away in English.

There was silence for an interminable length of time throughout which she kept her eyes tight closed. Whatever fate held in store for her she did not wish to know about it until the last possible moment.

"Good morning. Did George frighten you? He's terribly sorry about it. But in view of what happened over there, it is quite understandable you should be afraid. Do tell us you are all right."

A man's voice, quiet and well-bred. Astonished, Lila looked down.

He was about twenty-five, lean and tanned to a nutmeg brown, his fair hair cut without a thought to its appearance, and he had an equally untidy curly beard. He stared up at her with steady, wide-set eyes.

"Oh, sir!"

She scrambled down from the tree with his aid and stood before him, her hands clasped tight. It was all she could do not to fling her arms about his neck and kiss him.

"I cannot put into words how relieved I am to see a"—she paused, confused, and the man gave a sweet smile of encouragement that lit up his solemn face—"to see a civilized person the same color as myself," she finished eventually. "I am sure this young man is very nice and safe, but at this point I am suspicious of everyone."

He led her away from the massacre to where two horses were tethered, one saddled, the other bare.

"Do you ride? Take my horse, Neptune. George will walk back."

She alighted easily and sat sidesaddle as they began to trot sedately through the sparse forest.

The man spoke gravely, in a lecturing tone of voice.

"The incident you witnessed was most reprehensible, but rare. Two days ago a gang of drunken convicts came across a camp containing native women and their children. The men had gone to hunt. They set upon every female over the age of ten, and I will not go into detail of the outrages they committed before they murdered them all, before the eyes of the little ones. The men you saw were some of the husbands and fathers of those women and children taking their revenge upon white men. Unfortunately, they do not care whether or not the men they killed were those who committed the terrible acts against their womenfolk. All white men look the same to them."

"I see," said Lila. "Or at least I begin to."

He impressed upon her how trusting and childlike the natives were if properly treated. As if to prove his point, George ran happily along with them, chattering away in his own version of the English language which Lila could partially understand.

"Surely his name is not really George?" ahe asked, laughing at his antics.

"No. It is something unpronounceable which begins with a *G*, so I decided to call him after our king. I found him abandoned and badly injured three years ago when he was about twelve. He says his parents are dead and his other relatives did not want him."

The man smiled at her and once again his face lit up in the most charming manner. Lila decided she liked him very much indeed, and thanked God he had turned up in her life at a most appropriate time.

They had come to the top of a low hill, and suddenly before them stood one of the prettiest buildings she had ever seen. It was a single-story dwelling made of woodlap in the manner in which ships were sometimes built, its leaded windows framed with roses. Vines loaded with flowers, ivy, and other trailing plants climbed up onto the green roof and round the door, covering almost half the walls. The building was surrounded by fruit trees, and behind it stretched several acres of neatly laid-out squares containing an enormous variety of plants.

"Is this your home?" she asked in astonishment.

"Yes," he replied, clearly pleased at her surprised admiration.

"It is truly beautiful, it's like an oasis. Have you lived here long?"

They approached the small-holding and the familiar scents of flowers such as sweet William, pinks, and stock were in the air. Lila closed her eyes and for one wonderful moment was in the garden of Grassbrook Hall.

"I came with the first fleet in 1788. Let us go inside and I will make you some tea."

The interior of the house was as delightful as outside. A strange mixture of old and new resulted in a most unusual and attractive effect.

Both walls and floors were natural-colored wood which had been lightly waxed and had a delightful creamy satin appearance. All the drapes were white, so the main impression was of light and airiness. Despite the modernity of the setting, the furniture was old but chosen with the greatest care. Not one item was heavy or cumbersome; there were delicate, fragile pieces, with shapely, carved arms and legs. Here and there brilliant foreign-looking rugs were scattered and one particularly opulent one in rich, jewel colors hung on the wall.

"It is quite breathtaking," Lila said as her rescuer came in with a teatray bearing a silver teapot and white china cups and saucers. "I never thought to see such elegance in this land. I am not sure what I expected, but certainly nothing like this."

She fingered the little harpsichord, then sat on a velvet sofa.

"No doubt you thought we would be lolling about on benches roughly hewn from trees and eating off bare boards with scarcely a knife and fork between us," the man said dryly. "Well, now that you are in a civilized seat, drinking a civilized cup of tea, let me introduce myself. I am Roland Fairbrother, late of Bristol, England."

"Lilian Ward, sir, of Grassbrook, Yorkshire. No, stay! I was forgetting, that is no longer my name."

Roland Fairbrother raised his eyebrows. "You have forgotten your name? This morning's atrocities have had a more severe effect on you than I had thought."

"It is not that. On the boat here I married, though we were alone together for scarcely more than an hour a day and then only on deck. I have never been a wife in proper society, so

I am unused to introducing myself by my new name."

"And what might that name be?"

"Mrs. Timothy Bateson. My husband was a mere eighteen years old, younger even than myself, and press-ganged into service on the *Gabriel,* the ship that brought us here. Regrettably he died before we reached our destination." She blinked, suddenly remembering Timothy.

"I am sorry indeed to hear of your unfortunate and early widowhood. We must quickly get you to the friends or family to whom you were journeying yesterday. I take it the natives stole your horses and luggage?"

Lila lowered her cup and saucer onto her knee and regarded them sadly. This man did not know what she was. Indeed, Lila herself had forgotten her lowly station in life, and had spoken to him as an equal. What would his attitude be when he realized she was a convict?

"I had none of those things, sir. I was walking to Pitt's Plain to become a laundry maid at the farm of a Mr. Gouch. Those murdered men were fellow convicts. I am a convict, sentenced to be here seven years."

Roland Fairbrother stared at her in genuine disbelief. In fact, his jaw dropped, and Lila was flattered that he should find it so astounding.

She said quickly, "Without going into the ghastly story here and now, for I am mighty tired, I most positively assure you I am quite innocent of the offense for which I was sent here. It was all part of a wicked plot to get me out of England."

Fairbrother did not answer for several minutes, staring at his boots and frowning. He looked so stern Lila began to wonder if he was deciding whether to turn her out of his house on the spot. Suddenly he spoke.

"My dear Mrs. Bateson, please do not try to assure me of anything. I have not been good at many things in my life, but I have become a good judge of people. I hope you do not think me improper or too personal if I say I would only consider you guilty of anything if it were now a crime to look like an angel from heaven."

"Oh, my dear sir! How glad I am to find a friend like you in this foreign land."

Her eyes glowed with relief and gratitude. There was something so reassuring about this man, with his steady gaze and firm, fine-boned features. His thin, wiry frame had a gracefulness to it, yet his clothes were awkward and bulky, almost as if he'd stitched them together himself. Despite the beauty of his house, like many a man, he had come in wearing heavy, dust-covered boots. Tucked into these were brown britches of coarse, hard-wearing material, as was his shirt, though of thinner stuff, an oatmeal color. There was an air of honesty and openness to Roland Fairbrother which she found appealing.

A sudden clatter startled her, and she found she had banged her cup into the saucer because for the briefest of seconds she had fallen asleep, even as she sat conversing with her new acquaintance.

"I do beg your pardon," she cried. "It is just that I slept only in snatches last night, after having walked nine or ten miles."

She placed the cup and saucer on the tray. Roland Fairbrother was instantly concerned and got to his feet.

"You must rest immediately," he said.

He led her to a small room paneled in the same natural wood as the rest of the house. There was a single bed covered with a brightly colored woven blanket.

"This is my guest room, and in the eight years I have been here you are my first guest," he laughed. "Strange how customs are so inbred. I build a house on the other side of the world, never expecting to see a friend or relative again, yet into it I build a guest room!"

"Well, as you now have a guest, your instinct was not wrong," Lila told him. "Thank you, sir. A bed has rarely looked more welcoming."

He left her and she took off her dress and slept in her petticoat, as she had done for so many months now. Like the rest of her clothes, it had worn thin in places, for they had been washed and dried many times as she lay shivering in her bunk on the *Gabriel*. She had hoped to acquire a new set of clothing in Botany Bay.

This tiresome though unimportant worry occupied her mind until she fell asleep, feeling safe and secure in this house, scarcely moving and dead to the world for the remainder of the day and throughout the night.

Before he retired, Roland Fairbrother, feeling worried, opened the door to ensure his guest was still there and still breathing. For several seconds he watched Lila's sleeping form.

Her long lashes rested, quivering, featherlike, on her flushed cheeks and her tousled, uncombed hair lay in unruly curls on the pillow. Her lips were curved in contentment and one slim arm was thrown behind her. The bed clothes had fallen away revealing the worn white petticoat, and the swell of her breasts was just visible.

She was one of the loveliest things he had ever seen.

Lila would have been puzzled at the oddly wistful, oddly cynical smile that the watcher gave as he closed the door on his unexpected visitor.

She awoke refreshed, and the events of the previous day seemed a million years away. Having quickly dressed, she found the house empty and wandered about with interest, noticing the holy statues and crucifixes in every room. Her host must be a Catholic. There were books everywhere and she could not help but wonder how a man cultured as her new benefactor could live in such an isolated state. Did he never wish to converse with a like mind from time to time? Discuss politics, exchange books, play that pretty harpsichord to an audience? She had the impression that he saw no one.

At that moment he returned. She heard him enter the kitchen and rushed out to meet him. He greeted her with his odd, sweet smile.

"Good morning. I gave you up for dead last night and went to check to make sure you were still with us."

He removed five large brown eggs from the bag he carried and put them in a bowl on the table.

"I trust you are fond of eggs," he said. "For we eat them all the time."

"Indeed I am. And of chicken, too."

"Then I regret that latter desire must go unrequited. I too used to like chicken when they came to me dead and anonymous, but now I rear my own and have come to love all of them. I could not kill one. I certainly could not eat it. Maybe George could fetch a chicken killed by some other hand, from Sydney Cove, to satisfy your fondness."

"I assure you it is not a passion. I have not eaten chicken since I left England last August and have not come to any harm," Lila told him with amusement.

"Hopefully, you will have the same attitude towards geese

and duck, for I have made friends with them too. Even my two pigs have a place in my heart. I have become a vegetarian these last years."

"I think I could become a vegetarian too," Lila said happily, and then added hastily in case he thought her presumptuous, "that is, for as long as I am here."

He might want her to go back to Sydney Cove that very day for all she knew.

"Soon our small convoy will be reported missing and the bodies found. As mine is not with them . . ." She shrugged expressively.

"Do you realize they will think the natives took you?" he said. "They will not know where to search. You could stay here and escape your sentence, having completely disappeared off the face of the earth."

"That would be quite out of the question," cried Lila. "To let me stay here whilst I am in New South Wales would be a rare kindness on your part and I am sure a hundred, a thousand times better than being a laundry maid on the Gouch Farm, but I could not disappear! Word would filter back to my family and my friends. What would they think? Imagine their heartache if they were told I had been kidnapped by savages."

Roland Fairbrother smiled sweetly.

"I knew with all certainty that would be your answer, so yesterday, while you slept, I sent George into Sydney Cove with the wagon. I have been waiting for supplies off the *Gabriel* anyway. He took a note to the governor-general explaining your plight and saying I required a housekeeper and found you satisfactory."

He held up a piece of thick crested paper.

"Here is his reply. He concedes to my request, sends his regrets at your unfortunate experience, and expresses relief that you were spared. So, now I am your employer, Mrs. Bateson— and that is the last time I shall call you that. My name is Roland, and with your permission, may I call you Lilian?"

"I am generally called Lila," she replied, blushing with pleasure.

"Then, Lila, come with me." —

He led her into the spacious hall where the beautiful old grandmother clock chimed the hour of eight. A pile of boxes and packages were heaped by the front door and Roland took the topmost two.

"George had brought you toiletries and other things. He left it to the discretion of the storekeeper's wife to try and think of everything a young lady who had nothing might need. Dresses were unobtainable, I regret, but he has brought four lengths of cotton. I hope you do not mind his taste, which is a trifle bizarre, but I told him to get as plain as possible."

"How kind you are. Your thoughtfulness overwhelms me." Lila's voice trembled with emotion.

She took the packages and peeked at the material. It was perhaps a little bright. Blue muslin sprigged with very pink roses, a length of plain but vivid yellow, white with multicolored spots and a black and white check.

"You are handy with a needle, I hope?"

"Yes, indeed, sir—Roland. I shall look forward to making these up."

On the crates beneath her packages his address was scrawled.

"New Farm," she read. "That is the name you have given your home?"

"Yes," he said. "It lacks imagination, I know, but there were no memories of England I wished to commemorate here. I have even christened the area New Town, for it had no name."

"Timothy, my husband, had a wish to found a dynasty here, and had visions of some future city being called Batesonville or some such," Lila told him sadly.

"It must be nice to have such faith and hope," Roland said somewhat bitterly.

"I hope you do not mind my saying this," Lila blurted, eyes glowing, "but though you may not possess faith or hope, you certainly possess charity."

"That may be," he answered awkwardly pulling at his beard. "Now, I suggest we drink a toast to our—what should I call it—our partnership? Come."

He led the way into the drawing room and poured out two glasses of red wine.

"Perhaps you will advise me of my duties later," she said as she sipped the fruity liquor recalling that the last time she had drunk wine was at the Prince of Wales' reception, when—

She quickly stopped herself, not wishing to dwell on the injustices done to her.

"You have no duties," Roland Fairbrother replied abruptly. "The idea of a housekeeper was merely a ruse to allow you to stay here. I do not wish you to be my servant. I assume that in England we would be socially equal and I wish you to remain here as my guest."

Lila felt rebuked. Her host continued, "However, you are bound to become bored here with so little to do. My harpsichord is at your disposal, as are my books. I have cooked for myself so far and will continue to do so if using a kitchen dismays you, but my menus are somewhat restricted. If you wish to attempt more variety, then you are welcome."

It was difficult to imagine being bored in this haven of peace and quiet where Lila knew she was safe from authority and the iniquities it could inflict upon her. Cooking was one of the few things at which she was rather inept, but if there was a book of recipes anywhere in New Farm she would start experimenting tomorrow.

Roland Fairbrother excused himself, and Lila went to her own room to put away her new belongings. She could not stay in this heavenly place forever, but it would provide a wonderful and welcome respite while she thought of some way of getting back to England.

Chapter Eleven

Later that day Roland showed her around the house. In the kitchen at midday the heat was stifling, despite the fact that the range had been dampened down.

"It burns wood and there is always a goodly supply," Roland explained. "At the very height of summer it becomes unbearable, so I light it only for baking bread once a week and use this little oil stove for heating water."

Lila thought nostalgically that in England snowdrops would be thrusting their way through the frosty soil. Yet here! It was hard to imagine a few weeks ago it had been even hotter than this.

He led her into another room and explained where certain items had come from.

"This piece," he said indicating a little Chinese lacquered writing desk, "was for the Prince of Wales. Apparently in Carlton House there is a Chinese room, but this was not needed.

I have a man in London who snaps up such gems on my behalf."

"I have been in the Chinese Room," Lila said. "Believe me, it is not nearly so attractive as this house. More like a museum."

"You have been in Carlton House?" he remarked in surprise.

"I was a lady-in-waiting there." Roland Fairbrother looked even more astonished and Lila explained, "It is a long tale and each time I tell it another chapter has been added. I feel you have a right to hear it, so some time I will regale you with the story of my life. Or shall I say, of the last ten months of my life, for up until June last year, little of any consequence had ever happened to me.

"These are pretty," she said, changing the subject and indicating a set of boxes intricately carved in wood and decorated with mother-of-pearl.

They came to the hallway where the packing cases George had fetched from Sydney Cove waited to be opened.

"I have sufficient furniture now. In here are ornaments, a jade chess set and a clock. In the other are books and several months' editions of the *Times*. I had hoped to live a life divorced from everything outside, but the political intrigues of Europe never cease to fascinate me. I cannot remain ignorant of what wars are being fought and who is king of where. It would have been carrying my quest for quietude too far if it meant not knowing the French Revolution had taken place, for instance."

Lila had noticed the writing on the crates.

"My! You are a baronet, I see. Sir Roland Fairbrother. You did not mention that."

Roland said stiffly, "I inherited a baronetcy from my father."

"Would that be Sir Hubert Fairbrother?" She was too excited to notice the way his eyes clouded over. He nodded briefly. "He too was a member of Parliament, was he not? My father knew him well, for he was a Whig. I haven't mentioned it, but my father is Sir William Ward, Whig member for northwest Yorkshire."

"You had no need to tell me, for when you first told me your name, I realized your parent was a colleague of my own late father."

Lila's eyes opened wide with astonishment. "And you did not remark on the coincidence?"

Roland did not answer and Lila went on heedlessly, "I remember well my papa's grief when Sir Hubert died." She put her hand to her mouth and gasped, "I am sorry. I hope I haven't upset you.

"It doesn't upset me in the least. I was living here when he passed away, and we were not close."

He spoke tightly, with obvious reluctance, but Lila was still too carried away to notice.

"Strange," she mused. "But Papa never mentioned Sir Hubert had a son. Always he referred to a daughter, never a son."

"Mrs. Bateson!" His voice was hard and grating and Lila regarded him with some alarm. "I came here to forget the past and had largely succeeded in doing so. If you persist in constantly reminding me of it, then I regret I must ask you to leave New Farm and live elsewhere."

Turning on his heel, he marched out of the house.

Life at New Farm proved as tranquil as Lila had hoped. The small-holding Roland Fairbrother had established was of an experimental nature and Lila, who had never been the slightest bit interested in agriculture, found it fascinating to walk round the four acres of intensely planted grounds, an Aladdin's cave of exotic and rare plants.

"As this climate is almost tropical, it should be possible to grow anything here which can be grown in Africa or India," Roland explained.

Succulent black grapes weighed down vines covering the rear wall of the house. Neat patches of familiar vegetables grew next to fig trees from Africa, guava fruit imported from America, orange and lemon trees, their crop larger than anything in England.

One day Lila saw George putting a bucket full of roots onto the wagon he was taking to Sydney and asked what they were.

"Ipecacuanha, missie. Make good medicine. Take to doctor."

"I wonder what for?" Lila mused aloud thinking of Timothy's father and his seaweed physic.

"For bowels, missie. Mister R'land tell me, give you good clear out. Doctor, he swear it the best."

Roland made a good living from his little plantation. Once or twice a week, George took the wagon into Sydney Cove, loaded with fruit and vegetables, some of which were rare delicacies in this land. A mile or so to the rear of his farm

Roland had found a small stream which ran its leisurely way to the ocean, widening as it did so. He had dug irrigation trenches and his crops continued to thrive.

"Everybody is planting wheat, barley, or flax," he told Lila. "And it requires such a vast amount of labor to harvest that I decided to try a different type of agriculture altogether. I never thought I would find growing things exciting, but 'pon my soul, my heart leaps when something new pokes its little green head out of my soil, or a blossom bud appears on a tree transplanted from Morocco or South America."

He never accompanied George to the town and Lila had no wish to go either. Here she could forget that this and was a penal colony, and that a mere ten miles away there were people like Queen Lil.

Since the day she had made a faux pas referring to the past, Lila only mentioned England in relation to herself. She could not help but wonder about his background though, and as the weeks passed she tried to recall details of her father's friendship with Sir Hubert Fairbrother. He was one of Papa's London friends. He never came to the house, and Mama, who rarely went far from Yorkshire, had not met him.

There was something odd about Sir Hubert's wife, Fanny, for whenever she was mentioned, Mama would give a warning glance in the children's direction, reminding Sir William to be careful what he said. But this was nothing strange, for there were so many notorious goings-on amongst the London crowd that very little was fit for discussion in front of Lila and her sisters. Now she wished she had paid more attention to Papa's idle gossip. The only incident to stand out in her memory was the day of Sir Hubert's funeral, when Papa had come stamping in just before supper in quite a temper.

"Fanny all but danced on his grave," he'd stormed. "Brought along a pack of her disgusting women friends who grinned like Cheshire cats the whole time and made it plain she was glad to see the back of him. As for the daughter, no sign of her. Disappeared off the face of the earth, it seems."

Lila had been thirteen when that happened, for Mr. Partridge, her violin instructor, had been leaving as Papa came in, and she'd started the lessons just after her birthday. That was five years ago, and by then Roland had already been in New South Wales more than two years. He told Lila he had emigrated when he was eighteen. She felt sorry that a boy that young should have gained such a jaundiced view of life that he would travel some fourteen thousand miles to start a new one. Ruefully, she realized she herself was just that age and was also hiding from the world at New Farm.

But of late she had felt restless and somewhat fidgety after months of serenity. At night when they sat in the cool drawing room, reading, or discussing the parliamentary news which Roland gained from his old newspapers, she found her mind wandering. Roland was intensely interested in government and it was clear that he would have made a far finer politician than his father, though his inclinations were more towards a liberal type of Toryism. He was fascinated to learn from Lila the machinations of Carlton House and questioned her keenly about the politics of everyone involved.

On an October evening, with the lamps lit, and outside a sky of fiery red gashes against deep purple mist, Lila sewed lace on a petticoat and suddenly became conscious that Roland was staring at her rather moodily.

He was inclined to moroseness from time to time and she usually ignored it, as he always returned to his sweet natured self in time, but now she asked, "Is something wrong?"

"I have asked you twice if you would like a glass of wine but you were so taken up with your thoughts, you did not hear."

"I do beg your pardon."

She was instantly contrite for he was easily hurt. While sewing on the lace, she had been in the arms of Phillip Grenville in the little London basement room, and she wondered what he was doing at that very moment. It was nine o'clock, so it would be morning in England. He would be up, and she imagined him dressed in his red and gray uniform or his black civilian clothes. Where had he been the night before? Visiting Isabella's House of Sin, perhaps. Calling on—what was the name Isabella had called his favorite? Jenny. That was it. Had he held Jenny in his arms last night? Did he ever think of Lila . . . ?

"I am so sorry."

She apologized again to Roland who had not acknowledged her first and still stared at her intently.

"You are restive lately. Your mind spends more time away from New Farm than it does here," he said eventually, his voice dry and unemotional. Lila knew it was useless to deny this.

"I truly regret it has been so obvious," she said honestly. "But you are right. It is not that I am bored here. I confess this kind of existence would not suit me for a lifetime, but its pleasures have not dimmed one whit since I came to live here. No, I am anxious because I am doing nothing to clear my name, but stay here, enjoying myself, when I should be fighting to regain my honor, not only for my own sake, but also for the sake of my family."

Although Papa had been at fault placing her in a situation where she was so vulnerable, he had meant her no harm. Yet now he was ill, confined to bed when she last heard, all due to hearing the news of Lila's misadventure.

Roland sighed and Lila struggled to explain how she felt.

"You remember I told you Rawlesbury offered me money that awful night when I was moved to save the princess and her coachman from exposure? He also offered promotion within the Whig party for my father. I could have taken these and returned to the bosom of my family, but I refused and I stand by that refusal. By staying here, so safe and secure with you, I feel I am taking another easy way out. To serve my sentence without protest is to admit my guilt, just as I would have done accepting Rawlesbury's offer."

Unwittingly she had gathered the petticoat she was sewing into a bunch and clutched it to her heart. She desperately wanted him to understand so his feelings were not hurt. To her relief, he smiled.

"My dear girl," he said as though he were a quarter of a century older than her and not a mere eight years. "I appreciate your dilemma, but pray tell me, how do you propose to go about clearing your name? Even if you left New Farm and went to Sydney Cove, you would merely be sent elsewhere to work, perhaps further afield than this."

"I thought of appealing to the governor," she explained. "If the Prince of Wales was willing to listen to me, surely the governor would?"

"Captain-General John Hunter," mused Roland contemplatively. "I know little of him. Believe it or not, I read of our governors in the *Times* so I can be a year behind knowing even their names. George brings local news, but governors mean nothing to him. I understand Hunter is a bit of a religious fanatic. Such men I do not trust."

Roland practiced his Catholicism in a quiet and unobtrusive fashion.

"Even if this man gave you a hearing," he continued, it is not within his power to commute your sentence even if he should wish to, for a court of law in England has pronounced you guilty."

"There will indeed be difficulties," Lila conceded.

"Moreover, despite your experiences with your companions on board ship which has no doubt led you to believe all convicts are of a certain low class, there have been deportees from the highly born, so you are not unique. You cannot expect to be given preferential treatment because you are of the upper class. Furthermore, scores of prisoners are openly sent here on trumped-up charges."

"Surely that cannot be?" gasped Lila.

"Regrettably, it is so. In England and Scotland, men demanding a fair wage, particularly on farms where they often are treated as little more than slaves, are charged with incitement and sent here for life."

Lila's heart sank, and seeing her disconsolate expression Roland said encouragingly, "Pray, do not let me deter you. By all means approach John Hunter. In fact, I will write on your behalf, for my name will carry more weight—in New South Wales, that is. If you see him, I will accompany you and mention our fathers' acquaintanceship."

This was a sacrifice on Roland's part for he had nothing to do with Sydney and its inhabitants.

"Let us think on the matter for a day or so," he said. "I know it has preoccupied you for some time, but consider it in the light of what I have just said."

She went back to her lace trimming and he to his sketching, and they sat until bedtime in their usual companionable silence.

A few days later after she had eaten her breakfast, Lila fed the six hens. She too had become fond of them and had rather disrespectfully christened them after the royal princesses, convincing herself she could differentiate among them.

"Come along, Augusta," she called to one pecking moodily in a corner, whose beak she swore was slightly darker than the others. "Or there will be nothing left for you."

"Lila."

She looked up.

"Good morning, Roland."

That morning she wore the yellow dress she had made herself from the material George had fetched from Sydney and a matching kerchief on her hair. With the bowl of grain under one arm she looked to Roland like a character out of a fairy tale.

"Will you marry me?"

She stared at him for a long time while the hens clucked about her feet. The question was not entirely unexpected. She felt he was growing fond of her and it was a natural conclusion to their friendship. His next words took her by surprise though.

"It would be a marriage of convenience only. I would expect nothing from you, but I am inclined to think that once you were Lady Fairbrother you would be allowed passage on the next ship to England without demur. If difficulties were raised, then I could travel with you, at least to the first port of call where I could then await the next ship returning here."

Lila emptied the bowl on top of the squawking hens and went towards him. As usual he wore the roughest of working clothes, hard coarse material which must have been uncomfortable next to his skin. As a protection against the already boiling sun, he had on a most disreputable-looking hat. She felt she wanted to protect him, protect his innocence and goodness from the outside world, not let him become embroiled in negotiations in the town with government officials.

"Dear Roland," she said. "How flattered I am you should ask me to become your wife."

He gave an odd smile and led her to the arbor. When they sat, he made no move to touch her but said, "I have thought long and hard, and this is the most certain way to gain you your freedom and an opportunity to return to England."

"But . . ." Lila struggled for words. Roland had such a complex, mysterious nature that she reckoned it was a great effort on his part to propose. Lest of course he be in love. . . .

"But . . ." she said again and stopped, still unable to find words.

"No more buts." He smiled. "The sailing ship *Northern Star* is due here a month from now, at the end of November. I don't know if the formality of banns is required in New South Wales, but if so, there is just enough time for them to be called. I will send George this very day with a letter to the governor asking for guidance. Then we can be wed just prior to the ship's arrival."

"You must ask for a Catholic priest," she told him. "Else you will not be married in the eyes of God."

"No," he replied sharply. "All that is required to get you on board the *Star* when she returns to England is a wedding certificate. A church marriage will only create complications in the future. The minute you arrive in England, you must seek an annulment. I will give you the address of my solicitor, Quentin Burnett. Once you explain the situation to him, you will experience no difficulty."

He said this somewhat bitterly. She opened her mouth to argue but Roland raised his right hand dismissively.

"Please do not say 'but' again. I shall marry you by force if you continue to argue, and shall put you on board ship in a trunk. Now I am going to milk Gertrude and Genevieve. I can hear them lowing impatiently in the cowshed. George is away this morning clearing a ditch, for water is not reaching the orchard due to a blockage. I cannot bear to leave my poor animals in such discomfort."

It may well be, Lila reflected later as she sliced eggs, for lunch that at Carlton House she had come across many evil-doers who had wished her harm, but as a result of this she had met with much kindness. Now another man had offered his hand in marriage to help her.

She wondered why he insisted on a marriage of convenience only. Of course she had told him of Captain Grenville. Maybe he thought because she loved Phillip there was no room in her heart for anyone else. In a way this was true. Yet these last months she had discovered there were many different kinds of love, all likely to lead to a happy marriage. In fact she loved Roland dearly, though in a different manner altogether than Phillip.

Suddenly a thought struck her. So many men had wanted her. Ralph Curringham, the sailors on board ship, Phillip himself. Isabella had thought she would be a great asset in her House of Sin. She would offer herself to Roland. Let him see she loved him and wanted him to love her. He had done so much for her.

* * *

That night after Roland had retired, Lila stood before the small glass in her room, combing her sun-bleached hair onto her shoulders.

She looked down at herself, running her hands over her full, soft breasts, then onto her slim waist, her hips, and down her silky white thighs. Soon Roland would be touching her like this, and her heart gave a jump. At last the time had arrived for her to become a woman. With shaking hands she slipped on a thin cotton robe and went to Roland's bedroom.

He was sound asleep, and by the light of the full moon he reminded her of the Russian icon in the hall, a bearded Christ. She knelt beside him and touched the lean brown hand which lay upon the sheet. He blinked, opened his eyes, and she could not have been more horrified at his reaction. Struggling to sit up, his eyes burning without rage, he yelled at her hoarsely, *"Get out!"*

Bewildered, Lila stumbled back to her own room where she threw herself on the bed. What had she done? Why had he rejected her so violently? For a long time she lay, her body wracked with shame. She heard movements in the bungalow and a knock on her door.

"Lila?"

He sounded quite calm.

"Yes?"

"I assumed you would be awake. I want to talk to you. I have made tea."

She struggled into her nightdress, making sure it was securely fastened at the neck and tied her robe tightly about her. No doubt she would be told to pack and leave next morning.

He was in the kitchen, fully dressed and sitting on a stool away from the lamp so that his face was shadowed. She obediently sat at the far side of the table where he had placed a cup of tea.

"Are you a virgin, Lila?"

She was so taken aback that she banged down the cup before even taking a sip. She nodded affirmation.

"I thought as much. It was merely gratitude, not desire, that prompted your visit to my room."

Lila blushed, for this was not strictly true. While running her hands down her body as she contemplated calling on Roland she had felt a tremor of excitement and longing. This time she shook her head without looking at him. He gave his old cynical smile.

"I have no doubt dealt a shattering blow to your self-confidence."

"There has not been time to think of it," Lila answered.

His next question again surprised her.

"Have you heard of my mother, Lady Frances? Fanny Fairbrother, as she is known."

"Papa mentioned her occasionally. If you will forgive me for saying so, I don't think he liked her much."

He smiled again, almost laughed in fact.

"That is almost certainly an understatement. He probably loathed her. My father did."

"I had gathered they did not live together," said Lila. "I understand your father spent most of his time in the London house, while your mother remained in Bristol."

"True, except when Mother made one of her raids on London. Then my father would retreat to his club. He could not spend time under the same roof as that woman."

From the tone of his voice it seemed Roland shared his father's feelings.

"When you first came here, Lila, you said you could not recall your father mentioning Sir Hubert had a son, but only a daughter."

"That is true. I have wondered about that. I thought perhaps you were a black sheep and he would not speak of you."

"No, Lila, that is not the reason. It is because *I* was the daughter."

She looked at him, stupefied, at his bearded face and fine, masculine features.

Stammering, she replied, "I am sorry, but I do not understand."

"Let me tell you the story of *my* life, Lila. You have honored me with your history and if you are going to marry me—that is, if you still wish to after hearing this gory tale—you should know all there is to know about me."

He paused and took a deep breath.

"My mother was an incredible beauty. Black hair like velvet, eyes almost as dark, features as perfect as a porcelain figure. When she was a girl, suitors threw themselves at her feet. One man even tried to shoot himself when she laughed at his proposal. Eventually my father came along, and her parents, desperate to get her off their hands, for they could see something was not quite right with her, practically forced her to marry him. Of course my father was delirious with joy, for he worshipped his bride-to-be. The night they married he made love to her, and she responded with such passion, loved him back with such skill, that for an hour or two, he was in perfect heaven thinking that the beauty he had taken for a wife should turn out to be an accomplished lover too. Then, the minute it was over, she told him.''

Roland paused, staring unseeingly out of the kitchen window into the moonlit garden as though present at the very scene and remembering it. Then he seemed to recall Lila's presence and turning to her said, "You are perhaps wondering why my father told me these intimate details. It was during one of our rare meetings when he was trying to explain why he had deserted me and left me in my mother's clutches. . . . She told him she had never loved a man in her life and never would. When she was a child, she said, a gypsy had looked into her palm and declared her the reincarnation of the poetess Sappho. I reckon the gypsy was merely pandering to an inclination obvious to one with second sight. This filled my mother with pride, and from then on she had foresworn relations with men and committed herself to women in the manner of Sappho. She resented deeply her forced marriage and had let my father love her that night out of nothing less than cruelty.

"She felt it necessary for him to understand that she could give him intense happiness if she so chose, but she did not choose, and never again would she allow him in her bed.''

"My father left his own house, Bly Hall, immediately. He went abroad, distraught and ill for several months in Austria. Then he wandered about Europe not knowing that the one night of cruel love had resulted in my mother becoming pregnant. When he returned to England two years later, it was to learn he had a daughter, fifteen months old.''

Lila sat like a statue, fascinated by this lurid tale. Roland got to his feet and began to pace the floor as if he could not bear to remain still a second longer.

"He went to see his daughter, a baby dressed in the lace gowns all babies, boy or girl, wear until the age of three or four. Over the years he took gifts to the girl, never staying for more than a few hours, for he could not bear to be within the same four walls as the woman he had married.

"The daughter was about ten when he had a visit from the midwife who had delivered her. My mother had, within the first year of her married life, surrounded herself with women of similar desires to herself and when it came time for her to give birth, several of these were present to assist. Complications arose, and a midwife was hurriedly fetched to bring the child into the world. With some difficulty she accomplished this and she told my father that when she announced to the room that it was a fine boy, a wailing and moaning went up both from the mother and her friends. The women sneered and abused the newborn infant in a manner that horrified the midwife to the extent that she considered stealing the baby if she could and taking it to a place of safety. But then an older woman came forward, wrapped the child in a blanket and seemed more sympathetic to its welfare than the others."

The child must, of course, be Roland, Lila thought to herself, and a feeling of intense anger overwhelmed her for the sufferings inflicted on this man from the very moment of birth.

"The midwife was paid handsomely for her help, and she returned to the village from whence she came. In the years to come she often asked about the son of Lady Fairbrother, but was told none existed, there was only a daughter. She assumed my mother had given birth to another child and farmed out the hated son."

"Now my mother had been given a chance to cause real suffering to a member of the sex she loathed so much, even though the victim was to be her own child. From the very beginning, she dressed me in girls' clothes, gave me feminine toys to play with, encouraging me to behave as a girl would in every possible way. I was surrounded at all times by women who enjoyed pleasing their idol, Fanny Fairbrother, by tormenting her hated son-daughter.

"I grew up in anguish. I was never allowed to leave Bly Hall on a single occasion and received scarcely any education. There was an inexplicable imbalance in me, which I could not identify, could not even put into words.

"Then the midwife went to see my father. Someone had mentioned to her it was the tenth birthday of Lady Frances Fairbrother's daughter at Bly Hall. She recalled it was ten years to the day she had delivered the poor, unwanted boy. For all she knew the child could have been substituted by a girl, but nevertheless, the woman was so bothered by it all, she went all the way to London to see my father. He came post-haste to Bristol, storming into the house, waving his cane, and raving at my mother. I was hurriedly whisked out of earshot, though I remember his arrival quite clearly. He told me afterwards that my mother quite literally blackmailed him. Not only would his career as a member of Parliament be harmed if this unnatural state of affairs came to light, but how could *I* ever be accepted in society? I would be a freak, a laughingstock. My father was a weak man and gave in, allowing the situation to continue unchanged.

"When I was fifteen and beginning to mature I felt I was going out of my mind. I loathed putting on the dresses laid out for me each morning, yet my mother and friends reveled in my humiliation for I was gradually taking the shape of their mortal enemy, man."

Roland stopped talking and poured out two more cups of tea. "I am not used to talking so much. My throat is parched. Does this bore you, Lila?"

"No, no," she assured him. "But it is horrifying. My heart bleeds for you."

"I suppose I should worry I am distressing you."

"Please continue. Timothy once said, 'A trouble shared is a trouble halved.' It will ease your mind to talk."

"Very well, then. Our house adjoined a vicarage at one corner and four girls lived there, some younger, some older than myself and sometimes I would stare through the hedge at them, wondering why I felt such a misfit and did not want to become friends. In fact, the thought sickened me and increased my sense of bewilderment.

"One day, the girls' tutor noticed me watching them and called out to me. I immediately ran away, frightened. This was only the second man I had met in my life, the other being my father. But I was fascinated and returned the next day, mainly to meet the tutor, for at least I had come across a human being with whom I felt something in common. He was a Swede, Gunnar Andersen, aged twenty-one, and poor man, he fell in love with me. For the first time in my life I was in receipt of tenderness, and was happy and content. More than a year passed and inevitably the day came when he tried to make love to me and to his horror discovered I was a boy. That night he hung himself."

"Oh, no!" gasped Lila.

"I do not think he was a man made for women, and loving me had been a great relief. He had convinced himself he was normal. Then to find I was male after all, shattered it all. Nevertheless, this tragedy took the scales from my eyes.

"My feelings for my mother were of great hatred mixed with great fear. I could not face her, for I felt she had inflicted on me a fate worse than death, and if confronted she might well kill me—aided by her vicious friends. I took money and bought myself men's clothes. I resolved never to wear fine silks or lawns, velvets or laces again in my life. For the first time ever I felt comfortable, glad about the hair growing on my face and my strange, gruff voice. I went to London to see my father.

"I have already said I had never been outside the gates of Bly Hall. The world seemed a most odd yet fascinating place, and I thoroughly enjoyed my journey to London. My father was astonished when this youth appeared on his doorstep and turned out to be his son. Initially he was overjoyed and excused himself, apologizing for not having rescued me from my mother, whose household was notorious. It was then he told me of their first night together. I had nothing but contempt for him. He had sacrificed my life to his career."

Roland was beginning to pace again, nervously, as though what he now had to say was even more painful than before.

"I was a man in no time, a passionate man, my sexual feelings thoroughly roused. After a lifetime of neglect, I desperately wanted to love and be loved. But, and this is what I shall never, never forgive my mother for, I found I could not stand the sight of women. I hated their perfume and their powder, their lace and frills, their coquettish ways and their sickly smiles. Every single thing about a woman that makes her different from a man I loathed. All these things had been forced upon me against my nature for my entire life, and I reacted against them with such violence that for a long time I could not even stay in the same room with a woman. So who was I to turn to for the love I yearned for? Who else but to a man? The only person who had ever wanted me was a man. I fell in love with my father's coachman and pestered him to such a degree that my father had to dismiss the poor fellow. Not, you must realize, that anyone knew who I was. This still remained a secret. I was merely the son of an old friend who had passed away. In no time at all I discovered there were places for people with needs such as mine. I spent every night in a house in Blackfriars. I began to drink, was introduced to opium, and was well on the way to becoming totally dissolute when I discovered Catholicism. I considered becoming a priest, attracted by the idea of celibacy, but I did not have the calling."

"How did it come about, this conversion to Catholicism?" Lila asked gently.

"Somehow, I do not know how, for I was drunk, I found myself in a small private chapel. There was nothing dramatic about it. I did not hear voices or see visions. Just the quiet and the peace brought me to my senses and told me this life could not continue or I would be dead within a year. I came out confused, wondering what to do. Immediately outside was a news vendor, and on an impulse I brought a paper, and there was an item about New South Wales and the first fleet which was preparing to leave. I hoped I would find the peace and quiet I had just experienced in the chapel in the solitude of a vast, uninhabited country, and I booked a passage. My father was overjoyed to see the back of me and gave me the money due at twenty-one to set myself up here. My solicitor told me when my father passed away, and he deals with all my affairs in England. I hear nothing from my mother, nor do I want to."

He stopped talking and stared once again out of the window to where the lightened sky gave promise of the sun's arrival.

"So there, Lila, is my story. Beside that, yours pales, don't you think?"

He gave his gentle, wry smile, and Lila wanted to hold him in her arms, stroke his hair, comfort him. Yet he could not bear the touch of a woman. He would find her gestures of affection revolting.

"Are you disgusted?" he asked anxiously. "I have abstained totally from all forms of depravity since that night in the London church."

"Dear Roland. Your story is the most tragic I have ever heard. You have overcome your awful past with great courage."

"I do not feel confident that I can still resist the temptations which abound in the outside world. That is why I have no convict labor. Why I never, never visit the town. I keep myself well away from situations where I might give way to unwelcome impulses. And Lila . . ."

He paused and she said encouragingly, "Yes, Roland?"

"That first night you were here and I went to look to make sure you were all right, I thought most men would be overjoyed having someone like you come into their lives, and regretted I was unable to feel anything for you. Lately, though, I find myself drawn to you more and more."

Lila could have kicked herself for speaking out the other night and expressing a wish to leave. If she had only kept quiet, in another few months Roland might well have come to love her as any man loves a woman.

She said simply, "I am glad to hear that, Roland," but she did not approach him. Should they ever embrace, then he must make the first move.

Three weeks later they were married by the Reverend Samuel Marsden in a tiny wooden church in Sydney Cove.

The *Sir* before Roland's name at the foot of all his written inquiries oiled the wheels of bureaucracy, and there was no trouble arranging for the carriage and obtaining Lila's passage back to England.

The *Northern Star* was due to dock on November 25, the day of their wedding. Roland intended to confirm with the captain that a cabin was reserved for his wife. Then they would return to New Farm and stay until the boat was due to sail after Christmas.

The ship had not arrived by evening and the Reverend Marsden's wife, Elizabeth, was in a bit of a tizzy as to whether she should ask Sir Roland and his new wife to stay, for while she was impressed by her new title, nevertheless this young lady had been a convict until that very morning. But Mrs. Marsden was one of the very few entrusted with this secret information, and everybody else would welcome the young couple. She decided it would be politic to issue the invitation, which was so prettily accepted by the new bride that her hostess had to admit to herself that the young lady's manners were almost as perfect as her own.

Roland was not at all anxious to stay in Sydney Cove for a minute longer than necessary, but Lila was so delighted to be accepted in society once again as an equal, he decided she should enjoy, in one respect at least, the first day of her marriage to him.

After tea they went for a stroll around the town, though Mrs. Marsden warned them it was not really a fit place in which to wander after sunset.

"It is impossible to describe the depths of depravity into which the inhabitants have sunk," she told them, and her husband, who had not been in the colony long, remarked gloomily at the difficulty of the task of persuading the populace to adopt more Christian standards of behavior.

At this Roland suggested they stay in, but on that day Lila's excitement knew no bounds. Her return to England was in sight. The future held promise for the first time in more than a year. She didn't want to spend the evening of this glorious day sitting in the Marsdens' stuffy drawing room. And she was convinced they were exaggerating the dangers outside. Roland gave in. On that day, he could refuse Lila nothing.

They sat in the front seats of the theater, watching a performance by the "better class of prisoner" of a play entitled *The Revenge*. Lila had been thrilled to discover the little theatre in such an unlikely setting and found the downstairs occupied solely by government officials, military men or settlers, along with their wives, while the convict audience was confined to the gallery.

For her wedding, despite its unorthodoxy, Lila felt bound to make a new dress, and George had bought a length of cream silk. The style was plain, enhanced by a spray of rosebuds from Roland's garden on her shoulder. She had managed to fashion quite a respectable bonnet from the same material, and George had proudly obtained a length of cream satin ribbon for trimming.

In the theater she and Roland—he looking respectable in subdued brown—were the center of attention, for everybody knew everybody else in Sydney Cove and this new young couple who had appeared out of the blue created quite a stir. During the interval they were approached by numerous people, fascinated to learn this was Sir Roland and Lady Fairbrother of New Farm—surely, they remarked, that was the place where all those delicious rare fruits and vegetables grew? As most of the men had an interest in farming, Roland was inundated with questions about his growing methods.

Lila felt sure he would be glad of the opportunity to talk about his experiments on the small-holding and was so drunk

with her own sense of liberation that she failed to notice the
strain in his eyes. As the evening wore on, the old feeling of
being an incongruous misfit came over Roland more and more.
His distress was actually worsened by the mixed emotions he
felt for Lila. He could refuse her nothing. Half of him was an
infatuated, newly married husband, head over heels in love
with his bride. The other half tried to suppress the raw desires,
so long buried, for some of the men surrounding him.

A governor's aide, Michael Brandreth, a self-important,
anemic gentleman, invited them back to his house for drinks,
along with several other couples, and Roland, his head spinning
from the unaccustomed human contact, found himself sipping
glass after glass of rum in the hope it would blot out his unwelcome thoughts. The rippling feeling in his stomach and the
racing of his heart were uncontrollable, and he found himself
unable to take his eyes off a tall boy with the look of a Greek
god. He was the son of an army captain, and he reminded
Roland of the tutor, Gunnar Andersen.

Lila was the center of an admiring group and Roland was
willing himself to concentrate on her beauty and forget the boy,
when he was approached by a large, black-haired man who
placed a familiar arm around his shoulders and muttered, "The
strain shows, my friend. If you cannot stand it, come to Jubilee
House at any time."

The man was huge and muscular, his hands covered with
dark hairs, and Roland shivered in a mixture of ecstasy and
disgust. He approached Lila immediately.

"May we please go home—to the Marsdens', that is. I feel
unwell."

Lila felt guilty, for Roland did look feverish and was shaking
uncontrollably. She refused Michael Brandreth's offer of a trap,
for the house was a mere five minutes walk, and the fresh air
would do Roland good. To her surprise he did not hurry and
peered at the door of every house they passed.

Sydney seemed intent on proving itself to be the well of
iniquity it was reputed to be. After her experiences on the
Gabriel, Lila accepted the scenes of prostitution without turning
a hair, as did many respectable ladies and gentlemen, for people
of all classes and stations in life were out. Women sat at open
windows, their bodies bared for all to see. They lolled half-
dressed in doorways calling out to customers. As men outnumbered the fairer sex by ten to one in New South Wales, they

did not need to call for long, and outside some establishments men stood in line.

In a street darker and quieter than the others Roland stopped momentarily outside one house. Curtains were drawn on every window and the door was closed, yet as they watched, it opened and two people emerged, one a tall and well-dressed man of middle age, the other a boy no more than twelve or thirteen, wearing ill-fitting clothes, his face thin and gaunt. They hurried to the end of the street and turned the corner. Lila's innocence in the ways of the world was such that despite having so recently listened to Roland's life story, she suspected nothing untoward in this.

Roland was unnaturally quiet when they reached the Marsdens', and Lila felt inordinately sorry about her thoughtlessness. The evening must have been unbearable for him. If she hadn't been so engrossed in herself and her desire to walk the streets again, a free woman, then she would have recognized that the sensible thing to do was to go to their rooms after tea. It was shameful on her part to have subjected him to such stress, she thought as she brushed her hair. He was changing and would sleep in the little dressing room which adjoined hers. Lila hoped he would come in to say goodnight, but he still had not appeared when she fell asleep, exhausted from such an exhilarating day.

"Lila! Lila!"

She awoke to find Roland kneeling beside her bed, his head pressed into the pillow beside her.

"My dear! What is wrong?"

Unthinking, she stroked his thin, brown neck with one hand, placing the other gently on his face. She felt him stiffen.

"Let me kiss you, Lila."

"Of course, Roland."

He struggled to his feet as though drunk and sat on the edge of the bed, placing his arms around her and kissing her on the lips.

She kept her mouth to his, pressing against him, willing him to respond to the passion she felt mounting within her. She clasped her arms round his neck. There was no hint of desire or warmth in his rigid embrace. She leaned back, drawing him with her and together they lay, without speaking a word, Lila hoping he would find comfort in her still caress which asked for nothing. She fell asleep with him in her arms.

When he heard her light, even breathing, Roland disentangled himself, adjusted his clothing, and left the room without a backward glance at his lovely wife. He crept out of the house and was quickly swallowed up in the welcoming depravity of Sydney Cove.

Chapter Twelve

Lila arose late, and was not greatly surprised to find Roland absent from the breakfast table.

"He is used to rising early and has no doubt gone to make final arrangements for my passage to England," she told Elizabeth Marsden as they ate. "As soon as he returns we shall leave for New Farm. I will collect my few things and await him. I take it there is no sign as yet of the *Northern Star?*"

She was assured the ship had not been sighted, but its arrival was expected at any time.

"George will drive in daily to see if she has docked," Lila said.

Mrs. Marsden wondered why a young bride should look so radiant at the idea of parting from her new husband so soon after their wedding, but thought it tactful not to comment on this.

Lila was sitting in the little drawing room looking for Roland through the window when she saw Michael Brandreth, the government aide, approaching the Marsden house, and minutes later he was shown into the room.

She was surprised at the unpleasant expression on his face and even more surprised at his words.

"I did not know when I invited you into my house yesterday evening, Lady Fairbrother, that you were in fact a convict with a seven-year sentence for theft."

Lila threw back her head and declared, "Did you expect me to make a public announcement to that effect? In any case, I shall not be visiting your house ever again, for the minute my husband returns we shall be leaving here and in the near future I shall sail for England."

Michael Brandreth did not appear at all impressed with this announcement. Instead he said in sneering tones, "Sir Roland negotiated with the governor himself, and it was not until this morning that I discovered the truth about you and your blatant marriage of convenience."

A small, niggling worry beset Lila. What was the reason for this visit? Surely they could not wreck Roland's plans for her to leave. And where *was* he? It was ten o'clock. What could he be doing all this time? She looked out of the window, hoping to see his slight, graceful figure approaching, but the street was empty.

Michael Brandreth sneered again, and said, "There is no need to look for your spouse, good lady. He is dead."

"*What?*"

"Dead! Stabbed to death in a male brothel in a brawl over a boy prostitute. What a pleasant married couple you made, Lady Fairbrother. A felon and a pervert!"

Lila sat, feeling sullen and wretched, on a low wooden bed in one of the dormitories of the women's prison in New South Wales. It was hard to believe such a dismal building had only been erected a few years ago. The wooden floors and the walls were clean but scrubbed to a watery gray, dried and cracked. Ten beds lined each side of the long, dark room. The blankets and the women's dresses were gray as well so there was no contrast to the drab surroundings. The only faintly cheerful note was struck by the narrow shafts of sunlight which fell through the small barred windows. The room, the entire building, looked as though it had been there a hundred years and had aged with the suffering inside it.

She was in the temporary residents' section, which meant she could be sent to work somewhere as a skivvy, a laundry maid, or an agricultural laborer at any moment.

Elsewhere in the building were the long-term prisoners, those too violent or criminally minded to be allowed to mix with their fellow human beings even in the pit of Sydney Cove. There were also women either mentally or physically unfit to work, and there was a small section housing the expectant mothers. These had been taken on the pretext of becoming servants in a household, yet in fact were used as concubines by their masters, and sent back when their pregnancy rendered them useless in any capacity.

It was twenty-four hours since Lila had been told of Roland's murder, and her lips curled with hatred as she recalled Michael Brandreth's blatant delight in her misfortune. He had brought her to this building where she had been stripped of her clothes and ordered to bathe. The governor's aide made no attempt to leave, and indeed became so excited he dismissed the female warden who was supervising the proceedings and tried to wash Lila himself, his hand going immediately between her legs. She had flung soapy water into his face and he had cursed her, rubbing his eyes, and stepped back. Lila shouted for the warden to return.

The coarse frock she had to wear chafed her neck, but this was the least of her worries. She was tortured not only by the fact that it was partially her fault Roland had died, but also that the authorities were cruelly refusing to allow her to attend his funeral. He was to be buried in an unmarked grave along with all the criminals who had already perished in Botany Bay. Lila remembered Roland saying that when he died he wished to lie beneath the palm tree in the arbor at New Farm. She desperately wanted him to rest in the only place he had known true peace and happiness. It was the least she could do for that good and noble man, so warped and twisted by life from the moment of his birth. Lila swore if she ever returned to England she would kill Lady Frances Fairbrother with her own hands.

Through a window, the *Northern Star,* which had docked a few hours earlier, could be seen at anchor in the cove. With all her heart she wished it had arrived on time, and Roland was still alive.

* * *

Captain Phillip Grenville disembarked from the merchant-man *Northern Star* and breathed deeply the fresh air of Sydney Cove. He was aware only of the faint tang of tar which seemed sweet compared to the odors of vomit and rotten meat, and the stinging smell of blood which he had experienced throughout his seven-month passage to New South Wales. He was also relieved to be away from Captain Nathaniel Grey, the monster in charge of the ship, and his cruelty to the poor wretches being deported.

The men, the women, the child prisoners as young as ten, all were kept in chains for the entire voyage. Floggings were a regular occurrence, three times ending in death. All the crew and passengers were ordered on deck to watch these brutalities, and at the first beating, Phillip Grenville simply turned his back and stared out to sea. The awful cries of the beaten were enough to endure. To the chagrin of Captain Grey, more and more passengers emulated Phillip in showing their disgust at the treatment of the prisoners.

What Captain Grenville found intolerable was that Lila might have been treated this way on her journey to the new land. It was his intention to write a full report for submission to the governor, Captain-General John Hunter, giving details of the ill treatment bestowed by Captain Grey on the prisoners under his protection.

As his immediate concern was locating Lila Ward, he put the horrifying experience on board the ship to one side for the moment, and set off towards the small Admiralty hut close to the docks. Although it was a large country, such a tiny part had been inhabited that he envisaged no problem in locating his sweetheart, indeed imagined them being together in less than twenty-four hours, and, with the letter he had brought signed by the Prince of Wales personally, which pardoned Lila Ward from all crimes, they would embark on the *Northern Star,* hopefully under the command of a more humane captain, and return to England together.

He was therefore astounded when a clerk in the office very efficiently produced a list of prisoners who had arrived on the *Gemini* and Lila's name was not on it. There had been three Lilians on board with the surnames of Wheeler, Rawlesbury and Bateson. The clerk told the anxious captain that he had not been present when the ship docked, and suggested that if he was so convinced that this young lady had arrived on the ship, he should make inquiries about Sydney Cove.

A devastating thought hit Phillip. Suppose he had come on a wild goose chase. What if Lila had not been sent to New South Wales at all? Perhaps she had been done away with back in England, or was even held prisoner there. Such a notion scarcely bore thinking about. It might have been Lila's last-minute assignment to the ship that caused her name not to appear on the official list. He would give a description of Lila to the next person he asked and see if they recognized her from that.

To his intense relief, he was lucky almost straightaway. A gang of stevedores had begun to unload cargo from the *Northern Star*, and one recalled a young woman of medium height with bright golden hair and wearing a brown dress.

"Stuck out like a sore thumb, she did," said the man. "Came ashore by herself, looking proper lost and lonely. Didn't realize she was a prisoner."

Further inquiries resulted in what at first seemed like a strong lead.

"Yes, I remember her well, poor mite," said a man selling fish from a barrow at the quayside. "Sent her off with Jacob Evans to Pitt's Plain, they did, along with three or four proper ruffians. Felt right sorry for the young woman. She didn't look too happy, either."

"You're a good fellow." Captain Grenville handed the man a shilling. "Now, which way is Pitt's Plain, and where may I hire a horse?"

"Well, you can hire a horse off Nick McCarthy over there, Captain, sir. But there's bad news for ye, 'cuz old Jacob Evans and them ruffians, they was mudered by thunderin' savages."

Captain Grenville's heart missed several beats.

"The girl? What happened to the girl?"

"Well, now." The man pursed his lips and thought, which clearly proved a strain. The captain had to prevent himself from shaking the man.

"Well, now," the fishmonger said again. "I do believe there was talk she escaped, but where she went, I'm darned if I know."

Deciding he would not stop for food and drink until he had some good news, Captain Grenville kept on with his inquiries until once again he found someone who recognized Lila's description, though in an odd sort of way.

"New Farm!" shouted the man rather strangely in answer to his description of Lila. This time it was in a store piled high with merchandise of every description and the man was busy checking lists as goods were brought in and dumped on his floor.

"New Farm, that's where she'll be, I'll wager a guinea. The lad, George is his name, comes in here regular. Now about six months ago he asked for some lengths of cloth for 'Missie' to make dresses. Said his master—what's that nob's name now?—Fairbrother, Sir Roland Fairbrother. Well, he found this 'Missie' only that morning and the lad was impressed because she had hair 'like the setting sun' he said. Thought that was poetic like, for a savage."

"Have you ever seen the girl?" the captain demanded impatiently.

"No, never. But George has been buying, well, feminine sort of things ever since. Nice-smelling soap, buttons and bits of lace, a thimble and colored threads. Only two or three weeks ago he brought in a note asking for a length of white silk, but we only had cream so I sent that instead and three yards of satin ribbon to match."

"Have you still got the note?"

"No, Cap'n, but I do remember, those notes were always signed with the letter *L.*"

Joyfully, the captain left the store and found lodgings for the night. Then he visited Nick McCarthy's stables and hired a horse for first thing on the morrow.

The only thing to disturb his euphoria as he returned from the stables in the gray dusk was the sight of someone being buried in a corner of the makeshift graveyard reserved for criminals. The gravediggers laughed and joked as they roughly threw the sack-covered body into the hole. It did not seem humane for anyone to end his life so miserably that his poor, dead body was treated with such indignity and lack of respect.

There was a mourner, though. A young black boy, unseen by the gravediggers, watched the morbid scene from behind a bush. He was sobbing as though his heart would break.

When the wardress, a large, grim woman in a black dress covered with a stiff, white apron, entered the room, the women were supposed to stand to attention. In fact they rolled mutinously off their beds and stood in attitudes of defiance as a would-be employer was ushered in and walked round inspecting the inmates.

Usually a woman was chosen because of her strong arms or well-muscled legs, but often girls were picked for their charm and potential as a bedmate. A middle-aged man with a large, wet nose was brought in, and he inspected the girls with obscene delight, requesting that the overseer lift up the skirt of one and pinch the waist of another. He stopped before Lila, his protruding eyes glistening, and put out a hand to touch her. She spat full in his face.

"Pig!" she snarled. At this, the wardress stepped forward angrily and knocked her to the floor.

Looking affronted, the man passed on and chose a plump, happy-looking woman who declared in a strong Irish accent after he had departed that if he tried anything with her she would soon give him what for.

"Are you all right?"

The girl from the next bed helped Lila to her feet. In this place there was no suggestion of taunting the pretty, blond girl who someone said actually had a title. With her blue eyes hard and her mouth set in a grim line, Lila Fairbrother felt as tough and vicious as anyone there.

"Lilian," someone whispered urgently. "Wake up."

Lila opened her eyes cautiously.

"What is it?"

"Someone wants you. Go to the washroom next to the kitchen. The window in the last cubicle on the left is open and he is outside asking for you."

Dim lights burned in the gray corridors as Lila sped along and located the appropriate window.

"Who is it?" she asked in a low voice.

"Missie! George here. You get out and George take you 'way."

"George!"

Lila climbed onto the wooden shelf which held the bowls in which the women washed. In the moonlight she could just see his grief-stricken face. He was covered with dust, and tears had made shiny channels down his broad, flat cheeks. He sat in the front of the wagon, patting Neptune's rump, urging him to be quiet.

"I can't leave, George. There are bars on every window and the door is locked."

"Me go back to farm now with Mister R'land."

She was about to correct him when she noticed a still figure laid out on the wagon behind him, wrapped in a soil-stained sack.

"Roland!"

"Yes, Missie. George watch. George dig up just now. I bury Mister R'land under palm tree. Say to George many times, make sure me be dead under palm tree."

"Thank God, George. Look after the farm for Mister Roland too."

"No, Missie. Other people to go live on farm soon. Not want George. Me come back here for missie."

For the first time since her husband died, Lila felt tears flow as George took Roland back to his beloved farm.

Captain Grenville arrived at New Farm just after George had finished burying the body of his master in the garden. The boy had filled a bag with Lila's belongings and placed them in the cart, ready to leave, along with a box of fruit, when the captain rode up. He did not recognize the boy as being the one weeping in the dim cemetery the night before.

He looked so grand, thought George, so tall and kingly in his plain black clothes and white shirt, that he must be someone very important. George resented the authority which he held responsible for Roland's death. Why, only yesterday they had flatly refused to listen to his plea to bury him here. In fact they had told him never to return. He was not wanted anymore. They had put Missie in prison for no reason. This man looked as though he was likely to cause yet more trouble.

"Where is Sir Roland Fairbrother?" he demanded and George reckoned it would be wise to pretend total ignorance.

He shook his head and pretended he did not understand and the man muttered something irritably under his breath. This amused George, for would *he* understand George's language if it were spoken to him?

"I am looking for Miss Lilian Ward. Do you know where she is? Has she been living here?"

George stared at the ground and sighed. Every word the man said was clear to him, but he had no intention of getting

Missie into further trouble by telling this arrogant stranger where she was. Fortunately the man gave up trying to converse with such an ignorant savage and dismounting from his horse, began to investigate the farm.

Everything was locked, and although George had his own key tucked away in his shorts, he remained mute as the gentleman peered through all the windows. Lila and Roland had tidied everywhere before leaving to get married two days before. Drapes were drawn on the front windows to prevent the sun from scorching the lovely rugs and furniture.

With an agonized grunt, Phillip Grenville returned to his horse and was about to mount when he had a thought. Opening his saddle bag, he withdrew the dress, the torn red dress which Lila had worn that night in the Chinese Room at the reception for the Bohemian ambassador. The night when Phillip Grenville had known for sure that he loved her. He had taken it from the basement room in London, knowing how important it was to her. Tearing off a small square he handed it to George, though in his heart he felt sure it was a waste of time. This could not be the boy who spoke passable English that the shopkeeper had told him about.

Still, it was worth a try.

"Give to Missie," he ordered and George had no alternative but to take the square of silk offered to him.

Red stuff, the color of blood. No, he would not give to Missie, for he was sure it was bad and would upset her. Nevertheless, he put it carefully in the pocket of his shorts, just to please the gentleman.

When the wardress brought a tall, well-built man into the dormitory the following day, there was no chance for Lila to demonstrate how her awful disposition would make her an unwise choice. The man merely stood at the door, looked around the room at the slouching girls and whispered something to the woman who returned a few minutes later to inform Lila she was being sent to Mr. Holden's farm, fifty miles away to the north in an area called Toog'nah.

"Go to the kitchen and get your rations for the journey," she was told curtly. "One of the servants is to take you there by cart. Mr. Holden himself is staying in the port for a while."

At least she didn't have to walk, Lila thought with relief as she collected her few possessions. Most of her things were at

New Farm, which she assumed now belonged to her as Roland's sole heir. Some day she would ensure it was run in the way its creator had planned.

She took her bag of provisions to the side door where the vehicle waited for her, and there, holding the reins of the horse like some monstrous eagle, sat Queen Lil.

"Well, well!" her enemy chuckled. "If it isn't Miss Lilian Ward! Where did you disappear to on ship? I understand you acquired a protector who removed you from contamination from the likes of us."

"I acquired a husband," Lila told her coldly. "Though in fact I preferred death to you and your friends."

Having to travel with this dreadful person did not dismay her half as much as it once would have done. It was merely an unpleasantness she would have preferred not to undergo. After all, what could the woman do except use her dreadful tongue—and this she did for the many miles they traveled that day, bumping and jolting over the uneven track to Toog'nah.

Most of the time they stayed within sight of a river and Lila, having no intention of sitting beside the woman who never ceased to sneer and make fun of her downfall, inventing the most outrageous reasons for it, sat on the back watching the sparkling water and wondering what life had to offer on the Holden Farm.

Michael Brandreth, aide to the governor, composed his pale, plump face into what he hoped was a sympathetic smile.

"I am very sorry, Captain Grenville, but I have never heard of a Lilian Ward and do not recognize her description."

He offered the captain, who had a commission in the Prince of Wales' Own Light Dragoons no less, a glass of wine, which the man refused.

Brandreth had heard that only that very day Lila had been sent to some farm along the Hawkesbury River. Well, he wasn't going to tell *that* to this military busybody with a pardon from Prince George in his pocket. Michael Brandreth's career in the foreign office would go up in smoke if the woman were found and given a chance to tell of what he had tried to do to her in the washroom. Pretend ignorance, look helpful, be courteous, and hope and pray the man wouldn't track down Lilian Fairbrother before the *Northern Star* returned to England in a few weeks' time.

* * *

Outside the governor's office, Phillip Grenville felt like wringing his hands in despair. Everything seemed to be against him. How could Lila have arrived here and no one heard of her?

Was the girl at New Farm who signed her notes with an *L* really his Lila? He had never felt so frustrated in his life. He returned to his lodgings and tried to figure out where to turn next.

For once, help came to him rather than his having to seek it. The fishmonger, appreciative of the shilling he had been given yesterday, had discovered the whereabouts of the captain and called upon him.

"Captain, sir. Been a'looking for you all day. That young lady, the one sent off with Jacob Evans. I sees her this very afternoon, large as life."

"Where man, where?"

"If ye gives me me wind back, sir, I'll tell ye."

Captain Grenville released the man's shirt which he had grabbed without thinking.

"In a cart, Captain, sir. With big Queen Lil. Everyone knows Lil and I shouts to her, 'Where'ya going, Queenie, gal?' having recognized your young lady like and wanting to find out for your sake, and Queenie answers, 'To the Holden farm, fish-face.'"

"Bless you my man, and thank you."

The fishmonger was almost as chuffed at being blessed by a real captain as by being presented with a guinea, and went off happy as a lark, while Phillip Grenville left to seek advice on the whereabouts of the Holden farm, intending to travel there first thing on the morrow.

After some miles, Lila was surprised to notice a wagon following them some distance behind, until she joyfully realized it was George who had promised to come for her. She did not mention this to her companion.

The heat was unbearable, the journey slow. It was going to take three days and when darkness fell the frst night they stopped in the midst of a group of mountain ash trees. They had been provided with blankets and cooking utensils, and Queenie produced a fairly respectable stew followed by bitter tea without milk. The women ate in silence, then Lila retired to lie on the back of the cart while Queen Lil curled up at the foot of a tree.

Lila made no attempt to sleep. When she heard the snores of the big woman coming from under the tree, she slid off the cart and walked quietly back the way they had come, calling softly,

"George."

"Here is, Missie. He follow Missie."

"Did you bury Mister Roland, George? Is he safe now?"

"Yes, at home under palm tree."

"Thank God. Have you enough to eat?"

"Lots, lots fruit. Me take load from farm. You like, Missie?"

Lila felt indescribably sad as she ate the grapes plucked from the vine at the rear of New Farm. She was as comforted by George's presence as he was by hers. He was an orphan and used to white men's ways, unwilling to return to the life of a savage. She was all the family he had now. Her heart warmed to him even more when he handed her a drawstring laundry bag containing most of her clothes. He kept the piece of red silk the man had given him hidden in his pocket. He did not wish to worry Missie more than necessary.

"You sleep now, George. I'll go back to our camp."

"'Night, Missie."

She settled down on the cart feeling safe from danger with George nearby. After all, the last time she had slept in the vicinity of Queen Lil, her hair had been hacked off. In no time at all she drifted into sleep. She was rudely awakened by her shoulder being shaken violently, and she found George frantically staring down at her.

"Come, Missie. Come."

The sun was edging its way into the sky at the rim of the wide river, and everything was drenched in an eerie pink light.

George dragged her over to Queenie who lay, a still and silent lump under the tree. For one awful moment, Lila thought they'd been visited by savages again and Queen Lil would be headless or murdered in some other hideous manner, but as they approached, she could see the woman's body heaving as she took great breaths.

George pointed and at first Lila could see nothing, but then noticed a tiny snake slithering its way along the length of the sleeper, a mere six inches away from her body. Any second it would reach her outstretched arm.

"Me kill?" asked George picking up a huge rock and holding

it poised above the snake questioningly.

He did not know whether this woman was friend or foe, and if Lila preferred her to die, then he would let the snake do its deadly work.

Without a second thought, Lila shouted, "Kill!"

George brought the stone down onto the snake and smashed it.

Queen Lil woke up with a shout and reached for George but he was too nimble and leapt from her grasp.

"You perishin' savage," she shrieked. "You tried to kill me." She scrambled to her feet, stumbling over the stone beside her and revealing the crushed snake.

"Well! Bless me rotten soul. I'd be a goner if that'd given me a nip." She regarded George with a mixture of gratitude and astonishment.

"Who is he?" she asked Lila. "Where'd he come from?"

"This is George. He was my husband's servant and has attached himself to me—and I to him. He has nowhere to go."

"You saved me rotten life, George."

She turned to Lila in surprise.

"Why'd you let him? Would have thought you'd prefer me dead."

"Because I am a fool, I suppose," Lila retorted bitterly. Would she never learn? The same impetuosity that had caused her to rush out to Princess Caroline with her robe had allowed her to shout to George. All the tragedies of the past eighteen months had not taught her any lessons.

It would have not been her fault if her companion now lay dead of a snake bite, and whatever lay in store at Toog'nah would not be helped by Queenie being there.

"Come on," the woman was saying in a cheerful voice, "let's have a cup of tea and some breakfast. That fright's given me a fair appetite."

She gathered fuel for a fire and George went to get his wagon. To Lila's surprise, Queen Lil and the black boy got on like a house on fire. She ribbed him and joked with him until he began to look like his old, happy self.

To Queenie's uncomplicated mind Lila was now a friend, and from that moment on, her attitude changed so completely that it was hard to believe they had ever been enemies. Lila still felt animosity towards her, but this was difficult to maintain before such relentless friendliness. She prattled, gossiped, reminisced, asking for Lila's opinion on this and that, so that as the day progressed, Lila found herself answering, initially against her will, but eventually capitulating totally, and by afternoon they were chattering away like lifelong friends.

Life in the Holden household was better than in some places, worse than others, Queenie said. She'd worked in two other establishments since her arrival. In the governor's mansion she'd been employed as a cook which she was quite good at, but she became bored with the stuffy atmosphere so she burnt everything until they got rid of her. She was then sent to Parrametta to work in a small factory just opened in which she had to pick, spin and card wool, but the food was insufficient for her needs, and she deliberately began to make so many mistakes and waste so much material that she was soon shown the door by the overseer, whereupon she was assigned to the Holdens and at least had enough to eat, though the work was hard.

"Old Ma Holden keeps a strict eye on the girls, mainly because her husband will get his hands on 'em if she don't," she said. "But the chief cause of trouble there is Jim Smith, the overseer. The Marquis de Sade is a kindly angel compared to him."

"The Marquis de Sade?" queried Lila.

"Cor, gal, don't you know nothing? That French nob who gets a kick from torturing people. He's even written books about it. Enjoys it better than going to bed with a dozen women."

"How very strange," murmured Lila thinking there were never such odd people in Yorkshire, but this flattering view of her home county was given short shrift when Queenie said, "He comes from Yorkshire, same as you an' me."

"Who does?"

"Jim Smith, a'course. Right evil little monkey. Gives the men a rare old time, he does."

Time passed by quite enjoyably. Lil, her three chins wobbling, her hooded eyes disappearing completely into the sunken wrinkles of her face, laughed uproariously at George's antics as he did his utmost to impress and amuse his new friend.

The countryside improved as the large, shady trees became less sparse, and at times were so close they joined together overhead forming leafy tunnels. The river was always within sight on their right-hand side. Queenie explained that they had to travel in a big semicircle, sticking as close to the Hawkesbury as they could, as it was her only guide.

"Jim Smith is an ex-convict," she told Lila later on. "His sentence expired in ninety-four. Seven years for extortion he'd got, but many a murder he's committed in Hull where he was well known for his violence. For all their Christian principles, the Holdens know quite well what Jim's like, but they've made him overseer to the men. The work get's done and that's all they care about."

Lila hoped she would not have much to do with Jim Smith, and asked what her duties were to be at the farm.

"You're to help in the kitchen. They sent old Kitty Pegg back to Sydney Cove. She was so sick and weak she couldn't carry a pot and dropped all Sunday's dinner the other week."

That night Lila relished what she thought might well be her last night of freedom for some time. She lay on the cart, Queen Lil under a tree nearby and George in the wagon behind, staring at the blue-black sky with its spangles of stars and reflecting on how much more enjoyable it was to see stars, the moon, the sun, sky, clouds—all these miraculous things—when you were free. How long would it be, she wondered sadly, before she would be independent again? Able to enjoy all the world had to offer.

"There's summat wrong!"

Queen Lil sniffed as they approached the Holden farm. "It's siesta time, so everyone's abed, but I can still smell trouble."

The farm was a long, low building constructed of stout, bleached wood, but no effort had been made to make it attractive. Not a flower bloomed anywhere and all the trees near the house had been felled, leaving it bare and unshadowed. Behind stretched long cowsheds and barns where there were no signs of life. Compared to picturesque New Farm, it was a barren scene.

George had left to camp on the river bank.

"I reckon there's someone in the hole," Queenie said. "That'll be Jim Smith's work."

They drove up to the house and Lil tethered the horse.

"I'm right," she said. "See! There's the hole and there's a rock on the cover. Some poor soul's down there."

She indicated the sparsely grassed patch behind the house, in the center of which was a circular piece of wood, not much more than a yard in diameter, on top of which rested a large boulder. There was no shelter nearby, so the rays of the scorching sun, particularly hot now at midday, would burn mercilessly down from dawn to dusk.

"You mean there's someone down there?" Lila asked incredulously. "It must be like an oven. What can they have done to deserve that?"

"Not much, I reckon. It's Jim's favorite punishment. You can always sense if someone's down there. It's as if their suffering spreads and draws everyone in to suffer with them. How can you go about your business and have a laugh and a joke when some creature's being burnt alive."

Lila jumped off the wagon and strode purposefully towards the hole.

"Where are you going? Jim'll kill you." Queenie's voice was strangely hoarse with fright.

Lila knew exactly what she was doing. This was not the oft-regretted impetuosity, but outrage to think one human being had such power over another to cause such intense misery. She imagined how Phillip Grenville would act if he arrived here and found this torture in progress, or Timothy, or Roland. Even little Miss Prymm would surely do what she was doing now.

She was surprised that Queen Lil was so cowed by this Jim Smith, but then Lila had never met him, and it was easier to be brave when one had never come face to face with the enemy. Pressing her foot against the boulder, she managed to roll it off the wooden lid which she lifted to reveal the tormented man within.

Despite the uffocating, scalding steam which rose from the hole as if a fire was lit there, the man shivered uncontrollably. Every inch of his naked body was blood red and he was covered with sweat. His head was bent, and at first he did not seem to be aware of the daylight shining on him or the slight cooling of the air, but after Lila had spoken softly to him a few times, he opened his eyes, and to her horror, the whites were as violently red as his body.

She held down her hand to help him out, but he was too weak to move his arm.

Queen Lil came up, grumbling good-naturedly.

"I've managed to stay on the right side of Jim Smith ever since I came. Now you've put the cat in the pigeons. He'll have it in for both of us when he finds out what's been done. If there's one thing he likes more than putting someone down the hole, it's getting them out again and seein' them in this state or worse."

She leaned down and put her massive hands underneath the man's armpits, lifting him out of the hell pit as if he were a baby. Then cradling him in her arms, she carried him towards one of the crude wooden huts some distance away, with Lila following.

Inside Queenie laid the man on a low bed and covered him with a coarse sheet, while Lila fetched a pail of lukewarm water from just inside the door. Dipping her handkerchief into this, she bathed the man's forehead.

"It's one of the politicals," Queen Lil said. "Marcus Brady. There's three here and Jim really has it in for them. One's already at death's door, coughs blood all day long, but that don't stop Jim making him work in the fields."

Marcus Brady had recovered consciousness and eagerly gulped the water offered him. He ceased to shiver and before their eyes his skin and the whites of his eyes faded to pink, and he even managed a smile in their direction.

"What did you do, Marcus, me boy, to deserve incarceration down the hole again. That's the second time in a month, if I'm not mistaken."

"You're not, Queenie," the man wheezed, his voice seeming to come from a long way off. "This time I deserved it though. I managed a good punch on Scragg's jaw and the bruises on Jenkins' shins won't fade for many a week."

His voice had a soft Scottish lilt.

Queen Lil explained, "Jim Smith's got two protectors, Scragg and Jenkins. Enormous oafs who go with him everywhere, else he'd have had a knife in his back long ago."

"They were tormenting Charlie. Forcing him to eat when he was so sick he couldn't keep down a mouthful, so I set about them this morning during breakfast."

"You've been down that hole since breakfast?" gasped Lila.

"From just after five o'clock, miss," said Brady. His features were so distorted and puffed it was difficult to make out his age. "It wasn't so hot then, it was fair boiling when you got me out."

Suddenly he looked disturbed.

"Why get me out anyway? When Jim comes back, he'll skin you both alive."

"That thought had struck me too," Queenie said ruefully.

"I guess it's about time I took him on, Scragg and Jenkins too, though it fair scuppers me to think it's taken a slip of a girl to make me do it."

Lila was seething with indignation.

"You could have died down there. What time would this Jim Smith have got you out?"

"He might be back any time," wheezed Brady. "The men rest from one till three but whether they come back to the hut or not depends on how far away they are. If they're more than a mile or so off, they lie where they are till the sun cools. Anyway, miss, getting Charlie Duncan, Ian Campbell and yours truly dead is what Jim is aiming at."

"Come off it, Marcus. He's a fiend, to be sure, but he don't want you all dead," said Queen Lil scornfully.

"Believe me, Queenie, that's the certain truth. You know what we're here for? Sedition. Charlie and me, we formed a group in Edinburgh called the Society for Reform. We just wanted a fairer deal for the people. Better wages, better working conditions. Ian Campbell advocated parliamentary change and said so openly. He thought folks ought to be represented in government, not that seats should be bought up by the rich for their own advantage. Too many people had come round to our way of thinking. Putting us in a Scottish prison, we'd just be a constant reminder to everyone of what was wrong and it wouldn't stop us communicating with our friends, so they quietly deported us. Now they find we're doing the same thing here, speaking out against the rotten system, the corruption, and the inequality."

Brady coughed, exhausted from the effort of this long speech, and Lila wished he would rest, but his voice became stronger and he went on.

"This country is becoming worse than home. Do you know only a select few, the officers of both army and navy, are allowed to board ships when they dock, and there they buy up all the imports at the cheapest possible price. No competition is allowed. The cloth, the utensils, the food, the spirits. They make a profit on it all, but most of all the spirits, the rum. Ten shillings a gallon they pay for it and sell it for twenty-four and more if a man's desperate."

"Come on, Marcus," said Queen Lil as gently as her raucous voice would allow. "Shut your cakehole, shut your eyes and get your strength back."

But the man was too worked up to notice her. He turned to Lila.

"The government store where they buy in all the home-grown produce pay a pittance to the convict farmers, so it's not worth a man's while to slave all year round. Then they sell it at a monstrous profit, lining their own pockets at the expense of the poor farmer. *He's* not allowed to sell his own crops at a fair price. It's a crying shame the way greed has corrupted this new, fresh land so quickly."

"Please rest," pleaded Lila, dabbing at the man's forehead where beads of perspiration had reappeared, but he ignored her.

"They can't kill us outright," he said passionately. "Even from here news would get back home and there'd be riots on the streets of Scotland once it were known. So they're killing us slowly instead. Charlie's not got long to go anyway. Nearly rotten with the consumption he is and the journey over did him no good. I was a fit man when I arrived, but I've spent so much time down the hole it's beginning to tell on me. Soon Charlie'll be dead and when I've gone they'll start on Ian."

"But why give them cause to punish you so?" Lila asked reasonably.

"Ah, miss! You don't know what they do to ire a man. Wait'll you see Charlie. The blood fair flows from his throat sometimes. Could you stand by and watch your dying friend refused a mug of water because he won't go down on his knees and beg to Jim Smith for it? Would you let three bullies take your sick friend's Bible and watch them tear the pages out, slowly, slowly, one by one, crumpling them up and trying to make him *eat* them? Could you see that and do nothing, miss?"

"No, I couldn't, Marcus," Lila said frankly. "I hope I would have the courage to act as you have."

"Lila, go into the kitchen," broke in Queen Lil. "There you'll find a pan of stew simmering on the range. Bring some of the gravy in a bowl for this Scotich ninny, and whilst you're gone, I'll get some clothes on his rotten body. He'll be embarrassed if I do it in front of you, but it won't bother him if Queenie sees him in all his glory."

Outside, the silence took over. The farm could have been uninhabited it was so dead. Even the animals made no noise, no doubt stupefied by the sweltering sun. Lila entered the kitchen where a large black range with an open fire burned away, and stopped dead, encountering a wall of heat. Cautiously she approached the cauldron of stew, recalling the refreshing cold meals of fruit and vegetables washed down with cool wine at New Farm. After only a couple of minutes her body was soaked in perspiration.

Mrs. Holden clearly intended to run her household in New South Wales exactly as she had done in England, making no allowance for the different climate. Lila was apparently expected to work in this oven all day, preparing broths and stews and no doubt suet puddings and fried breakfasts. No wonder poor old Kitty Pegg had dropped the Sunday dinner. She'd probably done it on purpose, like Lil.

Lila found an iron cup and ladled gravy from the great black pot. It smelled greasy and unappetizing but nevertheless might do Marcus Brady some good. She carried it swiftly back to the hut to find him dressed in serge trousers and a striped shirt, far too thick for the weather, but few people seemed to wear light clothing and dressed as if it were an English summer.

He was beginning to look comparatively normal. The puffiness of his features had subsided and revealed a craggy, well-formed face with a large, friendly mouth and a shock of rust-red hair beginning to dry into crisp curls. He managed another smile as Lila knelt beside him with the broth, and made a face at the first spoonful.

"No complainin' now," warned Queen Lil. "There's goodness in it, which'll build you up."

"Ready for going down the hole another day," the man murmured with a wry grin. "In fact, I've got an idea. I'll get back down there in a minute so there'll be nothing amiss when the boys get back. Otherwise, Jim'll go berserk and you'll both be in trouble, even though he's not in charge o' the women. He's got authority here. It'll be satisfaction enough for me to get out of the hole under me own steam and not have to be dragged out by Jim or his henchmen. He'll begin to think I'm getting used to it and—"

"And think of summat worse," Queen Lil interrupted in an ominous voice. "Anyway, it's too late. Here's the men back now."

She was staring through the window, and Lila ran to join her. A group of weary, badly dressed men, some carrying spades and tools, others dragging carts laden with vegetables, came toward the farm. On all their faces were expressions of sheer hopelessness. Several yards in front of them came three healthier looking individuals, two of them huge, well over six feet tall, the third much smaller by seven or eight inches.

Queen Lil followed her gaze.

"That's the notorious Jim Smith," she said. "Looks more like the angel Gabriel than Satan, don't he?"

Indeed, Jim Smith had a shock of fair, golden curls and a pink and white choirboy complexion. From this distance he looked as if he wouldn't harm a fly. As they came nearer, Lila could see wicked lines etched into the soft skin of the foreman's face. Lines stretched from his nostrils down to the corners of his mouth giving the man a permanent sneer.

The three men were joking and laughing together and had virtually reached the hole before noticing it was empty. Smith uttered a cry and came bounding toward the hut where Marcus Brady lay. Despite their obvious fatigue, the laborers hurried after him, anxious to discover the reason for this strange happening.

The door was flung open and Jim Smith bounded angrily in, followed by the two louts who protected him, surprise on their faces.

Lila moved quickly to the foot of Brady's bed as Jim approached and she bobbed a neat curtsy, saying, "Good afternoon, sir. I am Lilian Fairbrother, just arrived at this establishment and come from Yorkshire, which I understand is the home county of your good self."

She smiled prettily into the foreman's stupefied face.

"Imagine, sir, when I drove into the farm I found this gentleman imprisoned in the ground over there, so I prevailed upon my good friend Queenie to help rescue him."

The other men had gathered round and even though they were so exhausted they could scarcely stand, they watched this performance with unaccustomed smiles on their weary faces.

"Who do you think, sir, could be so unchristian, so cruel and vindictive, to incarcerate another human being in a living grave like that?"

Lila's eyes began to sparkle with real anger. At the same time Jim Smith recovered from the shock of finding his prisoner removed and being cared for by a little golden-haired firebrand. She was making a mockery of him. His lips curled and the lines in his face deepened. He stepped forward ominously, but Lila held her ground and stared him in the eyes, declaring loudly, "I am not sure the authorities in Sydney would approve of the workmen being treated so badly, after being brought over to this country at such expense to the taxpayer. Perhaps someone ought to inform the governor himself of this ill treatment."

There was a gasp from the audience, and Jim Smith wondered wildly how to react to this unexpected development. Lila sensed his bewilderment, and not wishing to antagonize him too greatly, for it would only backfire on the men, decided to let things lie for a while.

"I am apparently to work in the kitchen here," she announced, "so I shall go there immediately and raise some refreshment for these gentlemen."

Flashing a brilliant smile at the gaping faces, she left the hut and sped across the yard to the kitchen. All was still silent in the farmhouse. It seemed that Mrs. Holden and her female staff took their siestas seriously.

Lila had no idea if the food in the cauldron was for the men's midday meal or not. She intended to use it anyway, and would prepare something else for the evening if she had done wrong. The men looked seriously undernourished anyway, and she didn't care if she got into trouble.

She was looking for receptacles for the meal when a sound at the kitchen door made her look up. Jim Smith stood there, his eyes smoldering with a rage that made her blood curdle. He didn't speak.

Lila could not stand the awful silence, and said chattily, "I do declare there is not a dish to be found. I daresay soon this kitchen will be as familiar to me as the back of my hand, but—"

"Shut your mouth!"

The voice was like a rip in cloth. She shuddered but carried on searching, opening and shutting doors, feeling as if she was taking part in a charade and must concentrate on her part.

"Here we are."

She discovered a stack of wooden bowls in a closet beside the range, placed them on the scrubbed table and began taking them one at a time to the cauldron of stew to fill.

"You're trouble, girl. I can tell that. Trouble, that's what you be."

It was a monotonous voice, without any expression, yet the

lack of passion made the words sound far more poisonous than ranting and raving.

"I don't want trouble on this farm. It runs smooth now, just as I like it. Just as Mr. Holden likes it."

"But not the way the men like it," Lila said with false brightness. "Or don't they matter?"

Eyes screwed to hateful slits, Jim Smith said, "I'm not arguing or discussing things with you, girl. I'll teach you a lesson here and now, so you won't ever interfere in my business again. You do one more thing like you done for Marcus Brady and you'll get more of this."

Lila's eyes were lowered deliberately, ignoring him, concentrating on the food, but when she glanced up her stomach twisted convulsively for Jim Smith approached her, a long, evil-looking knife in his hand.

"Don't worry, girl. I'm not going to kill you. Just give you my mark on your cheek, as a warning like."

He glided forward, the blade flashing like lightning in the dazzling sun and when he reached the table stretched out his arm towards Lila's face slowly, breathing heavily.

Without hesitation, she flung a bowl of boiling stew into his face.

He screamed in agony and fell back, screaming again when one arm touched the glowing coals of the kitchen range.

Instantly the dry cotton of his shirt burst into flames, and before Lila's horrified eyes, the flame spread up his arm, enveloping his shoulders, swiftly engulfing his entire body and immediately the smell of burning flesh was raw in her nostrils. The man writhed in shrieking agony, a human torch. He knocked over a chair containing clean laundry which also caught fire and in no time the chair itself was ablaze, and then the wooden floor beneath it. Then Lila began to scream too.

Queen Lil and the farmworkers, already alerted by Smith's roars of pain, dragged her from the room.

"Throw water on him!" she yelled to Marcus Brady, for Smith still jerked like a demon on the floor. "Put out the fire."

Marcus shook his head.

"T'would be a cruelty to save him. Let him suffer a few more seconds agony rather than a lifetime of it, for it would be far worse than anything he's ever inflicted on a man."

The other men were making efforts to suppress the fire in

the kitchen without much success. The dry wood was like tinder and burned fiercely.

A drum of water outside the door was soon used up without having any effect, and eventually someone shouted to raise Mrs. Holden and the other women before the entire building went up in flames. The three women eventually emerged, disheveled and hysterical.

"Pity there's no water left to throw over her," Queen Lil said as the farmer's wife danced around shrieking for someone to do something.

But there was nothing to be done except to save a few treasures. A piano, ornaments and some trunks of clothes were dragged from the flames. Mrs. Holden recovered sufficiently to fetch her jewelry casket which she clutched pathetically to her bosom while watching her home burn to ashes.

Eventually the entire building became an inferno and parts began to crash to the ground. The three women were taken to one of the men's huts to recover their senses, but the farm laborers remained, not minding the heat, reveling in their oppressor's misfortune.

It was then that George arrived, attracted by the smoke rising into the cloudless blue of the sky. He was relieved to find Lila alive and well.

Scragg and Jenkins, Jim Smith's henchmen, had quietly disappeared in the cart Queen Lil and Lila had arrived on.

Marcus Brady took Lila over to meet his two Scottish compatriots, Charlie Duncan, a painfully thin person whose smile momentarily blotted out the expression of real suffering on his face, and Ian Campbell, a broad ruddy-faced man whose accent was so strong his speech was scarcely comprehensible to Lila. The other men crowded around, shaking her hand as if she were a heroine and not a murdress.

In the background the last of the building collapsed, throwing up a shower of sparks, and Lila wondered aloud what was to do now.

"I have killed a man, albeit in self-defense," she said with awe. "An overseer, employed by the government. What will become of me, I wonder? Will they hang me?"

"We will hide the body or what remains of it when the heat allows us near," said Charlie Duncan. "And say he just disappeared."

"But there's Scragg and Jenkins to think of," put in Queen

Lil. "They know what happened and will be telling their tale in Sydney before long."

In a grave voice, Marcus Brady said, "Self-defense or not, I don't trust the authorities to act fair by Miss Lilian. What sort of witnesses are we to stand by her? We are convicts all."

Panic began to mount in Lila's breast as she imagined herself being sentenced to death for Jim Smith's murder, or even worse, committed to lifelong imprisonment in New South Wales. Justice seemed the last thought in the minds of many of the people appointed to administer it.

"I must run away," she murmured aloud. "But where to?"

The surrounding oceans were the prison bars of this great land. There was nowhere to escape to. Apart from the tiny piece of civilization established at Sydney Cove, the remainder was a barren wilderness.

At this point George intervened. "White men that way," he said, having understood Lila's dilemma. He waved to the north, and the laborers who had scarcely noticed his arrival in the recent turmoil turned to question him, intrigued by the savage who spoke English.

Lila explained who he was, and George, still vague, insisted there were white men in the direction he pointed.

"But how do you know, ye little heathen?" Queenie snorted, and George giggled and said word had reached him at this camp on the river bank.

"Many days' walk, but George take you, Missie," he said hopefully, and Lila declared that she would rather take her chances with George than with British justice.

The men expressed their doubts about such a course, eyeing George with suspicion, except for the three Scotsmen who urged her on.

"Ye don't stand a chance once they know you're connected with us," said Marcus Brady. Charlie Duncan, coughing so much it was painful to hear, seconded this.

"The Dutch reached this land afore the English," he added. "No one can say for sure it isn't inhabited elsewhere. Good luck to you, Miss Lilian, and write to us from England."

"I was going to say 'I'll go and pack me bag,' but I forgot me bag and everything to put in it, had gone up in smoke," said Queen Lil. "So I'll come as I am."

"No!" Lila was horrified. "There is no obligation on anyone's part to accompany me. If you do, you are implicating yourself in my crime. I must go alone."

"Bless you, gal, I want to stick by you. Life's more exciting when you're around. I was getting bored here anyhow."

Queenie strode towards George's wagon and patted Neptune on her shining flanks.

"Come on, ye little black snake-crusher, and let's travel into the unknown. And you, Lila Ward, or whatever your rotten name is nowadays, let's be off."

Chapter Thirteen

Captain Grenville did not depart for the Holden farm the following morning as he had planned. He discovered that Holden was still in Sydney Cove and intended to leave for home the next day.

"Yes, I hired a girl at the women's prison. Can't remember her name, no. Lilian rings a bell though, but not Ward," the man said. "Old Kitty got past it and we wanted a new girl in the kitchen. I just saw a girl who looked capable and said I'd take her."

This was not strictly true, for Mr. Holden had picked out the prettiest face in the room in the hope that he might get more than just help in the kitchen.

Although peeved at the idea of losing his new servant before she'd even started work, he suggested that the captain accompany him to the farm on the morrow.

"Directions are mighty difficult to give, Captain," he said.

"For there's no trodden path, only landmarks which I follow without hardly being aware of them."

Although reluctant to wait a day, even an hour, longer than necessary, Phillip saw the sense in waiting to travel with Farmer Holden and resigned himself to another night in Sydney Cove.

The captain would have found Alan Holden a boring companion, if they had been traveling slow enough to allow conversation. Relentlessly he urged the farmer on over the dry turf, through tall forests, quite oblivious to his surroundings.

As he galloped crisply over the yellow grass, the captain grew more sure that Queen Lil was the name of the kidnapper Lila had encountered in Blackfriars the night she had decided to go for a short walk. He smiled, remembering their coach journey home from Isabella's House of Sin where he had so surprisingly found Miss Lilian Ward. How embarrassed she had been, deeply resenting his assumption that he had a right to demand an explanation from her.

She was so proud and stubborn that he could not imagine her knuckling down to kitchen work and taking orders from people like Holden. He wondered what her position had been at New Farm.

Behind, the perspiring farmer wished he could bring himself to be a bit firmer with this imperious, military gentleman and refuse to allow himself to be hurried along in this way.

This resentment was suddenly swept aside by alarm, and he shouted, "Smoke! From the farm!"

There was no need for the captain to make the man hurry then, and they arrived at the smoldering remnants of the Holden residence half an hour later.

Phillip's recent conclusions on Lila's character were proved right when Mrs. Holden, her face blackened with soot, her servants wailing behind her, told of a girl who looked as if butter wouldn't melt in her mouth, who had ridden up, released one of the Scottish anarchists from the hole, murdered their foreman Jim Smith, and then set fire to the house.

"Where is she?" demanded both Captain Phillips and Farmer Holden, though for entirely different reasons and in entirely different voices.

"Gone off with that criminal, Queen Lil," screamed the enraged Mrs. Holden, "and a horrible little black savage!"

* * *

Killing a man was not an easy thing to live with, Lila discovered that night. She lay hunched in a ball, trembling, in the back of the wagon, recalling the afternoon's happenings. At one time she fell asleep and woke screaming, certain her hands were wet with blood from her slashed face. It was only perspiration. Then she twisted her head from side to side, desperately trying to rid herself of the smell of burning flesh.

Queen Lil dabbed her forehead with a wet cloth, but none too sympathetically.

"You'll come through," she said confidently. "Got a constitution like a horse. By hook or by crook, you'll be back in England living the life of Riley in no time at all, or my name's not Lilian Rawlesbury."

"There, there," said George comfortingly, looking down at Lila protectively.

Next morning she had recovered sufficiently to eat some of the fruit George had brought from New Farm, and in fact, despite the intense heat the small company took on a carnival atmosphere. Queen Lil sang several indecent songs which George pleaded to be taught. Lila hoped he did not ask for an explanation of the more obscene lines.

They were now traveling back along the far side of the Hawkesbury River in the direction of the coast and would reach the ocean some twenty or thirty miles up from Sydney Cove, as Queenie reckoned.

"How far are these flamin' white men?" she asked George, who shrugged his shoulders.

"Come in big, golden ships," he told them, wide-eyed. "Camp in palaces near water."

"Hope it's not some perishin' folklore," grumbled Queenie, her chins wobbling ominously. "And the white men arrived two hundred years ago. I'll skin this little black heathen alive if we don't find 'em."

George just grinned and repeated his previous statement.

"Anyway," Queenie went on gloomily. "Just because they're white doesn't mean they're civilized."

These dismal observations did not detract from the big woman's general cheerfulness, and after some doleful prediction that they might well be burnt as sacrifices or eaten alive, she would burst into song or tell a string of ribald puns which at first Lila tried not to laugh at. After all, she was a well brought up young lady, but eventually she couldn't resist the coarse humor, and shrieked with laughter at the gutter wit.

"You're an odd 'un," Queenie said slyly, glancing at her golden-haired companion. "I've heard of your father, William Ward, and he's a right dull cove, if you don't mind me saying so. How did he get a daughter so full o'spirit as yerself? Going round killing people, getting married like nobody's business, being deported? You're a right one, and no mistake."

"I have Medici blood in me," Lila said proudly and for the first time in her life she told someone about her mother and her relationship with King Louis XV of France. "I don't know how much, but there's a strain."

Queen Lil was not the least impressed.

"I wouldn't boast about being related to *that* lot," she said disparagingly. "Crowd of flamin' murderers, weren't they?"

"Well," Lila said flatly, "so am I."

Queenie roared with laughter.

"So you are." She slapped Lila heartily on the back so that she nearly fell forward onto Neptune.

"How have you heard of my father?" she asked curiously, for she couldn't imagine Queenie reading much or having an interest in politics. Sir William Ward was not exactly a national celebrity.

"Read the *Times,* don't I?" The hooked nose sniffed disdainfully. "Got to keep up with the antics of me darlin' brother."

"Is it true, Queenie? You said the first night we met in Blackfriars that Lord Guy was your brother. Is it really true?"

"True as I'm sitting here with a murderin' Medici and a little black savage," Queen Lil said with a huge grin, displaying her yellow stumps set in pallid gums.

"Then why do you live the way you do?" asked Lila. "First Blackfriars, now here?"

"I'm here for swiping a sheep's brain off a meat stall in Charing Cross, 'cuz Alf and me was hungry fit to burst. Blackfriars, well . . ." She paused for a moment, then said, "I'm no oil painting, am I?"

Not wishing to be rude, Lila stammered, "An artist can paint anyone."

This caused the three chins to wobble frantically as Queenie roared with laughter yet again.

"Well said. But I mean, I'm not exactly a beauty—no, there's no need to argue." She waved her hand dismissively as Lila opened her mouth. "I've seen myself in enough mirrors to know I'm enough to give little uns nightmares, but it don't bother me none. I'm not a sensitive soul and I don't give a flamin' fig that I'm no Cleopatra. In fact Anthony was probably better lookin' than yours truly."

Lila had once again opened her mouth to argue.

"Shurrup," she was told. "I must have been a throwback or summat. All the socializing, parties, politicking, made me sick. They didn't know what to do with me at home. I didn't know what to do with them. So, when I was no more than thirteen I ran off with a stable boy. He was the only person on the whole estate taller than me. A'course he hoped to line his pockets, attaching himself to the gentry, but me family wanted none of me and I wanted none of them. I got rid of the boy and in no time at all found myself in Blackfriars where no one gave a hang what I looked like. Indeed, there were worse than me. Believe it or not, gal, I lived there happily ever after. Me nose grew longer, me chin increased threefold, and me teeth fell out like confetti. But I never had a day in thirty years that wasn't happy in that rotten hole. I've been hungry, been cold, but allus happy. Just like I'm happy now," and she burst into vulgar song to prove it.

It was strange, but the longer one were with Queen Lil the less one noticed her appearance. After a while her monstrous features ceased to matter. She was far more entertaining than Sylvia, for instance, who'd been as pretty as a picture.

"Anyway, what trick did me dear brother play on your good self, Medici?" asked Queenie. "If you've had anything to do with him, he's bound to have done you down."

So once again Lila told her tale and Queen Lil interrupted with disgusted snorts when she described the marquess of Rawlesbury's behavior and Ralph's attack on her.

"Never met my nephew, not proper like. But I've seen him driving round with brother Guy. Insipid-looking worm he seemed."

Lila did not say she'd once considered Ralph incredibly handsome. She went on with her story until she came to being in the hold of the ship and finding her hair cut off.

"It was the girl in the next bed what done it," said Queenie. "She hated you, kept praying on that rosary you'd die."

Shuddering, Lila continued, telling Queenie about Roland. Her voice throbbed with emotion as she described his upbringing and his awful death.

"Timothy dying was sadder, in a way. He was so young and full of life, but at least he'd been happy. Roland's entire existence until he came to New South Wales had been a nightmare."

"I've heard of Fanny Fairbrother," said Queen Lil. "Fact, she and her cronies sometimes came to Blackfriars for specialized entertainment."

Through gritted teeth Lila said, "When I get back to England, I'd like to kill that woman."

"You should find that easy," Queenie said with a grin. "Now as you've had a bit of practice," and despite herself, Lila found she was grinning back.

They reached the ocean in three days. It stretched out before them blue and sparkling, curls of foam rippling onto the golden sands.

"This is my idea of flamin' paradise," said Queen Lil as the three of them paddled in the warm, refreshing sea, splashing their boiling faces and arms.

But as they traveled further, life began to feel a little less utopian. Several days later all the fruit George had brought was gone. As they had no large receptacles for water, each day's supply depended on whether George was able to locate a stream in the vicinity to fill their small wooden bowls. So far they had been fortunate, but a day came when none was to be found.

The trees thinned out, allowing the sun to beat down relentlessly. Only George remained unaffected by its scorching rays.

"A'course, we're getting nearer the flamin' equator," snarled Queen Lil, shaking her fist at the blazing orange ball.

"Maybe George will find water tomorrow," said Lila hopefully, her throat swollen, her voice cracked and hoarse.

But the next day George disappeared for hours and came back looking desolate.

"We go quicker. Find white men," he urged them, and the following day the two women lay on the wagon while he coaxed the thirsty Neptune into an unwilling trot.

That night Lila tossed and turned, her limbs on fire. This was retribution, she felt, for the death of Jim Smith. She tried to soothe herself with visions of Grassbrook Hall covered in snow, of walking through fine April rain, recalling old Thomas the gardener bringing pail after pail of water up from the well in the yard and carrying it into the washhouse where she would sometimes dip a cup into the smooth mirror of water and drink...drink...

"'Ere! Watcha moanin' for?" Queen Lil shouted from under her tree. "Woke me up, you did."

"I'm thirsty and I'm moaning for a drink," snapped Lila.

"Know what?" Queenie said, her voice husky with longing. "I was just dreaming about knockin' back a pint o'porter in Red Jock's bar. Imagining it, thick and strong, taking a mouthful, swishing it round and round me mouth like, then swallowing it. Never appreciated me porter when I had it."

"Nor I Mama's homemade lemonade. Tart and stinging."

"Or a cuppa strong tea you could stand the spoon up in."

"Cool wine that makes your throat tingle."

"Red biddy that knocks you unconscious."

They both laughed uproariously and after a minute or two, Queen Lil said, "Y'know, Lila Ward-Bateson-Fairbrother, if I was going to die of thirst and starvation in an unknown, foreign land, can't think of many people I'd sooner do it with than you, gal. You've got spunk, you really have. No moanin' from you."

"You just accused me of waking you up because I was moaning."

"Come orf it. You knows what I mean," Queenie snorted. "Don't count that sort. I mean wide awake, complainin'sort of moanin'."

"I know, Queenie. And the same goes for me. I'm sure you'd make me laugh if I was on my deathbed."

"Well, let's hope I don't have the opportunity," Queen Lil croaked ominously. "If that little heathen don't find some flamin' water, I'll skin him alive and drink his black blood."

Next day when the sun was at its height and the two women were groaning from every jolt of the wagon, George unhitched Neptune and said, "Me go fast alone and find water."

"And what'll ye bring it back in, ye little savage?" gasped Queen Lil.

"Find friends, other black heathens like George. Find something. Trust George."

He galloped away on the weary horse.

"I suppose that's the last we'll see of him," said Queenie scathingly, and dismissed Lila's indignant responses by saying, "Don't mind me. I just don't feel like seeing good in anybody."

It seemed to Lila that they lay for days half under the wagon, dragging themselves to the sea to bathe their baking skin from time to time. Later George said it was less than twenty-four hours, and when he did arrive Queen Lil saw him first and shrieked at Lila.

"Hell's bells! He's brought a crowd of white savages with him," and Lila saw approaching through a mist what appeared to be an array of bright, shining knights on horses resplendently decorated with jeweled harnesses and bright plumes, before she fainted in sheer relief only seconds before her friend. Theretofore, she never knew the giant woman was capable of such a feminine weakness.

Through half-closed eyes, Lila watched the huge Negro who was busy with his back to her. The canvas of the tent was bright green so the interior glowed like the inside of a great emerald. Stiff, pastel-colored paper shapes hung on threads from the roof. A hanging moon, stars, and flowers moved constantly, making a soothing swishing noise and creating a cool draft. Over a massive, brassbound trunk was thrown a black brocade dressing gown embroidered with silver thread and lined with fine gray silk. The four-poster bed on which she lay had white, gauzy curtains pulled back and tied with great gold cords. The silk sheets of the palest lemon felt beautifully cool against her skin.

As Lila began to emerge from her dreamlike state she became aware of the throbbing in her throat and realized how much she longed for a drink of water. The Negro, who was busy doing something on top of an ebony cabinet, his naked back shimmering like satin, didn't realize she had awoken. She opened her mouth to call him. For several seconds no sound would come and she thought she had lost the power of speech—and for the briefest moment she thought that Queen Lil was right and these were savages who had cut out her tongue—but then a croak emerged from her parched throat and the Negro turned and gave a shout when he saw her eyes open.

Fetching a silver goblet, he raised Lila's head with one massive pink-tipped hand and held the drink to her lips. She swallowed greedily and after a while sank back onto the pillow with a satisfied sigh.

"Is that enough?" the man asked in perfectly modulated English.

"Yes, thank you."

Lila was about to question him when two men entered the marquee, alerted by the black man's shout.

"Ah, Lady Fairbrother. You are conscious."

It was the first man who addressed her. He was slim and wearing a silk shirt lavishly trimmed with lace and frills, dark green tight-fitting britches with stockings to match, and well-polished, high-heeled shoes. Despite his rather foppish appearance, there was a sternness to his thin, middle-aged features. His black hair, the fine line of his mustache and his tiny pointed beard were lightly touched with gray.

"Your friend, Lady Rawlesbury, and your servant George are both well and quite recovered from their ordeal. I hope you are as well?"

His voice was light and pleasant, with the faintest touch of an accent which was immediately explained when he bowed, clicked his heels together and introduced himself, "General Benedetto da Porto of Venice, at your service, madam."

Lila struggled to sit up and took the beautifully manicured hand offered to her.

"Let me introduce my cousin, Count Carlo Ruzzini, also of Venice."

Without warning, Lila found her stomach fluttering as the second gentleman stepped forward and extended his hand. He was the most handsome man she had ever encountered.

Like his cousin's, the count's hair was gleaming black but with a slight curl which was also in his moustache and beard, giving him an engaging devil-may-care expression. He was younger, taller—six feet at least—with skin deeply tanned to a smooth gold. Eyes of a tawny, teasing velvet smiled into hers as he held her hand fractionally longer than necessary.

"I am charmed to meet you, Lady Fairbrother." A deep, husky voice, also practically devoid of accent.

As though feeling the need to explain their faultless English, General da Porto said, "Both my cousin and I spent a year at the University of Cambridge where we perfected your language, not merely to obtain a fluency in speaking, but in reading. Our families have a love of literature and to be unable to read the plays of William Shakespeare in their original form seemed too great an omission to bear, so all my cousins have been taught to speak and read English and French as well as their own language."

The Negro took the pillows from behind Lila, plumped them up, and placed them behind her back in a more comfortable position, so she was able to sit upright. Then he fetched two chairs and placed them beside the bed.

"May we sit down, Lady Fairbrother?" The general paused, placing his hand on the back of one chair.

"Of course," croaked Lila and on hearing her raw voice the Negro glanced at her in some concern, poured more water from a glass decanter into the silver goblet and handed it to her.

"More water, madam?"

"Thank you." Lila took the silver cup gratefully, her hands still a little unsteady. Bowing, the Negro left the tent.

"Pierre accompanied me to England to wait on me there." The general smiled, indicating the departing figure. "As you can see, he grasped the intricacies of your language better than I. His appreciation of your great playwright is also more sensitive than my own."

Count Ruzzini, more plainly dressed than his cousin, his shirt plain white cotton, britches black and boots covered with sand, sat in the other chair. Under their joint scrutiny, Lila felt the need of a comb and a looking glass, for she had traveled a week without a change of linen or a wash in fresh water.

"You must be as surprised to see us here as we were to find you," remarked the general, who seemed to have far more to say than the younger man. "I confess that when your servant arrived in a state of near collapse—his horse in the same condition—we suspected some sort of trap, for the natives, while not aggressive, are not friendly either. But when he spoke to us in English, we were inclined to believe there were indeed two ladies in distress. We set off at once. We were quite astounded to find it was all quite true. Your friend recovered some time ago and has told us of your adventures. We are kindred spirits, Lady Fairbrother, for while I am not under arrest, I left Venice in fear of my life because of my radical views. So we are all political refugees in a way."

Lila hid a smile, for Queen Lil had been deported for stealing a piece of meat, and she for taking a guinea off poor Nellie Dunn.

"My cousin, Carlo, has no interest in politics, but he is of an adventurous nature, and despite fierce objections from his family, he could not resist accompanying me on this great exploration."

The count smiled and spoke at last, addressing himself to his cousin.

"I must admit, Benedetto, that of all the strange experiences encountered since we left Venice twelve months ago, none has afforded such surprise and pleasure as finding two noble English ladies in the midst of this wilderness."

The general nodded his enthusiastic agreement and said, "Lady Fairbrother, now we have introduced ourselves, perhaps we should leave you to rest. Pierre will fetch you some light refreshment and I shall ask Lady Rawlesbury to come and see you."

"Ah!" he exclaimed. "Here she is now."

The two men leaped to their feet as Queen Lil entered, and Lila gaped.

Queenie's shoulders were thrown back, her expression was not her own mocking, slovenly one, but haughty and over-bearing. When she spoke, Lila gaped again for she sounded like an upper-class lady who had never set foot within a mile of Blackfriars in her life.

"Lady Lilian. You are recovered, I see. Now, if you would allow..." She paused impatiently, eyebrows raised, waiting for the two men to withdraw, which they did gracefully. Lila regarded her friend anxiously, worried that this transformation might be permanent. Her worry was short-lived.

"Gorblimey! Wot a turn up for the books," snorted Queenie raucously. "You should see the set-up these foreign geezers have got here. Like a flamin' court it is. Stables, kitchens, a barber's shop. Green tents for this, blue tents for that. There's even a pink one with women in."

"What on earth for?" Lila asked somewhat naively.

"What'd'ya think, ninny!" Queenie replied with a coarse laugh.

Most unreasonably after such a brief acquaintance, Lila hoped Count Carlo Ruzzini did not consort with the ladies in the pink tent.

"You're blushin'," snorted Queen Lil. "I don't know. Married twice and blushes 'cuz there's women here to service the men. Cor, you're a case and no mistake."

Lila ignored her.

"Why are they here?" she asked. "What brings them to this part of the world?"

"Well, that there general, he's a political. Told them we

were too. After all, you are, in a sort of way. Anyway, he got a bit unpopular and had always fancied doing a bit of explorin'. He'd heard of New South Wales, 'cuz he's a well-read sort of cove and got an expedition together. There's a hundred of 'em at least, just lazing about, having a good time, getting bits of trees and rocks and the like, to take back home."

At that moment, the huge figure of Pierre appeared in the open doorway of the marquee bearing a plate of sweetmeats, some cake, and two glasses of wine.

"You may enter," Queen Lil said graciously. "And thank you. Tell the general we shall drink his health with our first glass of wine in months."

As soon as Pierre left, she fell upon the food ravenously.

"Surely that's mine?" said Lila indignantly.

"It is, but you've only got a little appetite. Me stomach's rumbling like one of old Ma Holden's stews. Here, have half. They gave me food but barely enough to line me guts, let alone fill 'em. As I'm Lady Rawlesbury here, not Queen Lil of Blackfriars, I couldn't very well ask for more."

She handed Lila her glass of wine and raised her own.

"Drink up, Lila. A toast. To us! The future looks bright at the moment. Let's hope it stays that way."

Lila touched the other woman's glass with her own, then sipped the slightly fizzy drink which tickled her nose. Remembering the deep, golden eyes of Count Carlo Ruzzini, another unexpected little thrill shot through her, and she said, "To us, Lady Rawlesbury. And a bright future."

Three massive ships were anchored in the tiny cove. All were decorated with gilt carvings and each had a figurehead— an Eros, a mermaid, and an angel respectively, garishly embellished with bright-colored stones. In the early morning sunlight, with the multi-colored domed marquees scattered between the tall pine trees fringing the beach, the whole scene had a slightly pagan air to it, as though some exotic eastern conquerors had arrived in this unexplored land.

As yet only one or two people were about.

"Good morning, Lady Fairbrother. You are up early."

Lila recognized Count Carlo's voice behind her, and she turned to greet him, hoping he would notice the improvement in her appearance from yesterday. Despite her fair skin, she took kindly to the sun, which had also bestowed on her a light tan. She still had in her possession the bag George had fetched from New Farm, so she wore a fresh, not too badly creased frock of white spotted cotton. With some difficulty she had managed to get a comb through her tangled hair and now it was tied back with a pink ribbon, falling in curls onto her neck. She knew she looked pretty, wanted this man to notice and from the glow in his eyes she saw that he did.

"Good morning." She curtsied. "I slept so much yesterday that I woke at the very crack of dawn and could not bear to lie abed when I had not explored. This is all"—she gestured at the scene before them—"quite unbelievable. Like a strange Arabian fairy tale."

The count laughed, showing white, even teeth.

"I can assure you, Lady Fairbrother, you are just as unbelievable yourself. A Nordic princess, no less. An ice maiden in a tropical setting."

"How kind of you, sir."

She curtsied again in some confusion.

"It is not kindness, but truth," smiled the count and deliberately refused to let his eyes drop when they caught hers, till in the end she blushed and bit her lip, searching desperately for some trivial thing to say.

"How many people are here?" she asked.

"Roughly two hundred and fifty, counting the ships' crews."

"Really!" She was interested, despite the fact she had clutched at the question in embarrassment. "All residing under canvas?"

"No. The crews have remained on board. About one hundred and ninety of us are ashore, half of them servants of one sort or another. Benedetto has brought friends who came for the adventure, along with others such as botanists, geologists, anthropologists, all hungry for research in the real world. Then there are cooks, valets, hairdressers, grooms for the horses. Even a shoemaker." Count Carlo smiled affectionately. "Bene is a man of the utmost fastidiousness. He refuses to appear imperfectly groomed or to be without every possible civilized advantage just because he happens to be in an uncivilized country. Life in Goldoni Bay is not too different in many respects from life in his villa in Venice."

"Goldoni Bay?" queried Lila. "I have not heard of it before."

"That is not surprising. As Bene has explained, we are a literary family, so we named it after our great playwright. But no one knows that but us, and no doubt when we have gone and the English reach here they will call it something quite different."

They walked back across the beach toward the green tent where Lila had slept.

"You say 'when you are gone,'" she remarked. "Is it your intention to leave soon?" What would happen to Queen Lil and herself, she wondered, when these men departed?

They had arrived at her tent.

"May I breakfast with you, Lady Fairbrother? I would like to collect one or two things, if you do not mind, while I am here."

She was suddenly confused.

"Sir! I never dreamed I was taking from you your accommodations. Please, sleep here tonight and find me somewhere less sumptuous. Queen—Lady Rawlesbury and I can make do anywhere. I can assure you, we are used to it."

But he would not hear of such a thing and rang a bell which prompted the appearance of Pierre with two breakfasts on a tray, as if he had read their minds. Hard-boiled eggs chopped with herbs and covered with a creamy sauce comprised their first meal of the day, with fresh, crusty bread and highly scented weak tea, which at first sip, Lila did not like but soon found refreshing in the already humid atmosphere.

"To answer your question, Lady Fairbrother. One ship is to return to Venice in the very near future, taking those with family commitments or a wish to return home for any reason. I am still unsure whether to accompany them or not. The other two ships are to sail right around this great island, landing wherever they please, and will not head home for at least two years."

The long brown fingers trembled slightly as he took a silver knife and sliced an apple, offering her a piece. She wondered why he should be so nervous, but as she reached out to take the fruit, she felt her own hand shaking, and she realized that he was just as overcome by his attraction to her as she was to him.

Perhaps such realization came to him at that same moment, for he stared at her for a long moment with a lightly bemused expression on his sunburnt face, and his next question confirmed this.

"Please do not regard it as an impertinence, Lady Fairbrother, if I ask the whereabouts of your husband. I see you wear a wedding ring. Surely he did not remain in England and allow you to be deported here alone?"

Without going into detail, Lila explained that she was a widow. The count made no secret of his pleasure on hearing this news and informed her gravely that he was a single man, whose mother and father had both died when he was young.

"I have a sister, Maria, who is ten years my senior and who has been mother, father, tutor, and nurse to me. We were brought up mainly in Paris because that is where we were living when my parents died. The Ruzzini family is one of the oldest in Venice, and although on my mother's side our history is a little vague with roots in Austria, it is from this strain that our present wealth derives. My maternal grandfather, whom I share with Benedetto, was a great adventurer, traveling mainly on land through Russia to China, returning with a great fortune in precious stones, so that we are also one of the few noble families remaining in Venice who are still wealthy."

He said all this quite seriously, cataloging his family history for Lila's approval, and throughout his recital her heart seemed to move to the back of her throat and throb there uncontrollably. She almost expected a proposal on the spot, but to her relief he said little more. Lila felt sure that if he had, she would have collapsed from sheer emotion. At that moment Queen Lil swept regally in to ask politely if her young friend had slept well.

After Carlo had departed, she fell upon the remains of Lila's breakfast as if she hadn't eaten for a week.

"It's so long since I lived with the nobs, I can't remember whether they admitted to being hungry or not," she gulped as she chewed bread. "Will they think less of me if I ask for more to eat?"

Lila assured her that Princess Caroline ate like a horse and never hesitated to demand more, so Queenie decided to enlighten the cook as to the extent of her appetite that very day. Then she regarded Lila curiously.

"Did I see you making sheep's eyes at that Venetian swell?" she demanded, and laughed uproariously when Lila blushed in reply. "Well, I must admit he's a fine figure of a man, though there's another here I fancy more," said Queen Lil thoughtfully. "In fact, they're a grand lot of chaps altogether."

"I think," Lila said shyly, "that Count Carlo may well ask for my hand."

"As long as you don't give it to him, that's all right," Queen Lil snorted.

"Why on earth shouldn't I?" Lila said indignantly. "He is altogether the most prepossessing of men, from a rich and noble family. I find him . . . most appealing."

"Pshaw!" said her friend rudely, spitting out bread crumbs. "You've been out of England for a year and a half and have led a pretty horrible life. This is the first proper civilized attractive man you've come across. I mean, I know your other two husbands were decent chaps, and all that, but they were marriages of convenience. Don't fall into this one's arms, Lila."

"But he feels the same for me, I can sense it," Lila protested.

"Well, he's been away from home nigh on twelve months. He just feels like a bit o't'other." Queen Lil raised her eyes to heaven dramatically. "Strew me! What a better world it would be if we were born old and grew young."

"Queenie, shut up! Anyway, you said yourself there's a tent here with women especially for that sort of thing." Lila felt a shameful surge of pleasure, imagining that she was a member of the party of ladies brought to satisfy the Venetians and Count Carlo came to visit her. She visualized him caressing her shoulders, her breasts . . .

The big woman rudely interrupted her chain of thought.

"If you can't see the difference between having one of them and having you, then I'm not going to tell you," she said scathingly. "Anyway, what about this Captain Grenville you were telling me about. Have you forgotten all about him?"

"Of course not. But he is on the other side of the world. I may never see him again," Lila protested disloyally.

Little did she know that he was not many miles away, sick and injured after a futile search for her.

Chapter Fourteen

Lila and Carlo were married on Christmas Day.

One of the ships, the *Leo*, was set to sail for Venice on New Year's Day and Carlo decided to return with her. He had proposed to Lila the day the explorers met to plan their next move. That same night Lila had been upset to hear him having a heated argument with Benedetto. They were in the general's tent shouting at each other in Italian. She stopped when she heard her own name mentioned several times.

A servant entered and they began to speak in English.

"It is not fair on the girl," Bene said stiffly. "What will Maria—"

"What is it to do with Maria?" Carlo interrupted in outraged tones. "You are talking nonsense. I do not understand and I am deeply offended."

Benedetto's only reply to that was a deep sigh, and Lila

was about to hurry away when he said, "Perhaps you know nothing. I have often wondered."

What it was Bene wondered about Lila never knew, for she felt guilty about eavesdropping and hastily went to her own tent, firmly pushing any worries to the back of her mind. She looked forward eagerly to her marriage and the subsequent journey back to civilization. At the first port of call, she would write to her family and inform them of her well-being. To think she could visit them in the not-too-distant future. . . .

When she and Queen Lil had arrived at the camp they had been surprised to be reminded it was December and soon to be Christmas. The days of relentless, burning sunshine, of brilliant blue skies, had convinced their English minds it must be July or August, and constantly they would marvel to each other that at home it would be promising snow.

"Cook will have made the plum puddings by now," Lila said wistfully. "And Papa will have picked out the turkey for Christmas dinner—that is, if he is well enough."

"There'll be a roaring fire in Red Jock's," Queenie reminisced, "and they'll dip a red hot poker in the ale. That adds a tang, I must say. Gorblimey, I'd give me last remainin' six teeth to be in England right now."

Then she suddenly became her grand new self, but in a surprisingly coy sort of way, when Paulo Silvagni, a giant of a man with a face as red as the setting sun and a huge fluffy beard came up to speak to them. Her shy pleasure rather belied the recent wish she had just made, Lila thought with some amusement. Paulo Silvagni, from Rome, was the botanist of the expedition. She longed to tell him about Roland's farm and the experiments conducted there, but did not wish to make known her so recent widowhood and the manner in which it had come about.

That was the night Carlo proposed. He found Lila sitting in her favorite place atop a little grassy hillock, a distance outside the encampment. She was contemplating the newly emerging stars in the deepening sapphire sky. Some distance away the sea lapped gently onto golden sands, and from somewhere in the camp she could hear the strumming of a mandolin. Remembering her conversation earlier with Queenie, she wished she was in wet cold Yorkshire in the bosom of her family.

Carlo's proposal was brief, as though he knew her answer beforehand, and she accepted calmly, glad to be taking on a husband whom she loved. But the next day Queen Lil threw cold water on this view.

"It's just animal passion," she said flatly. "Sheer animal passion. It's not love at all, but just as much a marriage of convenience as your other two. Would you be marrying him if he said he intended staying on with the others?"

"Of course I would," Lila retorted hotly, but remembering the argument she had heard the night before just after Carlo's proposal, she wondered if Benedetto had been remonstrating with his cousin on the very same theme. Perhaps Queen Lil was right about her motives and about Carlo's.

The night prior to the wedding, Christmas Eve, Carlo produced an exquisite robe which he had bought in Rio de Janeiro for his sister. It was made from filmy, golden gauze and embroidered with heavy gold thread, and softly draped with huge flowing sleeves.

"Why I should buy such a garment for Maria, I do not know," Carlo admitted as Lila uttered cries of delight, "for she is quite uninterested in clothes. I saw it in a market and bought it on impulse. Perhaps some sixth sense was at work and without knowing it I bought it for my beautiful new wife."

Later Benedetto handed her a jewel-encrusted collaret.

"My wedding gift to you," he said bowing and clicking his heels together.

"Thank you!" breathed Lila, fingering the fiery rubies, alternating with diamond stars. "I never dreamed I would own such a fine piece of jewelry."

"It is said in my family that this necklet brings luck, and I hope the tradition holds true for you, Lady Lilian—Lila."

She was bothered by the concern in his eyes and in his voice. Perhaps he noticed her slightly puzzled look for he seemed about to speak further, but instead bowed again and left swiftly.

He had of course brought with them a priest, Father Giuseppe, for a well-attended Catholic mass was celebrated every morning. Lila decided such an elaborate gown and necklace necessitated a simple hairstyle and fiercely brushed back her thick golden hair until it became shiny smooth and then coiled it into a simple knot on the nape of her neck.

Queen Lil told her she looked like an Inca Princess. George stood staring at this new Missie, spellbound and speechless.

"Surely the Incas were dark," Lila argued.

"Well, if they were fair, you'd look like one," Queenie said. "Anyway, here's to you, Medici. I knew things'd turn up trumps if I stayed with you, and I weren't wrong."

The sight of the handsome young couple brought a lump to Queen Lil's throat as they stood together before Father Giuseppe to be joined in holy matrimony. Paulo Silvagni nudged her and handed over a great white handkerchief with which she made a great show of wiping away one or two unfamiliar tears.

The wedding was conducted in the great red marquee which served as a canteen for the servants and had been decorated with masses of flowers and greenery all around. A strangely beautiful Lila in her golden dress, her hair a shade or two lighter and the ruby and diamond collaret sparkling at her throat, was dignified and composed throughout the ceremony—and so she should be, thought Queenie, wondering why she was shedding a tear for her young friend. After all, she should be accomplished at this by now. It was her third go in eighteen months. Not only that, but the husbands got richer. This one, by all accounts, owned half of Venice and had properties in Paris and London.

Count Ruzzini looked nervous, and stammered his responses in English. Lila gave her answers serenely and confidently. Knows it off by heart, reckoned Queen Lil smugly, feeling proud of Lila. She rushed forward to be the first to congratulate Lila by her new title.

"Countess Ruzzini!" marveled Lila. "Is that really me? I hadn't realized I would gain such a grand appellation."

Three husbands or not, Queen Lil figured Lila Ward still had some milk behind the ears if she were *that* naive.

They sailed for Venice on New Year's Day, 1797. About fifty of the expedition were returning. Several were in ill health or had found the climate of this strange land did not agree with them. Others wished to see their wives and children again and one or two were unashamedly homesick. With them went their servants, including a cook and some kitchen staff, for General Benedetto da Porto would not allow his guests to suffer the food provided by the captain for his crew.

A carnival atmosphere prevailed as the longboats rolled gently close to the shore waiting to take the passengers out to the *Leo*. Within a few weeks the rest of the expedition was to leave Goldoni Bay on the other two ships. They intended to explore further down the coast of New South Wales and would land and set up camp when the inclination struck.

To Lila's astonishment, Queenie had decided to stay with the Venetians, and it was her turn to blush when Lila questioned this strange decision.

"It's a nice life they have," she argued defensively when urged to return to civilization. "I like the freedom. This place agrees with me."

This was undoubtedly true, for her normally sallow, spotty complexion had improved enormously from the sunshine and good food. She had a ruddy, healthy tan and her sparse hair had thickened and grew in short auburn curls which she cut frequently. If only she had more teeth, Lila reckoned, she wouldn't look nearly so gruesome.

But now she regarded her friend with streaming eyes.

"Oh, Queenie. I may never see you again."

"Shurrup, ninnie. Bet you a puddin' to a pea, I turn up on your doorstep in Venice some day. Stop snivelin', gal. It embarrasses me."

"Who is going to tell me off like that? Who is going to be rude to me?" wailed Lila. "I'll miss you terribly."

"Well, if you must know, I'll miss you too," Queen Lil said grudgingly, knowing this to be the honest truth. If the silly little creature didn't stop crying like that, she'd have her, Queen Lil of Blackfriars, pickpocket, thief, occasional prostitute, kidnapper, and escaped prisoner, crying as well—for the second time in a week.

"Look," she said accusingly. "See what you've done now. George is in tears."

"Oh, George!" Lila flung her arms around her young friend who was to stay with Queenie.

"Not want you to go, Missie," sniffed George. "Mister Roland go now Missie."

Tears ran gleaming down his black cheeks. From the pocket of his ragged shorts he took a scrap of red material.

"Not want upset Missie, but man came looking when George burying Mister R'land under palm tree at farm. He say, give you this. But everything bad then so George keep. Now everything good, so George give."

George reckoned he was right to have kept the scrap of

material, because when Missie saw it she went white and swayed as if she were about to faint.

"What kind of man, George?" she asked, her voice hoarse.

"Tall man on horse, dressed all in black. Eyes blue like Missie's, but darker."

Fortunately Queenie had turned away and missed this exchange, and Carlo was chatting to his cousin, so Lila was able to recover alone before saying her final good-byes. Throughout she was conscious only of the scrap of silk tucked up her sleeve, conscious of its different feel against her skin. It seemed to burn into her flesh, punishing her for having so little faith.

The *Northern Star* had been the first ship to arrive in Sydney since the *Gabriel* had brought her there in March. When it had docked she had been distraught over Roland's death, but even so, it had never crossed her mind that Phillip Grenville might be on board, come to look for her. She had failed him totally. If she trusted him, then she would have expected him to come in search of her. She should have waited for him, anticipated his arrival.

What a base person she was!

Self-recrimination overwhelmed her as they climbed aboard the *Leo* and she made her way to the cabin which Benedetto had specially altered to accommodate a married couple. Carlo remained on deck. The newly constructed double bed with its white lace covers went unnoticed as Lila sat alone, pressing the tiny square of red to her lips.

"Phillip! Phillip! What have I done to you?"

Then further self-condemnation overtook her. Why, when George handed her the scrap of red stuff, had she not leaped upon a horse and gone to him. Phillip Grenville would be frantic, wondering what had become of her.

Even as she stood, half-intending to demand that a longboat return her to shore, the *Leo* began to move and a cheer went up from everyone aboard and ashore.

It was too late!

Once again Lila was sailing for the other side of the world and leaving behind Captain Phillip Grenville. The only difference was that this time, instead of watching from the shore he was lying in a lodging house in Sydney Cove, trying to recover his health and strength by a supreme effort of will in order to make one last determined search for the mysterious and elusive Lilian Ward.

* * *

Carlo was an adept and satisfying lover. After a few nights, Lila had teased shyly, "You must have loved many women before."

"No," he answered surprisingly. "You are the first."

She felt bound to believe him but felt it was strange that he was able to understand her needs so well. His gentle caresses aroused them both to a fever pitch of excitement which culminated in an explosive and fulfilling climax, leaving them breathless and exhausted. Carlo would fall asleep almost instantly while Lila pushed to the back of her mind the unwelcome thought that all this was not as perfect as it appeared. Queenie's words would come to her, "It's just animal passion."

The first night on the *Leo* Lila felt bound to admit that Queenie was probably right. She felt unable to participate wholeheartedly in making love, for her mind was still filled with the picture of Phillip arriving at New Farm and giving George the scrap of red material. Tall, black-clothed, blue-eyed, George had said. His steadfast loyalty made her feel more and more sick with shame.

Yet Carlo did not appear to notice her abstractedness. He fell asleep after loving her, having no idea that another man occupied her mind. Phillip would have noticed straightaway, thought Lila. That is what is lacking between Carlo and me. An awareness, an understanding. She imagined that after sharing such ecstatic, rapturous passion, she and Phillip would lie in each other's arms, sharing secrets, reveling in their love.

"I gave Timothy Bateson my heart," she whispered to the blurred stars floating in the black sky outside the porthole. "And to Roland, that dear, kind man, I think I must have given my soul, and Carlo has taken my body." Tears, unchecked, ran freely down her cheeks onto the lace-trimmed pillow. "But to you, Phillip Grenville, in spirit at least, I render all, my body, my heart, and my soul."

As she lay beside her sleeping husband, Lila ached with sorrow to think she might never again see the man ordained for her by fate, yet from whom fate had so cruelly kept her apart.

What a way to spend New Year's Eve, thought Grenville as he lay on the bed in his lodgings, his forehead burning with fever and his legs too weak to even lift off the bed.

The last month had been a nightmare. After discovering the burnt-out wreckage of the Holden Farm, he had immediately galloped off alone in the direction vaguely indicated as that taken by Lila—or the girl he hoped was Lila—and her two companions.

He must have been mad to do such a foolishly impulsive thing, and was ashamed afterwards to have acted so hastily after all his military training and experience. He had no knowledge of the strange countryside and the dry land offered no clues to the route taken by the travelers. Within twenty-four hours he had become quite lost and spent over a week trying to find his way back to Sydney Cove, during which time he gashed his leg badly and could not even get water to bathe it. Poison set in, and he had arrived back in the settlement delirious and unable to walk for almost the entire month of December. During his saner moments he was disgusted with himself.

Fortunately, the *Northern Star* would be delayed several more months in her departure, mainly due to the statement which, despite his delirium, he had made to the governor regarding Captain Grey's disgraceful behavior towards his prisoners. A subsequent hearing had banned the man from holding captaincy again. Unfortunately, no one was available who was capable of sailing the ship back to England, so Grey would remain captain until he reached the homeland.

It just did not seem possible that Grenville had come all this way to look for his beloved without even getting a glimpse of her, without even the positive knowledge that she was here. True, the girl at the Holden Farm had fit the description of Lila exactly. But a murderess? She had spirit, yes, but was she the devil-creature described by Mrs. Holden?

Then he remembered the three Scotsmen and the other farm laborers whispering to him, "A girl to be proud of," they said. "A girl of courage. She saved our lives. It was an accident with Jim Smith. And he was an evil man."

With a supreme effort of will, Captain Grenville gritted his teeth and swung his aching legs off the bed to stand up shakily. He would make a last-ditch attempt to find the blond angel, the fair killer who had descended so swiftly on the Holden farm, caused such chaos, and departed for no one knew where.

One or two natives frequented Sydney Cove who spoke a fair amount of English, and Captain Grenville found one who agreed to guide him in the northern direction where the mysterious white men supposedly were.

"If they have been here long, surely they would be well known by now, and everyone would know their whereabouts," he reasoned as well as his groggy brain would allow. "If they have not long arrived, they will surely be near the coast for they would not venture inland to set up camp.

"We will stick to the coast," he told the native, who shrugged his shoulders, little caring where they went as long as he was paid enough to buy a plentiful supply of rum.

They set off at a fast, punishing pace, the native riding bareback and well able to keep up. Far into the night they rode, scarcely stopping for more than an hour, despite the intense heat. But as they had to circumvent the Hawkesbury River which took more than twenty-four hours, the distance they covered from Sydney was very little as the crow flies. There would only be time for another few miles before he would have to start back if he wished to return to England on the *Northern Star*. If he had thought there was a chance of finding Lila, he would have stayed. But now she seemed like a dream, a will o'the wisp who might never have existed. Perhaps she had never come.

Back in England he would continue his search through official channels. Someone, somewhere, must know where she was.

Late on the second day they were resting and Phillip was contemplating whether to risk venturing another few miles when he glimpsed something bright flashing in the early rays of the sun.

Benedetto, before leaving Goldoni Bay and embarking for pastures new, could not resist a visit to Sydney Cove after learning from his two lady visitors that it was only a few days' journey away. With Carlo and Lila gone, he decided to explore this fascinating new town, overcome with curiosity as to how a place peopled primarily by criminals could function, and what it would look like.

Having already found the Ladies Fairbrother and Rawlesbury in the wilderness, he was not at all surprised to observe a gentleman accompanied by a sullen native galloping towards him, apparently from nowhere.

"General Benedetto da Porto," he introduced himself courteously when the dusty, ill-looking man drew up and began to bombard him with questions.

Yes indeed, he informed the anxious traveler, a young lady answering to the description he gave had arrived at their camp a month ago, but, he was happy to announce, she had married his cousin, Count Carlo Ruzzini, over a week ago, and the newly married pair had sailed for Venice on New Year's Day.

Benedetto had mentioned it to no one, but had his cousin not instantly fallen in love with Lila, then he himself would have attempted to seduce her at the earliest opportunity. She was an undoubted beauty, destined to break many hearts. Now here was positive proof of that fact, for on hearing the news of the wedding, the pain in the man's eyes was almost unbearable to see, but he showed no other sign of weakness.

The weary captain did not stay with the foreigners long. After less than half an hour, he directed his horse towards Sydney Cove and galloped like the wind, even though he was in a state of near collapse. Despite his desperation, he could not prevent a smile at the idea of Lila and Queen Lil, who came from the gutters of Blackfriars, pretending nobility. Lady Fairbrother! Lady Rawlesbury! Political prisoners, indeed!

He laughed, a demonic sound which floated up and was lost in the branches of the trees looming above him. All he wished to do now was leave this accursed land behind forever.

Next morning Lila awoke still with a feeling of incredible sadness but determined to pull herself together.

What was done, was done, she told herself and threw back her shoulders, set her chin, and it was the old, determined Lila who appeared on deck to join her husband and watch the thin black line of New South Wales disappear into the horizon. He smiled and put his arm around her shoulders when she stood beside him.

"How much easier life would be," he said, "if we just sat at home and did nothing. It was a wrench to leave Venice a year ago. Now I feel just as dejected departing from Benedetto and New South Wales. If I had never left the Ruzzini Palace in the first place I would not have felt any unhappiness at all."

"Nor would you be married to me," Lila observed.

"I was going to say, also, if I had stayed at home, I would not have experienced such great happiness as we have so recently had together. Perhaps it is right to uproot oneself on occasions."

He kissed her ear and ran his hands over her breasts, and despite her depression, Lila felt a thrill.

She murmured, "Stop. The crew will observe."

"They they must have remarkable eyesight," Carlo grinned, "For you are facing out to sea. You are right, though. Let us go down to our cabin where we are safe from prying and envious eyes."

Had it not been for her frequent gnawing worries over Phillip, the long return journey to Venice would have been a thoroughly enjoyable experience. Even as it was, Lila could not help but yield to the luxury offered by the ship. Their cabin with its polished oak walls and fitted cupboards, and a carpet so thick her toes disappeared into it, was typical of Benedetto's perfect taste.

Sometimes the couple ate in their cabin, but more often they sat with the other members of Benedetto's expedition in the ornate saloon lined with thickly padded benches covered in velvet, the walls gleaming with polish and reflecting, particularly when it was dark, the light from the mounted glass lamps.

Benedetto and Carlo owned the three expedition ships, as well as many more. The maternal grandfather who had inflated the family fortune with the precious gems acquired in his travels, had the craft built some forty years before. Bene had just recently had them fitted out to an extraordinary degree of opulence for the trip to New South Wales.

Because she was the only woman aboard, Lila's fellow passengers made an enormous fuss over her and night after night she sat at the head of the long oak table, Carlo on her right, the object of twenty or more pairs of dark, sparkling eyes, all gazing at her with uninhibited admiration. Even the dour Swede, Captain Siwertz, was charmed and overcame his superstition that a woman on board was unlucky. Indeed, he began to think quite the reverse as the *Leo* passed the notoriously dangerous storm-ridden waters of Cape Horn without incident.

By then the *Leo* had already stopped at Valparaiso, and Lila, who had to wear one of Carlo's cloaks when she went on deck in cold weather, was at last able to partially replenish her wardrobe which consisted of the cotton frocks she had made in New Farm and her golden wedding dress which she wore almost every night at dinner. She found a seamstress in the port only too willing to sew into the night to provide this rich and beautiful countess with several outfits.

"I don't want you to be ashamed of me in front of your sister," she said, twirling round their cabin to show Carlo the new mulberry silk dress with its high neck, long tight sleeves and little velvet cape to match.

"I have already told you, Maria does not care about clothes. She will not notice what you are wearing."

Despite the fact that Carlo claimed she had been mother, father, tutor and nurse to him, he rarely mentioned his sister, and Lila wondered if they did not get on. Sometimes she tried to imagine what Maria looked like and wondered if she was as beautiful as her brother, why she had not married. If she was ten years Carlo's senior, she must be thirty-two.

"Shall I throw this away?"

Carlo picked up the black-and-white check dress she had discarded.

"No!" she cried involuntarily. That was the material George had fetched from Sydney Cove on her first day at New Farm, but after a while she decided to take it ashore with her other old dresses and give them to a convent for charity. After all, in New South Wales she had looked back on England with nostalgia. It was ridiculous to be sentimental about objects acquired in that alien country.

Remembering the passage outwards when she and Timothy had been confined to their cabins every time the ship docked, it was a delight to explore the sights of Rio de Janeiro, Teneriffe, and other ports of call.

Due to the fact that the *Leo* had to remain in Sierra Leone for two hot and steamy months for repairs to her hull, the entire journey to Europe took nearly a year. But despite this and despite Lila's frequent, heartbreaking thoughts of Phillip Grenville, the time spent on the ship was so pleasurable it seemed to flash by.

The day they left Sierra Leone was September 20th, Lila's birthday, and it was then that she felt certain she was with child. Carlo's face was a picture of delight when she told him he would become a father.

During a joyous Christmas dinner some months later it came as a surprise to learn that they were a mere seven days from Venice. Lila felt so elated to be so near to home that she drank too much wine, and on their return to their cabin, she and Carlo made love with such wild ferocity that the next morning she felt half-ashamed and half-delirious.

Chapter Fifteen

The *Leo,* proud and tall in the late December sun, sailed gracefully into the port of Venice. The city looked magical and exotic. Forests of masts lay before them, and among them stood stately buildings, so that it looked as though the entire city were afloat. On the quayside merchandise lay in high, untidy heaps, and crowds of boats and gondolas, their sails a multitude of colors, moved about like restless butterflies.

In the forefront of the grand square that they were approaching stood two tall granite columns, mounted by a statue of a man trampling a crocodile.

A young Genoese, Federigo Ariosto, stood beside Lila pointing out the sights. Carlo had retired to his cabin complaining of tiredness, which was so unlike him that Lila was afraid that he had only reluctantly returned home for her sake. She placed her hands comfortingly on the slight bulge that was her baby and with a sense of satisfaction felt the gentle movements within.

"That is the Piazzetta, the annex of the Piazza San Marco, and there is the Basilica di San Marco, the most famous landmark in all Venice," explained Federigo.

Lila was impressed with everything. The buildings had a noble, permanent air, as though they had been planted there at the beginning of time, and the people, the great variety of people in rich, fur-trimmed robes or in filthy rags, who sat around on the steps at the foot of the columns, also seemed permanent, as if part of an oil painting.

Her eyes sparkled with excitement as sailors jumped ashore and began to tie the *Leo* securely between the two columns. She was startled when Carlo suddenly appeared on deck shouting angrily to Captain Siwertz on the bridge. As English was the only language understood by both men, she followed every word.

"Why are we anchored in this spot?" stormed Carlo. "Are you not aware that this place is notoriously unlucky?"

Captain Siwertz looked amused, confessed that he had heard of no such thing, and said, "It is crowded here. Have you not noticed all the French warships about? We are lucky to find this place."

Carlo glanced around in surprise. Six or seven vessels flying the French flag were moored nearby.

"It is too late now."

He came over to Lila. "Between these columns gallows were set up for prisoners of note, admittedly many years ago, and it has been regarded as a doomed spot ever since. My grandfather scorned the superstition and yet died of a terrible rash and fever within a month of tying up here."

One of the old sailors shouted something to Carlo, and Federigo explained to Lila, "That man says it is an old belief which no longer holds true."

But Carlo's normally pleasant face held an unaccustomed frown, which deepened when he noticed something else that alarmed him.

Pointing to the top of the empty column he remarked in astonishment, "The lion of St. Mark is gone!"

He did not wait for the gangplank to be lowered, but leaped from the side of the ship. He started talking to a well-dressed man and pointing to where the statue should have been.

When Lila eventually disembarked he told her with amusement, "Benedetto will be sorry he has not returned home, for the revolution he hoped for has taken place—with the help of the French. An upstart Corsican general, name of Bonaparte, has laid siege to the city, and it was he who ordered our famous lion to be removed. Venice has been handed over to Austria, if you please, though life continues undisturbed, according to this gentleman. As for me, I do not think it makes much difference to the people, rich or poor, who is in power."

This news only added to Lila's feeling of intoxication, which was increased further when she learned that they would be traveling to the Palazzo Ruzzini by gondola. Carlo explained that his home was accessible by foot, but as several narrow bridges lay between it and the quay, a carriage was not possible, so the easiest method of transporting their vast amount of luggage was by water.

"You realize no one is expecting us?" Carlo said somewhat nervously. "I could not get word ahead of our arrival."

Lila smiled weakly, her mind and emotions confused, and nearly overwhelmed, not only by the odd behavior of her usually carefree husband, but also by the extreme beauty of Venice which was almost too much to absorb at once. The bulging domes towering on all sides gave a touch of the Arabian Nights; walls surrounding them as they drifted along the canals were decorated with fresco paintings or glittering mosaics; there was marble everywhere of all conceivable shades. Buildings were renaissance, baroque, and gothic, all elegant beyond words. But most strange of all was the light, a shimmering, shifting, subtle light.

Yet along with all this beauty lay horror. On the steps of the grand buildings, which on close examination were crumbling and rotting at their foundations, slumped beggars in rotten, lice-ridden rags. Many were missing arms or legs, the stumps raw and festering. Some were asleep, others cried out to the passersby for help or money, and cursed them when they were ignored.

And the stench! Different from the stench in the hold of the *Gabriel* which had at least been human, recognizable. Here it was fetid, sickly, and totally strange. Then something thumped against their boat, and Lila screamed when she saw it was the body of a large dog floating in the sewage-ridden water. She decided then that the smell was of death.

The gondolier laughed at her distress. Carlo appeared abstracted, and Lila began to wonder if it were true that evil fortune befell those who moored between the granite columns of the Piazzetta, for the dead dog and the pervasive smell seemed to smother the beauty of the place, and she felt only gloom and fear and misery.

The steps to the Palazzo Ruzzini led out from the water into a small arch in which stood a stout iron door. Carlo came out of his reverie and informed her that the entrance was seldom used, as this was the back of the building. The front led out onto the Piazza San Boldo.

"In uture, you can walk anywhere you wish and go to many places by carriage," he told her as they climbed the stone steps. He tugged at a bell and jangling tones echoed through the building.

She wondered why he did not ring again when nobody had answered even after several minutes, but he seemed resigned to a long wait, and it was some time before she heard heavy bolts being drawn inside and a fat woman, her face red and perspiring, opened the door. Whoever she was, she did not recognize Carlo, and he had to insist upon entering his own home.

He snapped at her curtly, and she shuffled away sullenly as he led Lila down a narrow passage, explaining as they went. "She is a new servant I have not seen before. A bit distressed, no doubt, for as I said, scarcely anyone arrives by water. I have sent her to fetch Maria."

Carlo had become a different person since arriving in Venice. He was taut and nervous, unconsciously snapping his fingers, and his normally gracious movements had become quick and clumsy.

They entered the front hall. A dim light filtered through the small squares of stained glass, making eerie, jewel-colored marks on the patterned marble floor. The hall was as high as the palace itself. Its domed roof was also of stained glass, and there were galleries running on three sides on the first and second floors. It was too lofty to be comfortable in, and Lila felt exposed, as though danger lurked in the vastness above.

Then like a breath of wild wind, she heard a cry, far away. "Carlo! Carlo!"

Then nearer, "Carlo!" A woman's cry.

The *r* was stretched out long and haunting, as if the caller was caressing the name with her tongue. Yet at the same time, it was an agonized cry, a wail, as though she had found his corpse and was pleading for him to come alive again.

"Carlo!"

The voice was on the second floor now and a girl could be seen running along the gallery and down the wide stairs, not holding on to anything. It was a wonder she kept her balance.

"Carlo!"

He was nearly thrown off his feet when she flung herself upon him, her arms tight around his neck, showering his face with kisses, patting his forehead, stroking his cheek.

"Carlo."

This last she said with quiet satisfaction, standing back, holding his hands and just staring as if to make sure he was really there.

"I had not expected you back for years yet. You said perhaps five years. You have only been gone two."

She spoke in French and Lila understood her perfectly. She was glad she would be able to communicate with her new sister-in-law.

Then the woman realized that someone else was present. She turned, and Lila was shocked to see that the left side of her face was completely disfigured by a bright red scar which covered all her cheek and forehead. The eye was distorted, dragged down at the outside, as was the corner of her mouth, as if a weight hung on them. It gave her a bitter, dissatisfied expression.

"Who is this?"

Lila was upset to see Carlo embarrassed by her presence. She had expected him to proudly introduce her to his sister and had expected that they would become friends, but Maria, who for all her thirty-two years looked no older than Lila herself, was regarding her with an expression little short of hatred.

"This is Lilian, my wife," Carlo said to his sister, then turning to Lila he spoke in English, "My sister, Maria."

As yet he did not know Lila spoke fluent French. After all, her own mother was of that nationality. The fact that he changed to English to address her caused Maria also to assume she could not understand French, and at that moment Lila felt inclined not to enlighten her, for Maria ignored her outstretched hand and stepped back as though she had been struck. Her gaze dropped in horror to the swollen bulk of Lila's stomach.

"You have betrayed me," she practically snarled at her brother. "Bringing to this house a wife."

Lila wondered why Carlo did not answer her sharply, for bringing home a wife was not exactly a crime.

"I will not look after her. I will do nothing for her."

"You are not expected to," Carlo replied somewhat impatiently at last. "Remember this is my home. Where else would I bring my wife?"

"I thought we had agreed... Never mind, perhaps you do not remember."

Staring stonily ahead, heart sinking into her gray kid boots, Lila gave no hint that she comprehended this discourse.

Maria was tiny, barely five feet tall. Her hair was black as night and drawn back from her face in an untidy bun. She wore a drab dress of dark green and a large apron. Even without the scar she would have been plain, for her skin was pasty white as if she never ventured out of doors and her nose was thin and long. In no way did she resemble her younger brother.

Carlo at last asserted himself and remarked stiffly that he and his wife would move immediately to a hotel if their presence was so unwelcome.

These words brought the angry girl to her senses and she swallowed hard, took a deep breath and said to Lila in halting English, "I am sorry. I have been unwell today. Excuse me, please."

She fled up the stairs as quickly as she had come, taking them two at a time.

Carlo said apologetically when she had disappeared, "Please forgive Maria. She leads a solitary life and is not used to meeting people."

Lila did not think this excused his sister's disgraceful behavior, but merely said, "Could I lie down, do you think? I feel so tired. It has been a taxing day."

"Of course. I will take you to my apartment, on the second floor. Our boxes will be brought up shortly."

As they climbed the stairs, Lila put her hand on the thick marble balustrade and when she withdrew it at the top found her pale gray glove thick with dust.

Surprised, she glanced about her and was dismayed to find cobwebs hanging from corners, and she shuddered to see a great nest of spiders within one. The first floor gallery was covered with wrinkled, moth-eaten carpets, and dirt covered the cut glass chandeliers and lovely paintings. What on earth would Carlo's apartment be like after an absence of nearly two years? Lila wondered with trepidation. To her surprise it was spotlessly clean, the bed linen a virginal white. Opulent gold brocade hangings gleamed dully and the furniture shone, giving off a faint hint of lavender. It was clear someone went through the apartment regularly, polishing and cleaning with loving care.

"I am sorry about Maria." Carlo sat in a stiff tapestry-covered chair.

"I should have come alone first to break the news. It was unfair for you to have to witness such ill-tempered behavior."

But why did Maria behave so? wondered Lila. What is so shattering about one's brother bringing home a wife?

Her puzzlement must have shown for Carlo went on, "I think I have already told you that my mother died giving birth to me. My father passed away soon afterwards. Maria gave up her life to rear me. She has always thought of nothing but my happiness and well-being."

"Surely your happiness and well-being should not exclude a wife?" Lila remarked somewhat coldly.

"We promised to stay together. It is hazy in my mind, I must admit, but I vowed to look after her when I became an adult. To protect her as she had protected me."

He looked miserable and guilty and Lila felt angry, not at him, but at this unreasonably possessive sister.

"But you can still do that," she said. "I do not want to prevent you from caring for her."

He answered in a far-away voice, "It will not be the same. Not for Maria."

Lila turned away impatiently and walked to the window which overlooked the Piazza San Boldo. Sunlight streamed across half the square and the dividing line between light and dark was like a knife, cutting the Piazza into two parts. Palazzo Ruzzini was in the dark half.

"It is my fault she is scarred! It was I who disfigured her," Carlo cried out suddenly. Lila turned to see him bury his face in his hands. "When I was just three, in Paris, a gardener left some chemicals in a bowl on a shelf, and I climbed up to investigate. I was about to drink the poisonous mixture which would have killed me instantly, when Maria came in. She knocked the bowl from my hands and it tipped onto her face, making her ugly forever. That is why we stayed in Paris for so long. She would not return here until after I had been to Cambridge."

"My dear love."

Lila crossed the room, kneeling before Carlo and enfolding him in her arms. She stroked the thick, dark curls, then, eyes glowing, touched his body until his eyes began to brighten with desire and she led him to the bed where they lay together.

It was not the same. It was as if they were different people altogether from the abandoned, reckless pair on ship who had reveled in their lovemaking. Carlo was awkward and could not fulfill her. Lila was worried throughout because she had not locked the door and she feared that Maria might walk in. She could not relax and almost began to wish they had stayed in Goldoni Bay and continued with the carefree life of exploring with Benedetto and Queen Lil.

At dinner that night, Lila wore the gauzy golden robe she had been married in and the collaret given her by Benedetto. Both these items inflamed Maria who had on the same cotton frock of the afternoon.

She remarked angrily to Carlo in French, "Surely that is the famous da Porto good-luck necklace?"

Carlo explained that Benedetto had given it to Lila as a wedding gift. This did not please Maria one bit, and her bad temper was increased when Carlo, in a tactless attempt to please, remarked that he had originally bought the golden dress for her.

Maria stared at Lila with unconcealed dislike. Carlo attempted to bring his wife into the conversation by chatting in English, but although she felt sorry for Carlo and the awkward situation he was in, Lila was in no mood to be amiable, and the three sat through the meal in silence.

Inwardly, Lila boiled with rage. She hated this place with its dust and dirt and high uncomfortable rooms. It was cold and damp. She hated this new sister-in-law who made no attempt to act in the most faintly civilized fashion. The food was unappetizing; the soup was too thick, the vegetables nearly raw, and the meat tough. Even the fruit seemed to be the bruised leftovers from some market stall.

The servant who attended them was a stooped, gray-haired woman who shuffled in and out with the nearly cold dishes without uttering a word. She did not wear a uniform, not even an apron, and her faded gray dress was none too clean. Having seen her nails black with dirt, Lila would not have relished the food even if it had been properly cooked.

Maria disappeared without a word as soon as the meal was over, and the second she had gone, Carlo said, "Lila, this situation is intolerable. I was crazy to come back here, and frankly, I do not know what possessed me to. My duty now is to you and our forthcoming child. I have houses in Paris and London. If you are fit, we will leave here within the week. I would go immediately, but I promised Benedetto I would carry out some business for him in Venice. I cannot let him down."

Maria was listening!

Lila glanced at the door through which her sister-in-law had gone and saw it tremble gently. Maria was waiting for her reply.

"If you so wish," she said, and saw the handle turn and the door fully close.

Sure now that they were alone she said to Carlo, "I have never felt better in my life. Childbearing agrees with me. However, the baby is due in three months and to embark on a long coach journey much later than this might prove dangerous."

"We will leave on Saturday," he promised.

Lila had imagined news of their intended departure would render Maria even more unpleasant, but the following day she was quite a different person.

She could not have been described as friendly, and she found her resentment of her brother's wife difficult to hide, but she attempted to be polite and took Lila on a tour of the palazzo, round the grand, crumbling rooms which smelled musty and unused, into the giant library full of leather-bound books whose spines had faded with age.

It was not as large as Lila had expected. She had imagined something like Carlton House, but this was only a fraction of the size. There was no ballroom and only one reception chamber. The Palazzo was about the size of Grassbrook Hall, but built in a more opulent style with marble floors and frescoes in every corridor.

Lila wondered why, with all the money supposedly at the disposal of the Ruzzini family, the palazzo had been allowed to deteriorate. Why were not more servants employed? She wondered if fresh paint would diminish the gloom that prevailed everywhere.

Maria did not take her up to the servants' quarters on the top floor. She said they were empty, thought Lila recalled that when they arrived Maria herself had come down from here. The only employees were the two women Lila had already seen and they did not live in.

"Where does this lead?" Lila asked curiously as they stood in the vast hall which she found so depressing. She was pointing to a small oak door at the foot of three stone steps.

"To the Chapel of Saint Cecilia," said Maria. "I show you."

The chapel was tiny with room for no more than twenty worshippers. The pulpit was of plain black marble. The stained-glass windows were narrow and let in very little light.

"You are not Catholic?" Maria remarked, her crooked mouth twisting into an ugly grin. She dipped her fingers into the holy water and made the sign of the cross.

"No," Lila answered shortly.

She was approaching the altar when she drew up short with a gasp of surprise, for on the altar steps a figure lay face down. It was a man in a habit of rough brown with a hood thrown back onto his shoulders. His feet and legs were bare and protruded from the hem of his garment, the skin blue with cold. He was so thin that his anklebones stuck out like knobs. So absorbed was he in his prayers he had not heard them enter.

Lila left hurriedly and Maria followed.

"Father Judas startled you?"

Did she mean to smile so sarcastically, or could the poor, deformed mouth not help but look unpleasant?

"Judas?" queried Lila. "I have not heard that name used before except by the Apostle."

"Then you will agree that it is an obvious choice for another betrayer of Christ?"

"What did he do?"

"Nothing so terrible. I do not know the precise details, but he took a married woman. Unlike many priests who take a vow of celibacy, Father Jude, as he was then, took his vows seriously. Too seriously. He changed his name to Judas, and has been begging forgiveness from God ever since."

"How tragic," murmured Lila.

"To me it is stupid," Maria sneered. "We are what we are and it is foolish to spend one's life expressing sorrow to God for doing what He made us to."

"That is one way of looking at it, I suppose."

Lila did not wish to argue with this spiteful little woman who seemed to be trying her best to be friendly.

"My English, which I have not used for many years, has returned to me surprisingly well," she said. "Before Carlo went to Cambridge, we spoke nothing but the English language for a whole year to prepare him for his studies."

"It is excellent," Lila told her. "You must have had a good teacher."

"Father Judas was my tutor; he speaks nine languages fluently."

"He has been with your family a long time then?"

"Since before I was born. But he lived here in the Palazzo Ruzzini until my parents died, then he came to Paris to help care for us."

Suddenly her morning's attempt at good humor seemed to desert her, and she said abruptly, "I must leave. I have much work to do," and she fled up the stairs two at a time, to the top floor which she had declared unused, and Lila saw her enter a door at the far end of the gallery.

Idly she wondered what work the woman got up to alone in an isolated room and decided to finish exploring the palace by herself. Opening the door through which she had seen the servants disappear, she found stone steps leading down to a basement kitchen below water level. The room was lit only by two dim oil lamps strung from the ceiling. The walls were blackened with age and the corners covered in green slime where water trickled down. Lila heard scuffling somewhere and felt her scalp prickle when she realized it was rats.

There was no fire to help lessen the dank, penetrating cold, and she shivered, wondering how on earth the women could stand working in this dungeon. She decided she would never eat another mouthful of food which emerged from it. Until they left on Saturday, she and Carlo would live on fresh food. She would shop that very afternoon.

In the kitchen the women regarded her sullenly, their black-rimmed eyes resentful, as if they were able to read her thoughts.

The idea of this palace becoming her permanent home was quite intolerable, yet Lila was irritated at her own capriciousness. Here she was comparing it unfavorably with New Farm, yet when she had lived in that lovely house, she had longed to leave and return to "civilization."

Carlo had been out all morning and when he returned she asked if they could shop later.

"Of course," he replied. "Anyway, Bene's wife has expressed a fervent wish to meet you."

"I did not know Bene was married," she exlaimed in surprise.

"He and Beatrice are separated by mutual agreement," Carlo explained. "She had endless lovers, which he could not stand, despite the fact that his mistresses outnumbered her partners by at least two to one. A most unreasonable jealousy, he conceded. They decided to live apart, though they are still great friends and occasionally great lovers."

"An unusual arrangement," remarked Lila, secretly shocked.

"Not for Venice," Carlo assured her. "On reflection, I am glad we are leaving here shortly, else I should be constantly worried that the loose moral climate might have some detrimental effect on you once our baby is born. A flower so fair as you, my love, will set numerous hearts afire, and you might not be able to withstand the onslaught of hopeful lovers."

"I am quite sure I would," Lila declared firmly.

She managed to avoid a midday meal by saying they would eat out, and she set off excitedly for her first proper look at the famous city which she had entered the day before under such a pall of depression.

Benedetto's wife was a charming, middle-aged woman of Austrian descent, with short black hair caught up in a pearl band. Her dress was cut daringly low, and she exuded an animal vitality, flirting outrageously with Carlo, even pouting seductively at her male servants. Nevertheless she had such a delightful personality that Lila liked her on the spot.

"I am so, so very pleased for Carlo," she sang, holding onto Lila's hands and staring intently into the thick-lashed blue eyes. "Bene and I have always worried about him being shut away with that awful sister of his."

"Hush, Beatrice. Do not speak of Maria in that fashion," Carlo protested.

"I won't hush and I shall speak of your awful sister in any way I like," Beatrice told him complacently. "She's a selfish young woman and I am glad my Bene tore you away to explore new lands—for what a find you have brought back with you."

She turned to Lila. "My husband argued, Maria screamed like a maniac, but Bene won in the end, I am glad to say. It was a difficult time, was it not, Carlo?"

Carlo frowned and murmured, "Do you know, I cannot remember. We had only been in Venice a year before I left with Bene, and the whole period is all quite hazy in my mind. When I came back yesterday, it was as if I was seeing the place afresh, almost as a stranger. Quite frankly, now I do not understand why I ever returned."

Lila was not surprised to hear all this, for she could not imagine the fastidious Carlo living in such sordid circumstances, whether it be a palace or not.

He left then to interview an agent of Benedetto's, and Beatrice turned to Lila and said, "You are definitely leaving on Saturday, I hope? I do not want to be rid of you, mind. I am fascinated to have such a delightful new cousin-in-law, and I love the idea of becoming a sort of aunt, but you and Carlo will be so much happier in a home of your own."

"We are going to London. All the arrangements have been made," Lila said. She had persuaded Carlo that England was far preferable to Paris, and she could not wait to see the Ruzzini residence in the Mall. There would of course be great difficulties to overcome in England. She had left there in disgrace, a laughingstock. There was her innocence still to be proved, and as yet she had explained nothing of it to Carlo.

"What does Maria do?" she asked Carlo later as they sat at a table under the arches bordering the Piazza San Marco. Ladies who were enceinte were not obliged to hide their condition in this liberal city but mingled as any other woman would. The tables belonged to a café called the Coach of Fortune. The café was tiny, but outside hundreds of people enjoyed the hospitality of its pavement seating. They faced the pageant of painted arches, colonnades, and balconies of the Doge's Palace, and the square teemed with people.

Carlo did not answer her question, but frowned, as if trying to understand it.

"I mean," Lila explained, "she said to me this morning she had work to do and she went onto the top floor of the house. What work?"

She was quite determined to find out more about her strange new relation.

"She is a scientist of sorts, a chemist. I am not sure how to describe her."

"The room on the top floor is a sort of workshop then?" Lila pressed.

"She refers to it as her laboratory. I have scarcely thought about it. It does not interest me."

Lila suppressed a smile for the more she got to know Carlo, the more she suspected that very little interested him. She had never seen him with a book and he had no hobbies, for all his Cambridge education and supposed love of literature.

"What does Maria do in this laboratory?" she insisted.

Carlo's tawny eyes twinkled with amusement. "Regretfully, little wife, you have married an ignoramous, for I confess I do not know. She is forever having flowers and plants delivered from all over the place, that I have noticed."

"Flowers?" Lila said in astonishment. Perhaps Maria was a botanist, growing rare specimens, pollinating and cross-pollinating seeds the way Roland had sometimes done.

Lila tried to bring in the bread, pastries and sweetmeats, fruit and wine, with a great deal of noisy bonhomie as though it was a treat, a special occasion, but Maria saw through the charade. She turned her back and marched off in a cold fury.

Feeling upset, Lila took Carlo down into the dungeon where the food was prepared. She said not a word, but let him see for himself the abhorrent conditions there. He was horrified and then nervously said he would have a word with Maria. Lila told him not to bother. There were only a few more days to go and it was not worth the trouble.

However, they ate their evening meal merrily in the library, boiling water on the fire to make fragrant Turkish coffee using a pot and cups Lila had purchased that afternoon, for she did not even trust the Palazzo Ruzzini's china and utensils. She put the washed dishes away in a small unused corner cupboard. They both felt like naughty children, waiting for the dragon sister to appear and scold them, and they giggled from beginning to end.

The next few days were odd and unreal, with Lila living in two quite different worlds. There was life outside the Palazzo Ruzzini. Lila and Carlo paid visits to Beatrice da Porto and met her outrageously eccentric friends and lovers, all of whom made an enormous fuss over the young pair.

Lila discovered the Merceria, a rabbit warren of intimate little shops, where she bought a jade necklace and earrings set in dull beaten silver for her mother, and identical gold chains with milky pearl drops for Mary and Hettie. Her eyes filled with tears as the shop assistant carefully packed the gifts in silk-lined boxes. Her sisters were growing up without her. Hettie would be seventeen. She might even be engaged by now. Lila felt a surge of anger against the cruel forces which had separated her from her family, but recovered her good humor when she thought of how she would soon be seeing them again.

Venice was fresher in the mornings. The hidden tides washed away the filth and refuse and the water sparkled. With Carlo by her side, she would stroll through the Piazza San Marco and sit for hours outside the Coach of Fortune, sipping coffee or wine, enjoying the bustle all about her.

Back in the Palazzo Ruzzini, all was dark with malice. Lila couldn't help shivering each time she entered the vast foyer, both from the chill and the bitter atmosphere.

Maria, always unpredictable, either ignored them both and stayed upstairs, or shouted angrily to Carlo in French, "So, this is how I am repaid for sacrificing my life for my little brother, eh?"

Her eyes were hot and passionate, like those of a jealous lover. Carlo would react with puzzled dignity as though unsure whether it was right or wrong to behave in such a manner.

Once he said when they were out, "Bene warned me not to bring you back here, yet I did not know, still do not really know, what he warned me of. It was not until we reached Teneriffe on our return journey I began to experience qualms, but even then I could not pinpoint my trepidation."

"I am amazed you escaped Maria's clutches to join Bene in his expedition," Lila said and Carlo frowned slightly in annoyance.

"Clutches? I am not such a milksop to be in any sister's clutches. I owe her a great deal to be sure. I hold myself responsible for her disfigurement, but I would not let her stop me from leading my own life."

"But Beatrice said it was due solely to Benedetto's efforts that you accompanied him. Why did you need his assistance if you say you are capable of leading your own life?" Lila asked her husband bluntly. She found his attitude towards Maria peculiarly muddled.

"I was ill, I remember that," Carlo frowned. "Bene came round, I think. He and Maria had a great shouting match. I faintly remember him calling in a friend from outside and they practically carried me out of the house. I recovered very quickly at Bene's and became fired with enthusiasm for his plans. When the expedition was due to leave I returned to the Palazzo Ruzzini to say good-bye to Maria, but she would not answer the door."

Away from Maria's influence, Carlo was almost his happy, carefree self, but his sister's disfigurement so distressed him that within her sphere he literally could not think straight. One minute he would be angry with her, the next apologetic or guilty, then suddenly angry again.

Lila felt she would like to talk to the priest, Father Judas, but every time he saw her, he would make for the Chapel of Saint Cecilia, disappearing down the steps like a brown ghost. They had not even come face to face yet and she was reluctant to force an audience with someone who made such a great point of avoiding her.

There was one occasion when Lila entered the front door, to be greeted by soft, enticing laughter which she was sure came from the top floor. Maria's laboratory door was open. The chuckling became louder, mocking, musical, like a witch trying to lure a child into her lair. Then it stopped abruptly and a door slammed.

Another time, as she stood in the great hall where she always felt danger existed, Lila was conscious of eyes upon her and there in the gloom of the third floor landing, Maria stared at her wordlessly, her eyes sending silent messages of hate. Instinctively Lila placed her hands over her baby as if to protect if from that penetrating glare and rushed to her room. She could not wait for Saturday to come so they could get as far away from the woman as possible.

One afternoon she asked Beatrice where she could find a woman to accompany her on the journey to England which she felt might be difficult without some feminine help, bearing in mind her condition.

"I know the very person," trilled her cousin, leaning forward to ring a little gold bell and exposing white breasts.

She fluttered her eyelashes at the footman who came in answer to her summons.

"Send Rosetta to me."

She turned to Lila. "Rosetta has cared for my wardrobe since we were young girls," she told Lila. "She is an excellent dressmaker and her daughter, Angela, is fifteen and anxious to find a place, though they do not wish to work in the same establishment."

A buxom, fair-haired woman entered and there followed a rapid exchange in Italian of which Lila understood nothing. The woman went away and soon returned with a pretty girl, also fair haired, and tall with a body already filled out. She was plainly dressed in a frock of dark blue with pale blue collar and cuffs.

"This is Angela," Beatrice said in French. "I greatly suspect my Bene is her papa, so she is of good stock."

Lila suppressed her surprise at such openness and asked Beatrice if she thought Angela would like to travel to England with the option of staying there. The girl's eyes lit up when the question was put to her.

"There! You do not need me to translate," Beatrice smiled. "She is delighted at the idea. I am sure she will suit for she is very mature and sensible. Now, promise me you will come and say good-bye before you leave."

Despite the fact that Lila brought Angela home with her and asked for extra bedding to be put in their dressing room, Maria proved unusually friendly that evening. She joined them in their meal for the first time. Lila had discovered many stalls in Venice which sold ready-cooked foods. They started dinner with *pidocchi*, a soup made from mussels found in the lagoon, followed by fried fish and fritters. Even cooked vegetables had been bought and altogether the meal proved quite delicious. Maria ate with relish, and Lila wondered if she had forgotten how nice good food could taste and that eating could actually be a pleasure.

During dinner, Maria insisted on searching out some beautiful crystal glasses for the red wine of Verona which they had bought. She went to the kitchen herself to wash the dust from them, then poured out the wine with a flourish and handed it to them with her awful, pathetic smile. Then she toasted them, wishing them well on their journey the day after tomorrow, and Lila thought that at last, at this late stage, she had become resigned to Carlo's marriage and was willing to accept Lila as her sister-in-law.

But Maria's good wishes were wasted, or perhaps they were a secret curse, for in the night Carlo awoke, groaning in agony, and by morning he had a fever that would keep him bedridden for that day at least.

Chapter Sixteen

Lila was heartbroken. She prayed hard, willing Carlo to recover in time to make their journey as planned on the following day.

She demanded a doctor and Maria brought in Father Judas. This was the first time they had met. His features were thin, almost skeletal, and his skin seemed stretched to the point of transparency, emphasizing his bony forehead and cheeks. His eyes were deep-set and his hair was a blackish gray. A thin layer of perspiration covered his brow. His feet were bare and dirty.

Carlo was flushed, his tongue swollen and black. To Lila he looked as if he was at death's door.

"Can you help?" she asked the priest impatiently. What good was a man of God when her husband needed medical help?

Maria answered her unspoken question, "Father Judas has a degree in medicine from the University of Florence," she said with sarcasm in her voice, and the priest looked at the woman sadly, with resignation, as though he was used to this tone of voice.

He examined Carlo thoroughly and announced, "In the place, *Terra Australis,* from which you have just returned, there is a tiny fly, the black ant, almost invisible to the naked eye. Its bite is unnoticeable and anywhere but on a surface vein is harmless. If its poison enters the blood, however, it can cause this fever."

He turned as if to leave, but Lila pounced on him. "But it is a year since we left New South Wales. How can this bite affect Carlo after all this time?"

She felt he hadn't the faintest idea what was wrong but was giving an explanation to placate her.

The priest regarded her courteously with his muddy eyes.

"Cases of the bite of the black ant causing immediate sickness are rare. It is far more common for the venom to stay in the system for as long as two years before ill effects are felt."

"Then what must I do for my husband? How must I treat him? Is he in danger?"

He answered with dry precision. "Keep him cool and use cold compresses. Give plenty of boiled water but no food at all. His life is not at risk, but he will be at least a week recovering."

Lila was comforted to learn that Carlo would get better, and the calm, knowledgeable manner in which the priest answered her convinced her that what he said was the truth and that no other medical help was required. Nevertheless, it was a blow to learn that it would be several days before her husband would be better. No doubt further time would be needed for him to recuperate. It looked as though their departure for London would be delayed at the very least by two weeks. In view of this she had a room on the third floor cleaned and aired for Angela to occupy, though the girl insisted on staying in the apartment for the next few nights to help care for Carlo while Lila slept fitfully on a sofa in the dressing room.

She was glad of the young girl's company. With the ingenuity of a child, Angela was able to make herself understood to Lila with gestures and facial expressions which would have been humorous if the recipient had not been so upset. In no time at all, she began to pick up some English and by the end of the first day was familiar with twenty or so of the more common words Lila had used.

If Angela had not been there, she would not have talked to a soul for Maria disappeared completely and Lila could not help but wonder why her fierce affection for her brother did not extend to helping care for him when he was ill.

Lila was pleased when Father Judas appeared a few days later to examine the patient.

"He is as well as can be expected," he pronounced, feeling Carlo's steaming brow and placing a hand on his racing heart.

"Should he be bled?" Lila asked, remembering that this was a favorite remedy practiced by their family doctor at Grassbrook for all ills.

"No, no!" the priest replied impatiently. "That is an old-fashioned and dangerous practice. Just leave him to me and the poison will drain from his system."

"But might it not return?" demanded Lila. "Once bitten by this insect is one infected forever?"

A friend of her father's had visited a place called Gambia where he had been bitten by mosquitos and had suffered intermittent fevers as a result of this most of his life.

Father Judas thought deeply and replied as though passing a judgment rather than an opinion. "I think it is probable that the fever will return."

With this depressing news he left.

As Carlo recovered, he emerged from the state of almost total unconsciousness in which he had lain supine, and began to behave in a strange and frightening way, suffering peculiar dreams in which he was mauled by wild animals. As invisible devils attacked him she had to hold him in her arms, soothe him, and assure him he was safe from his imaginary dangers. He swore his arm had been bitten off, that his legs were scratched and bleeding. Then the effort of fighting these mythical monsters would have its physical effect, and he would pant and gasp for breath.

Lila began to think she would not be able to cope any longer and told Angela that the following day she must call on Beatrice and ask for help. In fact, she wondered aloud, why hadn't her cousin been to inquire what was wrong when they had not called to say their promised good-byes?

At that moment help arrived unexpectedly as Maria glided

silently in carrying a tray with two small silver cups. Gravely she asked Lila if she might give Carlo a drink.

"Now that the fever is dissipating, it is safe to give him this. It will ease and relax him," she told Lila, and gently lifted her brother's head with one hand, coaxing him to sip the medicine.

"I suggest you have a little yourself," she said kindly, handing a cup to Lila. "You must be very tired, and a good rest is what you need."

Lila took the cup and sipped the bitter mixture. She felt she could sleep quite well without drugs, but was reluctant to refuse aid from the normally uncaring Maria.

"What is it?" she asked, making a face at the unpleasant taste.

"*Papaveraceae*," Maria answered with her awful smile.

After she left, Lila climbed into bed beside her husband for the first time in a week. Carlo was breathing deeply and evenly, and in no time at all she found herself floating into sleep herself.

When she awoke, Maria was at her side, persuading her to sip, sip from the silver cup to help her sleep more, to relax. Helplessly, Lila did as she was told.

"Carlo! Carlo?" she murmured.

"He is better. Much, much better," Maria said, and beside her Lila saw the drowsy form of Carlo being lifted and told to sip. Then Father Judas came in. Lila could see him through a mist, standing gravely at the foot of the bed, protesting something to Maria, who laughed in his face.

Suddenly, without warning, the lovely, sleepy feeling changed into a nightmare and the ceiling began to swiftly descend upon her. Her stomach heaved. She screamed, but then the ceiling stopped and floated slowly back into its proper place. Then the frieze suddenly turned into large white insects which began to run up and down the walls, then across the floor, up, up onto her bed and along the sheets to bite at Lila's face. Again she screamed and screamed until Father Judas reappeared and mopped her brow with a cold cloth, giving her cool, fresh water to drink. But Maria came in and knocked the cup from his hand, spitting in his face when he tried to argue with her.

One night when they were both conscious, Carlo turned to her and they made love in a feverish and violent way. Afterwards, Lila was sick.

"Somebody help me," she croaked and Carlo comforted her

before falling back onto his pillow where he sobbed uncontrollably for no reason at all. She watched him, unable to lift her arms to stroke the dark curls on his neck. His face changed to that of Roland and became still with death. Then he was Timothy, then Ralph Curringham, then her father.

Doors loomed large, then small, and ornaments, even furniture, drifted silently across the room. The curtains billowed and disappeared completely and cobwebs from the corridor outside seeped in from all around the door, expanding, filling the room, covering Lila's face until she could scarcely breathe.

Through the gray web Maria appeared.

"Sip," coaxed Maria. "Sip," and Lila obeyed, though her throat felt so swollen she doubted if there was room enough for the tiniest trickle of liquid to squeeze down.

"Where—where is Angela?" she whispered. "Angela?"

"Asleep. Like you, she sleeps," soothed Maria, smiling.

One day Father Judas stood at the foot of the bed and said, "What about Benedetto's wife? This is very dangerous. She is bound to ask for them sooner or later?"

"She has been twice," sneered Maria. "Many weeks ago. I convinced her that they had left for England and forgot to say good-bye."

One night Lila woke with a jerk.

"My baby!"

She had forgotten about the baby which suddenly kicked inside, nudging her into consciousness. She had forgotten about the new life waiting to be born.

When? She had quite lost track of time. Had she been lying here weeks, or months? "Mama, help me," she called silently. "Phillip. Am I still alive? Who is this beside me? Carlo, help me. When is my baby due?"

She threw back the clammy covers and stared at the mound which was her stomach. Her belly moved gently as the baby turned. She thanked God it was still alive and safe within her.

She tried to move, but her legs were quite paralyzed. She threw back the covers farther to make sure they were there, for she could not feel them.

"Sip. Sip," urged Maria and Lila drifted away again into an insane sleep in which a vast ship sailed on waves a thousand feet high and convicts tore out her hair at the roots. The girl who'd sat beside her on the ship put her rosary around Lila's neck and pulled and pulled. The beads cut into her skin, but fortunately the holy necklace snapped and Lila woke to the worst hallucination of all.

She herself was entering the room. She, Lila, opened the door in her lovely gold gauze wedding dress with Benedetto's collaret gleaming at her throat. Her hair, an unnatural orange color, was loose and hung down like damp wool over the left side of her face.

Lila watched herself approach the bed where she bent down to kiss Carlo full and long on the lips and saw her hand go beneath the sheets to stroke him.

She heard him murmur as he woke, "Lila, darling Lila."

"Come with me, my love," said the vision, moving back the bedclothes and lifting Carlo's legs from the bed. "Come with me."

Lila, the bed-ridden Lila, could sense her husband's body throbbing with desire beside her. He got off the bed like a sleepwalker, and the other Lila put her arm around Carlo to help him walk. But as her head touched his shoulder, the orange hair moved, and underneath was a bright red scar, a warped mouth. Carlo stumbled out with her.

Lila was wide awake for the first time in ages. The side of her face felt sticky where the last spoonful of Maria's potion had seeped when she had not had the strength to swallow it. Gritting her teeth, Lila tried to move her legs but they would not budge. Her hands were free, and with a supreme effort she managed to raise herself up but dropped back straight away from exhaustion. This small victory spurred her on and she sat up again, higher this time, and gasping for breath she looked around the room. Everything had returned to normal. Objects were in their proper places, and the ceiling stayed where it had always been.

Lila managed to move one leg off the bed, then the other, falling straight onto her knees when she tried to stand. She crawled towards a chair, clutching it and trying to drag herself upright. Never before had she been so conscious of the weight, of the bulk of the baby who lay still now.

"I *will* stand up, I *will*," she swore, and moments later, holding onto the chair, she stood erect and even managed to reach a lamp which she picked up.

With a feeling of triumph, she reached the dressing-room door and leaned, out of breath, against the frame. When she opened the door, the sight that met her eyes did not even cause her to blink. As much as her groggy mind had allowed, she had expected it. Carlo lay nude on the dressing room couch, and Maria was clumsily removing the golden dress, trying not to disturb the awful orange wig. Carlo's eyes were closed and he muttered, "Lila, Lila," over and over again.

Beneath the dress, Maria was naked, her skin coated with oil that gave her body a weird greenish tint. She climbed on top of her brother, and Lila softly closed the door.

It really didn't matter, she told herself, straining to sort things out in her still-clouded mind. The state she was in would make it impossible for her to defend herself against Maria. She must improve her strength, clear her mind, and then try to get Carlo away from his twisted sister.

Suddenly she remembered Angela. Maybe she could help.

Walking a little better now, straighter, she went onto the gallery. When she looked around she gasped.

Mist seeped through the edges of the front door, through the windows; feathery whirls of fog hung like bats in the high foyer and gathered at the top beneath the stained-glass roof, hiding it completely. Through a window she saw that outside a thick dirty cloud surrounded the house. She imagined it poised like a black angel over the canals of Venice.

Moisture dripped from the cobwebs making dull, mechanical *plops* in the passage and on the stairs as, holding her lamp high, she walked slowly up to the third floor and into Angela's room.

The girl lay on her bed, both hands clutching her throat, her tongue arched and black as it protruded several inches from her tortured throat. Her eyes stared, terror-stricken, at nothing.

She was dead. Poisoned. Had been for days; no, weeks— already her body had begun to rot and smell.

Lila stepped back, and with her horror every ounce of strength she possessed flowed forcefully back into her body. She walked along the passage to Maria's laboratory and went in. The room was lit by several oddly shaped lamps hung low over a table at one end. Strangely enough, it smelled pleasantly of English country lanes in spring, and was warm and comfortable. A low bed was made up in one corner and an old, well-used armchair was beside it.

Under the lamps were dozens of boxes of flowers, beautiful full blooms, a riot of summer colors, so incongruous in this fog-filled palace at dead of night. Foxgloves, pinkish-purple with dark spots, their leaves hairy, stems thick and erect and next to them buttercups, so fresh and dainty that they brought an ache to Lila's heart. To see again buttercups, little petaled suns. Ah! Celandine in little clusters, larkspur, and daffodils, Mama's favorite. Maria had labeled them something else, not daffodils but *Amaryllidaceae* and there were poppies. Red silk petals tired and listless. *Papaveraceae,* Maria had written on the box.

That was what she had called the medicine she'd given them. Medicine made from poppies. *Opium!* Lila shook her head in disbelief.

On the other side of the table single plants grew in pots and Lila recognized henbane and poison ivy, and remembered Mama pointing them out and saying they must not be touched. Never eat berries, or any fruit, without showing it to her first. There was hemlock and fool's parsley, mistletoe. How innocent the mistletoe looked, reminding her of Yorkshire Christmases, carols and pealing bells. Yet here it grew for its poisonous berries, of that she was sure.

Laying her lamp down behind her, Lila swept every box from the table so they fell, a jumble of soil and leaves and dirty petals in a heap on the floor.

A scurrying sound from her left made her heart leap, and she saw a row of rats in cages. Disturbed by the noise they were scratching at their prisons in frantic distress.

She ignored them, and moved on to another table where glass phials stood in wooden frames all filled with colored liquids carefully marked in Latin. Lila picked up a phial containing a virulent purple stuff and tucked it in the sleeve of her nightdress. Which color had killed poor Angela, who had just been in the way, and not worth torturing?

She wondered if Maria intended to kill her before the baby was born, or if she wanted Carlo's child for her own.

She swept every bottle, every phial, every bowl off the table, and they landed with an enormous crash on the floor. At last, satisfied with her work, she turned to leave the room.

Maria stood in the doorway in the gold dress, without the wig. Her face was brilliant and blood red on the left side.

"That was my life's work," she said simply.

Lila shrugged and walked past the woman without a word. Out in the mist-filled gallery chill droplets fell onto her shoulders and in her hair. She went down the stairs and into the library. A few cinders still glowed in the library fireplace where the servants lit a fire daily.

Shuddering, Lila took her lamp and went down into the dark kitchen to fill a pan with water and bring it back to boil on the flickering flames. Fetching the tin of Turkish coffee from the cupboard where she had last placed it, she carefully brewed some and poured it into her little silver pot. Then she prepared a tray with three cups, and into one she poured a generous measure of the purple poison, all that was left from Maria's evil experiments. Then she filled each cup with strong black coffee.

Carlo was sitting up in bed with a puzzled, almost insane expression on his face, but he gave a radiant smile when Lila entered, and his eyes lit up with boyish excitement. She had never seen him look more handsome.

"By jove!" he remarked, the words sounding too English and out of place in the room of their imprisonment. "I'm feeling much better now. Hopefully we can leave for England in a day or two."

"That is right, my darling," Lila said, and handed him a cup of coffee which he held shakily.

She took her own cup to the window and stood staring out into the black blanket of fog which filled the Piazza San Boldo. The third cup was left on the tray for Maria, who entered at that moment, her eyes darting from right to left as if expecting an imaginary devil to leap out at her.

"I have made a drink," Lila said coldly, indicating the tray with a nod. "This time it is to wake us up, rather than send us to sleep."

She turned away and watched Maria's reflection in the dark window. The woman sniggered as she lifted the cup, contemptuous of this weak angelic-looking sister-in-law. She took a gulp of the coffee, and then, as the burning liquid attacked her throat, stared at Lila in horrified surprise.

Lila saw all this in the reflection. Then turning, she took the purple phial from her sleeve and held it up. It was half empty.

"One *drop* of that would kill!" the woman screamed, and glanced frantically about her.

Carlo lay back, his smile dying as he observed this mysterious struggle between the two women. As his sister's glance fell on him, the last evil thought of her life came to her. She darted to her brother, the coffee cup still in her hand.

"Sip!" she commanded, and lifting up his beautiful head, she forced the remains of the coffee between his trusting lips. Carlo dutifully swallowed the poisoned drink before Lila could move a muscle.

Lila had stood motionless at the window while Maria and Carlo died clasped in each other's arms. Whether Maria's death was made more agonized because her brother whispered over and over again, "Lila. Darling Lila," as he embraced her stiffening body, Lila would never know.

Nor would she know what had prevented her from moving when she saw Maria dart across with the cup. Had it really happened too quickly for her to prevent it? Was her own drug-filled mind still too sluggish to realize what was happening?

For a long time she stood by the window until a sudden pain shot upwards through her body. For a second she thought Maria had won after all, and had somehow administered a poison, but then she realized it was the baby.

Donning Carlo's thick dressing gown, she rushed to the door to get help, though she didn't know where to go. Then, through the fog, Father Judas appeared and stood at the bottom of the stairs.

"Maria is dead," said Lila in a strange, cracked voice she had never used before.

He made the sign of the cross and his eyes closed for several seconds. Then he opened them and said, "She was my daughter," and pushing aside his coarse garment he bared a shoulder where on the blue flesh glowed a red and violent blemish.

"The mark of Satan," he said. "And never has Satan had a more cruel, unholy revenge than when he put his mark on my baby's face."

"But she said Carlo—"

"I know she told the boy that. She thought it bound him to her yet more tightly. I remonstrated with her."

He shook his head as though Maria had merely been a naughty child.

Lila said, "I killed her."

"I know," he said simply. "You were her match. I was glad when you came. I could not stop her, whatever she did. It was my fault, through my sin, that she was as she was."

"The black ant?" cried Lila. "It was a lie, all that?"

"She had poisoned Carlo to prevent him from leaving."

"But we might have died!"

"I think not. She would never have killed Carlo, at least not while there was a chance of keeping him for herself. And you. She was waiting for the baby to come. You were safe until then. She wanted Carlo's baby."

"Tonight," Lila said, wincing as the pain attacked again, but determined to know all, "she and Carlo . . ." She could not go on but the old priest knew what she wanted to say.

"It has always been like that. She loved him to the exclusion of all else in life. She was there when he was born, and from that moment on, he was her passion. Her mind was brilliant. I passed on to her all my medical knowledge, but it was the experiments that fascinated her."

"You mean the poisons."

"Yes. She found poisons in the most innocuous of plants. They were delivered to her from all over Europe. Daffodils, buttercups, hydrangea. Then, after she had brewed a toxin, she would find an antidote, sometimes from a different part of the same plant."

His eyes glowed with pride as he spoke of his terrible child.

"Sometimes she experimented on herself and would be covered in sores or a rash, with fever or ague, which she would then try to cure. Sometimes I would find her unconscious and hallucinating."

Lila grimaced, impatiently and uninterested in Maria's doings.

"But Carlo—" she interrupted.

The priest began to climb the stairs, the huge crucifix which hung down from the rope around his waist banging against his knees as the figure on the cross twisted and turned like a marionette. Perspiration glittered on his brow.

"Carlo was nineteen when he went to Cambridge. Until then they lived in Paris. Girls became interested, began to write to him, call on him, so, once back from England, Maria brought him here, where no one except Benedetto knew them."

"But he did not willingly . . . allow her . . ." She did not finish, but she knew she must have the answer to her unspoken question.

"Carlo was a good and pure young man." The priest gave

a ghost of a smile. "He knew nothing. He was drugged and hypnotized for almost the whole of the year they spent here and for part of the time in Paris. Then Benedetto realized what was going on and managed to drag him away."

"I think Carlo realized in a sort of way. At the back of his mind he knew things were not right." Lila turned on the gaunt priest accusingly. "Angela is dead too. Poisoned by your daughter. How could you *let* her?"

"How could I *stop* her?"

Father Judas stopped a few steps below her and stared at her with an agonized face.

"My baby girl, born through my sin. When the countess waited for the baby to be born, when we both waited, neither knew if it would be mine or the count's. We assumed it would never be known, but then I delivered her and there was my mark, the exact same shape but on her, poor girl, it was over her face."

Suddenly Lila gasped and doubled over, her hands on her belly.

"The baby is coming!"

Adjusting immediately to this new crisis, Father Judas said curtly, "It will not arrive so quick. Lie down in the bedroom."

"Not in there!" gasped Lila.

"Downstairs, then, in the library."

He reached up and took her arm. His hand was like an iron skeleton, his fingers pressing into her flesh as he helped her down the stairs.

He guided her into the library and made her lie before the dying fire, telling her firmly, "Relax there. And hold. Do not let the baby come yet. I will direct you when the time comes. First, I will get clean water and cloths from the chapel."

Minutes later, Lila's wail echoed up into the foggy reaches of the Palazzo Ruzzini as Father Judas hurried back. The baby's head had thrust its way into the world, and before he could reach her, Lila's second cry told him he would be too late to help. He returned to find a baby boy lying in a bloody mess on the silver lining of Carlo's dressing gown.

"It is a boy. A fine boy. Thin and small, and he has come early. But fine, nevertheless."

"Is he all right?"

"Everything is there," he said, an odd, joyous note in his voice. That this lovely babe should appear in the Palazzo Ruzzini within minutes of the death of the only creature he had cared for in thirty years, was little short of a miracle. A strange, tickling sensation in his throat surprised him.

He turned the baby upside down and smacked the small, creased bottom, and the little one opened his mouth and announced to the world that he was alive and well. Wrapping the child in a lace-trimmed cloth, Judas handed him to Lila, who was sobbing.

"We must get help for you," he said. I will cut the cord, but both of you must be washed in hot water. It will take too long to heat it here. This place is not fit for a newborn child, anyway."

He hurried to the front door and shouted until a wretched beggar appeared, not particularly caring whether such a call on an unearthly night like this meant good luck or bad. When promised ten silver ducats if he found a carriage, he was glad he'd followed the voice, and he set off in search of transport for this mad-looking priest.

When the beggar returned, Judas wrapped Lila and the child in a cloak and, with the help of the coachman, carried her out to the carriage.

Beatrice da Porto was awakened in the early hours of a wretched February morning to admit her cousin's wife whom she had thought to be in England many weeks ago. Lila was hysterical one minute and dead calm the next, but the baby, once washed, was beautiful. He seemed to be the image of his handsome father.

The entire household shed tears, Lila for her dead husband and her new child, Beatrice for she knew not what, and Rosetta for her daughter, Angela. All the servants who were summoned to help, to boil water and wash, find clean clothes, and prepare meals also cried, with wonder and pity.

Chapter Seventeen

"What will you call him?" asked Beatrice. She was sitting and holding a mirror up to her face, practicing a new smile which involved turning up the corners of her mouth a fraction, while keeping the rest of her face completely still. It looked seductive and hid the unwelcome little lines at the corners of her mouth which were so much more noticeable nowadays.

Lila sat contentedly on a sofa by the open French window in the morning room of Beatrice's mansion. It was an afternoon in early May, and for the first time that year the scent of spring was in the air, arriving at last to drive away the awful fogs which had imprisoned the city for nearly three months. The sun struggled to break through mild gray clouds, succeeding occasionally, and its unaccustomed warmth was a tonic to all who saw and felt it.

The colonnaded courtyard with its marble statues and bright green shrubs looked freshly painted in the bright afternoon. In one corner, a fountain tinkled merrily. The flower beds were as yet a mass of green, listless plants, but today they seemed stronger and fuller. The neatly clipped box and yew trees were unaffected by the climate and in and out of their regimented lines a peacock was strutting slowly.

Her legs tucked in a thick, cream shawl and with another shawl about her shoulders, Lila cuddled her baby boy to her breast. At three months he had lost his wizened redness and his skin was faint brown. His eyes were light blue, though Lila was sure they would later become a tawny brown like his father's.

"I have decided to call him Benedetto," she answered Beatrice.

Her cousin gave a small gasp of surprise.

"Had you not been on board ship and a thousand miles or more away from that lovable rascal of a husband of mine when you conceived I should immediately become suspicious." Beatrice laughed and looked curious. "But tell me, Lila. Who chose that name? You knew Benedetto only for a very short while, didn't you?"

"The obvious choice is Carlo," Lila replied sadly, "but I could not bear to say that name over and over again for the rest of my life. Carlo loved Benedetto so, and the name is a link with Venice. In England I shall call him Ben. A good solid name for a good solid boy."

She had toyed with calling her son "Phillip," but that seemed a betrayal of her husband. Lila sighed and leaned back against the arm of the sofa.

Beatrice rushed over. "My dear, you are tired. Here, let me take Benedetto, little Ben. Come, my darling cherub. Let Aunt Beatrice hold you to her heart."

Beatrice wondered why she had not had children of her own, and guiltily hoped it was not God's punishment for her preoccupation with keeping her youthful curves firm and inviting. Not that carrying little Ben had harmed Lila's shapely form. She looked as wonderful as ever, her waist having virtually returned to its previous diminutive size. Although a trifle pale, her golden beauty had come back in full force, heartened as she was by the child now dependent upon her.

Noticing her pallor, Beatrice asked anxiously, "Are you sure you will be fit to travel by the end of the month?"

"I am quite sure," declared Lila, opening her eyes and looking determinedly bright in the hope that there would be no argument against her going. "I feel fitter every day. See, watch me dance."

She flung back the shawls from her legs and shoulders and sprang to her feet, skipping a few steps out into the courtyard, stopping there to breathe in the lovely fresh warm air.

It was difficult to believe, thought Beatrice, that this was the same young woman who had arrived that nightmarish morning in February, with her hair dirty and wild, covered in Carlo's bloody dressing gown.

Because she had spent the last hellish weeks in the Palazzo Ruzzini in a drugged stupor, everything that had happened had the quality of a dream, and like a dream, it all began to fade, and Lila sometimes found it hard to believe that it had ever really taken place at all. But she would never forget Carlo, so tall and beautiful, and often she thought about that enchanted morning in New South Wales when she lay in the emerald tent and he had appeared and set her heart aflutter. And she thought about those tempestuous nights on board the *Leo*, reliving the feel of his caresses and the ecstasy when he would take her and they would become one.

"Carlo. I loved you," she whispered to herself at night. He had never known there was someone else she loved more, and she was glad of that.

She would not look forward to the journey back to England. It would be carefully planned, the route prepared beforehand. Her clothing, Ben's needs, would be packed, but she tried not to think about leaving until it was actually happening. Then, no matter how close her approach to home, she would not begin to imagine what it would be like until she was there. Anticipation was dangerous and best avoided. She and Ben, Father Judas, and Beatrice's maid, Rosetta, would be departing for England in two coaches which would travel through Switzerland, Germany and Belgium, avoiding France which was still in a precarious state after the revolution and at desultory war with England.

Father Judas had been reborn with Ben. The death of his tormented child had released him from an agonizing burden which had weakened him, body and soul. Now, having picked up the new baby from the library floor, making him take his first breath and utter his first cry, and getting mother and child to a sanctuary—all this had filled his veins with a surge of new life and vigor. He felt a will to live. His mind began to work again and his medical knowledge proved invaluable in aiding Lila's recovery. She had asked him to accompany her to England, but had insisted that if they were to remain friends, she would only call him by his proper name from then on. Father Jude.

Privately, Lila wished Rosetta were not accompanying them. The woman was still distraught over Angela's death. Indeed, sometimes it seemed that the murder of her daughter had deranged her mind. Without warning her face would become twisted with horror as she relived in her imagnation the last tortured moments of the girl's life.

Beatrice thought the journey to London and the responsibility of caring for Lila and Ben would return the woman to sanity. It was churlish and uncharitable to be reluctant to take the woman, Lila told herself. Although she was in no way to blame for the girl's death, it was under her roof she had died. She did not mention her concern to anyone.

Father Jude had purchased two fine brown coaches which would be kept on in London, and had insisted on the Ruzzini crest being painted in gold on the doors.

"Are you to deny who you are?" he said with his newfound firmness when Lila protested at this. "You cannot escape your past."

She conceded that she was being weak and silly, and so, one fine June morning, she climbed into the first Ruzzini coach and Beatrice tearfully handed over baby Ben after showering him with kisses.

"Can one ever become inured to saying good-bye?" Lila wondered as she waved until the coach turned and Beatrice was no longer visible. "I wish it were so, for no matter how many farewells I make, they become no less painful."

However, this good-bye was cushioned with joy for she was on her way home.

She felt liberated at last after nearly three years' imprisonment of one form or another as the coach left the environs of Venice. The countryside was lush, the trees green and covered with vines. Every scrap of fertile land was cultivated, and it was a perpetual delight to the eye. Her heart bursting with happiness, Lila felt that all this beauty had been especially prepared just for today in honor of her new freedom.

Their first stop was Padua, a poverty-stricken town, poorly lit by the candles illuminating small altars and by the occasional street lamp. The uneven paving-stones caused their carriage to rock dangerously despite its slow progress through the narrow streets.

Lila had wondered why Father Jude had arranged for a pile of bedding to be brought in the second coach, and this question was solved when they stopped at the White Cross hostelry and were shown their room. The beds were filthy, and Lila gasped as insects scurried away when the gray sheets were lifted. The mattresses were put in the corridor and their own fresh cots made up. All four travelers were apparently expected to share the same room. A large basket had been brought for Ben and this was placed on top of a chest to protect him from vermin. Downstairs the food smelled appetizing but Father Jude pronounced it suspect and brought in a small charcoal stove on which a sullen and reluctant Rosetta cooked their evening meal.

This was the pattern of their journey through Italy. During the day they traveled through fresh luscious countryside, and they would buy oranges, grapes, figs and a heady fruit wine that raised Lila's spirits joyfully. At night they stopped in small, dusty villages with unsanitary, sordid, often windowless accommodations; or they entered majestic crumbling cities such as Verona or Milan with their glorious marble palaces, which gave the towns an undeserved elegance at first glance, for on closer inspection, one found open sewers running past people's homes, polluting the lovely canals and rivers.

Everywhere they went children leaped onto their carriage, chanting and screaming for coins. Father Jude said to ignore them, so she just sat staring above their faces at the sky, or at her boots, for she was told if one gave a coin the carriage would be besieged by children sensing weakness, not generosity. Occasionally, to be rid of the poor mites when they were leaving a town, Father Jude would throw a handful of coins out of the window and the children would leap from the coach sides, descending on the money like a pack of rats on food and Lila would shudder at the horror of these children's lives.

Their final stop before entering Switzerland was on the banks of Lake Como, as blue as a bright summer sky. Well-known as a country retreat of wealthy nobles, the conditions in the Three Kings where they stayed for the night were an improvement on those suffered so far.

Ben was four months old that day. Lila touched his tiny hand as he slept. snugly wrapped in his basket. She marveled at the wrinkled knuckles, the miniature nails, his tiny finger-prints. That it should be such a perfect reproduction of an adult's hand seemed a miracle. Some day it would be wrinkled and spotted with age like the priest's. She would be dead, while this little defenseless human being would be himself an old man. She blinked away the tears, impatient with herself for such miserable thoughts. The present was all that mattered.

She placed a soft kiss on the baby's pink ear and retired to her own bed, but uncharacteristically on this wearying journey she was unable to sleep and lay tossing and turning, suddenly overwhelmed with worry at the responsibility of having little Benedetto to rear alone.

For hours she lay, trying to relax, counting sheep, then finding herself tense and worried again. At last she began to drift into sleep, but became alert when the bedroom door began to open cautiously. The room was drenched in moonlight, and she lay, strangely without fear, waiting to see who would enter. When she saw that it was Father Jude, she smiled and nearly called out to him, but his stealthy movements prevented her.

She watched him through lowered lids as he crept towards Rosetta's alcove, lifted the curtain and entered. Again she lay silent, this time waiting for the woman's cry of protest, but surprisingly none came, merely a muffled rustling of bed-clothes, and then subdued moans of delight.

Lila snuggled down into the bedclothes to hide her giggles.

People! They were a constant source of amusement. She would never cease to find them fascinating. With the faint sound of lovemaking in her ears, she eventually fell asleep.

The next morning Rosetta pleaded a headache and traveled alone in the coach behind them. Lila sat opposite Father Jude. The priest had filled out and his skin lay more thickly on his bones. Socks and stout sandals covered his feet, and he wore a shirt underneath his robe which was no longer of rough, coarse cloth but a finer serge. He had acquired a dignity which his vast learning and his two degrees entitled him to.

That morning she expected some sign of penitence, for after all, this straying from the path of celibacy had caused the change of name to Judas andthe abject atonement for more than thirty years with the Ruzzini family in Paris and Rome. However, there was no sign of repentance. Indeed, as they crossed the Alps into Switzerland Father Jude seemed contended and self-satisfied and stared out of the window complacently as though his mind was elsewhere. Lila decided that the night before with Rosetta was not the first, and smiled, thinking that if the priest's mind was elsewhere, then it was no doubt in bed with Rosetta.

He turned suddenly and caught her eye, and smiled. "So! You were awake last night. I thought so, and it worried me."

"It did not worry you enough to stop," Lila said with a laugh. She hoped he would not find her amusement offensive. Apparently he did not for he laughed back and said simply, "My need was greater than my concern."

Lila shrugged. There was nothing she could say to that.

"Are you—does it disgust you?" the priest asked hesitantly.

Eyes wide with amazement, Lila replied, "Of course not! It is your life, you must do as you think fit. As long as Rosetta does not object."

"Her need is as great as mine. We have both lost our daughters and it is a great relief to immerse oneself in passion, to know there are emotions other than misery and grief."

"I am sure you are right," Lila said earnestly. "But many years ago, you decided it was a sin—"

"It *is* a sin," the priest interrupted. "I am a man of God and took the vow of celibacy. Many break it. In fact, more betray the promise than keep it. But I have made another vow, this time not a holy one. My dear countess, I shall never say mass again, never partake of the host or enter a church. I have cheated on my Maker, but I no longer have the willpower to resist. In three years, I shall be sixty. I may not have much longer to live, for I have abused my body woefully in penance for my previous crime for more than half my life, and I am not strong. For the rest of my life I mean to give in to my weaknesses and pander to my passions. I shall go to hell and shout joyfully on entry for it will have been worthwhile. In other words, I intend to live my life to the full."

Lila had said she was not disgusted, but she was not at all sure if she approved. No doubt one thought differently about things at fifty-seven than one did at twenty, but she felt Father Jude should be able to control the weaknesses he spoke of. She was glad he had confided in her, however, and felt there was now an understanding between them, a friendship similar to the one with Queen Lil, and because of this she grinned widely and leaned forward to take both his hands in hers.

"I confess myself pleased for your sake that you have decided to be your own true self," she said and was not sure whether this was a tactful lie or not.

Some weeks later she was glad she had been so openly broadminded, for something was soon to show her that in matters of passion she herself was one of the weakest of mortals.

Chapter Eighteen

After the breathtaking beauty of Switzerland and the excellence of its inns, followed by the intensity of the German Black Forest, the countryside of Belgium proved flat and dull. The travelers began to feel tired and bored after their weeks on the road. Lila refused to stop anywhere for more than one night, despite Rosetta's pleas that they rest. Ben had begun to suffer from the colic and brought up much of his food and though Father Jude said this was quite normal, they slowed their pace to accommodate the baby, taking time-consuming detours to travel on better roads.

Not until she was within the bosom of her family, and she saw Ben asleep on English soil, would Lila feel safe again. Lord Rawlesbury, Lady Jersey—they could not touch her now that she was a countess, a citizen of Venice. Just let them try, she thought scornfully, and she would fight back with all the now ample resources at her disposal.

They pressed on. The two coachdrivers, experienced men hired in Venice, began to find their jobs tedious. Father Jude had thought it wiser to take on drivers they could trust rather than change men when they changed horses as most travelers did. The men were decent and honest and even guarded the coaches at night by sleeping in them. But they had behaved themselves for too long. One night, overcome by a feeling of homesickness for Venice, both had too much to drink and had to be sharply cautioned several times to drive more slowly and watch where they were going.

Lila had already noticed how suddenly night fell on this part of the Continent. Unlike England, where the evenings dimmed into dusk and gradually turned i into night, here it was broad daylight one minute, and then without warning the sun would disappear as if a huge hand had forced it down, and it would be pitch dark.

As they rode into the blackness of the night, Father Jude peered out of the window and complained, "We should have arrived at Liège an hour ago."

After another half an hour, both carriages stopped and the drivers could be heard shouting to each other.

The priest got out of the carriage and returned to report with disgust that the leading carriage had taken the wrong road despite the instructions he had given earlier in the day. Ben whimpered in his basket on the seat beside Lila, hungry for his evening meal. She climbed out of the carriage and stood on the dried mud road, staring around for some sign of life.

The landscape was flat. An isolated tree silhouetted here and there made crazy shapes against the dark blue of the sky.

"They should have guessed from the state of the road," the priest snapped irritably. "It is clearly little used."

"Then we must turn and make for Liège," Lila said impatiently, wondering why they had not done so immediately.

"We will probably have no choice but to do that," said Father Jude. "There is a small village a little further on. I am wondering if it would be quicker to press on and seek accommodation rather than waste time retracing our steps."

"As long as we do not risk losing ourselves yet further."

From inside the coach Rosetta expressed her disgust at the entire situation by giving a highly dramatic sigh. Then Ben began to give sad, subdued cries.

"Oh dear! What shall we do?" cried Lila, when her mind was made up for her.

From the distance came the sound of horses' hooves, loud on the clay surface and echoing crisply in the still night.

Father Jude crossed himself and muttered gloomily, "Should we prepare for rescue or for death?"

"Let us wait and see," Lila said irritably, and Rosetta, when she heard the approaching horsemen, uttered an agonized wail, at which Ben started to cry in earnest.

Lila opened the door of the carriage and was about to scold the woman for her lack of control when she remembered Angela. Instead she picked up her child, cuddling him close, and Father Jude helped her to the ground again.

The riders had reached the small party by now and the leader dismounted and came over to them.

"Can we help? Are you in trouble?"

To everyone's relief the voice was young and pleasant and spoke in French.

"Just travelers taken the wrong road," replied Father Jude.

Rosetta jabbered in fear and Lila told her sharply to be quiet. By now she was used to the darkness and could see that the men on horseback were soldiers, and the one who had approached them was an officer. Removing his hat, he bowed low before her.

"Madame! Lieutenant Jean St. Laurent, at your service."

He was little more than eighteen, bright-eyed and eager to help.

"Countess Ruzzini, sir."

She curtsied but was unable to offer her hand, for Ben was struggling, and his cries had reached desperate proportions.

"This is my friend, Father Jude. As you can see, our coachman took the wrong road and we don't know whether to go back or press on."

"Let me beg you to do neither, countess. Our camp is a mere mile ahead and I know my commandant will be delighted to accommodate you and your party for the night. It will be under canvas, I regret, but quite comfortable and clean, I assure you."

Lila did not tell the young man that she was quite familiar with life under canvas, but looked inquiringly at Father Jude. He quickly nodded agreement, and the young soldier's offer was gratefully accepted.

Two men were dispatched ahead to give notice to the camp. The travelers returned to their coach and conversed with the helpful lieutenant through the open window as the horses were directed gently over the bumpy roads. Both drivers had sobered enough to feel sorry about their misbehavior and glad the situation had turned out so well, though they would have preferred not to be rescued by a crowd of Frenchies, for it was the French who'd taken their beloved city and given it to the Austrians.

Rosetta was disgusted at the idea of a window being open at this time of night but her angry sniffs were ignored, and bobbing Ben up and down on her knee in an effort to keep him quiet, Lila learned from their new companion that a small detachment of the French army was returning to France from Westphalia where their commandant had been conducting urgent business. After some days of hard travel they had decided to encamp for the night, and Lieutenant St. Laurent and a dozen men were returning from buying wine and fresh food for their supper.

At the camp, a tent had already been set aside for Lila and her baby, and quarters for Jude and Rosetta were being organized. Rosetta came in to help her prepare to feed to Ben. She held him, while Lila removed her bonnet, also taking out the pins which held her curls neatly in place. Her golden hair fell loosely down, covering her shoulders in soft waves. Then she removed her tailored green jacket and quickly undid the buttons of her blouse, as Ben wailed in Rosetta's arms.

Baring one white breast she took Ben and guided him to the nipple, at the same time sinking down onto a stool and sighing with relief, smiling thankfully at Rosetta. She told her to go have her own supper and in half an hour or so bring in something light, for Lila was more tired than hungry, and she would appreciate a glass of the wine Jean St. Laurent had brought.

At first the baby sucked greedily, his gums pressing urgently into his mother's breast, but then the pressure became more gentle and Lila removed him. He sucked aimlessly while she put her hand inside her blouse and cupping her other breast brought it forth for Ben to continue his feed.

In about ten minutes he fell asleep still sucking, and she put him on her shoulder and rubbed his back, waiting for the burp to come.

It was then that Lila became aware that she was being watched. At first she thought it was Rosetta, and held back a sharp command that the woman should not creep up on her like that, but the hand she could see holding back the canvas flap was not Rosetta's, and the watcher, realizing he had been noticed, drew the cover back and stepped into the tent.

It was man, carrying a bottle of wine and some food on a small tray which he placed on a table near the bed.

He gazed at her insolently, his dark, somber eyes drinking in the exposed breasts and the tumble of golden hair, and she could see that desire was hot within him. He did not bother to disguise this with polite greetings or conversation. At first she thought he was a servant, but even if this had been so, his brooding, passionate stare somehow prevented her from crying out or telling him sharply to leave. She dimly realized that, against all logic, she did not want him to go!

He was not tall, and wore plain dark clothes. These, with his smoldering black eyes and skin almost as brown as an Asian's, gave a look of of unusual foreignness not often found in Frenchmen, exaggerated by the erotic desire so openly expressed as he continued to gaze at Lila.

At last he spoke. "Jean St. Laurent said you were pretty. He was wrong. You are the most beautiful woman I have ever seen."

What impudence, thought Lila, feeling her knees weaken and her heart race. How infuriating that she should feel a blush creep up and engulf her cheeks.

"Do you usually enter a lady's room without knocking?" she asked as icily as her trembling voice would allow.

"Knock? On a piece of canvas?" he replied mockingly, his sensual lips curving with a sardonic smile. His French was accented, but she could not place its origin.

Lila hid behind her baby, rubbing his back with unnecessary violence until he burped, and then she took him to his basket and he snuggled contentedly down with a deep, satisfied sigh.

This man was a magician, surely, a hypnotist. No ordinary mortal could have such fascination, such power. She wanted to belong to him, and as his dark eyes bored into her, all virtue, morality, and willpower melted away. She was her mother's daughter, a courtesan who would be this magnificent, this dreadful man's slave.

Still maintaining a façade of prim indignation, she started to button her blouse and cover her nakedness from his burning regard.

"Do not bother to get dressed again," he said in a hard voice.

She dropped her hands to her sides helplessly and stared at him, her eyes brilliant as sapphires, tears not far away as new emotions struggled for release. Just the light touch of his hands on her arms sent a shiver of raw delight through her body, and when he bent his head to her breasts she could contain herself no longer and cried out in a way she had not thought herself capable.

Then with his taut, strong arms he lifted her and carried her to the bed. The touch of his hands burnt her flesh, and she felt she would remain marked for all her life by this man's possession of her. No longer was she in a tent in Belgium, but in a world where every touch was emphasized a thousandfold, every thrust, every kiss an unbearable pleasure.

Much later, when it was over she gazed at him, still bemused and astonished at herself. Next morning he would be gone, which was as she wanted it. But the glorious joy of that night would stay with her forever, and she knew that even with Phillip Grenville, if fate should grant they would ever come together again, there would never be a night like this.

"I never want to know who you are," he murmured softly, kissing the corner of her mouth, her chin, the hollow of her neck. "St. Laurent was so dazzled he could not remember what you were called. And you will never know who I am."

"We shall never hear of each other again," said Lila. Tears appeared and he gently kissed them away.

"Tell me your first name though, for I shall never forget you. When I am old, I shall remember this night and draw comfort from it. I must know your first name."

"Lila," she replied.

"Lila." He said the word in an odd, clipped fashion. "Lila."

"And your first name?" she asked, stroking his naked shoulder.

His hand was heavy on her hip and both felt desire mounting yet again. He rose to take her once more but before they entered their own sweet world, he muttered his Christian name.

"Napoleon," he said.

* * *

England! It was there, within sight, not too many miles away. England. She had been sitting below, playing with Ben and had not been told it was so near. Father Jude said she was far too excited and would make herself ill, so he waited until the coast was almost upon them before calling her.

"I never realized it would be so quick. I am only used to long sea journeys." She chattered animatedly and Father Jude was charmed by her childlike enjoyment. So far she had always appeared so much in control of herself, and wise beyond her years.

There it was, under dark July clouds, white cottages nestling in gentle Suffolk hills. The flat plains of Essex were to their left, where waterways could be seen gleaming dully on which sat fishing boats, their sails hanging limply on this windless day.

Harwich was a bustling, lively port and Lila resisted the temptation to kneel down and kiss the ground—but she did bend down and pick up a piece of earth between her fingers.

"England. This is England, Ben." She touched his fingertips with the black soil and he immediately began to eat it.

Laughing, she cleaned his hands, and they waited for the Ruzzini carriages to come off the ship. The priest stared about him with great interest. This was his first time on English soil, and he looked forward to his new existence in the Ruzzini home in London.

Of course, Lila would not need a priest, even if Father Jude continued with the church, but she would require his assistance with her affairs. So he had appointed himself, without Lila's knowledge, as her secretary and manager of the vast Ruzzini fortune, the extent of which Lila was as yet little aware.

He vowed he would never admit it to another soul, but his new employer had captured his heart in a way he had not considered possible. Surely, only a very young man was capable of such foolish, doglike devotion? This was not the chaste love of an older man for a young girl, a father-daughter love, but genuine deep and passionate adoration.

Jude would never let the countess know of his love. It was his new, but not unwelcome cross. He would serve her, look after her interests before his own, and if anyone tried to harm her, as they had done once before, then they would have him to deal with, and he would lay down his life to protect his mistress. It was the Countess Ruzzini who had been the cause of his bitter withdrawal from life more than thirty years ago. Now a second countess had resurrected him.

It had taken a great deal of argument to keep Lila from taking the carriage and traveling then and there to Grassbrook Hall. Jude knew that once she was with her family it would be difficult to get her away, and there were many things he wanted to discuss before she hid herself in the countryside. He pleaded that she spend at least one night in London to sort out her affairs and inspect her new home.

Lila reluctantly agreed, swayed by the fact that she was unsure of the state her family was in. They were bound to have written to her over the years, but she had never been anywhere long enough to receive a letter from them. Mama could be dead; so might Papa, for had he not had a stroke three years before? She had written to them from Venice, telling them of Ben's birth and of her planned return to England in June or July. In fairness to them she felt they should be advised of the time of her impending arrival, so a messenger was dispatched immediately to give notice that she and her son were in England and intended to return to Grassbrook Hall the following day.

The gleaming white marble of which the Ruzzini London residence was constructed had been carted all the way from Volterra a hundred years before. The building was called simply Park House and the simplicity of its name was echoed in its architecture, both inside and out. No doubt its designer felt the richness of the materials was sufficient to its grandeur. And indeed the plain square of the house, with its steps the full width of the front, guarded by two white columns, had a regal beauty which more ornate buildings often lacked.

A London couple, Arthur and Gertrude Hoggett, had lived for many years in the basement of the house acting as caretakers. They had been warned in good time by Father Jude that it was the new countess's intention to make her permanent home in London, and anxious not to lose their comfortable quarters, they had Park House scrubbed from top to bottom. Dust covers had been removed from the furniture and every bit of wood had been polished with zeal. Drapes were cleaned, linen was brought out from long unopened drawers and washed, cupboards were aired and carpets beaten.

Lila, who had half-dreaded finding something akin to the

Ruzzini Palace in Venice, was delighted with this elegant home.

"Is this really mine?" she cried, dancing in and out of high-ceilinged white rooms, round and round the vast pillared ball-room, sitting on gold satin-covered chairs and on the edge of lace-covered beds.

"I hate dark, gloomy houses," she said laughing, while Rosetta watched this exhibition of happiness sullenly. "This is just the sort of house I would want if I could choose. Was the Countess Ruzzini responsible for all this lovely decoration?"

"They spent their honeymoon here," said the priest, "and the countess had the house completely redecorated and refurnished. They planned to spend at least half their time in London, but back in Venice—"

He stopped. Back in Venice, the countess had become infatuated with her priest and he had succumbed. She had never spoken to him again after Maria had been born, after she saw proof of her adultery branded forever on her baby's face.

The priest shook himself firmly. He must not keep returning to his guilt-ridden past, but must think of the future and of Lila, who needed him.

He explained her affairs to her that night as they sat in the drawing room, with the French windows open onto the smooth grass of the park behind. An angry-looking sun glimmered on the dark horizon as Father Jude told Lila how rich she was.

Carlo was half owner of the three ships that had gone to New South Wales, and of another five which traded with India and Ceylon, mainly in cloth and ornamental ware. These were stored in the Ruzzini warehouse in Marseilles, where there was also a small trading company which sold the imported goods to wholesalers. Father Jude had converted the money into English guineas and he reckoned the cargo on each ship was worth at least ten to fifteen thousand guineas. Normally all eight ships were in use, but Benedetto had requisitioned three for his expedition.

Venice held a traditional supremacy in the field of printing, and the Ruzzini family owned a firm which produced fine books, highly coveted throughout the civilized world. Also, the largest glass works in the republic was owned jointly by Benedetto and now, of course, by Lila.

She gasped, for although Carlo had explained that his family was rich, she had never dreamed his fortune was so great. But Father Jude had not finished. Adjusting a sheaf of papers on which he had made notes, he continued.

Carlo's father was a businessman of some skill himself, so there were other holdings which had been inherited by Carlo alone. A silk factory, about to close, had been purchased by the count and revitalized. It flourished, producing moirés, velvets, satins, damasks and a silk cloth in the Persian style so difficult to weave that its price was beyond the pocket of all but the wealthiest. The success of this venture had so encouraged her late father-in-law, the count, that he had deliberately sought out other businesses which were foundering for lack of new equipment or innovative management, and these he had bought, employing enthusiastic young men to haul the firms onto their feet again.

The count never urged mass production of inferior goods, but instructed his managers to concentrate on the finest quality and sometimes even to under-produce and so create a demand for the products. The little factory in Vicenza where small items of walnut furniture were made, for instance, had a waiting list of would-be buyers, all anxious to part with their money to become owners of the uniquely designed pieces.

Father Jude went on, describing holdings and investments, income from this, interest from that.

They came to the final piece of paper, and Jude delivered his summary. "Your yearly income is just in excess of one hundred and fifty thousand guineas. I find it difficult to put a figure on the total value of all your business assets, but I would hazard a guess that a figure of one million guineas is erring on the low side."

He lay down the documents and looked at Lila, waiting for her reaction.

"Thank you," was all she meekly said.

But still the priest had not finished. On the table before him stood a small wooden chest which Lila had noticed he kept close to him throughout the journey from Venice. Producing a large brass key from a cord around his neck, he inserted it into the ornate lock.

"Did Carlo tell you the family fortune was begun by his maternal grandfather who visited far off, unexplored lands and returned with a load of precious stones?"

Lila nodded numbly.

"Some of these were sold to provide the capital necessary

for the foundation of the commercial empire, but many were kept and fashioned into jewelry."

He brought over the box and knelt on the floor before her, lifting out one by one heavy gold necklaces set with flashing jewels, tiaras, rings, earrings, and bracelets; single jewel drops on delicate golden chains, jeweled pins, hair ornaments, and even a coronet. There were not only diamonds, sapphires, rubies, emeralds, and other familiar gems, but there were also some she had never seen before. Golden-brown brilliants and misty gray, purple, pink, and jet-black stones winked up at her. Lila did not touch a thing, but stared at the heap of priceless gems in fascinated horror. Men would kill for the smallest stone in that pile, yet she owned it all. She remembered the silver and jade necklace she had bought for Mama. How pathetic that appeared compared to all this!

There was yet more to come.

"I mentioned a silk factory. The count's wedding gift to his bride was an unusual one and his employees worked for nearly a year to produce it. A trousseau. Every garment designed by an artist and made by an expert."

Father Jude drew out another key and opened a trunk that had been deposited in the corner of the drawing room. Before Lila's astonished eyes he produced dress after dress of the most exquisite materials. Fairy-tale clothes she had never seen the like of, even in the court of the Prince of Wales. Satins embroidered with gold and silver thread in which nestled precious pearls. Velvets with real gems sewn on the waist, the cuffs, the skirt. Silks as soft as Ben's cheek with lace dripping from the sleeves and hem. A loose wrap in fiery hand-painted scarlet that ran through the priest's fingers like molten liquid. Garments fit for a princess, a queen, an empress.

"There is not another cloak like this in all the world," Father Jude announced proudly, and took from the wardrobe a garment that shimmered and twisted in his hands almost as if it were alive. "Sable, dyed black by a special process and lined with stripes of black and white crushed velvet.

"I think that is everything," he said with satisfaction. "It is all, I think, an inch or so too large for you. Rosetta can see to having it altered."

He looked about him at the pieces of paper extolling Lila's wealth, the heap of jewels, the unique clothes, and waited for her cries of delight. But there were none. To his amazement, Lila, her eyes large and bright with unshed tears, ran from the room without a word.

Down to the basement she fled where the Hoggetts were just settling down for the night and expressing to each other the hope that they had pleased the young countess.

"Hoggett!" she cried. "Call a carriage for me immediately."

"Why, milady. Your own carriages stand empty and I will gladly take you wherever you want to go. 'Twill not take a minute or more to harness the horses."

Hoggett appeared, rumpled, unsure if answering the countess's call immediately in a state of undress was better than letting her wait while he made himself respectable. He didn't think she'd have noticed if he'd come in nude, he decided as he hurried out to the stables. His wife came to help, fumbling with the stable bolts in her anxiety to please.

Lila hated their obsequiousness, and it added to her misery.

"Where did you want to go, milady?" Hoggett asked when all was ready.

"Hampstead. April Cottage, Hampstead. A new house. I don't remember the name of the street, something to do with a tree, I think."

"Myrtle Street, that's what it'll be. My wife's sister's in service that way and I know the area well. Get in then, milady, and we'll be on our way."

Yes, it was Myrtle Street. She recalled Rosalind describing the house with enthusiasm when it was being built. Just four bedrooms it was to have, and she had been in a tizzy trying to decide what sort of fireplace would suit the dining room best, and should the front door have glass panels to let in extra light, or be solid wood to keep out drafts?

Rosalind and Simon. They would bring her down to earth, remind her that she was really only Lilian Ward whose father was a nondescript member of Parliament. Better off than most girls, perhaps, but not as rich as some.

The carriage rattled apace through the darkening London streets, and Lila cursed Father Jude for waiting till now, her first night in England, before telling her of her unwanted wealth.

The village of Hampstead was quiet and dimly lit at ten o'clock on this unseasonably cold July evening.

"Here it is, milady. April Cottage."

Lila did not move but glanced at the small neat house through the glass. There were tasseled blinds on each window. The front door was solid and thick, protecting its occupants from the unwelcome drafts Rosalind had feared. A faint light shone upstairs.

They were in bed. It would be an adventure for Rosalind to receive a visit from her long-lost cousin late at night, but something made Lila hesitate. They were tight and secure in their own little world. Hoping perhaps for a raise in Simon's pay. Another ten pounds a year would open new horizons for them. A holiday, or new carpets. Maybe there were children in homemade trousers or cotton frocks which would be handed down.

She had no place in their lives now. She was calling on them for the wrong reasons, for comfort they could not give, for a problem she did not want to describe. Her enormous wealth had set her apart from ordinary people, and she did not belong anywhere.

Hoggett was astonished when the countess rapped on the carriage window and instructed him to return to Park House.

Chapter Nineteen

"Mama!"

They were expecting her and were standing at the drawing-room window. As the grand brown carriage turned into the drive, Lila could see the house, so comfortable and permanent, as if it had grown there, and everybody teemed out. Mama, Hettie, Mary, a young man she had never seen before, her old nurse Lucy, Norah, Thomas the gardener, Cook, a blur of other faces from the kitchen.

"Mama."

She could not fling herself into Mama's welcoming arms for she was carrying little Ben, but was enfolded instead, and then they all embraced the young mother and child together.

Hettie was taller than her older sister by two inches at least, and the young man was her fiancé, John Butler, son of a vicar, newly appointed curate at a church in nearby Halifax.

Mary had become as pretty as a picture and Mama looked

well. Lila could not get over her rosy cheeks and stout figure.

The servants, satisfied to see their Miss Lila back safe and sound and so grand, returned to their various duties.

"Papa?" Lila asked anxiously.

"Upstairs. He has not spoken now for three years. Since the day news reached us of the awful fate befallen you at Carlton House. He was stricken, and he lies abed, day and night, supping only warm milk or broth from a spoon."

Mama spoke matter-of-factly about her husband's illness, as though it was no longer a tragedy but something she had learned to live with.

"I can see him, can't I? Perhaps knowing I am safely home will have some good effect."

Hettie and Mary were left making an inordinate fuss of their new nephew, watched sternly by Lucy who had cared for all three girls since their birth, and by John Butler, who felt awkward and out of place in the presence of this brilliant sister-in-law-to-be.

William Ward lay propped up against a pile of bolsters and pillows, his eyes shut, his face turned away from the light which filtered in through shaded windows. His chin had sunk deep into his chest, and the only movement, apart from the barely perceptible rise and fall of his breast, was the occasional flicker of his eyelids.

"Papa," Lila whispered, sinking onto her knees beside him, then more loudly, "Papa."

There was no indication that he had heard.

"I am home, Papa. Here to stay, with a lovely grandson I know you will love." He had longed for a son. Benedetto would partly fill that need.

Although mother and daughter watched anxiously for a sign of recognition, William Ward remained in his own world.

Later that day, Lila wrote a note to Father Jude, who had remained in London to engage staff and arrange for the smooth running of the large London house. Rosetta had stayed with him. In the letter, she explained her father's illness and asked for his advice as a doctor.

Then she walked alone on the grounds, through the orchard where tiny apples grew in profusion, still almost hidden by the deep green leaves.

The earth was damp and moist, the sky gray, and there was a chill in the air quite unusual even for an English summer.

She remembered the lovely June day when Ralph had captured her in the long grass beneath that far tree, the day Lord Rawlesbury had asked her to carry out an important mission for her country.

Lila almost laughed aloud at the thought of how she had been taken in, and wondered how those two, that despicable father and son, would react when they came face to face with her. They were bound to once she set up home in London. There was nothing the social set there loved more than a new arrival, and as the Countess Ruzzini of Park House, she knew she would be welcomed in the Mall with open arms. There were few from that crowd who had known Miss Lilian Ward, and once established she would endeavor to prove herself ill-used by the Princess of Wales. Once the cream of society knew who she really was, she would see if they still invited her into their homes.

That night, discussing it with Mama, she was told impatiently to put the whole business behind her and try not to think of it again.

"No one, absolutely no one, thinks you were guilty of such a silly, dreadful thing with that servant," her mother said. "You have no idea what an ill reputation Princess Caroline has acquired. She has moved to her own residence, Montague House in Blackheath, where she entertains all sorts of gentlemen. It is even rumored that she has an illegitimate child."

"She is not an unpleasant woman, really," mused Lila, "though unfit to be a princess or a queen."

"Or even a wife," her mother laughed. Mama had acquired a down-to-earth manner, very different from her old refined and gentle air. She saw Lila watching her with some confusion, and laughed again, "I have changed, haven't I, my dear?"

"You are more . . . more . . ." Lila struggled for the appropriate word.

"Tough?" suggested Catherine Ward. "I had always rather cherished myself, you know. Ex-mistress of a great king. Coddled wife of an English gentleman. I basked in my own mystery and reputation."

"Mama! That is not true," protested Lila.

"Yes, it is, my dear child. It is all you saw of me and you are in no position to judge. Even I did not know I had it in me to be anything else until the dreadful morning that Margaret, Ralph Curringham's sister, came over and with awful relish

told us what had happened to you. I truly thought I would die
on the spot. The pains which had overwhelmed me for so long
attacked again in full force, and I began to gasp for breath.
But then your Papa fell to the floor as though a bolt of lightning
had struck him. Magically, my pains disappeared and I ran to
his side and called for Dr. Coates, who bled him copiously
over the next few weeks and gave him tonic after tonic."

"Bleeding is an old-fashioned and dangerous practice," Lila
said knowledgeably, remembering Father Jude.

"I do not know of that," her mother replied. "But I do know
it did your father no good. There I was, with two girls to bring
up, my older daughter in perilous danger, her whereabouts
unknown, and my husband paralyzed from a stroke. Then a
letter came from Miss Prymm saying you were dangerously
ill. My, what a load of tragedies! Simon rushed off to see you.
Lucy fed me eggs and milk, to build up my strength she said.
Indeed it did, and my body with it. I had no choice but to pull
myself together and cope, even when I heard you had been
deported to the farthest part of the earth. My pains never returned, and as you can see I am the very reverse of a shadow
of my former self."

She laughed yet again and Lila liked her this way so much
better. Before, Mama had been deeply loved and adored, but
a responsibility. Now she was someone to lean on and ask for
help. Yet at the same time, she was saddened that her mother's
amazing beauty had faded.

Catherine Ward leaned forward and picked up a large brass
poker to move the blazing logs so they spat and turned, showering sparks out onto the hearth. She shivered.

"Oh! If only this awful summer would actually become a
summer. It is so cold." She sat back in her chair. "Tell me,
Lila, are you all right? I have a heap of letters in my bureau
from all over the world. You have had three husbands and lost
them all. Whenever you feel the need, if you ever do, you
must tell me all that has happened. I am sure it must have been
a nightmare."

"It was indeed, Mama. You have no idea—"

She broke off, for the oddest thing happened. Memories
crowded in thick and fast. Images of the past three years. But
not nightmares. Anything but nightmares. Instead of the horrors, she remembered sitting on the deck of the *Gabriel* with
a laughing Timothy while he enthusiastically talked about their

future life together; the quiet evenings with Roland at New
Farm, when they sipped their home-made wine and watched
the breathtaking sunsets together; Queen Lil and George and
the wonderful camaraderie they had enjoyed on their journey
into the unknown; the nights with Carlo when he had taught
her to become a woman. Finally, with a thrill of desire that
almost took her breath away, came the vision of the French
officer who had loved her that heavenly night in Belgium.

She cried emotionally, "Suddenly, Mama, it has come over
me that it was not a nightmare at all. Well, only a part of it.
I am a lucky woman. So lucky, I want to cry. You will never
believe the friends I have made."

"Then my question is answered," Mama said gently. "You
are all right. Well-endowed financially too, I take it, for your
carriage outshines all others around here. The luggage you
bought and the clothes I saw being hung in your wardrobe are
all expensive and beyond my purse, of that I am sure."

"Mama! The most disconcerting thing has happened," Lila
said tragically.

Her enormous eyes filled with grief and Catherine Ward
waited anxiously for the awful tidings: Her daughter had stolen
the carriage, the luggage and the clothes; she was penniless,
in debt to avaricious moneylenders; worst of all, she had acquired the money in some criminal fashion. But the news was
quite different.

"I am rich, Mama. Not just ordinary rich, but wealthy beyond belief," Lila said in hushed tones.

Her mother smiled in sheer relief. She brushed aside all
Lila's fears and told her to enjoy her money and try to create
happiness for others with it.

"If you do not want it all, there are a multitude of good
causes you can embrace. We need a new almshouse here in
Grassbrook, for example. The present one is unsanitary and
unsafe and the poor souls who live there are miserably cold
and ill. I put in a bid here and now for a generous donation.

"But enjoy yourself, my love."

As is so often the case with the English weather, the summer
came upon them overnight. People flung off their clothes,
changed their heavy curtains for some of lighter weight, watered
their gardens, and complained of the heat.

Father Jude arrived in person to examine William Ward.

"He is in a state of shock," he said. "It is not a stroke at all and never has been. He has withdrawn from the world because he cannot take what it holds for him. I assume this collapse was caused on hearing bad news?"

"That is so," Lady Catherine said, finding this thin, ascetic monk cold and unlikable, and wondering where on earth Lila had found him. "His plot to achieve promotion within the Whig party resulted in our daughter, Lilian, being placed at great peril in the hands of dangerous men. This came as a great blow to us all."

"Indeed!" the priest cried, pleased to find his diagnosis confirmed. "Your terminology fits the situation perfectly. A blow. His brain suffered a blow and is refusing to return to consciousness."

Lady Catherine thought this sounded a load of nonsense, but Lila was listening to her friend and nodding as if he were the wisest man on earth.

"What must we do then?" Lila asked.

"Every minute that can be spared, you must talk to your father. He does not want to die. That is apparent by the fact that he allows you to feed him. Tell him over and over again that you are safe. That despite his unfortunate actions, here you are, alive and well. I guarantee nothing, but there is a chance that this message, if repeated often enough, might reach his stubborn mind, and he will wake."

Lila stayed peacefully in Yorkshire for several months. Against her mother's wishes, she asked the servants to keep her return as secret as possible. If asked, they were to say that lady from Venice was staying at Grassbrook, which was quite true.

As if to make up for its long delay, the summer was generous with its blessings, the sun appearing with glorious regularity to greet them morning after morning.

Lila went for walks with Ben who was now able to sit up, far sooner than any baby ever had before—or so said old Lucy proudly. It was a relief to have someone as trustworthy as her own nurse to care for Ben as she had never felt easy leaving him with Rosetta.

In September, Lila celebrated her twenty-first birthday with a quiet party to which only relatives were invited. Simon and Rosalind with their twin girls, John Butler, and two aunts. John had been prevailed upon to make a toast to this unnervingly lovely sister of his fiancée, and he managed this with dignity, stammering only very little while Hettie encouraged him with loving eyes.

"To Lila!" they chorused. "Many happy returns of the day."

"Now, you must wish," Mary told her when she blew out the candles on the cake. "But don't tell us what it is."

A jumble of wishes came to Lila's mind, involving Phillip Grenville, Papa getting better, and Ben growing up tall and strong like his handsome father.

As soon as tea was finished she went upstairs to see her father, which she had done regularly after every meal since coming to the house. Sometimes she took Ben with her. She told him about her party and how they all wished he had been there. She told him Mama needed him, that they all did, and would he please realize all was well, and it was quite safe to return to the real world again.

"Please, Papa. Please come back to us," she pleaded, stroking his thin, lifeless hand.

But Papa lay still and did not move. Her entreaties went unheard.

That night, when the aunts had gone, and Mary sat at the window in the fading light concentrating on a complicated piece of embroidery, and Hettie wandered about somewhere exchanging whispered confidences with John Butler, Catherine Ward asked her daughter the question she'd been longing to ask since her return in July.

"My dear, is it not your intention to contact the good Captain Grenville?" she asked gently. "I have never told you this for I was waiting for you to introduce his name, but the day after you were all but kidnapped and sent to New South Wales, he came here with your few possessions. He told us he would leave no stone unturned until he found you and brought you to England."

Lila was silent, the pangs of remorse which always attacked her whenever Phillip Grenville came to mind invading in full force now that Mama had actually spoken his name.

"Mama, you have no idea how badly I acted towards him. I had no faith. He came all the way to Sydney Cove to look for me, and I did not discover it until I was about to leave as Carlo's wife."

"Surely that is all the more reason for you to try to locate him. He is a fine man who impressed me deeply, and such devotion from one so distinguished and brave is a worthy thing."

"I do feel honored beyond words that he should think so lovingly of me, but I have let him down so cruelly that I should be ashamed to face him. Nevertheless, I asked Father Jude to send someone to Southampton when the *Northern Star* docked last month. This person reported that no one of the name of Phillip Grenville disembarked. It would seem that he has remained in New South Wales, perhaps to search for me, perhaps to make a new life. It may well attract his adventurous spirit."

Lady Catherine pursed her lips thoughtfully.

"Let us hope this is not the case and he comes back into your life shortly. A man like Captain Grenville is one in a thousand, in a million," she said fervently. "You must not let him go easily."

The leaves fell late because of the long delayed summer which stretched well into October. On All Souls' Eve a light rain fell, soaking the leaves which lay in piles against the railings and in the gutters of the Mall, blurring the reflections of the lamps in the glistening pavements.

Carriages clip-clopped busily to and fro, taking people to their evening engagements, and in the bedroom of her London house, Countess Lila Ruzzini prepared for her first social engagement since arriving in the capital.

A heap of cards awaited her appraisal when she came back to her residence from Yorkshire. Invitations to tea, to parties, soirées, receptions, concerts, and balls.

Rumors were rife in the parlors of the rich about the mysterious Venetian countess whose late husband was reputed to have been one of the richest men in Europe. The countess, it was said, was about forty, and wore a black lace eye patch, for she had lost an eye when a lover tried to blind her in a quarrel. No, said others, she is young with hair as black as jet, and olive skin. She was incredibly mean. No, generous to a fault. Had six children. No children, but was a passionate lover of horses.

At last the elite of London were to meet the new countess at a Halloween Ball to be given by the Duke and Duchess of Garth in their palatial home in Belgrave Square. The duchess had been quite wild with delight when she received an acceptance from Park House, for she had been sure her invitation would be politely declined—as everybody else's had so far—by the countess's secretary, who was a priest, of all things. Lila's acceptance gave her far more satisfaction even than that of the Prince of Wales, who could be counted on to attend practically any affair where there was plenty to eat and drink, pretty girls to flirt with, and people to talk to.

Despite Father Jude's opinion that her new clothes merely needed taking in a little at the waist, she had the clothes altered considerably into more fashionable styles. For her first venture into society, Lila was to wear silver tissue silk, as fine as a cobweb, lined with thick silver taffeta which was embroidered with tiny diamonds which shone dully through the filmy overskirt. The collar was high and so thickly sewn with jewels it gave the appearance of being a separate necklace, as did the similarly decorated cuffs which were caught in voluminous, sheer sleeves.

The color of the dress, the flashing diamonds in her ears and those on the simple tiara which Father Jude persuaded her to wear, seemed to overshadow the gold of her hair, giving it a silvery, unnatural sheen. When she entered the foyer of the Duke and Duchess of Garth's home, and the footman removed her shimmering fur cloak and announced her arrival, there was an audible gasp.

"By Gad! That's Lilian Ward," whispered Lord Ralph Curringham. He was leaning against a pillar sipping his fifth—or was it his sixth?—glass of the Garths' excellent brandy. He glanced at his wife, Lady Curringham, née Lady Sylvia Beauchamp, but the silly woman had not heard, and showed no sign of recognition as the brilliant, graceful figure of his ex-fiancée was led into the ballroom by her eager hosts.

In his surprise, Ralph stood forward away from the pillar, but stepped back quickly when he found himself losing his balance. He was in the process of drowning his sorrows, a daily necessity married to this inane, chattering little woman, who seemed to think having one baby gave her the excuse to become as fat as a cat and to forbid him access to her couch forever. Not that she'd ever been up to much in that direction, reflected Ralph. Provocative looks and little suggestive pouts before marriage, but once wed, all thoughts of keeping a husband satisfied in bed were thrown out of the window.

Whereas...

His eyes were on the silver-clad figure being introduced at

the far end of the ballroom. Whereas, Lila Ward . . . Damn it!
It *was* Lila. His lovely, down-to-earth Lila. No fluttering eyelashes and hiding coyly behind a fan with her. Yes, he'd known
there was passion, real passion there. If only he'd stuck by
her. . . .

She could have been his. That night he could have been
stripping the silver gauzy thing off the voluptuous curves of
the desirable creature being led gradually in his direction. He
imagined uncovering the white breasts, remembering them from
that day in Chelsea, when she'd fought him off. It seemed as
if brandy ran in his veins instead of blood, for his entire body
was on fire, throbbing, imagining, remembering. Lila. Lila
Ward. Countess Ruzzini.

Here she was now.

"May I introduce Lord and Lady Curringham," purred the
duchess showing off her prize, this unbelievably exotic Venetian noblewoman, to her friends. And, of course, her enemies.

"How do you do?" trilled Sylvia, thinking this shining figure
looked vaguely familiar. Of course. She had the look of Lila
Ward, the lady-in-waiting who had been so cruelly treated at
Carlton House.

She had been sorry about letting her friend down like that,
but her father had insisted, and Lila had just disappeared off
the face of the earth. There that night, so distraught and tearful,
then next morning, when Sylvia had sneaked along to see how
she had fared through the night, she was gone, forever, and
no one would tell her anything.

This foreign countess was so much older though. Not wrinkled or gray haired, but there was a look of experience and
maturity to her features that Lila never had.

How disgusting of Ralph to bend over the woman like that,
kissing her hand, staring at her with an invitation brazen in his
eyes. It was truly all he thought of.

All he said was, "Pleased to meet you," but there was an
insolent slur to his words.

Lila had never felt so powerful in her beauty. She was glad
Father Jude had insisted on the tiara. She was glad the unique
dress had been altered, for it was more elegant than any costume
here. People bowed to her, stammered their nervous greetings.
Men eyed her suggestively. A widow looking for a partner in
bed, maybe? Mothers regarded her speculatively; a wealthy
bride for their unwed sons. With the wives there was suspicion,

which they tried to hide, but could not. Did she look like an adulteress? Would she take their husband's love if offered?

In the midst of this adoration, this unanimous admiration, Lila suddenly smiled, for she thought of Queen Lil and imagined her thoroughly flattening Lila's conceited feelings with some remark, "Cor, ye don't 'alf fancy yerself, Lila-Medici-Ward. Don't forget you're a flamin' murderess, me old mate. Ye should see yourself, floating around like a puffed-up butterfly, whilst all these so-called ladies and gentleman cowtow to ye. Countess High and Mighty, that's what you are. Come down to earth, Lila, me gal."

These imaginary words rang in her ears again when the Prince of Wales entered, fatter than ever, dressed gorgeously in purple satin, smelling of lavender, his face white and wretched.

"Surely we have met before?" he said, puffy eyes gazing into the pure blue of Lila's.

"I would have remembered," murmured Lila, this ambiguous remark concealing the fact she remembered their one other meeting only too well.

Father Jude strolled down the Mall towards Belgrave Square. The grass, still saturated from the earlier rain, soaked through his sandals and socks, and there was a squelching noise each time he took a step. Yet it was pleasant. He actually enjoyed the discomfort and the wet hem of his cassock as it flapped against his ankles. Despite having renounced his priestly vows, he could not forego the gown he had worn for most of his life.

There was no moon, and the dim streetlights were outshone by the great lamps on the gateways of the tall houses that he passed, and dimmed also by the light from many of the rooms which fell out onto the shining pavements. He glanced, without curiosity, at the wealthy entertaining in their homes: the bejeweled ladies, simpering in their finery; the gentlemen, elegant in powdered wigs and snow white linen; rooms stuffed with riches and uncomfortable-looking furniture.

He sniffed the balmy evening air and decided that for the first time in his life he was happy. He liked London enormously. He liked the busy life he led organizing Lila's affairs. She relied on his judgment and it flattered him.

Most of all he liked his other life, when often, late at night, he would visit the high-class brothels of the capital. There, with women fresh and pretty and only too willing to satisfy his every whim, he would indulge in the carnality he had so long denied himself.

The only fly in this heady ointment was Rosetta, whom he knew he had treated badly. She complained of his neglect whenever they came face to face. Not only was the poor woman rejected by him, but Lila had brought her own nurse, Lucy, back from Yorkshire and she had charge of little Ben. All Rosetta had to do was fetch and carry for everyone. Lila thought they should write to Beatrice and say they were sending her home but was worried this might upset the woman more.

Father Jude kicked aside a heap of sodden leaves. Some clung to his gown, then fell. He gave a sigh of contentment and then saw Garth House just ahead of him. Every window blazed with lights. It seemed like a giant Christmas tree looming up into the sky. The front door was open and inside a pink tinted chandelier cast a healthy glow on all who stood near.

"What would ye be wantin', Father?" said a footman, respectful but firm as the priest stepped into the brightness, blinking, his gray-black hair wet from the dripping trees.

"I have called for the Countess Ruzzini," he said, his sandals leaving wet patches on the black and white marble floor, and he sat down on a pink chair. "I await her convenience."

Lila appeared about midnight, one of the first to leave.

Quite a crowd accompanied her to say good night, including a young man tall and blond as Lila herself, wearing a scarlet and blue military uniform and carrying himself with an elegance and ease which bespoke superior birth and upbringing.

Father Jude was feeling smugly satisfied at Lila's success when he noticed another young man who had also left the ballroom. He leaned against a doorpost and took frequent mouthfuls from his glass of brandy. This handsome gentleman was staring at Lila as if he wished to devour her on the spot. First his gaze would rest upon her face, then he would clutch his glass, and his gaze would drop to her bosom and remain there as though he could see the flesh through her jeweled bodice. Down her body his eyes moved, slowly, reflectively. Father Jude understood his reaction to Lila, but resented it all the same.

The young gentleman in uniform was murmuring something about escorting the countess home when Father Jude moved forward and Lila exclaimed, "Thank you, but no. See, here is my chaperon, come to see me safely under my own roof."

As they left, Father Jude saw the brandy glass shatter in the hands of the strange young man and his fingers start to bleed.

Departing as she did with the gaunt and shabby priest merely added to the mystery of the dazzling Countess Ruzzini. Who was she and where exactly did she come from? Venice, yes, but she was not Italian.

"There was no trace of accent that I could define," the Duchess of Garth pronounced, frowning as she tried to recall everything Lila had said.

"Yes, there was. Yorkshire or I'll eat my hat," said an elderly, unimpressed dowager. "No royal blood there, either. Could tell by the walk. Not used to being curtsied to, stuck out a mile."

"Don't talk nonsense, Patricia," snapped the duchess. "A Yorkshire accent from a foreign countess. Pshaw!"

The elderly lady, who usually spoke the truth and was therefore quite used to not being believed, shrugged her shoulders indifferently.

On the way home in the Ruzzini carriage, Lila was telling Father Jude about the evening.

"Lieutenant Geoffrey Rees, who is the eldest son of the Duchess of Garth's sister, is quite anxious to call. Did you see him? I danced with him a dozen times and he was quite rude to anyone who tried to butt in."

"A personable young gentleman," the priest conceded, envying the lieutenant's youth.

"The Prince of Wales was there and he made the most awful, mournful eyes at me. When he kissed my hand, 'twas like a wet sponge," Lila grimaced. "Poor man. I feel so sorry for him."

"You made many conquests I see," said Father Jude. "I noticed one gentleman in particular watching you, one who seemed to be partaking of a little too much brandy." He badly wanted to know who this person was.

For a moment, Lila was silent, staring out of the carriage window at the still busy London streets. She shook her head impatiently as though trying to rid the thought of the man from her mind. Then she said, "That was Lord Ralph Curringham. He and I were once engaged. He was the only person there to recognize me, but we did not acknowledge it."

By the time they arrived at Park House, Father Jude felt as pleased as if he himself had experienced the triumphant evening. The only niggling worry was the memory of the blood dripping from the hands of Lila's ex-fiancé.

Several letters and dozens of invitations arrived at Park House the following morning, most of them brought by special messenger. One gave Lila enormous delight and she called out to Father Jude who sat by the window adding up columns of figures.

"You will never believe this, but Mama writes to say that my father is beginning to recover. Each day after mealtimes, at precisely the times I visited him, he turns his head, opens his eyes and looks for someone, presumably me, for once he even uttered my name quite clearly. I must return home straightaway before he thinks it was all a dream."

Father Jude was pleased that his diagnosis had been right, and Lila rang for a servant to say she would leave for Yorkshire within the hour. She returned to opening her letters.

"Imagine!" she exclaimed seconds later. "Here is a love letter from the prince. I am the loveliest being ever to grace his gray and miserable world. I take *that* with a pinch of salt, I can tell you. I understood from the gossip yesterday evening that he is inundating Mrs. Fitzherbert with appeals to restore their former arrangements."

Also, she had learned that Lady Jersey had been banished from the court and was making the most awful public fright of herself trying to scratch her way back in. Even the prince, usually so gentle and courteous, had been forced to be quite rude to her.

"I take it, then," said Father Jude, "that you have not fallen prey to the prince's charms?"

"As far as I am concerned, he has none," Lila replied tartly.

She tore open another envelope.

"Ah! Lieutenant Rees wishes to call and pay his compliments. Will you write back for me and suggest a day next week?

"Oh, dear!" Her voice changed ominously. She was reading another letter and even from across the room, the priest could see the writing was large and black as if done by the claws of an animal.

"What is wrong?" he asked.

"This note. It is quite horrid. Please read it and tell me what to do."

The priest blanched at the signature at the foot of the five page missive: Ralph C.

It was a love letter which verged on the obscene. It told Lila that the writer had never ceased to love her passionately and hinted that if without a husband she felt in need of physical comfort, then he was most eager to provide it and thereupon went into detail regarding the delights which she could expect if she should so favor him.

"Ignore it," said Father Jude, crumpling the letter up and throwing it into the wastepaper basket.

Lila said worriedly, "He married my friend, Sylvia Beauchamp. I resent playing a part, even if it is entirely innocent, in his betrayal of her."

"Ignore it and forget about it," the priest commanded firmly, and to distract her, announced that the Ruzzini fortune had just become richer to the tune of fifteen thousand guineas as a consignment of rare silks had just arrived in Marseilles.

Lila's visit did her father a world of good. He did not embrace her, for that was not his way, but his eyes filled with tears when he opened them to find her truly there with a chubby, brown-haired grandson on her knee, pulling at her hair and trying to eat the fur bobbles on her jacket.

By the time she left a few days later he quite understood she was back in England to stay and was able to carry on a limited conversation with his wife and other daughters.

Happily, Lila returned to London but was disconcerted to find amongst the assortment of letters awaiting her, half a dozen more from Ralph, each more suggestive and indecent than the last. They were longer, wilder, with threats of suicide and murder in the final one delivered that very morning.

Father Jude was angry with himself that he had not sorted through her post and confiscated the letters before she found them. He offered to call on Ralph that very day to try and talk some sense into him, though from what he remembered of the man's behavior at the Garth home, he doubted if that would be possible.

He would make sure any future letters did not reach Lila, and to ease her mind, suggested she go shopping. Her young sister Mary was longing to try her hand at making gowns for her new nephew and Lila had promised to send several suitable lengths of material, together with all the necessary trimmings.

Ralph did not invite Father Jude in to sit down, but left him standing in the hallway of his gloomy Belgravia home. His eyes had an almost insane glitter which had not been there before. His hands were bandaged where the brandy glass had cut them, though now they held another, nearly empty. A pale stubble was growing on his chin.

He was clearly the worse for drink, even at midday, and swayed as he asked roughly, "What is it you want?"

"The Countess Ruzzini finds the nature of the letters you are sending her offensive and deeply upsetting," the priest said gravely. "I have come to ask that you cease this correspondence forthwith, else I shall be obliged to advise the countess to take legal action to restrain you from contacting her."

"The Countess Ruzzini is Lilian Ward, my fiancée. She belongs to me. I can write to her what I please." A vein throbbed angrily beside Ralph's left eye and once again his hands were tight on the glass he held.

"That is nonsense and you know it," the priest said quietly. "I have issued my warning. I leave it to you to take note."

As Father Jude opened the door to leave, he narrowly escaped a shower of splinters in his face as the glass Ralph held was flung in his direction, smashing against the back of the door.

"Get out, you filthy cleric," he screamed, and a voice sounded elsewhere in the house, "Ralph, dear. What is the matter?"

As he walked away into the vivid November sunshine, Father Jude was doubtful that his warning would have the slightest effect.

Chapter Twenty

For some reason, a name came to mind when Lila set out to buy material for Ben's clothes.

"Messrs. Hodges and Woolf," she told Hoggett as she climbed into the carriage. "Though I do not know where they are situated."

"I know them well, milady," said Hoggett, who seemed to have taken quite naturally to driving the coach. Indeed, the job suited him to perfection, for he knew London like the back of his hand.

At the shop an eager young man sprang over to the carriage door and escorted Lila to a chair at the back where several other ladies were being attended to, while older gentleman came forth and courteously asked her requirements.

Both had hurried off to fetch samples of cloth, when a tiny scrap of a woman sat in the next chair turned to Lila and said hopelessly, "I do declare I cannot make up my mind which

size buttons to have on my new black blouse. And should I
have silk or cotton lace on my nightdresses?"

Lila said, "Cotton would wear better but silk is more luxurious. As to the buttons," she eyed the petite figure whose
feet could scarcely touch the floor, "if I were you, I would
chose the smallest."

"Thank you, my dear child. I confess I am no good at all
at selecting my dressmaking needs. In the past, my good friend,
Annabelle Prymm advised me on every item, and even though
she passed away more than three years ago, I am still unable
to cope alone."

"Annabelle Prymm! You knew her? She was my friend also,
my dear savior," cried Lila, ignoring the two men who had
brought a dozen roles of cloth for her appraisal and who also
waited for the woman to make up her mind, for she had been
twittering away for almost an hour.

"Annabelle and I shared all our friends but one, so you must
be Miss Lilian Ward, whom I never met. My name is Esther
Larkin. I departed for Bath on the awful day my dear friend
died, and I did not know about it until I returned weeks later."

The little woman began to cry. Openly moved, Lila gave
her a handkerchief which she accepted gratefully. She eventually sniffed and said, "Tell me, my dear, are you living in
her house? I never could bring myself to even ride down Cotterell Street since she went."

"Why, no," said Lila, then asked curiously, "Why should
I be living in Miss Prymm's house?"

"Why? Because it is yours. She willed it to you, my dear.
I witnessed the document on my last visit."

"I knew nothing of this," said Lila in amazement.

"It is God's own truth, Miss Ward, I can assure you. I recall
quite distinctly dear Annabelle putting the document away in
her bureau."

Lila remembered George Prymm, so stern and respectable,
contempt in the curl of his narrow lips as he turned her out of
the house as if she were a criminal. Although there was no
excuse for his unpleasant attitude, she supposed it was possible
that the will had not been found in time. She expressed this
view to Miss Larkin who immediately denied that it could have
been the case.

"Ada, her maid, also witnessed the will. She is bound to
have told Annabelle's nephew. So, it is really your little house,

my dear. Should you ever need a roof over your head—" She
suddenly noticed Lila's rich fur-trimmed outfit, the pale cream
kid gloves, and the pearl drops at her ears.

"Rest assured, I am comfortably housed," Lila said with a
smile. "But if Miss Prymm's little cottage is mine, then *I* would
like to choose who lives in it."

"I wish to see a solicitor," she said to Father Jude that
afternoon.

"Certainly. I will make inquiries and discover who the best
man is," he replied, glancing up from his inevitable paperwork.

"There is no need. Quentin Burnett is the man I want."

"He has been recommended, I take it?"

"In a sort of way," Lila said. Quentin Burnett was Roland's
solicitor, whom he had advised her to contact immediately on
setting foot in London to seek an annulment to their marriage.
If he was good enough for Roland Fairbrother then he was
good enough for Lila Ruzzini.

"I have been meaning to see this man for some time anyway,
but today something happened that made me decide to go immediately," she said, and told him of her meeting with Miss
Larkin, and the disappearing will.

Father Jude laughed, "Surely you have property enough?"

"Do you think I am pursuing this matter out of greed?" Lila
asked angrily. "That man, Prymm, treated me abominably. I
want what is mine by rights. There are many good things the
property can be used for other than lining the pockets of a
dishonest man."

"I take your point," Father Jude conceded. "If you wish to
go today, I shall send Hoggett immediately to arrange an appointment."

"Is this woman, Esther Larkin, of good character?" asked
Quentin Burnett, his deep, melodious voice echoing throughout
his dark and dusty chambers in Gray's Inn.

"Impeccable," Lila assured him. "I questioned her, most
tactfully of course, for I knew it would be of importance. She
herself has always been deeply involved in works of charity,
and her only relative, a brother, is vicar of Craighorn in Kent.
She has an honest and open manner."

"Then I doubt if the case will even come to court," said the
lawyer scratching his bald head with an inkstained hand and

adding to the black smears already there. "The servant may well break down and confess if confronted by the majesty of the law, and this man, Prymm, is likely to hand over the property without protest if a reputable witness to a later will is forthcoming.

"I will commence with the matter today," he assured her, and thinking his client had completed her business, made to stand and bid her farewell.

"I have not finished, Mr. Burnett."

Lila raised her hand somewhat imperiously and the lawyer sat down again like a schoolboy.

"Have you received the tragic news regarding the death of my husband, Sir Roland Fairbrother?"

"Why, yes," said Quentin Burnett, astonished. "I was informed of this sad fact some months ago. I was also asked for instructions as to the running of his farm in New South Wales, which I understand is a thriving and successful business venture. I did not realize you—"

"Here is my marriage certificate. If you have the deeds to the farm, I should like them, please."

"I will ask my clerk to fetch them."

His large, inky hand pounded the bell on his desk, and he passed on this request to the elderly man who answered his summons.

Then a happy thought seemed to strike him and his eyes lit up. He waved the rather crumpled marriage certificate in the air and said, "Do you realize this piece of paper entitles you to ownership of Bly Hall in Bristol and the Fairbrothers' London house in Bloomsbury?"

"Of course it does," Lila said abruptly as if the idea that it should be otherwise had not entered her head. "Please inform Lady Frances Fairbrother to quit whichever of these establishments she happens to inhabit at the present time and never enter either again."

"I will attend to that without delay, Countess," answered the lawyer rubbing his pate gleefully at the thought of turning out the unspeakable mother of his late client.

"Give her the barest minimum of notice," Lila said. "Say by the end of this month."

"But, Countess," interrupted Father Jude, speaking for the first time, "where will the poor woman spend Christmas?"

"I care not," Lila declared frostily. "She may starve to death or perish of cold. I do not care."

The priest and the solicitor exchanged glances indicating that neither would like to get on the wrong side of the Countess Ruzzini.

Lieutenant Rees had come to tea and sat with a tiny cup and saucer in one hand and a ginger cake in the other. His mother and his aunt, the duchess of Garth, were urging him on as if he were a racehorse, insisting he press his suit with this new countess. Not that he needed much urging, for sitting there pouring out tea in a low-cut lilac dress, the lady looked as irresistible as a meal to a starving man.

He was dropping hints about engagements over the forthcoming Yuletide season, when she said, "I regret, Lieutenant, I must decline—though a Christmas Eve Party at the duchess's house sounds quite delightful. I shall be leaving a week prior to Christmas to spend the holiday with my family."

Remembering the interest expressed in the countess's antecedents he ventured to inquire where that family might be, and to his intense surprise, she replied, "Yorkshire."

Lila changed the subject for it was her intention to drop occasional hints as to her real identity until it was well-known who she was, though Mama kept on telling her this was quite ridiculous and far too sensitive.

Geoffrey Rees was asking if she would be back in town for the New Year to which she replied in the affirmative, and she was just about to condescend to accompany him to a ball on New Year's Eve, when there was a commotion in the hall, the door was flung open, and Ralph Curringham burst into the room.

He was quite intoxicated, and once in Lila's presence all the energy expended in getting there seemed to dissolve and he stood swaying and panting, while a footman entered, adjusting his jacket agitatedly, and exclaiming, "My apologies, milady. He would not be restrained."

Lila indicated she understood and the man went on, "I shall fetch Hoggett, milady, to help me remove him."

"There is no need for that." Lieutenant Rees had leaped to his feet. "I will deal with this intruder."

"No, pray!"

But Lila's plea went unheeded for the tall and fit army officer had Ralph by the scruff of the neck and was leading him to the door of the room, into the hall, and moments later the front door slammed and the lieutenant returned, rubbing his hands.

"How long has that blackguard been bothering you?" he asked angrily.

"That was the first occasion," Lila lied, leaving the letters unmentioned.

"Let me know instantly should he make a pest of himself again, and I'll give him such a thrashing, he'll never try a third time."

"Thank you," said Lila demurely, wondering why Ralph had come. It might have been to proffer a drunken apology, and she wished Geoffrey had not dismissed him so peremptorily.

This incident only made Lila appear more desirable than ever in the eyes of the lieutenant. The poor, defenseless countess needed protection and he was only too willing to give her this, though he could not help but wonder why she had not fainted or called for smelling salts as other women of his acquaintance would have done if gatecrashed by a drunken lord. Indeed, she looked quite unmoved by the whole incident.

Rosetta asked to see Lila as she was preparing for bed that night. She was without her usual sullen expression, which was a relief, for she bothered the entire household with her moans and sulks.

She had managed, despite herself, to acquire a few words of English, and without preamble, said to her mistress, "I am with child."

"Rosetta!" Lila wondered if the woman was glad or sorry but the expression of serene happiness on the servant's face answered her question. "When do you expect it?"

"Six months. In May, June. Then I have Angela back again."

"You cannot be sure it will be a girl," Lila protested, and then asked, "Who is the father?"

"Jude. Father Jude, father." Rosetta smiled at this joke and then her face contorted as she pleaded, "Do not turn me out, mistress. Beatrice, she keep me when Angela come."

"Of course I will not turn you out, Rosetta," Lila comforted her.

"People in the house make fun of me, but I don't care. I

have Angela back soon," she said proudly.

Lila assured her that she would be looked after and dug into her own wardrobe to find the frocks made for her when she carried Benedetto. She gave them to Rosetta, who looked pleased and grabbed them rudely. She also gave her the hand-painted scarlet robe that had been amongst the trousseau of the former Countess Ruzzini. Since that fateful night in the Princess of Wales' apartment Lila could never bring herself to wear that color again.

Rosetta departed happily, and as Lila sat brushing her hair she set to wondering what became of women who were made pregnant like Rosetta. Many employers, she knew, would turn the poor creatures out onto the streets without even the wages due to them. Where did these females go? Was there any place for them? Some women put in that position would have no recourse but to turn to vice or crime to support themselves and their child.

Lila smiled at her reflection. Mama had said there was no need to worry about being rich for one could do so much good with the money. What better use for Bly Hall and the Fairbrother house in Bloomsbury than as refuges for unwed mothers? She would discuss the matter with Father Jude next day.

Rosetta could not sleep. She lay feeling thankful her mistress had not been angry, though coming from the liberal home of Beatrice da Porto in Venice, this charity was not as unusual as it might have been to others in her place.

She could not sleep because her hands were resting firmly on her slightly bulging stomach, willing Angela to move. Just the faintest, tiniest sign of real life was all she wanted and this would be the next best thing to actually holding the little girl in her arms one day. It was too early, she supposed, and she tried to remember when the first Angela had kicked, but the memory of this time was hazy.

Rosetta sighed and got out of bed. By the light of her candle she saw the scarlet robe the countess had just given her. It was full and roomy and would cover her well in later months. She touched the material which felt as soft as petals to her fingers, and throwing it around her shoulders, she picked up the light and left her room.

Rosetta had not been subjected to the same rules which governed the other servants. She was almost regarded as a member of the family, and had no inhibitions about going downstairs and wandering restlessly in and out of the rooms hoping she would soon feel sleepy. She didn't know that a figure outside was darting from window to window, watching her progress through the house with murder in his heart.

The naked girl on the bed beside Ralph Curringham grunted in her sleep and he moved away in disgust, waking the second girl who lay on his other side.

"Come on, duckie," whispered the girl who had woken. "Let's do it again. Just us two this time."

Ralph shoved her and she fell onto the floor with a thump, giving an indignant yell which roused her friend. He crawled unsteadily off the bed and staggered to the dresser on which stood a decanter of Isabella's best brandy. He poured himself a glass and swallowed large mouthfuls, ignoring the foul insults from the girl on the floor and the questioning squawks from the other one who wanted to know what was going on.

They were like animals, thought Ralph, listening to their obscene noises. Disgusting animals. Why was he, a married man, reduced to finding satisfaction in a bawdy house? It was all right if one was single. Acceptable when middle-aged or old and one's wife had passed her prime. It was fine for a number of young, married blades to have a jaunt one night and round up the evening in a brothel.

But it was wrong that this nonstop aching in his loins could only find relief away from his wife, away from his home. He was sick of this place and all places like it. His father had brought him here at the age of sixteen and its pleasures had kept him well satisfied for more than seven years. Now these pleasures were beginning to wear thin. He wanted to love a girl who was not being paid for it, who would not demand more cash before granting some unusual little favor. He'd had to pay double for these two girls and now, what was so frightening, so utterly and unacceptably frightening, was that tonight, for the very first time, he'd been unable to fulfill his male role.

Just what was left in life if that went? Would he be reduced to wallowing in the troughs where his father now sought release?

There was no doubt in his mind that what he needed was a devoted and passionate wife. In his whole life he had never known what it was to make love to a woman who wanted him for himself. That was the sort of love he needed now.

He needed Lila!

He remembered the anticipation he'd felt when they were engaged and he'd imagined their life together, imagined himself taking the fresh and unsullied beauty, untouched by any other man. He would have been the first. Now she'd had three husbands, yet in a way this only made her more desirable than ever. She was experienced, more beautiful.

"Gad, Lila! I want you. You were made for me."

He spoke the words aloud and the girls stopped their complaining and listened to him. As he gulped down yet more brandy, a throbbing desire took possession of him, and the second girl forgot she'd just been so badly treated and came over to him, stroking his thighs with her hot and sweaty hand.

With a curse, Ralph flung her away and she fell, catching her head on the brass rail of the bed, and lay unconscious on the floor.

The other girl began to scream and as the drunken man flung on his clothes she yelled coarsely, "Go on ter yer Lila, then. If yer want 'er so much, well take 'er and leave us alone."

Outside, Ralph Curringham hailed a carriage and told the driver to take him to Park House. Rage engulfed him as he sat inside recalling the priest who'd visited him the other day to warn him not to write any more. He'd never written a love letter in his life until he met Lila again, and now he was being threatened with the law for putting his feelings on paper. He squirmed, reliving his rough dismissal at the hands of that lout of a soldier when he'd gone to pour his heart out to his loved one.

Why, oh why, had he listened to his father's stern instructions three years ago that marriage with Lilian Ward was out of the question? Why hadn't he just gone ahead and married her? Did money and position matter so much that one gave up everything good, everything worthwhile, to achieve them? Gave up Lila? His father had said at the time that the marriage would have ruined his life. But *not* going through with it had been Ralph's ruination, for Lila was all he wanted, was all he had ever wanted, and he'd been too blind to realize it at the time.

If he couldn't have Lila, he wanted nothing. And if Lila didn't want him, he reasoned in his crazy state, so she too would have nothing. He took out the two little pistols kept in each pocket of his greatcoat. Ralph frequently trod strange and dangerous paths and protection was necessary. So far neither gun had been used.

Park House was in total darkness. He entered through the high iron gates which were unlocked and walked unsteadily up to the house, a pistol in each hand and not the faintest notion of what he intended to do. He contemplated the front door. It was no use ringing the bell, for a flunky would answer it and if he barged in he still had no idea where Lila slept.

Wondering if a window had been left open, he turned, falling down the steps and grazing his cheek on the gravel. This did not bring him to his senses. Indeed the pain added fuel to the anger and desire that possessed him. Round to the side of the house he went, and there, through a window, he saw her!

She was in scarlet, flaming vivid scarlet, as she had been that night in Carlton House when it seemed the world came to pieces. He could not see her face, but merely the faint flicker of the candle she carried which lit only the color of her gown. The woman wandered out of the room he was watching and he darted along to the next window where the candle reappeared and began moving backwards and forwards as if she were pacing the floor.

She could not sleep! And why not? Because she needed a man. There was no doubt about it. And here was a man, ready and willing to provide her with everything she needed and more besides.

Then the candle moved towards the window, and Ralph seemed to step back in time. Instead of the dim figure before him, he saw Lila that night in Carlton House in her rich red gown, a rose in her hair and every man's eye upon her. He stepped up to the window to greet his angel, and she smiled at him, enticing and welcoming.

Why then was she shouting at the top of her voice? What was this screaming which shattered his eardrums? The bright figure faded and instead he saw Lila, both hands over her face, shielding the sight of Ralph from her eyes and shrieking as if her lungs would burst. So, this was how she welcomed him?

He raised his trembling hand and pointed the pistol at the hysterical, screaming woman and pulled the trigger. She dropped like a stone.

Then he put the other gun to his brow, and the life of Lord Ralph Curringham came to its tragic end.

* * *

Father Jude slept little and since the visit to the solicitors had decided to embark on a study of English law. He was reading his first volume on this subject by the light of a lamp when he heard the screaming and the shots. He left the room instantly and found Lila emerging from hers looking frightened. She made sure Benedetto was safe in his nursery, and then went downstairs with Jude.

The other servants at the back of the house on the top floor had heard nothing, but the Hoggetts who lived in the basement were both standing in the hall when Lila and Father Jude came down the stairs.

"It was in the morning room, I'll swear to that," said Mrs. Hoggett. "Right over me head, it was."

"A burglar by the sound of it, for I heard breaking glass," said her husband.

"But who did he shoot at? Who was screaming?" Lila exclaimed. Father Jude went over to the morning room door and kicked it open.

Holding his lamp high he peered cautiously inside and saw the prone figure of Rosetta just inside the window. It was not until he reached her that he saw the man lying outside with his head blown half away. He opened the French window and bent over the body.

"It is Ralph Curringham," Lila said flatly. She had, unbeknownst to him, come out right behind him. "Perhaps he is better off dead."

She turned and went back inside. Despite her calm words, she was shaking violently.

Mrs. Hoggett was kneeling by Rosetta, feeling her brow and pulse.

"Can't find out where she's hurt. It's more like she just fainted, yet there's an awful lot of blood."

"But she is alive?" Lila said with relief.

"Heart beating like a racehorse, milady."

Mrs. Hoggett was examining the woman for a bullet wound when Lila joined her on the floor beside Rosetta, saw the blood and said, "She has had a miscarriage."

"Poor lady. Though maybe she'll be glad of it when she comes to."

Lila doubted that very much, but for Rosetta's sake, she was relieved, for had not the other child of Father Jude been born scarred and ugly? How would poor Rosetta have acted if instead of another Angela, she'd given birth to a daughter like Maria?

She transferred her attention to the corpse, though Hoggett thought it was not at all right that the countess should view this horrible sight and he covered the mutilated face with his handkerchief.

Poor Ralph. She felt sorry for him, and at the same time she did not look forward to the scandal which would be caused by this happening on her property. The Countess Ruzzini wanted to establish a reputation totally free from notoriety.

Undoubtedly Ralph had mistaken Rosetta for her and tried to kill her, for two shots had been distinctly heard, and in daylight they would very likely find the first bullet somewhere in the room. Despite the close range, Ralph had probably missed because he was no doubt the worse for drink.

"I don't want him found here," she said. "Can he be moved?"

Father Jude turned questioningly to Hoggett who nodded.

"Don't worry, milady. We'll take him far away from here. Not your fault is it, if a madman tries to break in? You'll be pestered something shocking if it's reported."

The two men picked up the corpse unceremoniously and carried it away. The arms hung limply down, dragging along the grass, and the feet were twisted grotesquely. There was no sign that this figure had once been a lord.

"When will it all end?" Lila wailed some hours later. Outside the night was black. Trees waved softly, scarcely visible against the dark sky, and a few remaining leaves fluttered down unseen.

Father Jude, who had returned from disposing of Ralph's body, regarded her objectively.

Her hair was loose and in disarray and clouds of pink lace peeped from under her high-collared dressing gown. Her lovely blue eyes were misted from lack of sleep, which also added an unusual huskiness to her voice.

"Hopefully, you will marry again and have more children. When you belong to a strong man, have become established in your home, are busy organizing your household. Then, maybe it will end."

Lila sighed. There was only one person she wanted to marry, and that was Phillip Grenville. She had even sent a man to New South Wales in search of him. Inquiries had been made all over London. After all, she had returned to Europe by an unconventional route, why not Phillip? It seemed, however, that he had disappeared off the face of the earth.

Slowly Lila sipped the port which Mrs. Hoggett had given her before retiring to bed with her husband. Inwardly, she reproved herself for complaining so. After all, that night Sylvia had lost her husband and Rosetta who lay upstairs dosed with laudanum had lost her baby.

"We must find a husband for Rosetta," she said suddenly and Father Jude, who had thought she was feeling sorry for herself, was taken aback by this remark.

"Place an advertisement in the *Times* tomorrow," she told him. "Under another address, of course. Perhaps Quentin Burnett will allow us to use his, and he is sure to have a room where we can conduct interviews."

"But every scoundrel under the sun will apply," protested the priest. "You cannot do this to Rosetta."

"It seems rather more charitable than what *you* did to her," Lila said impatiently. "And it will not only be scoundrels who will come forward. The poor woman will be quite distraught when she awakes and finds she has lost her child. She is young, and there is time for her to have another baby, or even two or three."

Father Jude opened his mouth to speak and Lila held up her hand to stop him.

"I hope you are not going to offer your services in that direction," she said tartly. "I would like her settled with a gentleman who initially will be directed to court and propose to her in a proper and romantic manner. She must never know I have organized it and the successful applicant will be assured that his income will be withdrawn immediately should he reveal that fact."

"I was merely going to ask where they would live," the priest said meekly.

"Why, in Cotterell Street, Chelsea, of course," said Lila.

Next morning Lila woke late. She was annoyed to find that her maid had been instructed by Father Jude not to disturb her due to her late night, but she had the grace not to say anything to him as the order had been given out of consideration. Nevertheless, today was the twenty-fifth of November and she had a call to make. Dressing quickly in her plainest outfit, she instructed Lucy to prepare Ben for a journey, and sent for

Hoggett and told him they were going to Chichester within the hour.

"Chichester, milady?"

"Chichester, Hoggett. Furthermore, I do not wish to travel in my own carriage. Will you please hire a plain one and have it at the front door by ten o'clock?"

"Right, milady." Hoggett hurried away, and Lila remembered she must offer him a bonus for his help early that morning. It was quite beyond the duty of servants to dispose of dead bodies on their employer's behalf.

Also, she must get out of this highly inconvenient habit of refusing to plan anything in advance. Even if one's plans were thwarted by unforeseen circumstances as so many of Lila's had been, undertaking long distance journeys at the very last minute only led to chaos.

The trip was cold and uncomfortable and Lila had not realized how used she had become to the soft luxury of her own transport. She had insisted on traveling alone with Benedetto so she had only him for company. As his first teeth were beginning to grow in, he fretted and cried for hours on end, and the constant bumping and lurching of the coach clearly made him miserable. It was therefore with a great sense of relief she heard Hoggett shout when he drew the coach to a stop.

"Whereabouts in Chichester, milady?"

"Ask where a Dr. Bateson lives," she told him. "And go there."

Eventually they drew up outside a sprawling brick house, where, despite the chill of the evening, the front door was open to the world and several children ran screaming about the garden. She instructed Hoggett to wait at the local inn, and made her way to the door.

"Papa is out on his rounds," a young girl of about thirteen said in answer to Lila's query. "Do come into the waiting room. Is your baby ill? Shall I hold him? I'm afraid Papa might be hours yet, for Mrs. Sharp's expecting any minute and won't have the midwife."

"It is not for the baby I have come."

This was more difficult than she had supposed.

"May I speak to one of your older brothers or sisters?"

Not just one brother was produced, but two, Hugh and Robin, both red-haired and aged about twenty, and a sister,

Emma, a few years older, who had two children attached to her skirts so firmly they would appear to have been made with the frock.

"Sorry about the mess," apologized one of the boys, sounding as if he'd said those same words a million times before.

The girl snapped at the childern.

"Look at me as soulfully as you wish, John and Jimmie, but you are not having even the tiniest fragment of toffee until after your tea." Then to Lila, "Papa might be gone ages. Mrs. Sharp is expecting and has had words with the midwife, so he must deliver."

"So your sister said, at least I assume she is your sister."

"Yes. Geraldine is our family baby. All the others you see about who are younger are nephews and nieces. We are a large family, you see, nine boys and nine girls."

"I know," Lila said, "for I was married to Timothy."

At this news all three were so startled they nearly fell off their chairs, causing one of the children attached to Emma's skirt to become dislodged and start to scream. This noise reminded Ben of his own accomplishments of that nature and he started crying.

"Where is Timothy?" someone yelled and Lila was horrified to realize they did not know of his death. Surely the owners of the ship advised the families when their men died on board?"

Her distress must have been obvious to Emma, who picked up her own squealing child and handed him to one brother. She wrenched the other child away from the skirt, attached the empty clutching hand to the hem of Hugh's coat and told all four to shoo. Ben was removed from Lila's lap and placed in Geraldine's care, much to his mother's disconcertment, particularly when the girl was told to let the child suck on a piece of toffee to quiet him, "but on no account let him swallow it."

"It will help bring his teeth forth," said the young woman in the now unnatural peace and quiet. "I know why you have come today," she went on. "For it is—it would have been—Timothy's twenty-first birthday. In a family of eighteen, it is difficult to remember birthdays, but he was two years younger than me and we were always close. Our ages range from twelve to thirty-five, you see," she added, almost apologetically. "I can tell from your expression that the news you have of Timothy is not good. I cannot deny that after this space of time we ever expected to hear from him again."

"Regretfully, you are right. Timothy died," Lila said. "I thought you would have been informed long ago. The captain on the *Gabriel*—his name was Widdicombe—said he was a special friend of your papa. I am astounded that he has not called personally with the news."

"Ah, that will explain why we have heard nothing. Captain Widdicombe died of a stomach complaint on his way home from New South Wales more than two years ago. We knew, of course, that Timothy had been press-ganged, for we received a communication from him written in Teneriffe, and in this letter he speaks of a marvelous surprise which he would be bringing back with him. Would that be a new wife?"

"Indeed it would."

Then Lila told her how Timothy had died, and Emma smiled wistfully.

"I do recall how scared he was to climb a mere apple tree. What bravery to swarm up a great mast ten or twenty times as high."

"He did it without complaint," Lila told her. "He mentioned he was frightened, but that was all."

Tears came suddenly to her eyes. Timothy had come in and out of her life such a while ago, but suddenly he was there as if alive, so cheerful and good-humored.

There was a commotion in the hall and Lila strained her ears expecting the sound of Benedetto's dying screams. Instead, a tall, stooped man wearing a worn and darned frock coat came into the room with several children hanging onto his legs. His graying ginger hair flew about his head and he blinked vaguely at the light as if wondering if he had entered the right house.

He totally ignored Lila.

"Mrs. Sharp and the midwife have sorted out their differences, so I was able to get away."

"Papa!" Emma cried. "You will never believe it, but here is Timothy's wife."

Lila curtsied, feeling somewhat flustered for Doctor Bateson stared at her impatiently and said to his daughter indignantly, "What nonsense to introduce me to Timothy's wife when they have been married seven years and they and their children live next door."

"No, no, Papa. You are thinking of Thomas. Timothy was the one with red hair *and* freckles. A mixture you did not like, you told him. The one who disappeared three years past."

"Ah, *Timothy!* Did you say *was?* Timothy *was?*"

"Alas, Papa," Emma took his hand. "He died on board ship. But we were prepared, were we not. How many times have we all said, surely Timothy must be dead."

Doctor Bateson looked a forlorn and lonely figure just then, despite the fact that his house was spilling over with his children and his children's children.

"Whether you have one, or whether you have eighteen, a loss cuts just as deep," he murmured and Emma tried to smile encouragingly at him.

"Now we have yet another Mrs. Bateson. That makes five and six in January when Christopher marries."

"I am Lilian Ruzzini now, for I have married again."

Lila did not mention her title. She was determined not to impress or overawe these people with any ostentatious show of wealth or position. They were ordinary folk, not too different from her own people, and she wanted to be treated as one of them.

"Come then, Mrs. Ruzzini. I think I hear the bell for dinner. Please join us? The entire family will be eager to hear tell of Thomas's last adventures."

Emma raised her eyes to heaven and whispered, "He loves us dearly but can never remember our names. Now he gets confused with the younger ones and cannot tell which are his and which are his grandchildren."

Lila hastily sought out Ben who sat contentedly on the lap of another girl, a little older than Geraldine. Eyes glazed with delight he sucked on a large piece of toffee which the girl held in a rather grubby hand. His chin was a sticky mess and he had drooled onto his lovely white gown. Father Jude would have been outraged to see him, for he lectured Lila with great firmness on the baby's diet, in which toffee did not play a part. She decided to leave him as she was happy to have her child in the lap of a member of Timothy's family.

Dinner consisted of stew and baked sponge pudding, and Lila suspected there was rarely much change to this diet. The cook was assisted by two little servant girls who seemed as much a part of the family as the children of the house themselves. Several of the older girls helped to serve the meal and due to the great numbers eating, it was not considered necessary to wait for anyone else before starting. Consequently, many people had finished and were waiting for their pudding before some had got their first course. The smaller children ate in the kitchen.

They seemed to be a remarkably close family. Many of the older children were present with their husbands or wives and their own offspring, apparently all living nearby, and Lila began to wonder if the reason for her journey had been necessary, when, towards the end of the meal, they began to talk about Timothy. The way they spoke it was almost as if he were still alive. They laughed and joked at the things he used to say and do.

When she told him how he had rescued her from the lifeboat, one of the older boys chortled, "He always was a nosy so-and-so. Trust him to hunt you down and find out what you were up to."

Then she spoke about his plans for starting life in New South Wales, establishing a farm around which a town might grow, and Hugh and Robin began bombarding her with questions.

"Is it much, much hotter than here?"

"And is there no winter at all?"

"How many people actually live in Sydney Cove?"

"Are there many ordinary settlers? I mean, people like us?"

Lila tried as well as she could to describe exactly what life was like on the other side of the world, and the boys' enthusiasm grew great as she went on.

"By George! It sounds a fine life."

"I wish we could go."

Doctor Bateson said sternly, "Then go. You all know I have never attempted to stand in the way of any of you, whatever ambitions you expressed."

Lila could not help but wonder if the knowledge that they could leave home whenever they wished had the opposite effect of that which the good doctor intended, so that his boys all stayed firmly by his side, even when grown up and married. Perhaps if he had laid down the law and refused to let them leave, they would have run away in search of adventure.

Robin turned to her and said excitedly, "What do you think, Lilian? Could we make a go of it there?"

"I do not doubt it. You would soon learn to take care of yourselves, but don't forget, the majority of the inhabitants are convicts and many outright villains."

Doctor Bateson pointed out that neither of the boys knew

anything about animals, or farming, or trading of any sort. They had never supervised anyone, organized anything, cooked a meal, or mended their own clothes. Both, he declared, were totally useless at practically everything, but as far as he was concerned they could leave tomorrow and go with his blessing.

"Then we shall," cried Hugh with shining eyes. "Not tomorrow, of course, but as soon as a boat sails."

The conversation then continued animatedly as if the entire family were about to leave the country, and it was not until after the meal that Lila was able to get Doctor Bateson alone. She presented him with the deeds to New Farm which he was to give his sons just prior to leaving.

"I felt it was unwise to influence their decision by letting them know a homestead awaits them," she told him. "But I am sure they will be capable of continuing the work my—my friend began. He left the establishment to me, but I shall never return to that land."

"That is exceedingly kind of you, Cecily," said the doctor, at which point a breathless woman arrived to say that Mrs. Sharp's pains had begun in earnest, and she was in the midst of an awful row with the midwife, and would the doctor please hurry to sort things out.

It was far too late to leave for London by the time dinner was over, and then a child dispatched to the local inn to contact Hoggett returned with the information that he had partaken of a little too much ale and had fallen into a deep sleep from which no one could wake him. As he had been up half the night before attending to Ralph's body, Lila forgave him.

There was no room in the doctor's house, Emma said, but she invited Lila to stay the night in her little cottage in the High Street. A young man called Charles emerged from the crowd in the doctor's home and introduced himself as Emma's husband. Recovering her own two children, while Lila managed to prise Ben away from the two little girls who had adopted him, Emma led the way on foot to her home.

Lila stayed not one, but three days in Chichester. It was unusual and most pleasant to be regarded as a very ordinary young lady once again. She was not looked down on as a convict, or up to as a countess.

Emma confided that she was expecting her third child the following summer. For the first time, Lila was able to compare notes on babies with someone her own age. During the day they called in at the doctor's house to see how he was coping. This, Lila discovered, was the reason for the entire family's continuing presence in their childhood home. Their papa still had eight children at home to care for, so every day those who were married called in with their spouses to make sure everything was all right, thereby causing the chaos which existed, giving the poor servants double the amount of work to do, and making their poor papa more confused than ever. Yet it was a thoroughly happy and easygoing household, and Lila regretted having to leave and return to fashionable, glittering London where values were so different, and often so false.

But return she did, to find Father Jude peeved that she had been away so long and to news at last of Captain Phillip Grenville.

Chapter Twenty-One

"There'll be a roarin' fire in Red Jock's tonight. Gorblimey, I'd give me last remainin' six teeth to be back in England now."

These words of Queen Lil uttered in her raucous tones two years ago as they sat on the velvet sands in Goldoni Bay, came distinctly to Lila when she awoke on Christmas morning.

She glanced at her window. The snow which had been falling for three days had encroached onto the glass, making a thick white frame for the frost-tipped trees outside. She wondered fondly where Queenie was now, and as she got dressed in front of the spluttering fire in her bedroom, she thought that although Grassbrook Hall in Yorkshire was the most desirable place in the whole world to be at Christmas, it would be nice if it were just a little warmer. It was not until she had put on a woolen dress and thick-fringed shawl that she stopped shivering.

Outside, the fields were smooth blankets of white, and clumps of snow fell silently from overloaded branches when touched by just a slight wind. It was desolate, lonely, and incredibly beautiful.

Lila went out onto the landing. The house was beginning to warm up. Servants had risen at the crack of dawn to light fires in every room, and cheerful flames spurted in the grates. In the hall, branches of evergreen were tucked behind every picture and all the downstairs rooms were abundantly decorated with paper lanterns and chains, silver balls, holly, and mistletoe.

In the nursery where Lila and her two sisters had slept as babies, Ben, in his white-curtained crib, was just beginning to stir as Lucy bustled about preparing his breakfast. Already the smell of roasting turkey rose from the kitchens and Lila imagined Cook and the girls mixing sage and onion stuffing, preparing apples for the sauce and peeling the potatoes to go in the oven with the fowl. The puddings, cooked weeks ago, would be wrapped in muslin waiting to be steamed hot. Soon Mama and Papa would appear in their Sunday best, and together with their three daughters and any servants who wished to accompany them—apart from Cook who had to stay on guard in the kitchen—they would all go to church.

Lila ran down the stairs into the library, unable to keep still, she was so happy. The only single, solitary blot on the horizon was the unsatisfactory news regarding the whereabouts of Phillip Grenville. Several passengers from the *Northern Star* had been traced. The first two had no memory of anyone of Phillip's description on board, but the third, a trader who had boarded the ship at Sierra Leone, remembered his neighbor, a gentleman who emerged from his cabin only early in the mornings and late at nights, ate all his meals alone, and did not mix with the other passengers.

Rumor had it that the captain of the ship, Nathaniel Grey, an unpleasant, ill-mannered individual, was expecting to be court-martialed back in Englad due to charges brought against him by this mysterious gentleman over the treatment of convicts on the way out. Captain Grey had tried to refuse to carry this passenger on the return journey, and only the personal intervention of the governor himself had assured him of transportation home.

The ship's captain spitefully contented himself with totally ignoring this unwelcome traveler, even to the extent of omitting his name from the passenger list. For all the weeks the two were in adjacent cabins, the trader had never set eyes on his neighbor. And although he had not see him go, Grenville apparently disembarked when the ship docked at Gibraltar, for from then on there was no sound of him next door.

Could it be, wondered Lila, that he had come into contact with General Benedetto in New South Wales and received news of her, leaving the ship early in order to travel to Venice? Would he continue to look for her once he knew she was married? Did he know of her other marriages? If not, it would have made finding her in Sydney Cove virtually impossible. To set her mind at rest, she had sent a trustworthy man to Venice, but so far no reports had been received.

Lila sighed. She wanted nothing to spoil this longed for day, but Phillip would keep coming to mind and she would feel overcome with longing to see him again. If it had not been for Ben, she would have gone in search of Captain Grenville herself, even though she had no desire to leave England.

She sank down before the heap of burning logs in the library fireplace and stared deep into the flames, her imagination building strange and wonderful pictures deep in the molten grottoes, which a dislodged piece of wood or a shower of ash would suddenly obliterate. Was Phillip alone that day?

Also, she was slightly bothered about Father Jude who had decided to stay in London over Christmas. She hoped he too was not spending a miserable holiday by himself.

Father Jude woke in the arms of a black-haired gypsy beauty, a new recruit to Isabella's House of Sin. As a member of the clergy, a fact known only to Madam Isabella, he was allowed to use the upstairs part of the establishment along with the gentry.

He moved, and the slim brown arms tightened around him. The girl gave a tiny, satisfied sigh and snuggled her cheek against the red scar on his shoulder. Father Jude decided to lie and savor the feel of her thighs clasped round his leg, the softness of her breasts against his arm. Through the window he could see a weak sun just visible in the blue-gray sky. It was warm and cozy in the big, comfortable bed. As yet, he had not remembered it was Christmas Day.

* * *

The day was almost exactly as Lila had imagined it would
be. Not the smallest thing happened to spoil its perfection. The
aunts were staying for the holiday, and Rosalind and Simon
and their twins. John Butler came at midday after seeing to his
church services in Halifax. They all sat down to dinner at the
enormous oak table, with a bowl of chrysanthemums in the
center that Mama and old Thomas had carefully nurtured in
the greenhouse outside the kitchen. Candles in silver holders
flickered and danced beside the flowers and on the mantelshelf.
Every now and then, their brightness would be dimmed by the
watery sun which shone briefly into the dining room, then
disappeared as quickly as it had come, leaving the room illu-
minated only by the fire and candle flames.

After the sumptuous meal the servants were summoned and
each presented with a golden guinea. A point was made not to
interrupt their festivities until teatime. In the evening two neigh-
boring families arrived with their children. Mary took to the
piano and the entire company joined in Christmas carols, after
which people dispersed into groups, the men into the library,
supposedly to discuss weighty matters of state, while the ladies
gathered around the fireplace to gossip. Mary and the younger
children played guessing games in a corner, and Hettie, John,
and another boy and girl their own age held whispered con-
ferences in another.

At this point Lila felt a little lost, not quite sure which group
to join. She did not belong with the matrons before the fire,
nor with Hettie's group. Had she been allowed she would have
preferred to join her father and talk about politics—she urgently
wanted to discuss with him the conditions of prisoners sent to
New South Wales— but this was just not done. Besides, she
strongly suspected that if the truth be known, their chatter was
every bit as gossipy and inconsequential as that of the ladies.

Instead, she slipped out of the room to see Ben tucked in
for the night. He lay in his crib, ten months old now, chubby
and strong. His eyes were like stars, fixed on the night-light
burning on the table nearby, and he kicked his legs in excitement when Lila came in. She smiled as she bent over and
kissed him. Then she turned his crib so the light was behind
him; otherwise he would lie awake for hours staring at it.

His first Christmas on this earth.

"Please, please, let all his others be so happy," she prayed.
For some reason she thought of Ralph Curringham. He had

been a babe like this one. Who would have thought his end would be so tragic?

"A happy life, my dear son. I wish you this with all my heart."

On Boxing Day, Lila had an unexpected encounter with her greatest enemy.

Despite his long illness, Sir William Ward had not resigned his seat in Parliament and was now beginning to talk of taking up his responsibilities again as soon as the holiday was over. His mind was working as well as it ever had, though there was a streak of humor that had not been there before. Physically, he was still weak, but he grew stronger and healthier each day.

Lila returned from a short walk in the rose garden, Ben tucked cozily under her fur-lined cloak. Her cheeks were bright pink from the icy wind and as she came indoors and pushed the fur hood away, tendrils of golden hair fell onto her forehead. Carrying Ben into the library to warm, she stopped dead in the doorway, for Papa had a visitor, someone with his back to Lila. A stooped, elderly man whom she recognized straightaway.

With a sarcasm normally quite alien to him, William Ward said, "I believe you have met my daughter, Lila."

The visitor turned, and when he saw the girl on the threshold, he literally dropped the glass of port he was holding and a dark red stain appeared on the green carpet.

The marquess of Rawlesbury! So much older, wrinkled and bent, eyes screwed to slits, as though his entire body had been affected by the never ending twisting and scheming which seem to possess him.

"Lady Lilian!" he gasped. "I did not know—"

"Countess Ruzzini, if you please," Lila said shortly, wondering why she was not enjoying the discomfort of her most cruel foe. She noticed he was in mourning, and despite her loathing she felt pity for him. No doubt he had dearly loved his luckless son, and she expressed her condolences.

"The murderer has still not been found," he muttered.

His eyes twitched as he regarded this bewitching creature he had banished into the wilderness but a few short years ago. Yet here she was, seeming to light up the gloomy library with the dazzle of her beauty. Clutching her own bonny baby, too. Yet Ralph, poor Ralph . . .

Once he'd had the upper hand and she was at his mercy. Now he was a laughingstock in Parliament, his consuming ambition a source of amusement. Even his own party blamed him for their continued lack of influence and power.

Rawlesbury forgot what plan he had come to lay before his Whig colleague, and left the house immediately.

Father Jude was satiated and content when Lila arrived back at Park House. She thought this was due to the quiet, restful time which he had enjoyed while she and Ben were away. When she asked him if he'd spent his time studying law, he did not disillusion her, and said that he had indeed spent quite some time in bed and had also enjoyed several games of chess with Sian Reilly, the artist at present living in the house to paint a portrait of Lila and Ben.

Hopefully, Sian Reilly was to be Rosetta's husband. Out of nearly a hundred letters sent in response to the advertisement calling for a man of integrity to become husband to an attractive lady nearing middle age and offering a fair yearly income, more than ninety were rejected at first glance. Only about half a dozen seemed suitable and on interview it was Sian Reilly who Lila felt would appeal to Rosetta most.

Son of an illiterate Irish farm worker, he was robust and prematurely bald, quite unlike Lila's idea of what an artist should look like. Perhaps this was the reason he had been unlucky in his quest for a patron to subsidize him and encourage his undoubted talent. At forty-one he had long wished to take a wife, but spent every penny he could get on materials for his work and felt it unfair to burden some unfortunate woman with such a feckless husband. With a cheeky smile he said he saw no objection to Lila becoming his patron. While he could not guarantee to fall in love with Rosetta, he promised to try to make her a good husband. However, he insisted on seeing her first, for all the money in the world could not persuade him to take to bed a woman he did not fancy.

It was this last request which made up Lila's mind, for every other applicant had declared themselves virtually in love with Rosetta at the mere mention of her name. She was worried until Sian Reilly came to the house and found Rosetta pleasing. He was installed on the top floor in a room with large windows as his studio. So far the courtship seemed to be progressing well and for the first time since leaving Venice, Rosetta appeared happy and serene.

On the last day of the old year, Lila sat in Sian's studio wearing the silver dress inherited from the former Countess Ruzzini. The artist regarded this as a challenge to reproduce on canvas. They were chatting amiably for they had interests in common, one of his cousins having been deported to New South Wales on the *Gabriel,* when a visitor was announced.

"Lady Frances Fairbrother, milady," the maid said, and Lila's heart sank for she had been dreading such a visit for some time.

She was cross with herself for being unable to control the pounding of her heart as she entered the room where the woman who had ruined Roland's life was waiting.

"Madam," she said coldly, remaining standing as far away from her visitor as possible and making no move to extend a hand. "You wished to see me?"

"Ah! Countess Ruzzini, alias Lady Fairbrother, I believe." Clearly the woman had once been remarkably beautiful. This was obvious from the perfectly shaped nose, high cheekbones and black, thick-lashed eyes, but between those eyes was etched a furrow so deep it transformed the entire face.

Lila replied stiffly, "The word *alias* does not apply, Lady Fairbrother, for I was a widow when I remarried. Your son had regretfully died."

"Huh! Maybe you regretted the loss of that poltroon, but not I."

Lady Fairbrother wore a black velvet suit with a white cravat. As she spoke her eyes raked the silver-clad figure of the younger woman from head to foot. This bold regard made Lila's blood boil, and she almost choked on some stinging reply but managed to withhold it. She was not going to degrade herself by getting into an argument with this wicked person.

"I had some trouble tracing you, Countess. Your solicitor did not use your present name. It has taken this long to discover the whereabouts of my long lost daughter-in-law."

"And now that you have found me, what is it you want?"

"I want my house back. The London one preferably, for I find the capital more amenable than Bristol." She frowned and the furrow between her eyes deepened further. "My circumstances, since being so unceremoniously turned out of both my homes, have been unfortunate, to say the least."

"You mean both *my* homes," said Lila.

"As you wish." The woman shrugged. "Let them remain yours, but allow me to live in one, that is all I ask. I have huge debts and cannot afford to purchase other accommodation. Even many of my jewels have been requisitioned. I do not have rich friends, Countess. I am throwing myself at your mercy."

There was a hint of mockery in the voice, but even if it had been genuinely pleading and tearful, Lila would have felt no sympathy for her.

"Madam," she said, her voice icy, "I have plans for both houses which are at present under way. However, if you got down on your bended knees to plead with me, it would be to no avail. Never, never will I forgive you for what you did to Roland. He forfeited the happiness and contentment he had found in the new land to marry me, and I would consider it a betrayal to his memory to offer a helping hand to you."

"That is your final word?" Her voice was practically a sneer.

"Not only is it my final word, madam, but in order to emphasize the uselessness of appealing to me under any circumstances, should you ever be starving I would not give you a crust of bread from my table nor a sup of water for your dying thirst. All you will ever receive from me, Lady Fairbrother, is my utmost contempt."

The woman's eyes flashed with hate and anger. "I may not have *rich* friends," she spat, "but I have friends. Beware of threatening me or you may pay for your ill-will."

"I am not threatening you," Lila assured her with almost a laugh, "but merely making my feelings perfectly clear. You, however, have just threatened me. I would not normally boast of my past, but I have killed two people and should you attempt to harm me or my family, then I will have no scruples where your life is concerned. Now, perhaps, you will leave."

Frances Fairbrother glared at this slim, golden-haired girl and felt an uncalled-for surge of desire thrust through the bitterness in her heart. Once again Lila recognized this and openly shuddered as she stood back waiting for the woman to go. As the visitor swept towards the door, it opened in her face and Rosetta stood there holding Ben.

"Ben is ready for portrait," she said. "Mr. Reilly ask for blue gown, not white. Blue better for painting, he said."

Ben chuckled and held out his arms to his lovely mother who rushed over and grabbed him, nervous that even the gaze of this dreadful creature might do him harm.

"Ah! So you too have a son, Countess Ruzzini," her visitor remarked, and then made her exit without another word.

"That woman," Lila said, "must never, never be allowed inside this house again."

Lieutenant Geoffrey Rees danced constant attendance on the Countess Ruzzini over the first few months of the year. He was not the only gentleman to vie for her attention, but he was by far the most persistent. So far, however, he had gotten nowhere. He had held her hand—but only when helping her from her carriage. He had placed his arm around her waist—but solely when they danced. His flowers were always the largest and the most expensive to arrive at Park House, his presence the most frequent, his hints at furthering the relationship to a positive courtship more pressing and urgent than anyone else's. He was quite dazzled by her beauty, her maturity, her knowledge of the world, and her attitude to life which was so different from that of any other lady he knew.

He watched her through lowered lids as she sat opposite him in the carriage on the way home from a party. Every now and then the gold of her hair was caught in the fleeting light of the lamps they passed. The incredible fur cloak she often wore that everybody remarked about was flung loosely round her shoulders, and underneath he could see the bodice of the stiff white dress she wore, tantalizingly low cut and so tight about her waist that he felt sure both his hands could reach round and his fingers would meet at the back.

Just how long could she lead him on like this? He sighed, for she was not leading him on at all, that was the truth of it, and it drove him quite wild. She gave the impression that she thought him quite a decent chap, but that if she never saw him again it wouldn't bother her unduly.

The carriage drove through the open gates onto the gravel of Park House. He helped her down and led her into the hallway, bowing stiffly as he asked, "When do you return from Yorkshire?"

She was going to see her family the next morning. He was longing to be asked to meet them some day.

He dropped another of his hints. "I may visit my friend

Rodney Critchley shortly. He lives in Lincoln."

This was fairly close to Yorkshire. Surely she would take the opportunity to extend an invitation to Grassbrook Hall.

"I do hope you have a pleasant stay there," was all she said. "I will be returning within a week or two. I have not yet decided on the date."

So, she wasn't going to come back early for *him*, that was clear. Suddenly, he decided he must speak his mind.

"Can I confide in you, Lilian? There is a matter I can keep to myself no longer. May we go somewhere and talk?"

He stammered in his agitation, something he had not done since he was a child, and she looked at him sympathetically.

"Now is not the time for confidences, Lieutenant."

Of course he knew what she meant. She wasn't ready for him to speak out. Damn it though, would she ever be ready?

"But Lilian—"

She took his hand and patted it as if he were her little brother.

"Please, Lieutenant?"

He departed noisily, frustrated, and Lila smiled sadly at his retreating back. He was so nice and honest, and clearly he thought the world of her. What a pity she could never feel anything for him.

A footman, waiting discreetly at the end of the hall, came forward after Geoffrey had stomped away.

"There is a visitor in the drawing room, milady. I took the liberty of stoking up the fire and placing the brandy at hand for him."

Him! Was Papa in the capital and come to travel home with her? Or perhaps it was Quentin Burnett with urgent business. She opened the door and a tall figure rose from an armchair before the fire, placing the brandy glass on a table. Someone so achingly familiar that the minute Lila set eyes on him it seemed as though it was only yesterday she had last seen him.

"Phillip!" she cried running forward into his arms. "Oh, Phillip! I thought I would never see you again!"

Chapter Twenty-Two

He did not kiss her, but merely held her close, so close that she felt their bodies would fuse together for all time. Then he moved back and gazed into her face.

"You have changed, Lila. Changed so much."

He moved his hands up and placed them on her bare shoulders and a shudder of delight went through her.

"Yet, as I look more," he said, "I begin to think that you have not changed at all."

Lila said nothing, but noticed the faint graying at his temples and the tired look in his eyes, and this made him dearer to her than ever before.

"Where have you been? There is someone in New South Wales looking for you and I sent another man to Venice in case you had gone there from Gibraltar. Are you hungry? Shall I send for food? How long have you been in England?"

He laughed and replied, "I shall answer those questions in reverse order. I arrived in England today and came straight here. I have not eaten, my stomach rumbles uncomfortably, and something hot would be more than welcome. On two occasions I have been in Venice and the last time I ran into your man, which is why I am here."

Lila rang the bell and ordered some food to be brought to her guest. As soon as the footman left to comply with this request, she showered him again with questions until he held up his hand and said, "Let me tell you right from the beginning, shall I? Firstly, see what I have here."

He picked up a shabby leather bag and produced from it the torn scarlet dress Lila had sworn to keep.

"When you did not come to Carlton House that August morning nearly four years ago, with the greatest difficulty I discovered you had been sent to Newgate Prison. There I was told you were being deported to Botany Bay and your ship was due to sail that very morning. Like the devil himself I rode to Southampton, but I was too late."

He remembered his despair as he watched her disappear out of his life.

"Then I returned to your room, gathered together your possessions and took them to your family in Grassbrook. I kept the dress, for I knew how much you valued it as proof of your innocence."

"Mama was greatly taken with you," Lila murmured.

"And I with her," he said smiling. "Your father was so deeply shocked he had become bedridden. May I ask how he is?"

"Thankfully, completely recovered," Lila told him.

"I am gratified to hear that." He continued, "I spent eight impatient months waiting for the next ship which was to sail for Sydney Cove. I will not go into my experiences on the *Northern Star*, but I hope and pray that the captain of your ship was not as inhuman a rogue as Nathaniel Grey and you were not treated so abominably as the poor creatures in his care."

"No, no. Indeed, Captain Widdicombe was a reasonable and just man," said Lila. She would explain about Timothy later when it came time to tell her story.

"Thank God for that. In Sydney I could find no proper trace of you. I assumed perhaps you had changed your name to protect your family, for everywhere people recognized your description but not your name."

Phillip went on to describe his meeting with George, his arrival at the Holden Farm and his subsequent search when he injured his leg.

"I made a last attempt to find the mysterious white men who had been mentioned. I came across a General Benedetto da Porto who told me of your marriage to his cousin and your departure to Venice."

"I am a widow now," Lila said hastily and perhaps not too tactfully.

"I know," he said gently and the look in his brilliant, penetrating blue eyes caused disturbing quiverings in her breast.

"I arrived in Venice last August, and found the Palazzo Ruzzini without any difficulty, but it was empty. Several times I returned but I never found a soul. Inquiries of other residents in the Piazza San Boldo led nowhere. The palace had been empty for years, they said. People had come to live there a few years ago, but were rarely seen, never entertained or mixed socially. One person said he felt sure there had been some deaths there recently for he had seen more than one hearse outside earlier in the year, but he could offer no further information. The Ruzzinis were unknown and quite mysterious. They had disappeared as silently and as strangely as they had arrived."

A servant entered at that moment with refreshments and they did not speak while he arranged the hot soup and bread in front of the visitor. After he had gone, Lila took a glass of wine for herself.

When he had finished eating, the captain leaned back in his chair, sipping his own drink, and continued, "I must confess that by then, Lila, I felt a sense of despair. I had traveled many, many thousands of miles in search of you, without the faintest success. I began to think perhaps you did not exist at all, but were merely a figment of my imagination."

"No, no. I am not. I am here! I am real!" she cried, and as if to emphasize this, she rose and moved to kneel beside him, leaning her elbows on the arm of his chair. He gave his old, cynical smile that used to irritate her so much but which now turned her heart askew. His face was still weatherbeaten brown, a shade lighter than his hair, and his hands calloused from holding the reins of his horse.

"I am relieved to find that so."

Phillip raised his glass as though toasting this fact and wished he could get his story finished and take her in his arms. She looked like a Grecian goddess in that smooth, white dress, her arms and neck bare, hair coiled high, then falling thickly onto one white shoulder.

"I have nearly finished," he said. "When my inquiries in Venice proved fruitless, I traveled leisurely to Russia, a country I have long wished to visit, for my widowed mother lives there with her sister who married a Russian nobleman. I spent several months there, longer than I intended, for my mother is frail and both she and I felt this was probably the last time we would see each other. But eventually I felt I must return to England to see if there was news of you."

He took a long sip of his wine and stared intently at Lila.

"I cannot describe the wretchedness I felt throughout this time. You came into my life when I thought there was not a woman on earth who existed for me. Then you were snatched away, and I followed, thinking to find you, never for one moment imagining you would not be there to find.

"But wretched or not, instead of returning straight to England I had the initiative to visit Venice on my way back in case there was fresh news. To my surprise I found the Palazzo Ruzzini inhabited by nuns."

"It is to be an orphanage," Lila explained. "I had no further use for it."

"The sisters told of a Beatrice da Porto, a relative of your husband. I was, of course, still not absolutely sure that the Countess Ruzzini was Lila Ward, but suddenly information, so long denied me, came thick and fast. Your counsin-in-law, a charming woman, told me of your widowhood and your little son. She also said you had mentioned Grassbrook Hall in Yorkshire as being the home of your parents. Then your man found me and requested that I head for London with all possible speed. At last I had positive proof. I rode full pelt for Park House in London—and here I am!"

Both were silent for some time, staring deep into each others' eyes, until Lila blushed and lowered hers for she felt he could see into her very soul. Then he leaned forward, tipped her chin with one finger and kissed her softly on the mouth. Trembling, Lila lifted her hands, tangling her fingers in the dark hair at the nape of his lean neck. Reaching down he clasped her arms and drew her up to him, and their kiss became firmer, harder.

The tight bodice of the dress was not made for the wearer to be so roughly handled, and it came open, revealing her white breasts beneath the stiff stays. Her heart seemed to leap from her body as Phillip bent to kiss the creamy softness of her.

"Oh, Lila! Oh, Lila, my dear Lila!"

Afterwards, when she tried to remember how he took her, exactly what happened, what he said, what she said, she could recall nothing but the exquisite passion that possessed them both, a feeling of such overwhelming rapture, that what happened became submerged beneath their delight in each other.

He kissed her long and softly when it was all over, as if to seal their love forever, and asked, "When shall we be wed?"

"Tomorrow morning," Lila murmured. "Or now, this very minute, if it were possible."

"I wish it were. But I shall begin all the necessary proceedings first thing tomorrow—or shall I say today, for it is past midnight."

"You will stay the night? Come to my room and sleep there."

He stroked her cheek.

"My darling, you are still my old impetuous Lila. Much as I would love to stay, you have your reputation to consider."

She sighed. He was right, of course, for she was still establishing herself as a virtuous widow as the world gradually learned who she really was. The truth was beginning to leak out, and nobody seemed to care, but everything would be ruined by an open relationship, albeit with the man she was to marry.

She sighed again.

"Then I suppose you must leave. Where will you stay?"

"Down the road in Carlton House—the Prince will always accommodate me—or the barracks in Kensington. I will not want for a bed."

He began to dress. Lila lay naked before the fire, turning on her side to watch him and arching her hip seductively in the hope that she could tempt him again.

As though reading her thoughts he smiled and said, "It would seem I am more concerned for your public honor than yourself. Get dressed, my lovely harlot, before a servant enters and your indiscretion will be all over London tomorrow."

She stretched luxuriously and for a moment his determination to leave wavered as he watched her inviting body, sleak and gleaming in the glow of the fire, and she said with a wicked grin, "I have always wanted to be a harlot. It's in my blood, you know."

"You would do it well, my love. You would become a queen amongst such women, but from now on, you are to be my own, private harlot."

"I comply willingly," Lila whispered sweetly.

Instead of getting dressed, she cuddled into the sable cloak which she had so joyfully flung away on entering the room.

She picked up the scarlet dress and noticed the little square torn away, and Phillip said, "Tell me, did that tiny scrap of material ever reach you? I gave it to a native boy on a farm where it was said you lived, but he did not understand English."

"Indeed it did," Lila said. "But by then I was married to Carlo Ruzzini and ready to board a ship sailing to Venice. As for my friend George, the native boy, he understood English perfectly for my husband, Roland Fairbrother, taught it to him."

Captain Grenville, almost fully dressed, frowned as he put on his black coat.

"I thought you said a moment ago your husband was Carlo Ruzzini."

"That is perfectly true. Carlo was my third husband, Roland my second."

They had turned down the lamps a long while ago, and in the semi-darkness she could not see the thunder in his face.

"And who, pray, was your first?"

"Timothy Bateson," Lila answered innocently, too happy to notice the frigid tones in which the question was asked, so his following words were totally unexpected.

"So, madam, whilst I was crossing the world, searching for the woman whom I thought loved me as much as I loved her, you were abed with three different men. *Three* husbands in little more than two years! You are indeed a harlot, Lila!"

She stared at him, horrified. He had not asked for an explanation. He knew nothing of the circumstances of her marriages and assumed they had all been consummated.

"The man I heard arguing in the hall while I waited in here for you, was he next on your list if I had not turned up?"

The blood which had so recently run hot through his veins

as he made love to this woman turned to ice and he felt he wanted to take that slender white neck between his hands and squeeze it. While he searched the earth, she had been enjoying herself in other men's arms.

Dazed, not yet fully aware of what was happening, Lila struggled to her knees and the ermine cape fell away from one shoulder.

. Phillip Grenville stared at her, feeling he was about to choke with desire, with anger. He strode across the room and bent down, pulling the cloak away from her shoulders and clasping her roughly to him. Savagely he kissed her, his tongue digging deep into her mouth, his teeth bruising her lower lip, then flung her away.

"Good-bye, madam," he snapped and went to the door, laughing cynically when he found it locked. "You are experienced at this I see. Don't ever forget to lock it, Lila. Except to admit the next man!"

She stammered, her face ashen, "Phillip, please. Do not leave like this."

"There is no point in staying. I do not see myself cut out to be a *fourth* husband."

When the door closed with a slam behind him Lila woke from her stupor. She was visited by a rage so pure and violent it was greater than any experienced throughout her past trials and tribulations. She ran to the door and opened it to see Phillip Grenville on the verge of leaving the house.

Not caring whether the ermine cloak covered her or not, she yelled, "You are every bit as arrogant, as conceited and as hateful as I thought you were when we first met! I don't care if you ever come back!"

Phillip Grenville turned and bowed coldly at the half-naked, untidy, incredibly beautiful woman, and despite his hurt, he could not help but think to himself, *Any other woman would have been prostrate with tears. Trust Lila to have the guts to hurl abuse and not take rejection passively. Damn you, Lila Ward! Damn you!*

As she so often did when she was unhappy, Lila returned to her family, but she could not bring herself to confide even in her mother. How could she tell another living soul of that night when she went from heaven to hell within the space of one hour? Her thoughts were totally confused. He had proven his love for her so thoroughly that his sudden rejection seemed inexplicable.

She didn't realize men were so sensitive when it came to their women's relations with other men. How many bordellos had Phillip Grenville visited over the past three or four years, she wondered. If it were fifty, a hundred, she would not care. As long as it was she he came back to.

She spent a month at Grassbrook Hall, mooning about to the despair of her mother who knew something had happened but did not wish to pry. And Hettie was to be married in June, and the house was in a flurry of preparation.

Benedetto managed a few first faltering steps on his plump legs, and Lucy cried and said she'd never seen anything like it in her life. A baby walking at thirteen months! He was sure to be a genius when he grew up.

Back in London Lila tried to occupy her mind solely with Ben and business affairs. Sian Reilly's courtship of a suddenly starry-eyed Rosetta was progressing well, as was the portrait of mother and child.

Lieutenant Geoffrey Rees called constantly, as the servants witnessed. Almost every time the front door was opened, there would be the tall, fair army officer, holding a bunch of flowers or a box of bonbons for their mistress, and they all began to wonder how long she would be able to hold out under such an onslaught. Hold out she did, however, and she began to talk of going abroad after Hettie's wedding. It seemed ironic to her that after all those years of longing to come back to England, she wished to leave, but she was ashamed to inflict herself on her family so often.

Park House reminded her constantly of Phillip Grenville. Every time she entered she was on tenterhooks, willing the footman to announce a visitor in the drawing room, and whenever she entered that room she expected a tall figure to rise from the chair and hold out his arms.

How could he have such little faith in her? Then she would remember how little faith she had had in him.

Phillip, she mourned to herself, *please come back. Let me tell you what really happened.* But once again he had gone underground. She suspected he had returned to Russia to his mother.

*   *   *

She decided to go to Paris. The Ruzzini residence there was well looked after, Father Jude assured her, and so began the elaborate preparations necessary for transporting a countess and her baby, a maid, and all the necessary paraphernalia for a two-month stay abroad.

In the meantime, Hettie was married to John Butler. His father came to conduct the service and the bride, a taller, paler version of her older sister, in soft, floating white lace, wed solid, dependable John, who so clearly adored her. Lila felt unreasonably sad and at the same time unreasonably envious of the predictability of the life ahead of Hettie. She returned to London and the equally dull organization of her trip to Paris, feeling totally out of sorts with herself and the world at large.

The holiday was doomed from the start. Due to the long drawn-out war with France, it was necessary to travel to Belgium and enter across the border. Lila and Benedetto were citizens of Venice so were not in danger. It was a tiresome journey. The seas from Harwich to Ostend were choppy, causing both Ben and Father Jude to become seasick, and Lila felt heartily thankful when they landed on Belgian soil. However, she fell ill herself, and they had to stay in an uncomfortable hostelry where the food was bad and Ben missed Lucy, who was too old to attempt such a trip.

For a while Lila's sickness made her wonder if she was expecting Phillip Grenville's child, and her emotions were entirely split in two by this. Half of her visualized him riding like the wind to be by her side while the other half sourly decided that if he still held the unfavorable opinion of her expressed that awful night, he would declare that the child might be that of a dozen different men. Fortunately she discovered this was not the reason for her illness, and they continued with their journey.

At last the party arrived in the St. Germain district of Paris where the Ruzzini house was situated. It was a pretty, gracious building set in a lavishly flowered garden, but Lila felt uneasy straightaway. Everywhere she went within the rather dusty interior she thought of Maria. Of Maria treading the same corridors, entering the same rooms and sitting in the same chairs. She made sure she was not given the bedroom which had been her sister-in-law's, but nonetheless she had a terrifying dream one night that Maria took possession of her body and she rose and wandered down a passage to Carlo's room, wanting him, wanting him badly, but in a sinful, incestuous way. She opened the door to Carlo's room, but it was not the husband she had known. Instead, an old, wrinkled Carlo with gray hair and a wispy beard lay in his place.

At her insistence the next morning the entire party packed their essentials and moved to the best hotel in Paris. Lila told Father Jude she never wanted to use the Ruzzini home again. This time, before she could declare it an orphanage or some other charitable institution, he made arrangements for the house to be rented to permanent tenants.

Paris was not an enjoyable place to stay in so soon after the bloody revolution. It was difficult to forget the wretched scenes which had so recently taken place. Every sound made Lila think of a guillotine, and each old crone they passed seemed to bestow upon her a baleful look as if wishing to drag this hoity-toity miss to the tumbling block and whisk off her head.

The holiday was cut short, and one year and a week after she had returned so triumphantly to England, Lila once more made her way home, though this time her heart was heavy, and no matter how hard she tried, she could not rid her mind of the cruel rejection she had suffered at the hands of the man she loved so dearly.

Back in Park House she took herself firmly in hand. Rejected or not, she could not mope for the rest of her life. She searched her mind for a diversion and decided to hold a ball. Since her arrival in London, she had been invited to countless parties, dances, and events, yet so far in return had only had the courage to hold small dinners and parties for a dozen or so guests. She would arrange a splendid and magnificent ball to which she would invite her family, her friends and every socialite in London. If they accepted then she too would have been accepted back into the society, for by now her origins were known to all.

When to hold it, she pondered. There was her birthday next month, then not long after that All Souls' and All Saints' Eves. Perhaps Christmas would be a better time, but Rosetta made up her mind for her. She announced one day that she and Sian Reilly were to be married. Lila expressed her surprise and delight as naturally as if the news were truly unexpected and asked when the happy day was to be.

"New Year's Day," said Rosetta whose English had improved enormously. "Sian and I thought we would start the new century as man and wife."

The new century. Of course. The eve of 1800 would be ideal for her ball, and she excitedly went ahead with preliminary arrangements, with the willing help of Lieutenant Rees.

In vain Father Jude informed everyone that 1800 was merely the last year of the old century but no one was interested.

"When it becomes 1801, 'twill not be nearly so interesting," Lila said.

The first person to invite was the Prince of Wales. If he accepted, then all would follow. On no account must the Princess of Wales be invited, she was told, for her husband reviled her to all and sundry. However, an invitation must be sent to Mrs. Fitzherbert.

Unbeknownst to Lila, the Prince of Wales received the plain white card announcing Countess Ruzzini's Grand Ball one morning as he dressed, miserably perusing his figure in the looking glass. Why could he not retain the lean, elegant shape of his friend, Phillip Grenville, who was at that moment resting one arm nonchalantly against the mantelshelf? In vain he told himself he would eat less, drink less, sleep less, and exercise more.

Wrapping a vivid red brocade dressing gown around his ample middle he idly fingered the letters just brought in to him on a silver tray by his secretary.

"Ah! This is from the Countess Ruzzini. Was she not the one who inadvertently covered for my abomination of a wife in her indiscretion with that savage of a coachman?"

Captain Grenville affirmed that the Countess Ruzzini and Miss Lilian Ward were one and the same person, and turned away to hide his tortured face. Memories of Lila caused in him a turmoil of emotions and he was not sure if she appeared before him whether he would murder her or shower her with kisses. Usually when these thoughts assailed him he would hurriedly make his way to Isabella's House of Sin and submerge himself in the arms of one of the beauties there, and although his lovely, golden Lila never disappeared completely from his mind, at least her image would be temporarily blurred.

The prince was chattering on about a ball. Lila had invited him to a ball.

"What do you think, my friend? This is the third or fourth request for my presence on that night. Should I accept or will something better turn up?"

All Phillip could think of was Lila's eager, innocent young face. He told Prince George he should accept and managed to think up half a dozen good reasons why the countess's affair would be superior to all others. The prince was pleased to have someone make up his mind for him and told his secretary to send an acceptance forthwith.

When the royal personage went off for an appointment with his tailor, Phillip Grenville strolled out of Carlton House and along the Mall to Lila's residence.

It was a fine autumn morning. Somewhere a gardener was holding a bonfire of first fallen leaves and the pungent smell evoked childhood memories in Phillip. He recalled the impetuosity of his own youth and in that instant forgave Lila everything, particularly when he saw a tiny child tottering on the grass partly to the rear of Park House, closely followed by an elderly nurse bent over him like a guardian angel, ready to snatch the baby up if he should fall.

Lila's child. Her little boy!

He would call that very moment and beg her forgiveness, but even as his hand stretched out to open the iron gate, a young man emerged from the front door and stood outside looking satisfied and well pleased with life.

Phillip recognized him as Lieutenant Geoffrey Rees, in his opinion a useless clod. Not yet half past the hour of ten and a man coming *out!*

In disgust, Phillip Grenville turned on his heel and marched away from the woman who haunted him.

Geoffrey Rees came to the house at all hours on the assumption that the further he managed to ingratiate himself into Lila's home, the more she would come to regard him as a member of the family, and eventually find him indispensable. He was helping to draw up the list of five hundred guests for the Grand New Year's Eve Ball, or New Century's Eve as everyone had begun to call it. A quarter of the invitations had already gone to the most important names, and sometimes Geoffrey would come early to see what response there had been.

"The prince has accepted," Lila told him delightedly one

day, little realizing that Phillip was responsible for this swift and agreeable reply.

This meant the event could be organized in earnest, and for Geoffrey Rees it gave an excuse to virtually live in the house while he offered advice, which was given him beforehand by his aunt, the duchess of Garth, to whom arranging a ball for five hundred held no terrors.

Lila withdrew from the plans regarding refreshments when she heard that six cows and two dozen turkeys and geese were to be carefully and separately fed at a farm in Sussex, especially for her. She could not help but think of the much-loved animals at New Farm and did not wish to know about the animals being slaughtered for her guests. Cook and Mrs. Hoggett took over this side of things with enthusiasm, under Lieutenant Rees's counsel, of course.

There was such an amount of preparation to be done that Lila began to wonder if she should not have thought of the idea a whole year before and the weeks and months sped by so rapidly that Christmas was upon them before they knew it.

Despite the hectic dimension of her life, there was never a day that went by without Phillip Grenville's haughty and contemptuous face appearing before her, an when this happened it did not matter what she was doing or whom she was with. She always found it difficult to stop herself from crying aloud at the sudden pain his memory gave her.

Because Lila could not leave her house at Christmas, all her family came to stay with her. For the first time, Park House accommodated the number of people it was built for. Mama and Papa, Hettie and John, whose first baby was due in the spring, Mary, Rosalind and Simon and their children, and, bringing news from Robin and Hugh in New Farm came Emma and Charles and their three children from Chichester. Esther Larkin came too, twittering away happily throughout the entire holiday.

The house bustled with people intent on important tasks. Children ran about shrieking, their voices echoing through the high, white rooms. The servants, their numbers temporarily increased, had never been so busy.

Lila woke on New Year's Eve day feeling as if the world had stopped. There was literally nothing left for her to do. Everything had been so carefully organized that the flowers, the food, the furniture and seating, the prizes and gifts, decorations, attendants, uniforms, orchestra, and the dozens of other minor but important items were all being taken care of by other people. As the day wore on she even began to feel a little lost, for people scuttled everywhere intent on jobs which would make the forthcoming evening the most splendid and talked about social event of the year, while Lila literally watched the clock and waited for time to pass.

At one point she was concerned to notice Rosetta rushing by with a tear-stained face and hoped she and Sian had not had a tiff. Their wedding was due to take place the following day and their wedding present from Lila, Miss Prymm's old house in Cotterell Street, was furnished and awaiting their occupation. Sian's magnificent portrait of Lila, resplendent in her silver gown with baby Benedetto on her knee, had recently been hung in the library and was the subject of much admiration.

It was a relief when darkness fell. At last the house became quiet, for the children had been put to bed early. They were to be woken up and fetched downstairs at midnight for the chiming in of the New Year. The adults were resting and preparing themselves for the evening ahead.

Lila thankfully went to her room where, on the bed, lay the new dress she'd had made for the occasion. A daringly simple creation in hyacinth blue, with tiny sleeves, a low cut bodice and straight unadorned skirt. From the box of jewels from Carlo's grandfather she had chosen a sapphire necklace and matching earrings. The clear stones were almost exactly the same shade as her eyes and emphasized their blueness to an almost startling degree.

She began to brush her hair when the door was flung open without a knock and Lucy stood there looking wild-eyed and half-mad with panic. At first Lila thought she was ill, her face was so gray, but then she gasped out her message.

"Benedetto has disappeared," she croaked. "I have looked everywhere. Little Ben is gone."

Chapter Twenty-Three

Lila ran to the nursery to look in Ben's cot and see for herself that he was not there. It was empty. The covers had been dragged back so roughly that some of them lay on the floor.

"Mama might have taken him, or Hettie," Lila cried wildly, though she knew this was most unlikely. None of the family would dream of removing Ben without telling Lucy.

"I have asked them all," the old nurse said in despair. "I have knocked on every door to ask if Ben was with them. I thought one of the older children might have taken him to play with, but there is no sign of him anywhere."

Father Jude appeared. He seemed to have a sixth sense when there was trouble afoot. Lila explained what had happened and said, "We must search the house in case he has climbed into a cupboard or a chest," though her heart turned over to imagine Ben suffocating, or trapped.

"No. I do not think he is in the house," Father Jude said abruptly. He was by the window, leaning down and examining the floor.

"What on earth do you mean?" Lila cried in anguish but he didn't answer her, and turned to Lucy.

"Is this window always open?"

"You told me yourself it should be kept open at least three inches, even in winter," Lucy stuttered.

"Someone has been in here. See, here is a wet leaf and there is soil on the windowsill. Benedetto has been kidnapped."

"Do not disturb the household," Lila said, for she could not bear the thought of all her guests running around in a panic.

She would keep a cooler head with just Father Jude to help. She looked at him questioningly. He stood blinking, staring into space, and she waited for him to sort out his thoughts. Lucy had sunk into a chair sobbing hysterically and Lila told her not to cry, they would get Ben back, at the same time wishing someone would convince her this was the case. Lucy was exhorted on no account to tell anyone else about Ben's disappearance. Her tears reminded Lila of Rosetta.

"Rosetta?" she breathed. "Could she—?" but he interrupted irritably.

"She had a quarrel with Sian earlier on, but all is now well. I agree there have been times when she could have been suspect, but not now. Come downstairs and we will question Hoggett and any other servants who have been out recently."

Lila recognized the description straightaway. The young footman who had offered to eject Ralph Curringham had noticed a carriage waiting outside, a little farther up from the gates of Park House. He had passed it on the way to Charing Cross to buy an extra supply of candles.

A woman inside the carriage had attracted his attention, as well as the two boys standing on the pavement talking to her. "The boys were odd because . . ." He struggled for the words he felt he could use in front of his mistress. "Because they were of feminine shape," he said at last.

The woman inside the coach he had noticed because as he approached it from afar she seemed quite unusually beautiful with huge dark eyes, but when he passed by he was surprised to see she was not lovely at all but was actually quite strange looking. "Like the wicked witch in a fairy tale" was how he put it.

On his way back the carriage had passed him going in the direction of the Cross, and the woman and both boys were inside, all laughing fit to burst. When Lila asked him if they were holding anything, he could not say, for it had all been too quick.

Hoggett had already been told to get the carriage ready. Lila snatched a cloak from behind the kitchen door, and outside Father Jude was astounded when she commanded the coachman to take them to Isabella's House of Sin.

"It is Frances Fairbrother who has taken my Ben, for she would think it an ideal way to get even with me," she said as they sat in the rocking vehicle. Hoggett was making all possible speed. "She ruined Roland's life. I know she would kill my son if she could. Isabella is the only person I can think of to approach who might know her whereabouts."

Hoggett was having a hard time keeping up any speed in the mounting traffic, and when it slowed down altogether, Lila looked through the window and saw they were not too far away from their destination. She opened the door, leaped out, and was nearly run down by a trap going in the opposite direction. The driver reigned his horses frantically and swore at her. Father Jude descended more carefully and hurried down the street after Lila to Isabella's front door. She hammered loudly.

Isabella was sitting at the head of a table laid for twenty guests, made up of her ten favorite customers and the upstairs girls. She heard the banging but gave it not a second thought. For one thing, she knew her maid would answer it, and for another, she was used to people demanding urgent entrance to her establishment at all hours of the day and night. She excused herself only when the maid came in and whispered something in her ear.

She recognized the woman who had asked for her when she entered the hall. It was the hair she remembered—such a unique shade of gold—and also the perfect hourglass figure beneath the carelessly tied cloak. Of course! This was the little girl Roger had brought along one night many years ago, the one who'd turned out to be someone from the court. What on earth did she want here and what was she doing with that half-mad, over-sexed priest, whom several of her girls clamored to partner whenever he visited the house? She thought it tactful to pretend she did not know the cleric. He kept his eyes firmly on the floor as she approached.

Lila came straight to the point.

"My child has been kidnapped by Lady Frances Fairbrother, I am sure. Do you know where she can be found?"

Isabella replied indignantly, "You don't think I cater for the likes of her, do you?"

"No, no. But surely you know the names of the places she might frequent? She is infamous, I am told. I am sure she is somewhere in London, even in this vicinity. My little son's life is in danger. Surely you can help?"

In her anxiety, Lila clutched hold of Isabella's arm and the woman's lovely gray eyes softened before this plea for her help.

"Well, rumor has it she's got no home of her own nowadays. Turfed out of her house in Bloomsbury for some reason. I hear she tried to start a place of her own, but even amongst her own kind she's none too popular. I understand she's sunk so low as to frequent the Stocks nearby London Bridge, or if not there, then Spanish Julie's in Mutton Street."

Calling her thanks, Lila rushed from the house, followed by Father Jude who had not uttered a word. Isabella watched their departing figures and wished the golden-haired beauty had been interested in the employment offered all those years ago, for she would have indeed been an asset, but it looked as if she had done better for herself through other means. She returned to the dinner table and continued with her meal, but was unable to get the distraught young mother's face out of her mind. Eventually someone asked why she was so quiet.

As she looked up to answer, she caught the eye of one of her guests, Captain Phillip Grenville, and remembered it was he who had taken the girl home after her first visit to the house. Some instinct told her to acquaint him with the plight of the young woman he had once rescued.

She was not at all surprised, indeed was much relieved, when he shoved his chair back, threw his napkin onto the table, and left the room without a word.

Spanish Julie's was a bar, dimly lit, but clean. Lila was set to leap from the carriage as it drew to a halt, but Hoggett scrambled down first and waylaid her.

"Oh, no, you don't, milady," he said firmly, and went into

the bar, pushing his way through the crowds of customers Lila could see within. At first she wondered what was so odd about the occasional bursts of laughter which could be heard, and eventually realized there were only women in the bar.

Hoggett returned, dragging a sallow-skinned woman with him who hissed at them that Frances Fairbrother was not present and persisted in her denials even when threatened with the law.

"Do what you like, you won't find that bitch under my roof," she snarled viciously.

All felt inclined to believe her. Hoggett resumed his place and they raced towards London Bridge. Lila began to pray aloud, and even the priest took brief refuge in the religion he had foresworn.

In this less affluent area, fewer vehicles were about and Hoggett was able to get up some speed.

"Here it is, milady," shouted Hoggett.

They got out of the carriage in a dank, cold street beside London Bridge. An acrid fog covered the river. Before them stood a row of high, rickety houses leaning forward and criss-crossed with rotting beams. In parts they were open to the damp air where plaster had fallen away leaving jagged holes in their walls.

Hoggett banged on the door of one with dirty, broken windows, and when no one answered, lifted his huge boot and broke down the door as if it were little more than cardboard.

Dirty fog rolled in as, holding aloft a carriage lamp, he motioned them to enter and they walked onto the straw-covered floor of the grimy entrance hall.

A man with eyes that were swollen slits and a nose almost eaten away by disease came from a back room, his face twisted in fright.

"Lady Frances Fairbrother?" demanded Father Jude. "Where is she?"

"Upstairs, I think. There's a lady what speaks well up there with two others. The second floor at the back."

From behind doors, strange noises could be heard as they climbed the creaking stairs. Unearthly moans followed some-times by the fierce flick of a whip on bare flesh. On the first floor a door was open, and when Lila turned to look inside, Hoggett who was behind roughly twisted her head so she could not see.

"Sorry, milady," he said, "but there's men and women comes

here who are the very dregs of the whole world."

Damp had attacked the plastered walls so that half had fallen away leaving rough and dirty patches which made the very walls, lit by the flickering flames of Hoggett's lamp, appear to be covered in running sores.

To think Benedetto might be in this horrible place.

"Please, please, let us find him soon." Lila was unaware that she had spoken these words aloud.

On the second floor, two doors faced them at the back. They stopped and listened at both but could near nothing.

"Try that one," Lila said to Hoggett, pointing to the door on the right. He lifted his boot, and with a crash it swung open. Lila screamed in fright and once again both men tried to shield her eyes, but it was too late. In the center of the filthy room were a set of old-fashioned stocks after which the establishment was named, and in this contraption knelt a man, his back bare and covered in bloody streaks from a whipping. His eyes were closed, and spittle ran from his open mouth onto the dusty floor. Their noise did not disturb him, his eyes did not even flicker, and Hoggett closed the door when Lila cried, "We must rescue him later. He cannot be left there."

"Damn him, milady! That is what the wretch wants. He has *paid* to be there."

Without another word he kicked open the other door, but Lady Fairbrother had been warned by the din outside, and as her two young friends cowered in a corner, she darted to the open window and held a struggling and screaming Benedetto out over the river.

"Come another step and I drop him," she said in a voice of steel, her black eyes sparkling.

The three stood helplessly on the threshold of the room. There was nothing they could do that would not endanger Ben.

"He will catch his death of cold," cried Lila in anguish. "Bring him inside, I beg of you."

"Perhaps I would rather drop him," said the woman, with a horrid, cunning grin.

"Bring him in," Lila pleaded again. "You can have back your house. Both houses. Anything, if you will give back my son."

"What sickening, maudlin mush for a male baby," the woman

sniggered. "How I wished when my child was being born that it would be a girl, in my likeness. But no, I was cursed with one like this."

As if he understood her words, Ben screamed louder. Lila could see him wriggling precariously in mid-air.

She bit back a sharp retort for fear of her child's safety, and the woman continued, "I did not think you would trace me so quickly. Tomorrow, early, we leave for the Isle of Lesvos, which is where I belong, where I have always wanted to be. It has been my intention for several months to capture this creature and take him with me."

"But why?" Lila beseeched. "Why?"

Frances Fairbrother shrugged.

"Revenge," she said. "Revenge on you, on my unwelcome son and your son, on life itself."

"If you hand Ben to me, then we will leave and say nothing about this to a living soul. You can go to your Isle of Lesvos. I will even give you the money. I will give you—"

She screamed, for Ben disappeared out of the hands of his kidnapper and Frances Fairbrother fell forward, balancing precariously on the windowsill. Hoggett rushed outside and Lila ran to the window waiting for the splash when Ben's body hit the gray, ice-cold water. The shock alone would kill him.

But there was no such sound. Instead, there was Captain Grenville hanging by one hand from a rotting beam, his feet on another which had already begun to creak beneath his weight. Ben was tucked under his right arm. He had climbed out the window of the room next door.

Lila wanted to reach out for Ben, for Phillip could not move an inch with only one hand. But Lady Fairbrother was in the way, balancing half outside, half inside. Lila could have pulled her in. It would only have taken seconds longer.

But all she thought of was Ben as she pushed the woman aside, and the heartless Lady Fairbrother hurtled down to the swiftly flowing water of the Thames below. She never surfaced.

Lila reached for Ben, and it was only then, when she had him back safe and secure, that she began to cry.

Back at Park House, the baby was rushed upstairs and Lila examined every inch of him to make sure his kidnapper had not harmed him. He was as perfect as ever and already quite recovered from his misadventure as he climbed off Lila's knee and tried to clamber onto the rocking horse his grandparents had brought him for Christmas.

"I am reluctant to leave him," Lila said to Lucy. "But I must prepare for the ball."

Although it seemed impossible to believe, the entire ordeal had taken an hour and half. In just over an hour her guests would be arriving.

Then Mama and Hettie appeared, already fully dressed in their new ball gowns, wanting to know what on earth was going on and why Lila was wearing Mrs. Hoggett's old cloak.

She promised to tell them everything the next day, though in fact intended to leave out a great deal. She was about to go to her room when the footman announced two visitors in the drawing room who had been waiting nearly an hour.

"A Mr. and Mrs. Silvagni," Peter said.

Suppressing an inclination to tell him they must be asked to come back tomorrow, Lila ran downstairs and into the drawing room.

Two figures rose at her entrance, and at the sight of one she cried out in delight, "Queen Lil! Oh, dear, dear Queenie!"

She launched herself at the woman and showered her with kisses and hugs. Lil looked embarrassed and shoved her away none too gently.

"Gerrof, yer sentimental twerp," she grunted but there was no doubt she was pleased to see Lila and gave an affectionate grin.

Lila stood back and stared. There was something different about Queenie. Something that made a vast difference in her looks but was difficult to spot at first glance.

Queen Lil grinned again and Lila gasped, "Your teeth! You've got teeth."

An entire mouthful of white glistened as Queen Lil smiled.

"That's right, gal. Had me last six out and put in a set of thirty-two brand new ivories. Took a whole pair of elephant's tusks, did this set of choppers."

"Oh, Queenie. You look beautiful," Lila lied.

"That's not all. Got a husband too. Remember Paulo? Well, we got hitched."

"Queenie, I'm so happy for you. And for you, Paulo."

She took his hand and then kissed his great red face. He

mumbled a few indistinct phrases made up of Italian and his wife's cockney slang.

"You must tell me everything that has happened to you since I left on the *Leo*. I want to know about George and Benedetto da Porto and everyone else from Goldoni Bay. But not until tomorrow, for tonight I am giving a ball to herald in the new year. Can you stay? Have you something to wear? The prince is coming and Mrs. Fitzherbert and just about everybody in the whole of London."

"I suppose it'll be a bit grander than Red Jock's in Blackfriars," Queenie said with a grin. "A'course we'll come, me old mate. Got some posh togs outside in our trunks and I'll put me posh voice on with 'em."

When Lila eventually emerged, having taken less than a quarter of the time to prepare herself than she had planned, the events of the evening added a sparkle to her eyes.

She felt relieved beyond words that Ben was safe again, and touched by the loyalty and devotion shown by Father Jude and Hoggett when she was in trouble. She found her emotions in a state of positive turmoil at the way Phillip Grenville had turned up out of the blue. *He must have been at Isabella's House of Sin,* she thought, and she was surprised at the fierce stab of jealousy this thought engendered in her breast. At that moment she understood his feelings. What would her reaction have been if he had turned up and announced he had been wed three times since she sailed for New South Wales? She did not doubt she would have been outrageously shocked.

At the very earliest moment she would seek him out, beg his forgiveness and insist that he listen to the reasons for her first two marriages. If necessary, she would go down on her bended knees and beg him to take her. She no longer cared for her reputation. He had enjoyed her that night. Let him take her at his will for as long as he wished. There was no need for him to marry her if he did not care to become a fourth husband. She was his, heart, body and soul.

By now the entire household was at a feverish pitch of excitement. Maids, footmen, doormen, musicians scurried about, and recrossing each other's paths. Mama, Papa, her sisters, her friends, were all ready, fidgeting as they waited for the first guests to arrive.

The ballroom shone with a thousand candles, as if the stars themselves had come down to earth to light up the Countess Ruzzini's New Century's Eve Ball. The orchestra was already tuning up, and behind the musicians was a mass of chrysanthemums, gold, rust, orange, cream, and brown, piled high against the wall, so it looked as if they sat before a huge glowing fire. Three tables were loaded with sides of beef, whole turkeys and geese, pastries, and such a variety of food that there was barely room left to place a single spoon.

Lila felt her heart would burst with emotion and, afraid that she was about to cry, retired hurriedly to the drawing room where great logs burnt in the fireplace. Impulsively she took from a drawer the torn red dress which Phillip had taken round the world with him and began to rip it into shreds, flinging the pieces onto the crackling flames.

It was silly to keep it another minute, she thought, for everyone knew who she was. Everyone was coming to her ball.

The last piece had gone up in flames when she heard the door open and close behind her. Because no word was spoken, she knew who her visitor was.

She remained silent, without turning, as he came up behind her and placed hard, rough hands upon her shoulders. Sighing deeply, she turned and began to speak, wanting to say all the things she had thought of only minutes before.

But he would not let her. He kissed her, over and over again. Kissed, caressed, and kissed yet again.

"I don't care if you have had a dozen husbands, my darling, darling Lila. You were made for me. Sent by heaven for me."

She could have sworn she saw tears in his eyes.

"Lila! Where are you?" called Mama. "The first carriage has just drawn up."

"She is with me," Phillip called back, and they went out of the room hand in hand.

"And she will stay with me," he whispered, "for as long as we both shall live."

Sweeping Stories of Historical Romance

☐ 79119-0	SWEET FIRE Kate Fairfax	$2.95	
☐ 05227-4	BEAU BARRON'S LADY Helen Ashfield	$2.75	
☐ 06585-6	BLAZING VIXEN Elizabeth Zachary	$2.50	
☐ 43233-6	KATYA Lucy Cores	$2.95	
☐ 16663-3	DRAGON STAR Olivia O'Neill	$2.95	
☐ 48325-9	LILA Maureen Lee	$2.95	
☐ 70809-9	RAVENSTOR Elizabeth Renier	$2.50	
☐ 70885-4	REBEL IN HIS ARMS Francine Rivers	$3.50	
☐ 71324-6	REMEMBER CAROLINE MARY Dorothy Wakeley	$2.25	
☐ 83288-1	TWILIGHT'S BURNING Diane Guest	$3.25	
☐ 81465-4	TO DISTANT SHORES Jill Gregory	$2.50	
☐ 88531-4	WHISPER ON THE WATER E.P. Murray	$3.25	

Available wherever paperbacks are sold or use this coupon.

 CHARTER BOOKS
Book Mailing Service
P.O. Box 690, Rockville Centre, NY 11571

Please send me the titles checked above. I enclose _____
Include $1.00 for postage and handling if one book is ordered; 50¢ per book for
two or more. California, Illinois, New York and Tennessee residents please add
sales tax.

NAME _____

ADDRESS _____

CITY _____ STATE/ZIP _____

(allow six weeks for delivery)

A-5

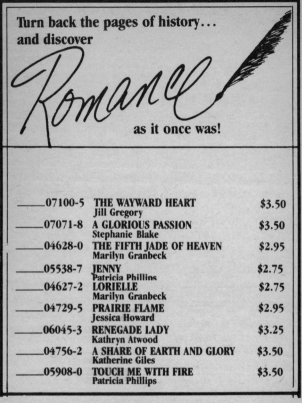